MONTAN...

Wed i...

*Welcome to V...land —
a place of passion and adventure.
Seems this charming little town has some
Big Sky secrets. And everybody's talking about...*

Cleo Kincaid Monroe: Her Kincaid roots ran deep, and Cleo was ready to start a new generation. She'd thought Ethan Redford was The One. But he'd swept her off her feet, only to leave town. Now he was back with one burning question: Would she marry him...for baby's sake?

Ethan Redford: Ethan knew Cleo was The One to help him keep custody of his orphaned nephew. But would this heartless tycoon resist the temptation to take his temporary bride's innocence?

Frannie Hannon: She was definitely more Hannon than Kincaid, with her flair for the understated. But then Frannie found herself the recipient of a NASCAR champion's attentions...and amorous *intentions*....

Austin Parker: He'd never understood the ties that bind...till he met Frannie. Though he could tell *she* was inexperienced, nothing in his past could have prepared him for the feelings Frannie inspired....

Raven Hunter: When the bones of this Kincaid rival turned up, everyone started talking about the ill-fated affair between Native American Raven and the Kincaid beauty who once defied her family for love. Was Raven's disappearance all those years ago truly an accident?

CHRISTIE RIDGWAY

thinks she has the greatest job in the world. She loves writing stories, and the only thing she loves more is her family: a supportive husband and two sons who often are forced to remind her that kids are entitled to three meals a day.

A native of California, she now lives in the southern part of the state. A typical writing day can include rescuing the turtle from the pool and finding frogs in the shower. When not writing or chasing down errant pets, she volunteers at her sons' school. Finally, because there's really nothing better, Christie always finds time to curl up with a good book.

You may contact her at P.O. Box 3803, La Mesa, CA 91944. Send a SASE for reply, or e-mail her at christie@christieridgway.com

ROBIN WELLS

Before becoming a full-time writer, Robin was a hotel public relations executive whose career ran the gamut from writing and producing award-winning videos to organizing pie-throwing classes taught by circus clowns. At other times in her life she has been a model, a reporter and even a charm school teacher. But her lifelong dream was to become an author, a dream no doubt inspired by having parents who were both librarians and who passed on their love of books. Her first book won RWA's national 1995 Golden Heart Award.

Robin lives just outside New Orleans with her husband and two young daughters, Taylor and Arden. Although New Orleans is known as America's Most Romantic City, Robin says her personal romantic inspiration is her husband, Ken.

Robin loves to hear from her readers and can be reached at P.O. Box 303, Mandeville, LA 70470-0303.

MONTANA MAVERICKS

MONTANA
Born

Christie Ridgway

Robin Wells

Published by Silhouette Books
America's Publisher of Contemporary Romance

Special thanks and acknowledgment are given to
Christie Ridgway and Robin Wells for their
contributions to MONTANA BORN.

SILHOUETTE BOOKS

MONTANA BORN
Copyright © 2002 by Harlequin Books S.A.

ISBN 0-373-48484-4

The publisher acknowledges the copyright holder
of the individual works as follows:

THE MARRIAGE MAKER
Copyright © 2000 by Harlequin Books S.A.

AND THE WINNER—WEDS!
Copyright © 2000 by Harlequin Books S.A.

Printed in U.S.A.

CONTENTS

All underlined places are fictitious.

MONTANA MAVERICKS: WED IN WHITEHORN
THE KINCAIDS

Affair w/ Ruth Whitefeather

Barton Kincaid m. Beatrice Lambert

Garrett m. Laura Hart (d)   Arthur   Louise

Larry (d) m. Sue Ellen Edwards (D)   Alice m. Henry Brooks

Collin   Melanie   Lyle

m.   m.
Hope Baxter   Eli Forrester

Brandon Harper   Trent Remmington — Blake Remmington   Mitch Fielding   Gabe Reilly

m.   m.   m.   m.
Emma Stover   Gina Henderson   Elaine Sinclair (D)   Joanna Larson (d)

2nd m.   Taylor   Ashley
Serena Dovesong

Nate   2nd m.
Heather Johnson

Jessica   Patrick   Andrew

Symbols
..... Child of an Affair
— Twins
d   Deceased
D   Divorced

The Marriage Maker

Christie Ridgway

To my editor, Lynda Curnyn.
Thanks for everything.

Prologue

Never in her life had Cleo Kincaid Monroe schemed to get a kiss.

"But there's a first time for everything," she muttered to herself as she moved around the spacious kitchen of the Big Sky Bed & Breakfast.

"Did you say something?" The deep voice of Ethan Redford, her evening's date, came from the direction of the small den off the kitchen.

"Say something? Not me. Uh-uh. Nothing." And nothing was exactly what had happened between Cleo and Ethan. Not tonight when he'd taken her to dinner at the Whitehorn Country Club, not last week when he'd flown her in a private plane for lunch in Bozeman, not all the times they'd run into each other at the B and B where he was staying and where she lived with her mother and sister.

Cleo scooped coffee into an unbleached filter, vowing to change that nothing to something, to a kiss, because for the three weeks since Ethan had arrived in Whitehorn, Montana, she hadn't been able to think of anything *but* kissing him.

Aware that it was after midnight, she dumped another generous scoop of grounds into the filter and clicked on the coffeemaker. Drowsiness wasn't going to get in the way of this kiss, either, by gosh.

Another woman might have thought Ethan didn't *want* to kiss her, but Cleo figured it had more to do with all the interruptions that came with living at the family business. Why, after their Bozeman lunch they'd stood in this very kitchen and she'd actually *seen* the kiss in his eyes, even felt his warm breath rush across her mouth as he leaned toward her. But then her sister Jasmine and their mother had bustled in, wanting every detail of Cleo's first-ever private plane ride.

She could have killed them.

But tonight, ah, tonight the B and B was blissfully quiet. Ethan was their only guest right now—early February not being the high tourist season in Montana—and Jasmine went to bed early. Cleo cast a glance down the hall that led to the family's bedrooms and didn't see a light under her mother's door, either. That was good, too. Celeste hadn't been sleeping well lately and maybe she was finally getting a chance to catch up on her rest.

Cleo loaded a tray with the coffee carafe, mugs, cream, sugar and spoons, then took one bracing breath before stepping into the den.

And there he was.

Her stomach gave that funny little hiccup it always did when she looked at Ethan. There wasn't much call for elegant dark business suits, white shirts and ties in Montana, but Ethan wore them with the ease most of the men she knew wore down jackets and cowboy boots.

He'd thrown his suit jacket over the rocking chair in the corner, rolled up his sleeves and loosened his tie. Cleo's tummy hiccuped again. Who'd have thought "corporate rumple" could look so delicious and complement so well that glint of gold stubble on his chin?

She let her gaze wander up to his blue eyes. Guilt pinged her. "You look tired," she said, and here she was, ready to feed him megadoses of caffeine to satisfy her own sensual curiosity. She knew he'd been working long hours on a merger deal between the local ATI Com company and the Kyoto-based Sokia Industries.

But he smiled—grinned really, that confident Ethan grin—and stood to take the tray out of her hands. "It wears a man out, talking about himself all night." He set the tray on the small table in front of the love seat he'd been sitting on. "Don't think I didn't realize you were plying me with questions."

With her hands unoccupied, Cleo found herself suddenly nervous. The den was small and the love seat—the only sitting space available since Ethan's jacket occupied the rocking chair—was even smaller. She swallowed as he sat back down, his tall frame taking up more than half of the cushions. "My questions were legitimate," she said, trying to hide her nervousness with a smile. "I didn't know a thing about a merger and acquisitions consulting company."

He grimaced. "And now you probably know more than you ever wanted to…and about the man who owns one."

Cleo remained standing, her hands clutching each other. Yes, Ethan had told her about his company, United Mergers, Inc., and about the deal he was trying to put together here in Whitehorn. He'd told her about his penthouse condo in Houston and about the constant travel his work required. But did she know much about *him?* He hadn't shared one word with her about his personal life. A little shiver of apprehension tickled her spine. Maybe kissing Ethan wasn't such a good idea, after all.

"Are you cold?" Ethan patted the love seat beside him. "Come and sit down and let me warm you up with some…coffee."

Was Cleo imagining that little hesitation? What about that little gleam in his eye? "Maybe…" She glanced back toward the kitchen, as if some excuse might conveniently present itself.

"Cleo." Two of his fingers curled in her direction, more commanding than coaxing. "Come here."

That shiver sped down her spine again, but there was no saying no to the decisive tone in Ethan's voice. She didn't want to, anyway, of course. Not really. Not when she'd been staring into his intense blue eyes all evening. Not when she'd been wondering for days what his crisp, dark gold hair would feel like between her fingers.

She slid onto the cushion beside him, pressing against the upholstered arm. To hide her nervousness, she busied herself arranging the soft gathers of her long, violet-colored, thermal-knit dress. Small buttons ran from the hem to the modest neckline, and Ethan reached out and touched the topmost one, right below the pulse beat at her throat.

"This dress matches your eyes," he said quietly. "Did I tell you tonight how beautiful you look?"

Goose bumps prickled her skin and she felt her cheeks heat. She kept her gaze on her lap. "I think you mentioned it, right after you noticed the green fingerpaint in my hair."

He leaned forward and picked up a long wavy tendril of the stuff in question. The green had been quite a startling contrast to its usual russet color. Cleo couldn't believe she'd missed it when she'd gotten ready for their date. But even then, the idea of kissing Ethan had been distracting her.

He idly toyed with her hair, brushing the end against her cheek with a teasing flick. "Occupational hazard, right?"

"I suppose so." As the director of Beansprouts, Whitehorn's only day care center, fingerpaint was merely one of life's daily surprises. She grinned. "But I tell you, a couple of occupational-type presents made up for it. Brandon Rye brought me some fat earthworms from his family's compost bin along with a big ol' sloppy kiss."

Ethan's hand, still tickling her with her hair, froze midstroke. "A sloppy kiss? And who is this Brandon? Should I be jealous?"

Cleo looked up at Ethan then. Her cheeks burned and her heart pounded, but she didn't let either sensation stop her. "I don't know if you should be jealous," she answered. "Are you?"

He smiled, and grooves appeared in his lean cheeks. "That depends on whether you like sloppy kisses."

Cleo liked to breathe, but it didn't appear she'd get air soon, not with how it all seemed to be sucked away by the contrast of Ethan's playful smile with his intense, darkening gaze. "I...like all kinds of kisses."

Ethan's smile died and the heat in his eyes intensified. "Is that right?" He leaned closer.

Cleo watched his face near hers, her heart pounding hard and loud. The kiss. It was coming. And the idea scared her all over again so she put her hand lightly on his chest to slow his obvious intent. "Ethan..." she said.

His gaze was trained on her lips. "Hmm?"

It was the first thought that popped into her head. "Brandon's three years old."

That cocky, confident Ethan grin flashed again. "Cleo?"

"Hmm?"

He cupped her face with both his big hands. "I'm not." Then he touched her mouth.

His lips were warm and his scent spicy and she breathed him in, her stomach hiccuping again in excitement.

He held her face firmly with his hands, his fingertips against the pulses pounding at her temples. He angled his mouth to taste her deeper, but it was a gentle, thorough taking, his lips persuasive as his tongue slid softly into her mouth.

It was Ethan making a deal, she thought fuzzily as he curled his tongue coaxingly against hers. Smooth and slow, but ruthless, too. He trailed one hand from her face down her throat and held her there, too, the pulse at her throat beating against the vee made by his thumb and index finger. Goose bumps followed his path and Cleo found herself crowding his mouth, trying to press harder.

But he refused to be hurried, instead backing off a little himself and continuing to stroke his tongue softly, slowly—too soft, too slow—into her mouth.

She made a little sound of frustration and then finally remembered she had her own ways of getting what she wanted. Her fingers flattened against his shirtfront and she let him have that slow kiss as she explored the crispness of his shirt until she slid two fingers between the buttons beneath his tie.

She stroked once. Hot skin. She stroked twice. Hot male skin.

Ethan groaned, and then he widened her mouth with his and slid his tongue fully, wildly, inside.

Another rush of heat ran through Cleo, speeding from where their mouths met to run between her aching breasts. She took her free hand and touched the back of his head, pulling him closer with her palm against his thick golden hair.

He grunted and she made him pay for those three weeks of thinking of kissing by taking what she wanted—a slow pass of her tongue against his. She felt him shudder, and then she did, too, because he took her breasts in the curved cups of his palms.

Someone broke the kiss, and they stared at each other. Ethan's nostrils flared and there was a flush on his cheekbones. Cleo couldn't catch her breath; it just heaved in and out, pushing her breasts against the palms of Ethan's hands.

With slow intent, he dropped his gaze, and she watched

him watch himself rub his thumbs across her beaded nipples.

Cleo jerked, startled by the sweet sensation, surprised by how, how much she craved Ethan's touch.

He looked back up and met her eyes. "I'm going to see you," he said, his voice full of the kind of conviction that probably made CEOs in business meetings roll over and play dead.

Cleo didn't even have that much will. She only knew she wanted what Ethan wanted, his gaze on her, his hands on her. *Please.*

Never hurrying, not appearing the least bit nervous, his fingers started on the row of small buttons holding her dress together.

Cleo closed her eyes. There were too many buttons. He was taking too long. And then he peeled the dress off her shoulders.

Ethan groaned one more time. "Cleo. Hell. Cleo."

Her eyelids lifted and she saw his body was tense. He was looking at her breasts, and so she looked, too. Between the parted violet fabric of her clingy dress showed the lace of her darker violet bra, and rising from that was the swell of her breasts, taut and trembling.

Ethan's hands tightened on her shoulders. He leaned forward, kissed her mouth hard, ran his tongue along her bottom lip.

Cleo shivered, only aware of how badly she wanted him to touch her. "I usually don't..." she said, feeling almost bewildered by the power of the wanting. "I'm not—"

Ethan kissed her swiftly again, then rested his forehead against hers. "I know. And I wish—"

The distant sound of glass breaking cut him off.

Cleo jerked and half rose from her seat. Another sound—

a woman's stifled cry—made her rise completely. "My mother."

Ethan hastily stood, too, and he pulled Cleo's dress together, trying to button it. He looked around wildly, as if searching for an intruder or some other explanation. "What could it be?"

She pushed his hands away and quickly fastened the most crucial buttons as she ran through the kitchen. "A nightmare," she called back, now speeding down the hall. "She has terrible nightmares."

Cleo threw open the door to her mother's bedroom. Just as she expected, Celeste was awake. With the help of the dim hallway light, Cleo confirmed her mother had had another run-in with the terrible dream. Tears still ran down Celeste's pretty face.

"Don't come in!" she ordered.

Cleo grabbed the doorjamb to halt her forward momentum. "What? Why?"

Instead of answering, Celeste struck a match, her hand wavering with nightmare aftershocks as she lit the candle that was always at the ready on her bedside table.

The scent of Louisiana—that was how Celeste always described the aroma of her special white candles—filled the air. In the light the flame gave off, the light that Celeste believed burned the dream's evil from the room, Cleo saw why her mother had ordered her to stay by the door.

Somehow she'd broken the delicate glass vial that always sat on the small bedside table, as well. In the incongruous shape of a skeleton, the vial had been filled with bergamot oil. Inspired by her time on the bayou, Celeste conferred upon the oil a special power, just as she did the candles. She believed rubbing the stuff on her skin would ease the almost-arthritic cramping of her left hand that invariably followed the horrible dream.

Cleo watched her mother take a long, deep breath. "Are you all right, Mama?"

Celeste closed her eyes, opened them, and a faint smile moved the corners of her mouth. "I'm all right for now, Cleo."

"I'll get a broom." Her heart heavy, she whirled around, and headed back toward the kitchen.

To find Ethan lingering by the sink with his back to her, staring out into the snowy February night.

Cleo automatically lifted her fingers toward the remaining undone buttons of her dress.

Ethan turned around, catching her.

She froze.

His gaze flicked in the direction of her breasts, flicked back to her face. He swallowed. "Is everything all right?"

Cleo self-consciously dropped her hands to her sides. "She has a recurring nightmare that is very…unsettling."

"Ah." He shoved his hands into the pockets of his slacks. "Please tell her I'm sorry."

"I will." Cleo backed toward the utility closet where they stored the broom. "And, um, Ethan." Her cheeks burned. She wondered if he would want to wait for her to settle her mother back to sleep. She wondered if she had the nerve to ask him to wait. "I'm, uh, sorry, too."

His mouth curved up but there was no smile in his eyes or his voice. "Don't worry about it." He took a step in the direction that would take him to the guest stairs and his second-floor bedroom. "Good night, Cleo."

Good night, Cleo. Her courage didn't show itself to ask him for something more than that. Biting her bottom lip, she just watched him head out of the kitchen.

"Wait!" Her voice was squeakily anxious.

Ethan halted, then slowly turned around. One dark gold eyebrow rose. "What?"

Cleo swallowed. "Before...before..." She gave up and just gestured toward the den and the love seat that she'd never look at quite the same way again. "Back there, back then, you..." Impatient with herself, she ran a hand through her hair. "You were saying something. What was it?"

Ethan's expression didn't give any of his thoughts away. Cleo supposed his kind of work made that an important trait, too. "Tomorrow, Cleo. We'll talk tomorrow."

And this time when he turned toward the stairs, Cleo let Ethan go. *Tomorrow.*

But when tomorrow came, Ethan Redford left the Big Sky B and B, without a word of excuse or explanation to anyone. As a matter of fact he disappeared from Montana altogether, leaving Cleo with only two imprints as a reminder of him—one of his credit card and the other of his kiss.

One

The thirty-year-old nightmare was older than Celeste Kincaid Monroe's daughter Cleo, but it gripped Celeste ruthlessly all the same, dragging her instantly from sleep to terror.

The bayou again. Moss hanging like sticky, gray spiderwebs in the trees. The scent of wet decay.

Thunder. Once. Twice.

Then, as always, he appeared, a dark figure carrying something even darker. Fear surged like adrenaline through Celeste's veins. It sang in her blood, an eerie, high-pitched dirge. She dug her bare toes into the mud.

Turn! Run!

But escape was impossible. The tall silhouette of her brother, Jeremiah Kincaid, kept coming toward her, the water swishing around his knees. The burden in his arms didn't seem to trouble him. He carried it to Celeste as if it were a gift.

"No, Jeremiah," she whispered. No, he shouldn't be here in Louisiana. He'd never come to see her once she'd done his bidding and married Ty Monroe.

"Look," he said, his voice commanding her, always telling her how it was, what she must do. "Look what is yours."

"No." She kept her gaze away from the limp body in his arms. It would be her sister Blanche, who had died after childbirth. It could only be Blanche, and Celeste refused to look at her. She couldn't bear to see her sister's vibrant fall of hair trailing through the stagnant, murky water. Just the thought made her heart stop, then disappear altogether.

In the cavern of her chest, only pain remained, echoing over and over.

"Look," Jeremiah insisted.

Fear again, with its high-pitched song. *No.* But then she obeyed, her gaze angling down, down, toward the dead body of—

No! Celeste jerked up her head…

…and jerked right out of the nightmare's grasp.

Lying against the soft sheets in her bedroom at Whitehorn's Big Sky Bed & Breakfast, Celeste tried to catch her breath as tears rolled down her cheeks. She wiped at them with her hands, then turned her face against the pillow. Still, the dream clutched at her.

"Montana," she whispered to herself, sitting up and lighting the white candle beside her bed. She'd left Louisiana with her husband after only a year, coming back to Whitehorn and buying this house on the lake that with her sister Yvette she'd turned into the Big Sky Bed & Breakfast. This was where her daughters were born and lived. Montana.

Forget the dream. But despite the steady, bright flame of her candle, the emotions the dream always roiled up still lurked in the dark corners of the room. She shivered.

And the past. The past lurked, too, hovering above her bed like a dark cloying canopy.

Celeste threw off the covers. Though her clock said it was only 5:00 a.m., she wasn't going to find any more sleep. Dressing in jeans, sweater and lambskin boots, Celeste told herself a cup of coffee would burn away any last traces of the bad dream.

She quickly made up the bed, blew out her candle, then

stepped into the hall, shutting her bedroom door firmly. Just as decisively, she shoved the memory of the dream to the back of her mind.

She couldn't help being a victim to her nights, but she refused to let her waking hours be tainted, too. Today she wouldn't let the one emotion that always stayed with her after the nightmare—that one unnameable emotion—overshadow her every daytime hour.

Celeste took the long route to the kitchen, walking through the public rooms of the B and B as if inspecting the intricate, natural-hued woodwork of the arts-and-crafts-style house could bring her quickly and fully into the present. Through the large living room windows she could see the last of the stars reflected in the glassy surface of Blue Mirror Lake. She stared out at the water, her hands absently stroking the Native-print blanket thrown over the back of one of the room's rattan couches.

After the years she'd spent alongside the bayou in Louisiana, this house, overlooking the water of the small natural lake, had drawn her, and not just because it was a respectable distance from the controlling influence of her brother, Jeremiah Kincaid. She'd always been grateful to her late husband Tyler's agreeing to return to Montana and to buy this property. He'd recognized that she'd needed something to call her own, especially when he travelled so often. And the house was a true gem. There were a few others scattered among the pines surrounding the lake—vacation places, all of them—and most newer than her three-story house. It had been an ideal location to raise a family, an ideal home for her and Yvette to turn into a ten-bedroom bed-and-breakfast, and an ideal way to support themselves while they also raised Summer, the orphaned daughter of their sister Blanche.

Blanche.

Celeste shivered as that dream-born emotion she was trying to bury struggled to surface. She hurried away from it by hurrying out of the room, past two more rattan couches and overstuffed club chairs, through the massive dining room with its long mission-style table and heavily beamed ceiling.

Letting herself think only of coffee, she swore she could almost smell it as she pushed the swinging door that led into the kitchen.

Celeste blinked in the dazzling overhead light. The room was bright, there *was* coffee already brewed, and she wasn't going to keep her insomnia a secret because it seemed another Monroe woman shared it.

"Mama!" Celeste's twenty-seven-year-old daughter Cleo looked up from the mug she'd been frowning at.

"Sweetie, what's wrong?" Celeste crossed the hardwood floor in the direction of the scarred oval table where Cleo was sitting. "You're looking at that coffee as if it's your worst enemy."

Cleo's full lips raised in something that wasn't quite a smile. "It is *my* coffee, after all, Mama, not Jasmine's."

Well, her younger daughter was undoubtedly a master in the kitchen, but Celeste knew Cleo was just avoiding the real question. "C'mon, sweetie, this is your mother you're talking to. You don't usually have trouble sleeping."

Cleo's eyebrows came together in concern. "No, it's you that usually can't get any rest. Another nightmare?"

Celeste gestured with her hand as if to brush the subject away. She didn't want to discuss it. "I'm asking what's keeping you awake."

There was a long pause, then Cleo looked balefully back down at her coffee mug. "Beansprouts. I'm worried about the day care center."

Celeste let the admission go for a moment and moved to

the counter to pour herself some of Cleo's less-than-stellar coffee. She was proud of her daughter's success as the director of the day care center and knew that Cleo also took a lot of pride in what she did. The man she leased the building from had told Cleo last week he was going to sell the property as soon as possible. With her lease agreement up for renewal, Cleo had a legitimate worry that her business might not survive.

"You haven't found another possible site, honey?" Celeste added a dash of milk to her mug then held the hot ceramic against the knuckles of her left hand. Their deep arthritic ache was as unpleasantly familiar as the dream that brought it about.

"Nothing," Cleo said, shrugging. "And Gene came by again yesterday. He's putting up a For Sale sign next week."

Celeste came forward to lay a hand on top of her daughter's head. "Maybe he won't find anyone interested in buying."

"Mmm."

Celeste's eyes narrowed. If she had to guess, she would say that Cleo wasn't thinking about Beansprouts or For Sale signs or anything to do with business. There was a sad, faraway but dreamy look in her daughter's beautiful violet eyes. "This is about something else. Something besides Beansprouts."

Cleo didn't look up.

Celeste's heart squeezed, and she used her aching left hand to tilt up her daughter's chin. "Oh, Cleo," she said. "This isn't about him, is it? He's been gone three months, sweetie. You wouldn't still be mooning over a man like Ethan Redford?"

A new voice broke in. "Of course Cleo's not mooning over Ethan, Mama. Cleo is much too sensible, much too practical to be letting a big shot, here-today-gone-tomorrow man like Ethan Redford even give her heart a tickle.''

Celeste chuckled as her younger daughter Jasmine glided into the room. At twenty-three, with her short-cropped black hair and a slender face, she looked too fresh and wide-awake for five-thirty in the morning. ''You're up early.''

''Mmm.'' She took one sniff at the coffee carafe, grimaced in mock disgust, then dumped its contents into the sink. ''Cleo would be in a better mood if she could learn to make better coffee.''

Since Jasmine's coffee was universally acclaimed as fabulous—as well as anything else she created in the kitchen—neither Cleo nor Celeste bothered disagreeing with her. As a matter of fact, Cleo only said, ''Sit down, Mama,'' and then took both their mugs to the sink. She poured out the contents, then set the cups on the counter to wait for her sister's heaven-blessed brew.

She gave Jasmine a significant look. ''Mama had another nightmare.''

Both young women turned toward her. Celeste froze under her daughters' worried gazes. ''No—'' But she stopped, because they were pointedly looking at her hands, and she realized she'd been massaging the painful left one with her right. She sighed.

''Please, girls, let's talk about something else,'' she pleaded. Talking about her nightmare might allow that disturbing, unnameable emotion she was keeping under strict control to rise again. ''Please.''

Jasmine surrendered first, sliding her gaze toward her more voluptuous sister. ''Okay, Mama.'' She grinned, that devilish grin of a younger sibling who knows just how to push the older one's buttons—and revels in it. ''Let's talk about what's bugging Cleo.''

"Watch it," Cleo threatened. "I can still hide your Barbie dolls, brat." She propped her hands on her hips.

Jasmine's grin widened. "I've hidden them from *you*. At your insistence, I recycle, Cleo. I compost our kitchen scraps. I'd never wear fur. But you're not going to make me give up my precious fashion dolls. Uh-uh."

Before Cleo could retort, the kitchen's back door opened and Frannie, Celeste's niece, stepped over the threshold. In a brown, knee-length business suit that matched the brown of her hair and the brown of her eyes, she looked completely prepared for another day in her job as a loan officer at the Whitehorn Savings and Loan.

At five-nine, Frannie towered over her cousins. In a familiar morning ritual, she automatically took the cup of coffee Cleo poured for her. "What are we talking about?" She lived at her parents' house, located just behind the B and B.

Jasmine started bustling around the kitchen, getting ready for the breakfast she'd serve the guests. "Fashion, I'd guess you'd say."

Frannie touched the brown tortoiseshell clip that held her hair at the back of her neck. She sighed. "I guess that lets me out, then."

Jasmine shook her head. "Only because you won't let me make you over, Frannie. If you'd just give yourself a chance, you'd be stunning."

Frannie flushed. "Let's talk about something else."

That mischievous smile twitched at Jasmine's lips again. Uh-oh, Celeste thought. Prepare yourself, Cleo.

"We could go back to discussing Cleo's love life," Jasmine said, taking eggs out of the refrigerator.

"Oh, no, you don't." Cleo's face blushed just as pink as Frannie's.

Jasmine acted as if she hadn't heard her. "Mama wondered if maybe Cleo was still smitten with that Ethan Red-ford who was here three months ago.''

Frannie blinked owlishly. ''Who?''

''You remember.'' Jasmine took the juicer out of a lower cupboard. ''He took Cleo out a couple of times, and I admit the looks he gave her could have melted that old wallpaper off the downstairs hallway, but then he just—poof!—left Whitehorn. What do you think? Is Cleo in need of romantic repair?''

''Of course not.'' Frannie blinked again and her voice was absolutely certain. ''Cleo is much, much too practical to make any kind of romantic mistake.''

''Sensible, too. You missed sensible, Frannie,'' Cleo added. Her face had regained its normal color and her voice was without animation.

Something in the nonemotion of Cleo's voice niggled at Celeste and her mother radar went on the alert. ''Cleo, sweetie—''

''Good morning!'' The back door had opened again to admit Frannie's parents, Celeste's sister Yvette and her hus-band, Edward Hannon. The smell of a cool spring morning accompanied them as they headed for the countertop and Jasmine's coffee.

The girls exchanged pleasantries with the new arrivals, and soon they were all savoring their morning ritual. Jas-mine continued preparing breakfast for the guests, but the rest of them took their places around the large kitchen table. Edward unfolded the newspaper and smiled at the faces circling him. ''And a good morning it is. No better way for a man to start the day than with a glimpse of the harem that has kept him happy all these years.''

Celeste joined the others in the groan that invariably ac-companied Edward's usual comment. Someone wished that

David, Frannie's brother, was around to keep his father in check.

Thinking of her nephew, Celeste could only wish David was nearby, too. An FBI agent in Atlanta, Georgia, he hadn't made it to Montana for a visit in too long. And she needed her loved ones around her. The nightmares were trying to tell her something about the past, and she felt certain she'd need all those she held dear when the day of reckoning came.

Yvette touched Celeste's arm. "Are you all right?"

"She had another rough night," Cleo said.

Celeste felt like a specimen in a bottle with five sets of serious eyes regarding her. That desperate, unnamed emotion swirled up inside her like a tornado, and she had to take a deep breath to find the strength to push it back down. "But I'm looking forward to an interesting day," she said firmly. "Edward, tell us some good news."

With one more searching look at her face, Edward smoothed the front page absently, then bent his head. "Well," he said, smoothing the paper again. "Lyle Brooks finally broke ground for that resort/casino complex he's been talking up all over town."

Celeste frowned. That young man was some sort of kin on the Kincaid side and she'd never felt comfortable around him. "But isn't the casino part of the Laughing Horse Reservation? How is Lyle involved?"

It was banker Frannie who answered. "Because Indian laws allow gambling, the casino will be on the Laughing Horse reservation, Aunt Celeste. But the accompanying resort will be on Kincaid land. Lyle's put together the financing for both projects." She didn't look any more at ease about the young man than Celeste felt. "In ten years the whole thing will move out of Kincaid/Laughing Horse hands and into those of a joint corporation, headed by Lyle.''

Celeste should have been happy that they were off the subject of her nightmares, but suddenly the whole notion of Lyle and the disturbance of Kincaid land chilled her. A shiver racked her body. Yvette's hand moved across the table to cover Celeste's left one, the ache in it more pronounced than usual.

"Celeste, what's the matter?" Yvette asked.

Another shiver rattled over Celeste's spine. "There's just something about Lyle I don't like," she said to her sister. "Maybe it's because he reminds me of Jeremiah.''

At the mention of their elder brother's name, silence fell around the table. When he'd been murdered, the violence had been shocking, but they hadn't mourned him. He'd been cold and controlling all his life.

Celeste took a long breath, sorry to have brought her brother's name into their warm circle. She looked from face to face, trying to gauge their moods. Edward and Yvette were concerned about her, she could see, while Frannie looked almost embarrassed. Standing behind Cleo, two worry lines bisected Jasmine's smooth forehead. And Cleo—her beautiful, motherly Cleo—looked ready to fight tigers on Celeste's behalf. But even underneath all her bristling protectiveness Celeste sensed in her older daughter another kind of sadness...

Yvette squeezed Celeste's hand. "We love you," she said.

Oh. And she loved them all and wanted them so much to be happy. With her right hand she lifted her coffee cup to her mouth, intent on moistening her throat to tell them so.

But the coffee sloshed over her hand instead, and she didn't even notice the slight scald, because suddenly that frightening maelstrom of emotion, that nightmare hangover, rose up within her once again. There was no controlling it.

She looked around at the faces of her family, but the feeling stayed, pulsing inside her.

It was powerful and dark and she finally, finally, knew its terrifying name.

The emotion that always remained with her after the horrible dream was…shame.

Celeste dropped her gaze, unable to meet the eyes of her caring, beloved family. Because just as certain as she was that it was shame trying to claw its way out of her heart, she was quite sure her family would condemn her if they knew that long ago she had…she had…

What?

Oh, God. Despite the acknowledgment of that feeling of shame, despite thirty years of terror-filled nights, Celeste just didn't know.

She didn't know what terrifying, shameful thing she had done.

TWO

Ethan Redford sat in his newly purchased Range Rover outside Whitehorn, Montana's Beansprouts day care center. Out his tinted windows he had a perfect view of the center's fenced playground. Under the watchful gaze of several women he didn't recognize, little kids built sandcastles, slid down a wavy slide, made imaginary meals in a gaily painted playhouse. Pleasing though the sight was, Ethan's fingertips drummed the saddle-colored leather armrest.

He was stalling.

As humbling as the confession might be, he had to admit to himself that the idea of confronting Cleo Monroe after his abrupt, three-month absence was making his palms sweat. Hell! And this from a man who'd faced down his drunken, raging father at nine years old and brokered his first multimillion-dollar merger at thirty.

He rubbed his hands against his deliberately casual khaki slacks. Though the deal he wanted to propose today was the most important of his life, he knew it wasn't the moment for an Armani suit and his best silk tie. For Cleo, he needed to appear approachable instead of powerful. Friendly, not frightening.

Cleo.

As if thinking her name had summoned her, the woman he'd been fantasizing about for three months stepped from the back door of the stucco building onto the fenced play yard. Instantly she was surrounded, little kids clamoring for her attention, little hands patting her legs, little fingers grabbing her hands.

Kind of like what he wanted to do. Grabbing her sounded good to him, too.

Ethan closed his eyes and groaned, remembering the sweet, silky feel of Cleo's skin. He saw the voluptuous rise of her breasts over her lacy bra and felt again the tremors shaking her body as he brushed his thumbs over her nipples. He groaned again.

When he'd left Cleo that night, he'd considered himself pretty damn heroic for backing away from the wildfire of their mutual physical attraction. He hadn't wanted to lead her on. She was the marrying kind, and he wasn't. She deserved a man prepared for the type of family life she undoubtedly desired, and that hadn't been him, by any means.

Fate must be laughing its head off about right now.

To the faint echoes of its capricious guffaws, Ethan forced himself out of his car and then reached into the rear seat for what had brought him from Houston back to Whitehorn, back to Cleo. He wrestled a bit with the latch that released the baby carrier from its car seat base, letting loose a soft curse.

Guilt gave him a little jab and he quickly apologized to the blond, wide-eyed baby staring up at him. ''Sorry, Jonah.'' And sorry to you too, Della. The boy's mother wouldn't appreciate the child's first word being something better suited to a locker room than a nursery. He took a breath, pushing away the pain that came when he thought of Della. The only thing he could do for her now was to take care of Jonah.

That was where Cleo came in.

At the reception desk inside Beansprouts, Ethan asked to speak with the center's director—Cleo. The young receptionist gave him a friendly smile and after rising from her chair to peek at Jonah, told Ethan they didn't take children until they were two years old. She would be happy to place his name on their waiting list.

Ethan bared his teeth in what he hoped would pass for a smile, and mildly asked once again to see the Beansprouts director. When the still-friendly but outright curious receptionist gave in and showed him into a small office, she asked his name.

Ethan told her he wanted to keep it a surprise.

He sure as hell hoped Cleo liked surprises.

When she walked through the office door, it was obvious she didn't. As she caught sight of him, her feet stopped before the rest of her body did and she grabbed the doorjamb to keep herself from pitching forward. Expressions chased themselves across her face. Ethan couldn't separate them all—but the last one he read loud and clear.

It was as cool and distant as her voice. "Ethan Redford," she said as if he'd never tasted the hot wetness of her mouth. Then her gaze dropped to the infant carrier he held against his chest as if it were a shield. She blinked, shook her head a little, blinked again.

"Who? What?" Her cheeks flushed a deep pink. *"Oh,"* she said.

Oh? What did she mean by that significant *oh?* And then it hit him.

Uh-oh.

"The baby's not mine," he said quickly. But then he had to correct himself. "Well, he is mine, but—" From the look on her face this wasn't going well. He sighed. "It's complicated."

Cleo took a breath and Ethan pretended he wasn't aware of the way her breasts pressed against the long-sleeved white T-shirt she wore. "What do you want, Ethan?"

He sighed again. ''That's complicated, too.'' The smile he gave her was supposed to be charming, but she looked distinctly unmoved. ''Could we talk?''

With a little roll of one of her shoulders, she fully entered the room and shut the office door behind her. Then she walked past him, the familiar, delicate flower scent of her perfume brushing by him nonchalantly. Cleo's T-shirt was tucked into a long denim skirt that showed off her small waist and rounded hips and he had to look away until she was completely seated behind her desk.

She linked her fingers on the surface of a blotter-size calendar full of notations in neat, rounded handwriting. ''What would you like to say, Ethan?''

He'd like to say he wished like hell they'd not been interrupted by her mother's nightmare that evening. He'd like to say that he'd been thinking of her kisses, of her skin, of the beauty of her wavy, russet hair for the past three months. He'd like to say that even in the midst of grief and worry, the memory of her smile and laughter had been a warm beacon.

Instead he sat in a chair across from her, the infant carrier resting on his knees. ''This is my nephew, Jonah,'' he said simply. ''And the day I left your mother's bed-and-breakfast, I was called away because Jonah's mother, my sister, had been the victim of a carjacking.''

One of Cleo's hands rose to cover her mouth.

He went on doggedly. It wasn't an easy story to tell. ''I probably should have left you some word, or called you when I reached Houston, but all I could think about was Della and Jonah. She was in intensive care with head injuries and Jonah was missing.''

''Oh, my Lord,'' Cleo whispered. Suddenly she wasn't in her chair, but kneeling beside Ethan, her attention focused on the baby. One fingertip stroked his nephew's downy head. Her gaze turned Ethan's way. In her violet eyes was the sudden awareness that his story didn't have a happy-ever-after. "But the baby was found."

Ethan nodded. "In an alley, in Della's abandoned car." His hand curled into a fist, as the useless waste of the tragedy cut through him again like an acid burn. "Two days later the carjacker was killed in a police shoot-out. A day after that, my sister died." His voice was hoarse.

"Oh, Ethan." Cleo's warm hand covered his fist and he closed his eyes, her touch soothing and so damn welcome. "You must have loved her very much."

"She was my little sister." He opened his eyes and saw Cleo still kneeling between Jonah and him, one hand touching his, one hand on the baby's hair, linking all three of them together.

Just as he knew she would.

"Tell me about her, Ethan. You never even mentioned to me you had a sister."

Guilt stabbed him again. When he'd been in Montana three months ago he'd been carefully impersonal with Cleo. To tell the truth, he was carefully impersonal with everyone, but Cleo was the kind of woman who invited you to bare your soul. And because he'd been interested only in baring her body, he'd steered completely clear of anything that would even vaguely hint of any deeper intimacy.

But things were different now. *Everything* was different. Not him, though. He hadn't changed. But his needs had. So that meant telling Cleo what she wanted to know.

He cleared his throat. "Della was twenty-nine years old. She worked for me, at my office in Houston."

Cleo looked at little Jonah and smiled. "Was she blond like you?"

He pictured his sister in his mind. Not as he'd last seen her, her head swathed in bandages, bruises on her face and tubes everywhere, but as she'd been before the carjacking. "She was tiny, shorter than you, and she did have blond hair. After Jonah was born, she cut it short as a boy's."

Cleo nodded solemnly. "Easy to take care of."

"*She* was easy to take care of." Ethan broke off, suddenly embarrassed. Yeah, he missed his sister, but he wasn't about to get all maudlin in front of Cleo.

Maybe she sensed his reluctance, because she turned her attention back to the baby. "How old is he?"

"Seven months," Ethan replied.

"And where's Jonah's father?"

"His *biological* father abandoned both Della and the baby before Jonah was born. They were engaged, but let's just say Della found it a little…distressing when Drake gave her a black eye instead of a welcome home kiss one evening." Ethan and Della knew a lot about black eyes and the kind of men who dispensed them.

"She decided that she and the baby were better off without him and he didn't put up a fuss." With Ethan there, backing Della up, the cowardly bastard wouldn't have dared.

"And now that Della's…gone?" Cleo asked quietly.

"As far as Drake's concerned, Della and Jonah were gone from his life a long time ago." Ethan paused, because now they were getting to the important part. "I'm Jonah's f—"

Damn. He ran his hand through his hair. It was hard to say the word because he'd never considered himself suited to the job.

Cleo rose and leaned against the back of her desk, smiling a little as she looked down at Ethan. "His f—?" she asked, her almost-teasing voice easing the moment. "His what? Feet? Fiddle? Filly?"

Ethan's lips twitched and his brows came together. "Correct me if I'm wrong, Montana lady, but this city boy seems to recall that a filly is a *female* horse, right?''

At her little nod he couldn't resist reaching out to stroke one finger against the back of her hand. ''Well, now, Cleo, you gotta know I'm all man, don't you?''

Her face pinkened and she snatched her hand away, and for the first time in months, Ethan's mood lightened. Cleo. God, it was right to come back to her. When his lawyer had made what should have been an outrageous suggestion, he'd instantly thought of her, of her wavy hair, of her warm touch, of the way she looked at him.

And the lawyer's suggestion was what he had to tell Cleo about now. Jonah had drifted off to sleep and Ethan carefully moved the carrier to the carpet beside him. He casually rested his hands on the arms of his chair, though the situation he found himself in was anything *but* casual.

''I'm Jonah's family now,'' Ethan said. ''Nothing and no one is going to take him away from me. Della named me as his legal guardian.'' He paused.

''I think I hear a but,'' Cleo said slowly.

He nodded. ''After Della...died, I hired a nanny right away. I was able to postpone the deal I had going on here in Whitehorn, but there were a couple of others I couldn't put off. You know what that means.''

''You were out of town a lot.''

Ethan stared down at the sleeping baby. ''Yes. But I was cutting my trips as close to the bone as possible and the nanny was working out fine. Then Drake's parents entered the picture.''

''The baby's grandparents.''

Ethan nodded. ''They're rich, they're socially prominent and they don't think much of me as Jonah's...father since I'm away from him so much.''

''But the nanny—''

"Isn't a mother." Ethan looked up into Cleo's unsuspecting but sympathetic violet eyes. "They're suing for custody of Jonah."

"Oh." Cleo kneeled again, putting one hand on Ethan's shoulder. They were face-to-face, and hers was full of concern and sadness. "I'm so sorry, Ethan."

He looked at her steadily, and suddenly she dropped her hand and jumped to her feet. "Well, well." Something was making her very nervous, and he wondered if she'd figured out what he was about to ask.

She swallowed. "So now you're back in Montana," she said briskly. "The ATI Com-Sokia deal again?"

Ethan captured her hand and stood. "I've been thinking about another kind of merger altogether."

She swallowed again, but didn't say a word.

"I need something from you, Cleo."

"Me?" Her voice sounded breathless and her hand tried to slip from his. "What could *I* possibly do for you?"

Ethan held her fingers firmly. "You could marry me, Cleo."

Marry him. Marry Ethan.

Cleo's heart lurched, as if it were trying to find a way out of her chest. "Are you kidding?" she said, her voice sounding very far away.

Ethan's blue eyes were scarily solemn. "Not kidding."

Cleo's heart pitched again, like a boat ready to capsize. Marry Ethan? This whole episode was like something out of a fantasy, a too familiar fantasy born the first moment she'd seen Ethan last winter. A fantasy that had only grown in detail and proportion every time she'd encountered him after that.

But the reality of Ethan was right in front of her, too close, really. She could smell his delicious, sophisticated scent and see new lines of tiredness, or grief maybe, etched around his serious mouth. His sister had died. He had a baby now.

Little Jonah was real, too. Cleo looked down at the sweet baby, snoozing in his carrier. With his blond hair and the blue eyes she'd glimpsed, he could really *be* Ethan's.

A husband. A child. Ethan and Jonah.

"Cleo?" Ethan rubbed his thumb across the backs of her knuckles, and she suppressed a shiver. A fantasy couldn't come to life this easily. "What are you thinking?" he asked.

She swallowed. "Ethan, I need to know—"

A light knock on the office door interrupted her.

They both started and with the distraction Cleo was able to reclaim her hand. She moved away from Ethan and hoped she appeared calm.

"Come in," she called.

The door opened and Lynn, one of the caregivers on her staff, peeked in. "I'm sorry, Cleo, but Bessie had a fall and needs your expert touch in the bandage department." Lynn's gaze slid toward Ethan and her eyes widened. "That is, if you have the time."

"I always have time for Bessie," Cleo said, almost glad for the temporary reprieve. She smiled as Lynn escorted the four-year-old into the office.

Bessie had platinum-blond hair in pigtails and her eyelashes were spiked wet with recent tears. A painful-looking scrape slashed across one knee.

Cleo knelt by her side. "What happened, sweetie?" she said softly. Though Ethan had stepped out of the way, she continued to feel his gaze on her.

Bessie frowned fiercely. "Kenny G.," she said, her gravelly voice always a shocking contrast to her angelic features.

Lynn, who stood behind Bessie, must have seen the puzzlement on Ethan's face because she suddenly grinned his way and explained Bessie's statement. "Not the famous musician, mind you, but an infamous three-year-old. We have four Kennys at Beansprouts." Her fingers ticked them off. "Kenny E., Kenny K., Kenny T., and—" she paused, "—Kenny G."

Bessie's truckdriver voice took over. "Kenny G. pushed me down."

Lynn smiled in Ethan's direction again. "Kenny G. is currently having a time-out."

Cleo tamped down a little spurt of irritation at the other woman. There was no need for Lynn to explain things to Ethan, or to even be looking at him with such appreciation. But she focused on Bessie instead, brushing back a stray strand of the little girl's hair. "You're okay now, though?"

Bessie nodded and held out a bandage. "But I want you to put this on for me."

"Sure, hon." Cleo swung the little girl into her arms and sat her on the edge of her desk. With gentle hands she lifted Bessie's right leg and propped her sneakered foot against her own thigh. "Did Lynn clean this for you?"

Bessie looked as though she wanted to say "yes," but Lynn produced a bottle of hydrogen peroxide and a soft cloth. "She wanted you to do that, too."

"No problem, kiddo," Cleo said. "We'll get it taken care of pronto." She hadn't met a child yet who didn't detest getting his or her scrapes and cuts cleaned, but she also knew that handling it with confidence and without cringing was best for everyone.

Within moments she ensured the scrape was free of dirt and then she applied the bandage, the whole time chattering with Bessie about what was scheduled for the afternoon's snack and the new kitten in the little girl's household.

Aware the entire time of Ethan's focus on her, Cleo was proud that her hands didn't shake once. She ended the first aid with her usual healing kiss on Bessie's forehead and then she took the little girl's light weight in her arms to lift her off the desk.

Bessie looked over Cleo's shoulder. "Who's that?" she asked in her improbably rough voice, pointing at Ethan.

"Um…" Cleo froze, and noticed that Lynn's expression was as curious as Bessie's. "That's Mr. Redford. He's my, uh, friend." She set the little girl on her feet.

"He's cute," Bessie said, and she gave a little wave then skipped out of the room.

Lynn backed out more slowly, her gaze flicking between Cleo and Ethan. "Well, I'll just, um…" She seemed to have forgotten who and what generated her paycheck. "I'll just…"

"Go watch the kids?" Cleo prompted.

Lynn sighed. "Yeah." But then, as if she couldn't help herself, she sent Cleo a thumbs-up sign before shutting the door behind her.

Cleo hoped her cheeks weren't as red as they felt when she turned to face Ethan. "I'm, uh, sorry about that."

An echo of that old, confident Ethan grin flashed over his face. "Why? One female says I'm cute and another appears to have given me her stamp of approval. I'm thinking that's good for my case."

Apparently his proposal wasn't just a daydream, after all. Cleo leaned against her desk, gripping the edges with tight fingers. Marriage to Ethan! But as appealing as the idea was…

She inhaled a long, deep breath. "Why me?"

His eyes widened. "Uh." He shoved his hands in his pockets as he retreated to the far side of the small room, where he leaned his shoulders against the wall. "'Why you'?" he echoed.

Cleo tightened her grip on the edge of her old oak desk. "It's a hard question?"

"No. Yes." He groaned and pushed his hands impatiently through his hair.

Cleo had never seen the golden locks so disordered, not even the night she'd touched them herself as they'd kissed. She ignored the little hot rush of her blood at the memory. "Talk to me, Ethan," she said quietly.

His fingers raked through his hair once again. "My attorney in Houston—the one handling Della's estate and all the legalities regarding Jonah—he's very experienced in custody issues."

Cleo nodded. Ethan was no fool and money was no object. He'd hire the best.

"The Covingtons—Jonah's grandparents—have a lot of influence in Houston. If it comes to a court battle, they have the time and the money. To ensure I keep Jonah the attorney thought I needed something better than fat bank accounts, a trust fund for Jonah, and a top-ranked nanny. He thought I needed—"

"A wife." Cleo wasn't a fool, either.

"A mother for Jonah," Ethan corrected quickly.

Cleo's blood was running cooler now, but there was still hope in her heart. "That still doesn't explain why you came to see me, Ethan. Certainly you know plenty of women in other places. Someone from Houston, for example."

He shifted uncomfortably. "Cleo…"

"I never thought you were a man who didn't appreciate your share of women, Ethan."

He shifted again. "Sure, I have 'appreciated' women, but it's not like I have a harem of them all dying to wear my ring."

Cleo wanted to disagree, certain there were several—if not dozens—of women who wouldn't say no to Ethan. Women who'd be thrilled to wear his ring.

Such as herself.

Without warning, she remembered again that night on the love seat in the little den. She remembered how needy she'd been for him, how her pulse leaped when he'd touched her with his big hands. How she'd craved to have all of him against all of her.

No man had ever made her so excited and so hungry. And now she could have it all if she agreed to wear his ring. But still...

"You're in Montana, Ethan. Looking for a wife in my office. Please, just say it. Why me?"

"Because you're perfect, Cleo."

Her heart went crazy again, hopping around like a high school cheerleader. She released her grip on the desk, just about to launch herself into his arms.

"Because you're so...capable."

Capable? Cleo's heart tripped, and then fell with a long *whoosh*. Going cold, hot, cold, she sagged back against the desk, but he didn't seem to notice.

Instead Ethan smiled at her and continued. "You see, you're a childcare provider. How ideal is that? You have the education and the experience to be an unbeatable mother. My attorney couldn't be happier."

"Your attorney is happy?"

Ethan smiled wider and nodded. "'Unbeatable mother material.' Those were his exact words."

"What about a wife?" she said quietly, her words tinged with just a bit of sharpness. "What kind of wife material do you suppose I am?"

Ethan looked suddenly wary and he tried to step back, but his heel hit the wall with a soft *thump*. "Cleo, I—"

"What kind of wife material do you suppose I am, Ethan?" she asked again, her voice steelier this time.

He looked down at his hands for a moment, as if the answer might be written on them. Then he looked back up, his blue eyes guarded. "You're a practical, capable, sensible woman, Cleo. I think you make fine wife material or I wouldn't be here."

Capable. Practical. Sensible.

Maybe it was because she hadn't slept well the night before—she hadn't slept well in three months—that the words sounded more like insults instead of flattery.

Ethan needed a mother for Jonah and she had the right credentials. Ethan was willing to take a wife to get that mother, and she fit the bill because she was practical, capable, sensible.

Was that really the best thing anyone could say about her? It certainly echoed the sentiments her mother, sister and cousin had expressed this morning. Everyone was so darn certain that Cleo was sensible and practical.

Or maybe she was really just boring.

She crossed her arms over her chest, suddenly mad at the world, but especially mad at Ethan, her family, herself. What kind of woman gave a man the impression she'd be swayed by "practical" and "capable" and "sensible"?

She took a fast breath through her nose. "No," she said.

He blinked. "No, what?"

Cleo stared at him. What an idiot. "No, I won't marry you."

He blinked again. "Cleo—"

"Go find someone else, Ethan." She cast a look at Jonah and found herself softening when she saw the baby's sweet round cheeks and silky eyebrows. So she looked back at the rotten, gorgeous, and unpleasantly surprised Ethan.

Practical. Sensible. Ugh. "Goodbye," she said briskly.

"Goodbye?" he echoed stupidly.

"Goodbye."

He swallowed. "We can't talk about this some more?" He came toward her and she backed around her desk. "If not now, sometime later?"

So what that he was so darn good-looking he made her heart flutter? "*No*. I'm too busy. I have Beansprouts to run. Children, the staff." She looked out the window and remembered the most pressing problem. "I have to find a new building. My lease is running out and this one is up for sale."

Without waiting for him to answer, she sat in her chair and pulled a list of phone numbers from her desk drawer. "If you'll excuse me, Ethan." She put her hand on the phone.

He could be as belligerent as she. "What if I won't?"

She refused to look at him, even for one last time. "Please," she said.

A long, tense pause and then there was a flurry of movement and firm footsteps. Her office door opened, closed.

The room was without Ethan.

Cleo instantly folded, bending over to rest her flushed cheek on the cool desktop. Hot tears stung her eyes and she was unsure whether she was elated or disappointed that Ethan had given up.

Three

It was past 6:00 p.m. and Cleo was still sitting at her desk. The last Beansprouts's child had been picked up and the last staffer had gone home. She told herself she was taking advantage of the unfamiliar quiet to catch up on her bottomless stack of paperwork, but the only paper she'd put pencil to was a leaf from one of her "list pads"—stacks of tear-off sheets preprinted with lines.

Cleo had more list pads than most women had shoes. Yellow ones edged with flowers, white ones with a teacher's apple bulleting each line item; list pads printed on graph paper with thick, no-nonsense lines of military blue.

A sheet of that pad lay in front of her now, and she would have sworn she was just doodling as she stared out her window at the May twilight, but then she looked down. Her "doodles" were words, and what she'd really created was a list of the many practical, sensible things she'd done with her life.

Line one listed "Accounting 303." That was the class she'd taken the summer between her junior and senior years at college. A group of her friends had invited her to join them traveling through Europe for three months, but she'd needed the accounting class to graduate and it was hard to get into during the regular school year. So she'd taken the wise, practical route and given up Paris for profit-and-loss statements and the Alps for accounts receivable and payable.

Part of that same group of friends had urged her to join them in an Internet startup business after they graduated. That was why she'd written "Refused Internet Startup" on the second line. It hadn't seemed a safe choice, not when it meant moving to Las Vegas, of all places, and not when it meant they'd all be dirt-poor at the beginning. In the end—two years later—of course, that group of friends spent half the year vacationing in Europe. They'd struck it rich.

Next she'd written "Lives At Home." Cleo sighed. As much as she loved her family, it did seem as though a twenty-seven-year-old might want to have her own place. But it was so practical to live at home. Sensible.

Lastly were the words "Yearly Lease." She sighed again. When she'd opened Beansprouts two years ago she'd been relieved to sign up for a mere twelve-month lease. That way, if the business didn't fly, she wouldn't be chained to a monthly payment for too long. She'd done the same the following year, even though by then the day care center had a foot-long waiting list.

Irritated at herself, Cleo tapped her pencil against the desktop. The building's owner, Gene, would have let her sign for something longer, but she'd wanted to be practical. Sensible. Just look where that had led her—to Gene suddenly wanting to sell and Cleo suddenly facing disaster.

She jumped up from her chair, depressed by the turn of her thoughts. Thanks to that annoying man, Ethan Redford, she was viewing her best traits as her worst faults! No thank you.

Anyway, it was time to go home and consume a crate of brownies or something else decadently chocolate. Maybe on her way back to the Big Sky B and B, she'd think of a suitable bribe to get her sister in the kitchen, and baking.

Cleo drove down the winding country road, appreciating late spring in Montana and watching eagerly for her first soothing glimpse of Blue Mirror Lake. Yes, the B and B was a sensible, practical place for her to live, but it was a choice she didn't regret. She'd like to travel, sure, but this piece of Montana and the lake would always be home. She was glad her mother had convinced her father to leave Louisiana and open the business all those years ago.

Thinking of Louisiana reminded Cleo of her mother's nightmares. There. Another reason that living at the bed-and-breakfast was a good choice. She wanted to be near Celeste while these terrible dreams continued to plague her.

What the heck were they all about? Cleo pursed her lips and vowed to sit her mother down for a little heart-to-heart this evening. She could picture Celeste already, her eyes shadowed and her manner subdued, as it always was the day after the dream.

Cleo parked her Volvo sedan in its usual spot and let herself inside the back door. The kitchen was immaculate, but Cleo sniffed hopefully, wondering if Jasmine had done any particularly delectable culinary experimenting that day.

A soft, delighted laugh froze her midsniff.

It was followed by another. Her mother's laugh. And then came a giggle. A baby's giggle.

Cleo gritted her teeth, a terrible premonition overcoming her. With quick steps she passed through the kitchen and dining room to the living room.

Her mother sat on one of the long couches, cradling an adorable blond, blue-eyed baby. A man, golden-haired and devastating in a dark suit, watched them from a spot by the windows.

Cleo frowned at him. For all her sniffing, it was quite a surprise she hadn't smelled a rat.

She tapped her toe against the honey-pine floor. "You're not staying *here* are you?" she asked, her voice cool, she hoped, and not crabby.

Ethan's head came up and so did his eyebrows.

Her mother smiled at the baby but addressed Cleo. "Ethan and Jonah have rented the Atchinson house."

The Atchinson house. Oh, great. Another lakeside property not more than half a mile away. She crossed her arms over her chest. "So if you have your own place, what are you doing here?"

Her mother spoke again. "Ethan came to introduce me to Jonah. And I'm thrilled to meet this very handsome young man." Celeste nuzzled the baby's cheek and the little boy giggled again, his hands patting her hair.

Cleo softened a little. Her mother looked happier than she had in a long time, and obviously distracted from the terror of the night before.

Then Ethan spoke for the first time. "And I came to see if I could persuade you to go to dinner with me at the country club."

Cleo took a step back. Oh, no. That wouldn't be sensible *or* practical. Not when he was looking like the Golden God of Business in that Italian suit. Not when the last time they'd had dinner at the country club the evening had ended with her half dressed and nearly begging him for more.

"No," she said firmly, and then smiled to herself. Sometimes sensible and practical felt darn good.

"Please, Cleo," Ethan said quietly. "It might be the last time we ever meet."

Cleo's heart jumped. The last time. But then she narrowed her eyes, staring at him suspiciously. He didn't look like a man who thought they would never meet again.

"Go ahead, sweetie," her mother added. "I told Ethan I'd watch Jonah, and I can't think of *anything* that would make me happier than watching this little angel."

Cleo softened again. Her mother *did* look so darn happy holding that baby. To be honest, she itched to hold him herself. Without even thinking about it, she walked forward and sat beside her mother on the couch, then reached out toward Jonah. He immediately grabbed her hand and gave her a grin that made mush of everything inside her.

"Please come with me, Cleo," Ethan said.

Looking at the motherless baby and sharing the joy her own mother had in just touching him, Cleo discovered her backbone had dissolved completely. She sighed and stroked Jonah's cheek with her free hand.

"All right," she said grudgingly. "This last time." Because, anyway, could she really resist just one last time with Ethan? "I need a few minutes to change."

He nodded. "Take all the time you need."

In her room, Cleo whipped through a refreshing shower and then stood in her underwear, staring into her closet. What did a woman wear for a last dinner with the man she'd refused to marry? The man who considered her so practical and sensible?

The answer was obvious, of course. A woman should wear something completely impractical and as far from sensible as possible. Something that would make him sweat and make him drool.

But Cleo being Cleo, she had nothing remotely close to that in her closet.

She went wild, double-checking, flinging hangers aside with abandon until she had to admit the closest thing to "vamp" in her closet was the black witch's costume she wore at Beansprouts on Halloween. And even that was something that had been Jasmine's first.

"Jasmine," Cleo whispered. Her mother had said her sister was out for the evening, but Cleo dashed through their adjoining bathroom into her room, anyway. Without a moment's compunction, she went double-fast through her sister's double-stuffed closet and emerged clutching a long-sleeved black knit dress that was deeply veed in the front and back.

Not allowing herself to give in to doubt, she ran back to her own room and slipped into black stockings, black heels, and the dynamite black dress that had been bought by her less-curvy sister. Sitting at her dressing table, she twisted her wavy hair behind her head and held it back with a jeweled comb. Then she applied her makeup heavier than usual, not daring to look past her chin.

Once she'd blotted her lipstick, a shade named Derring Do, Cleo stood. With a deep breath, she turned around and looked at herself in the full-length mirror.

"Eek," she said breathlessly. Where the dress had displayed a lot of Jasmine's fragile clavicle and just a hint of her bust, on Cleo, the dress displayed a lot of bust and nothing, but *nothing* was hinted at. "Oh, boy," she whispered.

Could she do it? With fingers that trembled just a little, she pulled a couple of wavy tendrils free from the twist of her hair, letting them drift softly around her face. Could she walk out there and face Ethan in something so...well, sophisticated instead of sensible?

Taking a deep breath—and then swearing to herself to not take another after what she noticed it did to her cleavage—Cleo gave herself one more objective, assessing look in the mirror.

And liked what she saw.

She strutted a couple of steps in her high heels, then made an about-face and walked past the mirror again. Yes, she thought. I'm going through with it.

Because she'd be darned if she was going to send Ethan out of her life with him remembering a boringly sensible, practical, capable Cleo. And if this dress didn't make him look at her just a teensy bit differently, then her name wasn't Cleo Kincaid Monroe.

By the time they'd left the B and B, settled into his Range Rover and driven to the Whitehorn Country Club, Cleo was pretty sure that Ethan didn't know *what* to think when he looked at her. While her mother had smiled and told Cleo how nice she looked, Ethan appeared to have swallowed his tongue. The miles to the country club had been covered in virtual silence and Cleo got the distinct feeling that Ethan was glad to have something to focus on besides her and the dress she was wearing.

Which was why she smiled at him smugly as he took his seat across from her at their intimate table for two. She didn't need to be embarrassed about the marriage proposal any longer. Ethan could now see that she was a woman who didn't have to resort to convenient marriages.

She figured that was what he was coming to grips with as they gave the waiter their orders and were served a bottle of excellent wine. Ethan was terse, a fact that made Cleo even more warm and gracious.

Once they were finally alone, Cleo held up her wineglass, watching the golden wine glow in the soft candlelight. "What should we drink to?" she said lightly.

Regrets came to mind. The kind of regrets she hoped he had for underestimating her qualities. Of course, he might suggest they drink to her beauty—no, her sexiness, she thought, wiggling in her seat. Drinking to her sexiness would be just right.

Ethan suddenly closed his eyes, opened them. "To my apologies," he said tersely.

Cleo blinked. Okay. Fine. Apologies would work. There was regret in apologies, though no acknowledgment of sexiness, darn him. But apologies certainly meant Ethan realized she wasn't the type of woman to leap on a man's proposal when all he wanted from her was her capability.

She shrugged and clinked her glass against the rim of his. The first sip of the delicious wine was slipping over her tongue when he continued.

"My apologies for not presenting my proposal in a more businesslike way," he said. "I wasn't thinking clearly earlier. Blame it on the mess my life is in."

Cleo held on to that mouthful of wine, uncertain she remembered how to swallow. He was apologizing for not proposing in a *more* businesslike way?

He sighed. "I didn't present any reasons *you* might be interested in the deal—I mean, marriage. But let me assure you I've thought that through now." With a flick of his wrist, he downed the contents of his glass in one gulp. "First, let me assure you that the physical aspect of our merger—uh, marriage—needn't happen until and unless you're ready."

The wine still in her mouth, Cleo blinked. He was just shrugging off the idea of making love with her—until! he'd said, unless!—when she was wearing the most sophisticated, most sexy dress she'd ever worn in her life.

He must have taken her silence as a prompt to go on, because he now looked her full in the face. "And, Cleo, second, and best of all…" He paused a moment, dealmaking charisma oozing off him. "If you marry me, I'll buy the Beansprouts's building and list the deed in your name."

That's when Cleo finally tried to swallow, quickly, so she could get right to telling him what she thought of such a businesslike…bribe. Yes. That's what it was, all right, a bribe. But either the wine went down the wrong way or her throat was as angry as the rest of her and forgot to actually accept the liquid.

In any case, instead of telling Ethan off, Cleo found herself fighting for breath. She choked and coughed, thinking she might die from lack of oxygen, instead of at the hands of the state, a much more predictable fate considering what she felt like doing to Ethan.

"Cleo! Are you all right?"

Her napkin to her mouth, she looked up, into the concerned face of John Riker. His wife, Rosemary, bustled over and started patting Cleo briskly on the back.

Thanks to Rosemary and a couple of sips of water, Cleo managed to catch her breath and then smile at her longtime friends. "I haven't seen you two in ages," she said, her voice only a little hoarse from all the coughing.

She stood to hug Rosemary, and then turned to John. A sweet smile transformed his craggy face to something just this side of beautiful. He took her hands in his huge ones. "Cleo, my love." His arms came around her and he swept her up for a bearlike squeeze.

Cleo giggled. Embracing John was like embracing one of the ageless pines surrounding Blue Mirror Lake. He was as dear as he was sturdy. With an appreciative smack, he kissed her on the lips.

From the other side of the table came the sound of an ominously cleared throat. Cleo ignored it. Ignored him. Ethan. She still couldn't believe he would so cold-bloodedly frame his second proposal of marriage, and she needed a little time to decide exactly how she was going to tell him no, no way, no how.

But he cleared his throat again, and John set her on her feet. "Won't you introduce us?" John asked in his booming voice.

Cleo sighed, but turned toward Ethan. His eyes looked kind of glittery and he was staring at John. "Rosemary and

John Riker, this is an…acquaintance of mine, Ethan Redford.''

He stood as she spoke and came around the table to shake first Rosemary's, then John's hand. "I'm a friend of Cleo's," he corrected. "A close friend." His palm came to rest on her shoulder.

Cleo ignored the heat running down her arm. "I've known John since we were kids."

John teasingly tugged one of the tendrils of hair around her face. "But you sure look all grown up tonight."

As if Ethan even noticed it, darn him. Cleo pushed lightly against John's shoulder. "Flatterer," she said fondly.

Ethan's fingers squeezed her shoulder. "Don't let us hold you up."

Cleo turned her head to look at him. His face was a perfect mask of politeness, but she could feel the tension in his body. Of course, he'd just asked her to marry him and she'd yet to give him her answer. She liked the idea he might be a little anxious about it.

She smiled gaily at Rosemary and John. "Please say you can join us. It would be *so* much more fun as a foursome." Cleo ignored a second squeeze from Ethan's hand.

Rosemary cocked an eyebrow and darted a look at Ethan. "Oh, I don't know…"

But John didn't need to be asked twice. "For a drink, Rosie. Then we'll get our own table. I want to know what Cleo's been up to." He chuckled. "And who she's been up to it with."

Rosemary rolled her eyes. "John."

Cleo just whacked him with another light punch and grinned. She didn't mind John's teasing if it meant Ethan would have to squirm for a while.

Once they were all seated at the table and the other couple's drinks served, John leaned back and gave Cleo another once-over. "Have I mentioned you look like a million bucks? You're going to break my heart a second time, I swear."

Cleo grinned. "I may take you back just for the compliments."

Ethan's chair made a loud *crrrck* as he scraped it closer to the table.

Rosemary smiled and put her hand on her husband's massive forearm. "You're making Cleo's date nervous, John, with all this talk." She turned toward Ethan. "Cleo and John were an item once upon a time. She was the best thing that ever happened to him."

John grinned. "Until she tore my heart out of my chest and stomped all over it."

It was Cleo's turn to roll her eyes. "We were in college, John. You loved beer more than you ever loved me, admit it."

John's grin died. "Nah, Cleo, honey, I really loved you." But the light in his eyes was for his wife when he turned his gaze to her. "But then I met Rosemary."

Cleo smiled, remembering, and sent a significant look Ethan's way. "Whom *I* introduced him to, by the way."

"How…fortunate for all three of you," he said. He wore that deal-maker's poker face of his. "How long ago did you say this was?" he addressed this last to Rosemary.

She sipped at her glass of red wine. "Hmm. Five years ago? We've been married for two."

"That's right," Cleo said. "You were married the same week I opened Beansprouts."

"A business that certainly deserves to remain open," Ethan murmured. Beneath the table, he touched her hand. He linked his fingers with hers and held on tight when she instantly tried to pull away.

Rosemary smiled, unaware of the undertones beneath

Ethan's compliment. "Cleo does wonders with the business *and* the children."

"Always knew she'd make a success of it," John added. "Cleo is a detail person."

"Hey, come on, you guys." Cleo squirmed in her seat, embarrassed.

"Now you shush," Rosemary answered. "There's no reason we can't tell Ethan about you."

Cleo groaned, feeling pretty certain that for some reason her friends had decided to foster the romance they supposed—oh, so wrongly—was going on between her and Ethan.

"I'd like to know everything about Cleo," Ethan said smoothly. "Please go on."

Cleo groaned again. The only thing he needed to know was how quickly she could spit out the letters n-o. "Really, guys—"

"She's the most sensible woman I know."

Rosemary's obviously heartfelt words penetrated Cleo like a blade. *Sensible?* She stared at her friend. Is that how Rosemary saw her, too?

"Why I remember a time in college when the rest of us were gung-ho for a road trip to San Francisco. While we were throwing stuff in backpacks and arguing about how to divvy up the driving, it was Cleo who checked the road conditions, called the weather service, and determined that not only was our car without a first-aid kit, it didn't have a spare tire, either." Rosemary smiled. "And you were right, Cleo. We should have listened to you. We ran into a storm two hours out and had a flat six hours after that."

"And I bet Cleo was the only one who knew how to change a tire," Ethan said.

A chill ran down Cleo's back. "I didn't go," she said

slowly. "I had an early class on the day they were planning to get back and I was worried about missing it."

Rosemary beamed. "What did I tell you? Always sensible."

Cleo swallowed. "But, remember? You had a terrific time. You brought me back one of those little cable cars from a souvenir shop. I keep it at Beansprouts." Now that she thought about it, she didn't know what made her give it that place of honor on her desk. To remind her of what? That she'd never seen San Francisco because she'd made the wise, sensible choice?

"Don't pout, honey," John said teasingly. "If we all followed our bliss who would be around to mop up the mess we left behind? We need you practical, capable types."

Cleo hid behind her glass of wine. *If we all followed our bliss...* John did that. He'd taken the same business courses she had and ended up with his own successful enterprise—he made a fortune in woodworking, crafting unique custom cabinetry and such with his own two hands. His bliss.

Conversation continued around the table and Cleo let it go on without her. John said they needed the practical, capable types. Like her.

Was she this sturdy old stick that everyone saw her as? Sure she loved Beansprouts and was happy working at her business, but when she thought of following her bliss...

She slid her gaze toward Ethan. And like that, she remembered his kiss, the sensation of his palms cupping her face, the catch in his voice when he peeled her dress from her shoulders....

Her fingers tightened on the stem of her wineglass and she tugged on her other fingers, the ones Ethan still claimed. Without a pause in what he was saying to John and Rosemary, he held on.

Cleo swallowed, her gaze following his handsome profile. *Bliss*.

"Are you okay?" Rosemary's voice snuck under the louder conversation of the men.

Cleo swallowed again. "I'm…not sure." Which even to her own ears sounded odd. She was always sure about things. Sensible, safe choices. Practical decisions.

"He's to die for," Rosemary whispered, her gaze flicking toward Ethan. "And when I saw the way he looks at you and the way you look at him…whoa!"

Cleo raised her eyebrows and thought maybe her friend should consider another line of work. Rosemary was an artist, which should have made her an excellent observer, but though Cleo might be guilty of going moony over Ethan, the reverse was definitely not true. He saw her as a sensible-practical-capable person.

Not as a to-drool-for woman.

Anyway, people shouldn't marry someone they think of as practical and capable any more than someone should marry over a little lust.

"He has a child," she told Rosemary suddenly. "A baby. His sister died and he has custody of his nephew." The thought of Jonah's blond chubbiness made her stomach clench. And then clench harder, when she thought of the hard, golden man who cared enough about his dead sister and her child to do anything to keep him close.

"Like your mother and Summer," Rosemary said softly.

Cleo nodded. Like her mother and Summer… When Cleo's aunt Blanche died, before Cleo was even born, Yvette and Celeste had raised Blanche's daughter Summer. Yvette looked after her while Celeste was in Louisiana, but when Celeste returned and Yvette married and moved to the house behind the B and B, Summer had continued to live with Celeste. Summer, Cleo and Jasmine, and their cousin Frannie had been raised as sisters, loved each other as sisters.

That was what Ethan wanted for Jonah. Love and family.

"I—" she broke off and looked desperately at Rosemary as a scary, life-altering realization crystallized in her mind. "Marriage is forever, isn't it?"

Rosemary smiled softly. "It doesn't seem that long when you're in love with the person you're married to."

In love.

Cleo gripped her wineglass again. "Rosemary, talk me out of something. Tell me to think sensibly. Tell me to be practical."

Rosemary's smile widened. "Are you talking to me? I went to San Francisco, remember? I'm an artist."

"You follow your bliss."

Rosemary nodded. "Always, Cleo. And if I take a wrong path or two, well the bliss more than makes up for it."

Oh, God. Cleo wished Rosemary hadn't said that. But though she could wish the whole conversation away, could wish they'd never run into Rosemary and John, none of the wishing would change the truth.

Cleo met her bliss the day she met Ethan Redford. She'd fallen in love with him that instant, as improbable and impractical as it sounded.

And sensible, capable Cleo just couldn't deny it any longer. Maybe she didn't want to. Maybe at twenty-seven years old it was time to damn the consequences and embrace her bliss.

Embrace Ethan.

A delighted, thrilled shiver wiggled down her spine. She squeezed Ethan's hand and he stopped talking to John and gave her a questioning look.

Cleo took a deep breath. There would be time to make

him drool later. "Why don't we go ahead and tell them?" she said.

Ethan stilled and his eyes widened. Oh, they were so heartbreakingly blue. "You mean...?"

She nodded and then tried smiling, but she wasn't sure how it came off when she knew there was more than a hint of tears in her eyes. "John, Rosemary. Ethan and I are going to be married."

Around the table, she noted varied reactions. Rosemary wore an expression of gentle delight. John was out-and-out grinning, which told Cleo that somehow Ethan had worked his deal-maker magic and already made a buddy.

As for Ethan himself...he didn't look at all surprised that the sensible woman he'd asked to marry him had made such a practical decision as to commit to a man who offered brick-and-mortar buildings instead of tender emotion.

She sighed, letting the reality of what she'd just done wash over her. She, practical, sensible Cleo Monroe, loved Ethan Redford. There was no question about that.

But would she ever be capable of getting Ethan to love her back?

Four

The next evening the doorbell rang at Ethan's rented house. Seated in the deep, comfortable couch, he threw down the report he'd been reading.

"That's her," he told his nephew. Jonah sat in a hammock-like baby chair on the coffee table in front of the couch. "It's Cleo."

The baby blinked, and then rolled his eyes in the direction of the striking view of Blue Mirror Lake from the room's huge picture window. Ethan followed his gaze, then stared at the French doors leading to the spacious deck—the last possible escape route before he made what could be the biggest mistake of his life.

"I wanted a mother figure, bud," he whispered to the baby. But instead, the certainly attractive, yet maternal Cleo of his memory had turned into a tantalizing siren last night. Oh, he'd known she had that side to her, too—it wasn't as if he'd forgotten the time he'd kissed her mouth and touched her luscious skin—but he'd thought he could focus on her mothering qualities.

Well, hell, not in that piece of shrink-wrap she'd called a dress last night. He'd barely kept his hands to himself and then his irritation under control when another man's hands—those of her old boyfriend John—had so naturally touched her.

The doorbell rang again. With a sigh, Ethan stood. It wasn't as if he had any choice. He'd proposed, she'd accepted, and then they'd calmly discussed their future plans. Plans that included getting Jonah accustomed to her as soon as possible. Hence tonight's dinner.

He pulled open the door just as Cleo rang the bell once more. He hoped the echoing sound would account for the stupid expression he figured took over his face, because even in a casual pair of jeans and a lightweight apricot-colored turtleneck, she made his blood chug hotly through his veins, just as she had the night before in the slinky dress.

"Hi." Cleo held out a bottle of wine and smiled.

Chug-a-chug-chug went his blood, pulsing a slow burn through his body. Hell. Ethan set his jaw. How terrible would it be if he grabbed the wine but then shut the door on her pretty, tempting face?

Cleo stepped closer and lifted the bottle she held higher. "Jasmine said this would go well with the meal you conned her into making us."

Ethan found his voice. "I wanted the meal to be something special." That was before he'd been having these doubts. Really, it wasn't too late to call the whole thing off. Some other woman, some woman who looked less like something he wanted to savor for dessert and more like a Mrs. Cleaver mother-type who would *make* desserts, would be better. Safer.

If this marriage—if Ethan himself—took the sparkle out of Cleo's wide violet eyes, he'd never be able to look himself in the face again. "Cleo—"

But her gaze drifted past him and her face changed, her mouth softening. "Oh," she said softly. "There he is." The wine was thrust against his chest and he caught it as she brushed by him and headed for Jonah.

Something contracted painfully inside the emptiness in Ethan's chest. There had been tears in Cleo's eyes. He closed his, damn grateful. No matter what risks, Jonah deserved a woman who cried the first time she saw him after agreeing to be his mother.

Ethan shut the door and turned to see Cleo pluck the baby from his chair. She held him up, so they were nearly nose to nose, and Jonah gave her that hopeful don't-I-know-you smile of his that never failed to stab Ethan. It seemed to be the smile of a baby who was desperately looking for his place in the world.

Cleo fussed over Jonah, praising his intelligence, size and beauty. The baby listened avidly to each soft word and his hands reached out for Cleo's face. She cuddled him against her chest.

Ethan swallowed. "Can I get you something? A drink?"

Cleo didn't take her gaze off the baby. "How about a glass of the wine I brought and some directions?"

"Directions?"

She flicked a glance Ethan's way. The sparkle was there, bright as Christmas lights. "To the diaper changing area. I think this guy could use my services."

Ethan pointed her down the hallway to the baby's bedroom, then poured a glass of wine for each of them. He trailed her to Jonah's room, following the sound of more feminine nonsense talk. Her diaper-changing skills were a lot more professional than his first efforts had been.

"You're good," he said admiringly. "When I first started changing Jonah I had pangs of guilt over my contribution to the landfill problem. About one in four diapers actually stayed on him."

The fresh diaper fastened, Cleo leaned down to kiss the baby's tummy. Jonah kicked in delight, and Ethan thought about her lips on *his* body... Anywhere close to his stomach would do.

She looked over at Ethan and he quickly schooled his features. "We should consider using cloth diapers for that

very reason," she said. "Do you have any objections?"
With a few efficient movements she redressed the baby.

"No objections at all, but I don't want to make too much
work for you," he answered.

Cleo lifted the baby off the changing table and against
her shoulder again. "I'd like to raise him, even from the
beginning, with a concern for the environment."

Ethan just nodded, his mind not going past "I'd like to
raise him." His pulse did that *chug-a-chug* again, but this
time the heat was accompanied with a sweet feeling of relief. He'd found someone to raise Jonah. He'd feared all
along that he didn't have what it took to nurture a child to
adulthood. No good example to follow, no notion of how
to figure it all out.

But Cleo. Cleo would know what to do.

Even if he failed her, she wouldn't fail Jonah.

She was looking at him strangely, so he tried to put a
smile on his face. "What about dinner? Are you ready?"

"Sure," she said. "Show me how I can help."

In the kitchen, she bustled around, finding plates and silverware to set the table. Ethan was nonplussed again. When
he was caring for the baby, he never was quite sure what
to *do* with him. Well, Cleo did everything with Jonah. She
managed to accomplish her tasks with the baby sort of bal-
anced on her hip, and Jonah appeared enthralled by all the
movement and the constantly changing sights.

For his part, Ethan felt pretty lame as all he did was fill
their plates with what Jasmine had prepared. When everything was on the table, Cleo sat with Jonah still in her arms.

"Let me take him," Ethan said. "Or I can put him in
his baby chair. He's not much of a complainer."

Cleo shook her head. "Do you mind if I keep him
close?"

"How are you going to eat?"

"I'll manage." She smiled. "It's more important that Jonah gets used to me than I clean my plate."

Another wave of thankfulness rushed over Ethan. She was putting Jonah first. That was what the baby needed and deserved. If he just concentrated on that, maybe he could ignore the desire he felt for Cleo. The entanglements of sex and need might lead them straight to disaster. He wasn't going to risk Jonah's welfare for a few hot times in the sheets.

He cleared his throat and toyed with his salad. "Jasmine said you told your family we're getting married." But Cleo's sister hadn't spilled a hint of what their reaction had been.

Cleo's expression didn't give anything away, either. Despite Jonah, she'd managed a mouthful of Jasmine's chicken and she nodded as she chewed.

Ethan cleared his throat again. "So, um, what did they think?"

Cleo shrugged. "They're my family. They like you. They respect my decisions and will always be behind me."

Family was what he wanted for Jonah. And he felt certain that all of Cleo's family would take the little boy to their hearts. "Is next week still okay for the wedding?" That was what they'd decided last night.

Cleo's cheeks flushed, but she nodded. "Just fine. Friday, right?"

"Friday. And then I thought we could live here, at least for a few months. I have it leased through the summer. After that we can find something else."

Cleo looked down at Jonah and made funny faces at him. "This is really going to happen, isn't it?" she said softly. "I'm going to have a son...and a husband."

"Cleo, look at me." He waited for her gaze to meet his.

"I'm not playing. Next Friday, if you're sure, we'll get married. It will really happen."

Her eyes were so incredibly violet and so wide that he would find it much too easy to be mesmerized by them. But he had promises to make before those wedding vows. "I want us to marry." He really did, he realized.

For Jonah's sake.

"And I'm going to do my damned best not to screw it up. I've got to be honest, I've never wanted to be married and I've never wanted to have a child. But that's in the past. Now I'm committed to providing for you and Jonah. I work hard and I make good money. Better than good. And every dollar I have will be yours and Jonah's."

Two worry lines appeared between Cleo's brows. "This is not about money, Ethan."

"It's what I have to offer, Cleo." All he had to offer. "And speaking of business, don't forget that Jonah and I have to head back to Houston tomorrow evening."

Those worry lines continued to mar the smooth skin of her forehead. "About that…I was wondering if you'd leave Jonah with me. I'm planning on going part-time at Beansprouts for a few weeks and doing a lot of my administrative tasks from home. Jonah would work right into that."

Ethan frowned. "Oh, I don't think so. The nanny in Houston said she'd be available."

"I'll take good care of him."

"It's not that, it's—" It was that Ethan couldn't imagine coming home at night to his Houston condo and finding it empty. "Let me think about it."

Jonah, tiring of sitting in one place, distracted their attention. Ethan welcomed the new focus, though it meant more opportunity to notice how very natural Cleo was with the baby—so much more natural than he had ever been. He turned on the stereo, having at least discovered that the

baby enjoyed country music, and it made him feel...
something he couldn't quite name when he watched Cleo
two-step around the kitchen with Jonah in her arms.

"We should go dancing sometime," Ethan said suddenly.

Cleo's feet stopped their cute little shuffle. She looked at
him, all wide-eyed again, and Ethan wondered what it
would be like to hold her curvy body against his chest and
to have that remarkable hair tickling his chin. He remembered the sweet scent of it, and his blood *chug-a-chug-
chugged* toward his groin.

She licked her lips, and Ethan almost groaned. "I'd like
that," she said. "Very much."

Damn. He wasn't supposed to be thinking of her lips, her
curves, or her scent. No embracing. No dancing. Because
if he got too close to Cleo and their romantic relationship
went sour, where would that leave Jonah?

He turned away from her. "Yeah, well, sometime.
Maybe," he said, his voice gruff.

Hers was carefully neutral. "Would you mind if I gave
Jonah his bath?"

"No problem. I'll just finish the dishes."

Which only took a few minutes. Yet by the time he'd
put them away and wandered toward Jonah's bathroom,
Cleo had the baby's safety seat in the warm water and Jonah
already in it. She was singing something about a spider as
she gently washed him.

The baby's gaze was glued to her face. Ethan leaned
against the doorjamb and watched the picture they made,
feeling as if he'd wandered into someone else's life. It all
seemed so normal and natural, so much the way it should
be, but so much what he didn't know about.

He wanted to reach out to stroke Cleo's hair, and then

Jonah's pink, just-washed skin, but it was as if a glass wall had been erected between the door and the bathtub.

"Are you okay?" Cleo looked over her shoulder at him, her face flushed from the warmth of the water.

Ethan's mind instantly conjured up an image of Cleo, pink and glistening from her bath. He imagined himself washing her, touching those beautiful breasts, his soapy hands running along the curves of her hips.

Her nostrils flared. "Ethan?"

He shook himself out of the fantasy, afraid she might read his thoughts. "Hmm?" Even his "hmm" sounded hoarse.

"What were you thinking about?" Her voice sounded a little hoarse, too.

He swallowed. "About tomorrow," he lied. "I think it will be fine if Jonah stays with you while I'm on this trip to Houston." There really had never been any doubt. He wanted the baby to become accustomed to Cleo—the mother Ethan had brought into Jonah's life.

Of course there were no guarantees that Ethan himself would ever become accustomed to Cleo. And if the fantasies he'd been indulging in and the hardened state of his body were any indication, the resounding answer was no.

It was one thing to say you were going to do something impractical for once, Cleo thought, and an entirely other thing to actually *do* it.

In the kitchen at Ethan's—no, *their*—house, she stared down at the brand-new platinum-and-diamond wedding band on her fourth finger. She'd married Ethan Redford three hours before. Jonah—her son—was asleep for the night in his bedroom. He'd gone down like a dream, wearing a teeny smile that she pretended was because he understood they'd created a family for him today.

The one thing that had been easy about this whole situation was caring for Jonah. She'd fallen for him almost as quickly as she'd fallen for his uncle. At first it was because a motherless baby was a certain draw to her maternal heart.

But then, quickly, it was for Jonah himself. Because he was a morning person, as she was. Because of the way he snuggled his head into the hollow of her shoulder. Because his smiles beamed at her now with a confidence and familiarity she was sure wasn't there the week before, when she'd first started caring for him full-time.

A light rap on the back door of the kitchen startled Cleo. She looked over to see Jasmine, illuminated by the small porch light, peeking through the curtains that swagged across the glassed upper half of the door. Cleo quickly crossed to turn the knob, but instead of stepping over the threshold, Jasmine merely handed over a brown grocery bag that was mouth-wateringly fragrant.

"Here," she whispered. "Take this."

Cleo looked inside and spied Jasmine's famous cashew chicken and steamed rice in clear-topped containers. "Yum, but—"

"Shh." Jasmine's eyes widened and she kept her voice hushed. "It's dinner. I thought you might need fortification or—" she giggled lightly "—inspiration."

Cleo's cheeks went warm but she ignored her sister's teasing. "Excuse me, but why exactly are we whispering?"

"So you can tell Ethan you just whipped it up yourself. You said he hadn't had a chance to eat any of your cooking yet, and I thought—"

Cleo groaned. "Jasmine, sooner or later the man's going to have to find out I'm cuisinely clueless." She'd only been able to postpone the inevitable because Ethan had been out of town since the day after they'd last eaten one of Jasmine's meals. Cleo had lived at the house with Jonah all week, but Ethan had only arrived back early that afternoon, just in time for their four o'clock wedding.

She bit her lip. "He's exhausted and I said I'd make us a light dinner. You don't think I'll mess up sandwiches and soup, do you?"

Jasmine rolled her eyes. "Just tell me this. Has the marriage been consummated yet?"

"*Jasmine!*" Cleo's face turned even hotter and she inspected a nearby pristine countertop. "I just put the baby to bed."

"Well, you better get yourself and Ethan there, as well— before you do any cooking."

"Jasmine," Cleo muttered again.

"Hey." Jasmine grinned. "A sister has to tell it like it is. Get him in the sack before you give him any of your soup and sandwiches. Otherwise, go with the good stuff." She nodded toward the bag. "'Bye!"

"'Bye," Cleo echoed faintly, but then her sister turned around. Cleo raised a brow. "What? More advice?"

Jasmine smiled. "Just a thumbs-up. Ethan's *gorgeous*. If you hadn't seen him first…"

Cleo shook her head. "Ethan's too old for you, baby sister."

"Uh-uh." Jasmine backed into the twilight. "The males my age are boys. I want a man like Ethan, and I want my man to look at me the way Ethan looks at you." She turned and melted away into the darkness.

Cleo frowned. Great. Gone before she could pin down exactly what that "way" was. She set the bag of food on the counter and rubbed her midsection. Just hearing the words "Ethan" and "bed" in the same sentence had her stomach hiccuping again.

What way *had* he looked at her? Jasmine and Cleo's mother, cousins, aunt and uncle had all been witnesses to their civil ceremony. To her eyes, Ethan had appeared pre-occupied when not downright tired. The kiss he'd brushed across her lips at the conclusion of the ceremony had less emotion than the one Uncle Edward had pressed against her cheek.

He'd seemed relieved that she'd told her family they'd save the celebrating for another day. Cleo had broken the news to them six days before, when Ethan told her he had to make an immediate and unscheduled trip to Japan, though he swore he'd make it home in time for the wedding ceremony.

Tonight would be quiet, just the three of them. Well, two actually, with the baby already asleep.

Leaving them to discuss the bed issue uninterrupted—the issue being that Cleo didn't know which one to choose tonight.

For the past week she'd been in the guest bedroom across from Jonah's room. But there was the stately master suite just down the hall, with the echoes of Ethan's spicy scent and the huge bed made for a man and a woman's…uh, comfort.

Her stomach hopped up and down again and Cleo closed her eyes. Ethan had said the physical side of their marriage would be up to her. Well, it was pretty stupid to pretend the idea of making love with him was something she even needed to consider.

She wanted to make love to him.

She wanted Ethan.

But how to broach the subject? With a frown, she swung around to look out the window over the sink and caught sight of her reflection, clear against the night's darkness. Dang, if every nervous, anxious, but aroused thought wasn't written all over her face.

Once he saw her, he'd know.

With a deep breath Cleo started across the gleaming kitchen floor. Find Ethan, she thought. Then he'd take care of the rest.

With cold fingers, she pushed through the swinging door. The faint sounds of country music came from the direction of Ethan's office at the far end of the house. She smiled to herself, remembering he said they should go dancing sometime. Maybe tonight they could begin that way, a little slow dance in each other's arms before a long, delicious night of lovemaking.

"Ethan?" she called softly, but her voice was so squeaky she had to swallow and start over. "Ethan?"

To give him fair warning she made her steps distinct and firm. "Ethan?" she said again.

Still no answer.

She peeked through the office doorway. His desk was in one corner of the room and a leather couch, its back to the entry, faced a small fire crackling in the brick-and-stone fireplace. Clint Black sang softly to the empty room.

Cleo shifted, anticipation building unmercilessly. At this rate, by the time she found him, one touch would shatter her into a zillion nervous pieces. Clint stopped singing, and there was a brief segue of silence before the next song on the CD began. That was when Cleo heard it.

A sigh. No, a breath. Another one. Rhythmic breathing.

With a sinking heart, she walked up to the couch and peered over its high back.

Oh, there he was. Ethan. Tie loosened, ankles crossed, gold stubble starting to bristle along his square chin. Her bridegroom. So asleep, Cleo guessed a marching band wouldn't wake him.

A nervous bride certainly wouldn't do it.

Would she?

She cleared her throat.

She cleared it again. Loudly.

Ethan didn't stir.

She stomped over to the fireplace and poked at the small fire until a satisfying shower of sparks hissed in the grate. Over her shoulder, Ethan continued to sleep soundly. She poked again. More sparks. More rhythmic breathing from the man on the couch.

Sighing in defeat, she walked around the end of the couch and plucked an afghan off the plump bolster by his feet. She tossed it over him, and even when the crocheted corner smacked him lightly in the nose, he didn't move. Sighing louder, she folded the offending—and useless—corner back from his face.

She slipped his loafers off his feet, letting them fall to the floor with noisy clunks. When he still didn't rouse, she turned out the lights and turned off Clint Black.

Standing in the firelit darkness, staring down at the man who she wanted naked and next to her more than anything else, she considered herself one of the most understanding—frustrated—women in the world.

With Jonah perched on one hip, Cleo sipped a fresh mug of her sister's awesome coffee. Jasmine stood nearby, chopping walnuts for the waffles she was serving that morning to the B and B guests. "What are we going to do about Mama?" Cleo asked her sister. Upon arriving at the bed-and-breakfast earlier, she'd discovered Celeste had been up since 4:00 a.m., when another nightmare had woken her.

Jasmine shrugged. "Until she tells us more about the darned dreams, or is at least willing to tell *someone* about them, what can we do?" She looked over her shoulder and raised her eyebrows. "And to tell the truth, I'm almost just as worried about *you*. Don't you think you should be home with your husband the morning after your wedding?"

Cleo turned her gaze on Jonah and gave him a big smacking kiss on his nose. He grinned. She grinned back. "Please. Mama already fussed at me. But Ethan's exhausted from his overseas trip, and Jonah and I didn't want to disturb him, okay?"

Jasmine lips quirked up. "Exhausted, you say? That sounds promising." Her eyes narrowed. "But shouldn't you be exhausted then, too?"

Cleo shook her head. "Shut up, Jasmine."

Jasmine's gaze darted toward the dining room and she lowered her voice. "Seriously. I saw it on 'Oprah.' If you don't know what I mean, there are manuals—"

"Jasmine!" Cleo set her mug on the countertop and used her free hand to cover one of Jonah's ears. "There are children present. And I don't need any manuals, thank you very much."

Jasmine blinked. "Okay. But does Ethan?" she asked seriously.

"Does Ethan what?" a new voice asked.

Both Cleo and Jasmine whipped around, to find that the man in question had just slipped in the back door. Jonah kicked and so did Cleo's heart. Ethan had changed into jeans and a T-shirt, but he hadn't shaved and his dark gold hair stood on end. He crossed his arms over his chest. "Does Ethan what?" he asked again.

"Noth—"

"Need manuals," Jasmine said over Cleo. "L-o-v-e manuals." She wiggled her eyebrows.

The look in Ethan's eyes was unreadable as he transferred his gaze from Jasmine to Cleo. Lord, but she hoped tomato-red was her color, because her face was so hot it just had to be that particular shade. Then his gaze slid off her face, and down, down to— Oh, please, don't let her nipples be hardening from the mere brush of his gaze.

She shifted Jonah so that he covered both strategic areas. Then she tried on a sickly smile. "Sleep well?"

He drifted closer to her, picked her mug up off the counter and sipped from it. "I'm sorry," he said quietly. "I went comatose on you, didn't I?"

The back door opened again and a handsome, tanned man came in, carrying two stacked produce boxes. "Hey, ladies!" He slid the boxes onto the kitchen table. "The asparagus looks good today, Jasmine."

Then his gaze snagged on Ethan, standing so close to Cleo. His eyes widened. "It wasn't just a rumor?" he asked, looking again at Jasmine.

"Nope, Cleo really got hitched yesterday afternoon." Jasmine performed introductions with the point of her wicked-looking butcher knife. "Ethan Redford, this is Jeremy Ricksley, our local organic farmer. Jer, this is Ethan."

Ethan held out his hand, but Jeremy ignored it to sweep Cleo—Jonah, too—into a green-smelling embrace. "I'll be damned." He released her, kissed her cheek, hugged her again, then gave her another kiss, this one on the mouth. "Congratulations."

Cleo smiled and gave his cheek a pat. Jeremy was such a dear, dear, old friend. "Thanks, sweetie," she said.

Jeremy spun in his work boots. "And you," he said to Ethan. He slapped him on the back, causing Ethan to hop forward a few inches. "You hooked the best woman in town," Jeremy said.

"Is that so," Ethan replied carefully, rotating his shoulders as if checking to see they still worked.

"Man, yes! Broke my heart a dozen times, I'll tell you, but it was worth it. She gave me the best kiss of my life."

Ethan froze. "Is that so," he said again.

Cleo rolled her eyes. "In fifth grade, Jeremy. Mention that part."

Jeremy smirked. "Okay, but that was just our *first* kiss."

Cleo rolled her eyes again. Yeah, Jeremy had caught her once beneath some mistletoe, but he'd smelled like beer and been on the rebound, so she'd quickly left him to his own devices.

"Oh, well. Fifth grade." Ethan seemed to relax a little. He even smiled.

Cleo looked at him sharply. Wait a minute. Maybe she liked it a little better when he was wondering what kind of kisses she'd exchanged with Jeremy. Ethan certainly hadn't given her any worth talking about yesterday.

He started small-talking with Jeremy, apparently now quite at ease with her elementary school conquest. Jeremy went on and on about her virtues, which would have been all right if he'd concentrated on her great kisses, Cleo thought. Maybe then Ethan would regret what hadn't happened the night before.

Instead, Jeremy was telling Ethan how businesslike Cleo was. He told Ethan they served on a committee together for the local chamber of commerce. Everyone knew they could rely on Cleo. Practical, sensible Cleo.

Ugh.

Cleo sipped her coffee, tuning out the men's voices and stealing little glances at her new husband. Ethan seemed plenty rested now, all ready to be sociable. But could he have saved a little something of himself for her last night? No. When she was all hot and flustered and thinking lusty thoughts, he'd been sawing logs as though deep winter was coming.

She frowned. Then there was that smile of his when Jeremy'd mentioned fifth grade. Oh, yeah, immediately Ethan's interest in who else she'd kissed had cooled way down when he'd heard those words. Maybe he didn't think a woman as practical and capable as she could attract a *grown* man.

Cleo bit her lower lip. And maybe she couldn't. After all, she and Ethan had only had that one brief interlude of passion months ago. If it was as memorable for Ethan as it was for her, why *hadn't* he been able to stay awake last night?

A cold dousing of embarrassment ran over her. Suddenly she was thankful he hadn't woken up. He probably didn't want her *that* way. After all, he'd been willing to postpone the intimate part of their marriage indefinitely.

Another sip of Jasmine's coffee tasted bitter in her mouth. Cleo had almost made a fool of herself last night by putting the moves on him. Well, that wouldn't happen again.

Unless she was positively, absolutely, certain he did want her.

Five

Three days into his marriage, Ethan hung up the phone in the room he used as an office and sought out Cleo. He wasn't accustomed to discussing his plans with anyone, but he realized that his upcoming schedule had to be presented to his...wife.

It was still hard to think the word. Wife. He had one.

He found her in Jonah's room, standing at the changing table. Ethan hesitated in the doorway, watching her spread lotion over the baby's freshly bathed skin. Cleo was whispering something to Jonah and smiling, and he stared back at her with all the intent of a man—albeit an infant one—deeply in love.

Cleo picked up the lotion bottle and as she upended it, she glanced over her shoulder and spotted Ethan. She froze, in the act of squeezing apparently, because a huge dollop squirted into her hand and threatened to overflow her cupped palm.

"Whoops." She hastily set the bottle down and stared at her hand in dismay. "Did you need something?"

Ethan came closer. "Sorry to startle you. Can I, uh, help?"

"Thanks." She shuffled a bit to the side. "Take the baby, will you?"

Ethan hesitated, then gamely reached for the wiggling body of his nephew. He held him awkwardly against his chest.

"Hold it right there," Cleo said. She dabbed two fingers into the lotion in her palm and rubbed the stuff into the skin of Jonah's back above his soft cloth diaper.

Ethan held the baby awkwardly and breathed in the powdery scent of the lotion. Jonah's eyes were wide as they took in his face, and guilt pinged Ethan. With expert Cleo on the scene, he left most of the baby-tending to her. He'd never quite gotten the hang of what Jonah needed.

And for his sister Della's sake, he'd been determined to find someone who could.

Hence the marriage, hence this moment, hence the uncomfortable task of sharing his life with another person. Of course, marrying Cleo had been his idea, but it still took some getting used to.

He cleared his throat. "I wanted to tell you— I mean, talk to you about my schedule for the next couple of weeks."

"Okay." Cleo dabbed her fingers into the lotion again but this time rubbed it on herself instead of the baby, her hand moving against the smooth skin of her arm.

Ethan forgot what he was supposed to be talking about. He watched her fingers make circles, circles. Then she bent and started stroking her calves with the stuff, lifting the long hem of her skirt to new heights.

His muscles tightened. Maybe he'd never before seen Cleo's knees.

Which led his thoughts instantly back to their wedding night. If he hadn't had to bust his butt getting from one side of the world to the other... If he hadn't gone to sleep on her... would those knees be something he was intimately familiar with by now?

He imagined his hands where hers were, his palms just there, on the inside of her knees. He imagined pushing them apart so he could push the part of him that was going hard this moment into her...

"Ethan?"

He shook his head to clear it. "What?" he said hoarsely.

She straightened and cocked an eyebrow. "Your schedule, you said?"

His mind whirled, trying to refocus. His schedule. Yeah. Right. He automatically handed Jonah back to her and shoved his hands into his pockets. To tell the truth, it was damn awkward accounting to Cleo. Maybe because his old man had never bothered to give Ethan's mom a why, wherefore, or the courtesy of a what-do-you-think.

Maybe it was because Ethan couldn't stop thinking about Cleo's knees.

He cleared his throat again. "We need to work out a few details."

She gently laid the baby back on the changing table and deftly started dressing him. "Okay."

"I need to head back to Houston in the next couple of days." He winced at the decisiveness in his voice. "I mean, if that's all right with you."

Cleo shrugged. "No problem."

No problem. That should be good. But instead it bothered him a little that she was so cavalier about his comings and goings. "I might have to be gone for a week."

"Fine."

"Or two," he added, an unfamiliar feeling coming to life in his gut.

"Okay."

It was a hot feeling in his gut, completely foreign to him. She didn't blink when he said he might be gone for *two weeks?* What kind of marriage did she think they were going to have?

Maybe she had counted on him being gone most of the

time. There *were* all those men who couldn't wait for chances to kiss her.

But of course that was stupid. Cleo was as loyal as he was business savvy. That fire in his belly subsided. "I don't like to be gone that long," he explained, "but I want to get my business moved to Whitehorn as soon as possible."

"What?" Her attention finally garnered, she picked up the baby and turned to face him. "You're moving the business from Houston to Montana?"

He blinked. "Of course. You didn't think I was going to add out-of-town headquarters to a business that already keeps me from home, did you?"

"Oh." She fussed with the baby's wispy hair. "Of course I didn't."

But it was obvious she had. He thought of those kissing "old friends" of hers again, but dismissed the idea again. "Anyway," he said, "if I remained headquartered in Houston, it wouldn't look very convincing to Jonah's grandparents. They need to see that we've created a two-parent, stable home for him."

"Mmm." She gave a little nod. "Jonah's grandparents. That's right. This is all about that custody issue."

There was a little edge to her voice he didn't understand. "Yes," he said quietly. "And don't think I don't appreciate what you've done, Cleo."

"What I've done," she echoed.

"Taking on the baby, me…"

She gave Jonah a big kiss on the top of his head. "Taking on the baby has been a pleasure."

Ethan noticed she said nothing about taking on him.

"But since you're going to be gone so much," Cleo continued, "do you mind if I return to Beansprouts?"

She'd taken the past couple of weeks off, though yesterday she'd driven in while Jonah was napping. "Well, uh, sure," he said. "Whatever you want."

"I'll take the baby with me, of course. I can set up a portable crib in my office and I've already increased my assistant's hours. It won't be as if I'll ignore Jonah's needs."

"I didn't think for a second you'd ignore Jonah's needs," Ethan said. The only person ignoring needs was Ethan himself. The sudden need to kiss Cleo's little frown away.

He ran his hands through his hair. "Look, I know this is weird, trying to accustom ourselves to a life together, but I trust you to do the right thing, Cleo."

"Thank you. And I trust you, Ethan."

God, he wished he was so certain. This woman had gone out on a limb for him and Jonah, and he wanted to do right by her. He figured that meant slow and cool, but all he felt was this hot, quick need to bury himself inside her and know that she couldn't get away.

Only the thought that if he got close to her he might hurt her—emotionally—stopped him. He couldn't take the risk.

Because all that heat and all that quickness reminded him much too much of his father and the way he'd hurt his family. Ethan had survived by evicting emotion from his life. But that meant he didn't know how to have the kind of relationship a woman such as Cleo would want.

He sighed and stepped back. "By the way, when I'm in Houston I'll also be moving my bank accounts. I'll do it first thing, and then call to give you the numbers."

"What would I need the numbers for?"

"Because it's your money, too. I'll have the checks and debit card sent directly here, okay?"

Cleo shook her head. "You don't have to do that. I don't want your money."

"What are you talking about? Of course I have to do that." He didn't like the stubborn expression on her face. Money was what he brought to the table, damn it. If he couldn't do anything else well, he knew he could provide for them.

"It just doesn't seem…right, somehow." Cleo frowned and looked at Jonah, who appeared serious, as if he understood the adult talk.

"Hell, Cleo, what's mine is yours. We *are* married, after all."

She looked up, her violet eyes holding questions he didn't have the answers to. "Are we?"

But that answer he knew. "Yes." The little burn in his belly had fired up again and he frowned. "We're definitely married." Before he could say something stupid, he stalked off.

Entering his office, he managed to not slam the door, but he did throw himself into his chair in front of his laptop computer. Damn, damn, damn.

He'd thought he was the one who needed to get used to being married. Ha! The joke was on him, because it was Cleo who suddenly seemed the more uncomfortable.

But they *were* married. More than half of him wanted to take her to bed right now to prove that point.

But more important was Jonah and the promise Ethan had made to his sister before she died. Jonah would have the love, the nurturing, that he and Della had missed out on. That meant Ethan couldn't take a chance on messing things up with Cleo.

Cleo sat at her desk at Beansprouts, trying to ignore the calendar that reminded her of how long Ethan had been gone. She knew he regretted the necessity of leaving

Whitehorn. It was the only soothing balm to the rawness of their new and to-date tense marriage.

He'd left for Houston, as physically distant as ever.

It made her nuts, because she was aware of him every moment they were together in the house. She would catch him watching her, and her skin would prickle in awareness. He would walk past her and she would follow him with her gaze, drinking in his lean strength and the graceful, male way he moved.

Though they still weren't comfortable in their marriage, he'd called her every night over the past week. No surprise, Ethan wasn't a chatterer, but the sound of his voice in her ear created a new intimacy between them. They talked of their child—that's what Cleo was careful to do, refer to him as "our boy." Ethan seemed to be getting used to it, though the first time she used the term, there had been forty-five full seconds of silence before he'd spoken.

They talked of whatever deal he was working on and Cleo would entertain him with Beansprouts reports—Bessie had recently forgiven Kenny G. and laid a big kiss on the little boy, which had sent *him* to Cleo's office in tears.

For a few minutes each night, they laughed together.

Cleo treasured the moments because they reminded her of the first time Ethan had been in Montana. Then, she'd known he saw her as a woman, not as a sensible, capable, practical caretaker for the child who had been dropped into his life.

Last night Ethan had even mentioned a gift. "Be on the lookout for its delivery tomorrow," he'd said.

Cleo had melted with tenderness. She was lying in his bed in the master suite—she would change the bedding so he would never, ever know she'd slept there—her body a warm puddle of breathlessness. "For me?"

His voice was soft, but rough, like the tongue of a cat,

and she wiggled against the sheets. "For you, Cleo. Because…" He'd let the last word trail away.

Because why? Oh, how much she'd wanted to ask.

But she hadn't managed another word, and so all morning she'd wasted time looking out the window for a delivery truck, visions of lingerie or champagne or perfume or all three in her mind.

"Cleo?" Her assistant Nancy's voice sounded from the door.

Cleo straightened her spine, trying to appear businesslike, but afraid her daydreams were still written on her face. "Yes?"

"There's a package here for you."

Cleo's heart jumped. Ethan's gift? "I can't believe I missed something being delivered." Then she flushed and tried explaining why she was suddenly so interested in deliveries. "Ethan said he was sending me a present." Then her cheeks went even warmer. The last thing she needed was someone looking over her shoulder while she opened it. But knowing Nancy…

Oh, and she was right. Not only Nancy, but the three other staff members who'd managed to find the time to wander by her office as she stared at the overlarge envelope on her desk. An envelope, she noted, made from the kind of paper guaranteed to resist water as well as dynamite.

Cleo sighed, supposing she could send them all on their way. But a sisterhood developed when there was an all-woman staff. Frank opinions, unqualified support, and the right to watch someone open a present—especially one sent by a new husband!—were givens.

She tested the package's weight. Not soft enough for lingerie, not liquid enough for champagne. A book, maybe?

Nancy reached over and poked the package. "I think it's

a book," she confirmed. "Poetry, do you suppose? How romantic."

"Come on! Open it!" the others urged, and Cleo used her scissors to cut across the envelope top. Then, she hesitated, suddenly remembering Jasmine's talk the other day about love manuals. How much had Ethan heard? Her heartbeat sped up. *Thump-thump-thump.* Surely he wouldn't—

Impatient, Nancy grabbed the package and shook the contents onto the desk. A stack of paperwork—sandwiched between two pieces of cardboard and held together with a thick rubber band—slid out. Instead of a card, a yellow sticky note was slapped on the front.

"For you," it said, in a masculine slash. "As promised, and thanks again." No name.

No name was necessary. Not once Cleo freed the sheaf of papers. Because the romantic gift she'd been daydreaming about wasn't really a gift at all. *Thump.* Her heart sank. *Thump.* The pages were Ethan's half of their marriage deal. *Thump.* He'd been as good as he'd promised and bought the Beansprouts building for her. Her heart settled to a slow, resigned, disappointed beat.

Thanks again.

Not surprisingly, her friends realized her disappointment and tried to cheer Cleo up by sharing the worst gifts they'd ever received from their husbands. There were some doozies—Nancy's Glen had given her a new garage door opener for their anniversary, and for her birthday, Lorna's husband of thirty-two years had recently presented her with a squishy toilet seat that played show tunes.

"Well," Nancy finally said, shepherding the other staff members out the office door, "at least it proves he knows you, Cleo. A woman like you appreciates a practical gift."

"Yes, that's right," Cleo said, sadder than ever. It

seemed that everyone saw her the same way. "'Practical' me should feel happy."

But when her friends were gone, she whispered into the empty room, "But 'practical' me also feels 'capable' of wringing that man's neck."

She tamped down a sudden urge to jump up on her desk and scream to the world that she wasn't who they thought she was. She suppressed a second impulse to call Ethan and whisper scandalous things in his ear, just to shake him up.

Why couldn't people—Ethan—see that practical didn't cancel out passionate and that capable could exist alongside carnal?

Two days later Cleo waved from her office window as her mother and Jonah took off down the street. Being a grandma thrilled Celeste, and she had even bought her own stroller for her "grandbaby." She turned up her nose at the one Ethan had arrived in Montana with—it was as large and sturdy as the brand-new Range Rover he'd also purchased—but she adored touring Jonah through town in her simpler model.

Cleo relaxed against her chair. If all that her marriage gained was a new focus for her mother, something other than those disturbing dreams, then Cleo was happy.

But the soft, warm glow inside her sparked high and hot when fifteen minutes later she looked up to find her husband standing in the entry to her office.

"Ethan!" She gulped. "I didn't expect you back today."

He paused in the doorway, filling it with six plus feet of Italian suit and expensive shoes.

Cleo put down the unexpected heat rising up her neck to the clothes, not the man. She just wasn't used to power dressing.

He walked toward her, and she gulped again. "I was able to get out a day early," he said. "I wanted to see you."

Without thinking, Cleo rose from behind her desk. Her simple, Oxford-cloth cotton dress was probably wrinkled from a morning of sitting, and she automatically tried smoothing it with her palm. "You wanted to see *me?*"

He nodded.

Cleo tried slowing everything—her footsteps toward him, her pulse, her explanation that Jonah was with her mother. But then she stood in front of him and she wanted to touch his golden hair more than she wanted to kiss his mouth, and she wanted to kiss his mouth more than she wanted him to touch her.

Slow down, she reminded herself again. This is the man who gave you a piece of property as a thank-you gift.

With a renewed sense of self-preservation, she took a step back. "Why did you want to see me, Ethan?"

"Because, uh…" He blinked, as if the why hadn't occurred to him. His hand reached out and tucked a stray tendril of hair behind her ear.

Goose bumps prickled on her cheek and ran down the too-warm skin of her neck. No. She took another step back. Sure, she wanted him to want her, but she wanted to make certain he was moved by passion and desire, not by convenience and gratitude.

She cleared her throat. "Your trip was successful?"

He nodded, and his expression suddenly lightened. "I know what I came to tell you," he said, grinning. "I just, uh, forgot for a minute."

Despite the temptation of that gorgeous grin, Cleo retreated one more step, the backs of her thighs hitting the edge of her desk. She leaned against it, but couldn't help smiling a little in return. "Good news?"

"Great news." His grin widened.

Cleo folded her arms over her chest to stop herself from reaching out and tracing his mouth with her fingertips. "Okay," she said. "Out with it."

"The Covingtons have dropped their suit."

For a moment Cleo puzzled over the unfamiliar name. But then it hit her. "Jonah's grandparents?" She couldn't put a name to the euphoric bubble that burst inside her. "Jonah's grandparents have given up fighting for custody?"

Ethan's answering grin made her head spin. "Yep."

Cleo didn't know what was wrong with her. The edges of the room started going black and Ethan seemed too far away. "He's going to stay with you?" she said over the lump in her throat.

"He's going to stay with *us*."

The room shrank to a tunnel.

"Cleo? Cleo?" She heard Ethan's voice but, like the rest of him, it was distant. Then large warm hands grasped her shoulders. The funny thing was, she thought dazedly, she knew those were Ethan's hands, even though he was so very far away.

"Cleo, honey." He pulled her up against his chest. "Breathe, honey. Breathe."

As instructed, she sucked in a breath. Then another. The room lightened, the tunnel opened up and suddenly her vision completely cleared and she was staring at the lapel of an olive-colored, lightweight wool suit jacket.

Ethan took her chin in his hand and made her look up. His gaze ran over her face. "Your color's coming back. Are you all right? What was wrong?"

Cleo licked her lips. "I knew...I knew you were going to see your attorney in Houston about the custody, but I didn't let myself think about it."

He frowned, his eyebrows coming together over his concerned blue eyes. "Okay."

"And you'll notice I didn't ask you about it, even though we talked almost every night."

He nodded. "And I didn't say anything to you, because there wasn't anything to tell until today. I visited the Covingtons, too, and told them about you and about our marriage, but I wasn't sure of their response."

Cleo swallowed to ease her dry mouth, aware of what she'd been hiding from. *I was supposed to be the reason they would let you have Jonah,* shewanted to say. *I was terrified I wouldn't help.*

What would their marriage have been about then?

And she had been hiding from something else, too. She hadn't acknowledged how worried she'd been about one more thing. One more very important thing.

He frowned again. "What aren't you telling me, Cleo? I want to know why you almost fainted on me a minute ago."

She bit her bottom lip. "Oh, Ethan," she said. Tears stung the corners of her eyes and she blinked them back. "I don't think I could bear to lose him." The truth was wrenched from her heart. "I've been too scared to even think about it. I care about that little boy so much."

The tears in Cleo's eyes kept her from seeing Ethan's expression, but it didn't matter, because he jerked her against him and held her close. "Cleo." He murmured her name gruffly. "Oh, Cleo."

She wrapped her arms around his waist and breathed in Ethan's scent. His solid warmth comforted her. "Thank God, we get to keep Jonah."

His cheek rubbed against the top of her head. "Thank God," he echoed.

"I didn't know how easy it would be to love him," she said.

Ethan stilled. Two heartbeats passed, and then he pushed her a few inches away, just enough to look down into her face. "Cleo..." he said hoarsely.

She reached up and touched his mouth, just as she'd been wanting to. "What?" she whispered.

There was something in his eyes she'd never seen before. His fingers tightened on her shoulders. "I wish—"

"Am I interrupting something?" boomed a loud, male voice.

Cleo automatically swung toward the door, breaking her connection with Ethan. He stepped away, and she stared at the newcomer in her office. "Stuart?" she said stupidly, her mind still caught up in Ethan's embrace and the second time he'd started an "I wish" that he couldn't finish.

Her longtime friend Stuart Smith smiled wickedly and leaned one rangy shoulder against the doorjamb. "Forgotten me already?" His gaze flickered toward Ethan. "You won't be forgiven, sweetheart, unless you tell me that this guy in the Eye-talian apparel is your brand-new husband."

She ignored his "Eye-talia"—she'd punish him later by telling his Nona Marchetti, who would then withhold Stuart's favorite cannoli dessert—and made quick introductions. "This is my husband, Ethan Redford. Ethan, this co-median here is a half-Italian cowboy with the unlikely name of Stuart Smith."

Stuart shook Ethan's hand. "Ropin' and rigatoni. With one I caught Cleo. But it was the other that held her." His smile took on that wicked edge again. "Do you know how much Cleo loves pasta, Ethan? Well, any kind of food if a man is cooking for her. It's because—"

Cleo gripped Stuart's forearm and dug in her fingernails. "Are you looking for your daughter? Bessie is probably at storytime with the four-year-olds." She tugged him in the direction of her doorway. "Don't let us stop you."

Stuart winced, but the teasing light didn't leave his eyes as he firmly planted the heels of his cowboy boots into her carpet. "Something tells me Ethan doesn't know that you once wore my ring."

"I didn't know." A funny expression crossed Ethan's face and he looked at her. "You wore another man's ring?"

Stuart chuckled and Cleo shot him a mean look. He always did have lousy timing. When he saw that she and Ethan were…close, couldn't he have just left them alone?

She sighed. "I wore Stuart's *class* ring. I was fifteen years old."

The teasing was gone from the tall cowboy's brown eyes, leaving only fondness behind. "For two years, though, Cleo. You wore it for two years, and it was the darkest day of my life when you took it off and gave it back to me."

Her jaw dropped. "Stuart, you went out with Dinah Marcus behind my back. *Two times.*"

Stuart nodded. "I was an idiot." He looked over Cleo's head at Ethan. "Don't be stupid, Ethan," he said, and Cleo thought he even sounded a bit serious. "Don't let go of this woman."

There was an ironic edge to Ethan's voice. "I've heard that from more than one man, believe me."

Cleo shook her head. Men were so funny sometimes. "You big silly," she said to Stuart. She went on tiptoe to kiss his cheek, and then pat it, as if sealing it there. "Dinah Marcus went on to become your wife, and a happier couple I've never met. You don't have to pretend anything for Ethan. He sees me for what I am."

And then she frowned at the disquieting notion. Was she really just the practical, sensible woman he thought?

Stuart bent to give her a goodbye peck on the mouth. "I know *exactly* what Ethan sees, sweetiepie." With a two-fingered salute and laughter in his eyes, he left them.

Cleo pursed her lips and turned toward Ethan, shaking her head. "That man…"

The strange, intense look on Ethan's face had her stumbling over her tongue. He walked toward her with purpose and she found herself stepping back, toward the safety of the open door.

Ethan continued to advance. "I've been wondering, Cleo." His words were thoughtful, though his voice was tight. "Have you dated and kissed and broken the heart of every man in Montana, or just Whitehorn?"

Cleo's eyes widened. Her hands found the knob of the door, and she hung on to its solidness. There was something new in the way Ethan was looking at her, something she'd barely remembered from months ago when they had first met. There was a kiss in his eyes. Suddenly nervous, she squeezed the knob.

He must have noticed. "What a good idea," he said. In one fluid movement, he plucked her fingers free and kicked the door shut with his foot.

Six

Driven by impulse, Ethan took hold of Cleo by her upper arms and maneuvered her back against the now closed door of the office. She licked her lips nervously and the coil inside him heated and tightened.

"Ethan?"

"Mmm." His muscles were tense, too, and he didn't know if it was because of the three airport terminals he'd sprinted through to make his Montana flight, or because of something else.

"Um, you know that Stuart was only teasing me... you...um, I guess us."

Oh, yeah, and it was just about as funny as he was feeling right now. Annoyed-as-hell funny. Because when he'd first walked into her office just the sight of her had wiped everything else from his mind. He'd wanted to taste her ripe mouth and put his hands on her ripe curves and take her, take her, take her.

But when he'd come to his senses and told her about the Covingtons's decision, she'd floored him again. Knocked him flat on his butt by the depth of her feelings for Jonah.

God. He'd never known a woman who cared this much. The tears in her eyes had been more precious than diamonds, and it had half thrilled and half chilled him that he realized it...and yet couldn't offer her anything as valuable in return.

Ethan Redford was a man who always paid his debts.

But he suspected Cleo's bill was something he could never clear. He would never have that much cash.

Or whatever else she wanted it paid in.

"Ethan."

He ignored her, and the fact that his bill was just about to go up. Way up.

That hot coil was burning inside him with undeniable insistence. It had been twisted and heated by every man he'd watch kiss her, by every man who had known her longer than he had, by every man who had at one time wanted her.

She was his now.

And he was going to have her.

He lowered his head and brushed her lips with his. Sweet. Cleo tasted like a sugary treat.

He'd known from the beginning she'd be bad for him.

He stroked her mouth another time and she made a little sound, but he didn't even bother to figure out what it meant. He wanted more. The sweet taste of Cleo's mouth was just too good.

He crowded her against the door and kissed her again. Her lips were soft and pliant but he didn't even try to open them with his tongue. He wanted to, damn, he wanted it bad, but anticipation was almost as addictive. And he had to prove to himself he had some kind of control when it came to her.

She made another noise and wiggled against him. He groaned and his hands left her upper arms. To hold her head still, he drove his fingers into her hair, and then bent again to her soft lips.

Control, he reminded himself. Anticipation. He brushed against her lips, brushed once, twice, but when she made that anxious little noise again, he couldn't stop himself from following her breath inside her mouth.

Anticipation fled. Control disappeared. Inside Cleo's wet heat, Ethan lost all sense of timing, all notion of the tactics that made him a winner in the boardroom. He pressed his tongue deeper, pressed his heavily aroused body against her belly.

Her arms looped around his neck. She lifted herself against him, tilting her hips to move him closer. His heart ricocheting in his chest, he angled his head to explore her mouth from another direction, and he rubbed his tongue along hers.

Her body jerked against him, and the movement made him lift his head. Her mouth was wet and her violet eyes were at an erotic half-mast. He groaned silently, needing her again, more, closer.

Desperate to touch, he ran his palms down her back to cup her round bottom. He shuddered and instantly craved more.

"Cleo," he whispered. His mouth trailed over her lips, her cheek, and down her neck. He wanted to devour her, in huge gulping bites.

He rubbed his pelvis against hers and that coil of desire inside him wound tighter. His fingers moved with a will of their own, pulling up the fabric of her long dress in great bunches. As he took her mouth, thrusting his tongue inside, he thrust his hands beneath her silky panties.

Her silky skin filled his palms.

She moaned.

Something slammed hard in his chest, as if it was knocking against it.

The something slammed again, and the knocking—

Someone was knocking on Cleo's office door.

Ethan lifted his head, withdrew his hands, stepped back. Her skirt fell around her calves like a curtain going down on pleasure.

She stared at him.

He buttoned his suit jacket to hide his erection.

Cleo was still staring at him, despite another insistent knock.

"Cleo, someone's at the door," he said.

She blinked.

"And if it's another one of your old boyfriends," he said flatly, "I can promise you blood will be shed."

Blinking again, she whirled around and opened the door. Maybe it was because of his threat that Cleo stepped into the hall, leaving him alone with his thoughts...and his lust.

He dropped into an empty chair, rubbing his palm over his face. What the hell was he doing?

If he wanted to seduce Cleo—and God knows he did, but he still wasn't at all sure it was right—why had he acted like a oafish hothead and pushed her against the door and then pushed his tongue in her mouth?

The slow tease, the gradual courtship, and then the well-timed union of two separate entities were steps he'd studied in business school and then perfected in the business world. Wooing a woman had never been any different for him. Or to him.

But with Cleo... When it came to Cleo he forgot all his lessons and let impulses, neediness, and cravings drive him.

He hungered for her in a way that was at once familiar and terrifying. He'd experienced that single-minded focus at work before. It was a hunger that reminded him too much of the anger that had been his father's driving force.

An anger that led him to hit and rage...all in the name of love.

Ethan's gaze snagged on Jonah's portable crib, tucked away in the far corner of Cleo's office. A corduroy elephant stared at him down his long, long nose, and a yellow bunny sat up on its fluffy tail. Ethan sighed.

He wasn't afraid he'd ever physically hurt Cleo. God, he knew he could never raise his hand to her, or any woman or child.

But there were other ways to cause her pain. If they became intimate, she would have every right to demand from him the depth of caring that she herself was capable of. And Ethan just didn't have that to offer. He had a sick feeling that he had *nothing* to offer Cleo.

Because growing up with a man such as Jack Redford hadn't shown Ethan how to be a husband and father. Only how not to be one.

When Cleo walked into the house with Jonah that evening, she was met by the delicious smell of pizza. Relief mingled with the awkwardness of seeing Ethan again after this afternoon's mind-blowing kisses. She'd managed to avoid the whole cooking issue so far in their marriage. And today of all days, she didn't think she would have been able to pull off a meal even the least bit palatable.

Not when the only thing she could think of was the heady sensations of his hands in her hair and on her skin, of his mouth so soft one minute and so greedy the next.

She shivered as Ethan walked out of the kitchen. To smooth over the moment, she held up Jonah. "Here he is! My mother was sorry to have caused you to miss him." After their...interlude, Ethan had quickly left Beansprouts and told her he'd meet her at home.

Cleo approached Ethan and lifted Jonah toward him. Instead of taking the proffered baby, Ethan slipped the over-stuffed diaper bag off her shoulder. "Let me get this," he said.

Her eyebrows rose, but she didn't say anything as Ethan set the bag on a nearby table. When he turned, she tried for a natural smile. "Pizza, huh? Shall I serve us while you entertain Jonah for a bit?"

Ethan's gaze shifted away from the baby. "Let me serve you," he said quickly.

Cleo narrowed her eyes. Ethan needed to spend time with Jonah and vice versa. If they were going to build a family, that is. And with the memory of those kisses as incentive, she was determined that they both give this marriage a real go.

Without giving him a chance to get away, she walked to Ethan and thrust the baby into his arms. He automatically grabbed hold of him, thank goodness, though he appeared as if he didn't want to. Without a backward look, Cleo headed into the kitchen.

Ethan trailed behind. "What do I, uh, do, exactly, to entertain him?"

Cleo slid him a glance. He stared down at the baby as if Jonah were a piece of fruit Ethan couldn't quite figure out how to peel. She almost relented and took the baby from him, but then she remembered how happy he'd been to tell her that Jonah's grandparents were giving up their custody battle. Ethan wanted the little boy in his life, no doubt about that.

"Cleo?"

She ignored the tiny note of panic in his voice. "You can keep me company in the kitchen. Jonah will let you know if he finds it boring." At the sink, she washed her hands and then tied on an apron.

She slid another look at Ethan. He still held the baby stiffly, a couple of inches away from his body, as if he wanted some distance between them. Pursing her lips, she breathed out a silent, frustrated sigh.

Distance was the problem. Ethan's job allowed for plenty of physical distance between the three of them, and she'd known from the start that Ethan liked to keep an emotional distance, too.

She didn't know why.

When they'd met months ago he'd been the same. Then, he'd talk to her, the conversation easy and charming, but he'd share nothing of himself. Now, despite the fact they were married, he was as reticent. Even during their nightly phone calls, the subject matter had never been anything personal.

Cleo took silverware from the drawer and began setting the table. Ethan leaned against a nearby countertop, looking uncomfortable. She ached to tell him to hold Jonah against the warmth of his body. She ached to ask him to hold *her* against him again.

Never before had passion risen so hot and so fast inside her. If he'd asked, she'd have made love to him right there in her office! Well, maybe she was a little too sensible for that, but she'd have gone somewhere with him. Gone anyplace they could be alone and indulge in touching and kissing and—

Cleo had to shove her hands into the apron pockets so he wouldn't see them shaking. Only a fool wouldn't realize there could be something special between her and Ethan. But their marriage wouldn't go anywhere if she couldn't get him to open up to her.

She didn't want to be married to a stranger, no matter how passionate that marriage could be.

The pizza took only a moment to serve. When they sat at the table, with Jonah in his infant seat as a centerpiece, Cleo bit into her slice with relish. "Nothing beats pizza," she said after swallowing the first mouthful.

Ethan cocked an eyebrow her way. "Pizza's number one with you? That surprises me."

"Why?"

He shrugged. At some point before she'd come home he'd changed from a suit to jeans and a T-shirt. Ethan without his Armani always took a little getting used to. "I would have thought you'd like something…I don't know, more sophisticated, maybe."

Cleo set her slice down on her plate. "Sophisticated? Me?"

He shrugged again. "You forget. I've eaten a lot of meals at the B and B. It's the kind of fare a person could get used to. You've been around that for quite some time."

"It's Jasmine who's in charge of the food. Not just the breakfasts for the guests. She's always experimenting. So most of what I've eaten has been Jasmine's choice and Jasmine's cooking." Someday Cleo was going to have to admit to Ethan that not only was delivery pizza the best dinner she could imagine, but the best dinner she herself knew how to prepare.

"Do you, uh, like sophisticated food best?" she asked. If he answered in the affirmative, she would definitely have to break the news that all that kind of cooking was going to have to be done by him.

"Mmm. I don't know."

Cleo frowned, tamping down a little spurt of irritation. See, even in the littlest things he wouldn't open up to her. If Mr. Armani had grown up on foie gras and imported truffles, what was the harm in telling her?

She picked up her pizza slice again and then looked him straight in the eye. "What's the best meal you've ever eaten?" she asked.

"Easy," he answered promptly. "October 1998. The Field House in St. Helena, California. It's a small restaurant in the wine country." He smiled. "I ate lunch there and then I offered to make them rich."

Cleo wondered if he'd shared that special lunch with a woman. "Rich, how?"

"I offered them the capital to open a place in New York or San Francisco." Ethan chuckled. "I begged them to do something in Houston so I could eat there more regularly. But they turned me down flat."

"They?" she asked.

"A husband and wife team. But the two of them liked St. Helena. They liked raising their children in a small town."

"Like Whitehorn," Cleo found herself saying.

Ethan lifted his water glass in a little toast. "Like Whitehorn."

Cleo gave her attention back to her pizza.

"How about you?" he said. "What's the best meal you ever had?"

Cleo pursed her lips, then lowered her voice to a whisper. "You have to promise never to tell my mother."

Ethan's mouth twitched. "Why?"

She shook her head. "Promise first."

He smiled now. "I promise."

Cleo leaned over her plate and whispered, "My cousin Summer, Jasmine and I had a party at the house once."

Amusement lit Ethan's eyes. "So?"

"I can't remember where the adults were—my mother, my aunt and uncle—but they thought we were old enough to stay overnight alone. We invited just a few girlfriends over, but…" She gave him a knowing look.

His eyebrows rose and he sat back in his chair. "I'm guessing you had a few more guests than you expected."

She nodded sagely. "And they were boys."

"Cleo," Ethan said, amusement in his voice, but his expression harder to read, "have you been a man magnet since the day you were born?"

"'Man magnet'?" She waved the idea away. "Yeah, right. When you are sandwiched between two beauties like Summer and Jasmine, you get real used to being the ordinary one."

"The 'ordinary one'?" Ethan echoed. "You've got to be kidding."

She appreciated how surprised he sounded, she really did, but she was the practical, sensible, capable one, correct?

"Hey," she said. "I accepted it long ago and I don't mind, honest. I'm the girl that was every guy's buddy. You know, the one who'd introduce them to the girl they didn't have enough nerve to strike up a conversation with. The one they'd take to a dance because they didn't need to impress me. If a guy got in a jam, he knew he could turn to me for advice or...whatever."

Ethan's brows came together. "What's 'whatever'?"

"Maybe he needed the notes from biology class. Maybe an idea for the perfect gift for his girlfriend." She shot him a look. "Maybe he needed a wife."

Ethan straightened. "Cleo—"

"But anyway, back to my party and the best meal I've ever eaten. So about a zillion kids show up, and we don't know how to turn them away. Or maybe we didn't try *that* hard, I don't know. But we paid, believe me. We spent the entire night turning the stereo down and rescuing furniture from irreparable damage and shutting the refrigerator and kitchen cabinets after the latest forage.

"It was 2:00 a.m. before the last partygoer was gone and we'd finished filling four trash bags. Summer drove off to find a place to dump them so Mama wouldn't find out. Jasmine and I sat in the kitchen and ate the only food left in the house. I was so relieved and so hungry that it is indelibly etched on my brain as the best meal of my life."

Ethan looked amused again. "And it was...?"

"Cap'n Crunch cereal. Brownies that weren't fully cooked—we couldn't wait that long to eat them. And pizza. The kind that comes frozen in a box and isn't much more than a saltine cracker with tomato sauce and a sprinkle of cheese."

"That's disgusting." He pushed his plate away.

"Hey, don't knock it until you're that hungry and have been that terrified your friends are going to break a lamp or something."

"It's still disgusting." He gave her a mock frown. "And promise or no promise, I just might tell your mother on you. You girls could have gotten yourselves in a bad situation."

"Don't go holier than thou on me now." Cleo wagged a finger at him. "You can't tell me you didn't crash a few girls' parties in your time." She tried imagining him as a teenager. Blond, and with that devastating smile. No girls would have hesitated to welcome him in.

Ethan was quiet for a moment, his gaze distant. "I crashed a few parties, all right," he said slowly, as if he wasn't aware he was speaking. "The kind thrown by untouchable girls who loved the darkest corners and the daring idea of taking the dirt-poor boy from the wrong side of town into them."

"What?" Cleo tried putting it together. *Dirt poor. The boy from the wrong side of town.* No. Not Ethan. Not the man who wore European suits the way other men wore baseball caps.

"I wouldn't have come to your party, though, Cleo."

She was still grappling with the first insight he'd ever given her into his past. Ethan hadn't grown up rich, as she'd always thought. He'd been poor, dirt poor. "You wouldn't have come to my party?" she echoed stupidly. "Why not?"

"Because I would have known you weren't ordinary. Not

ordinary at all.'' He pushed away from the table. ''And I wouldn't have wanted to taint that.''

Cleo just stared at him, her jaw agape. ''You're not— You're not—'' What did she want to ask? He didn't think she was ordinary? He was afraid he might taint her? ''You're not going anywhere, are you?'' she finally finished lamely.

''Not until I apologize.''

Again, she stared at him dumbly.

''Listen. I grew up with a rough, brutal man. I'd cut off my right arm before I was ever either one to you, Cleo.'' He looked away, out the window, where it was just beginning to go dark. ''So I'm sorry for the way I...kissed you today. So very, very sorry.''

Before she could say anything in return, he was gone.

Cleo might have sat there all night, stunned, if it hadn't been for Jonah. He began to fuss and she left the dishes where they were to fetch his bottle, feed him, and then get him ready for bed.

Once he was finally tucked into his crib and asleep, Cleo let herself think about Ethan again.

Dirt poor. Wrong side of town. Father was a rough and brutal man.

She didn't know Ethan Redford. She didn't know him at all.

She'd married a stranger. A stranger who might have very good reasons for the distance he liked to keep. And one who felt he needed to apologize for the most passionate, most exciting kisses of her life.

Cleo wanted her mother.

Once she drove to the B and B and located Celeste reading in the den off the kitchen, Cleo found herself tongue-tied. Maybe it was because of the love seat—where she'd first encountered the power of what Ethan could do to her. Maybe it was because she couldn't explain how someone as capable as herself was married to a man who ran from emotional entanglements.

But she had to say *something* about why she was there. So despite the fact that a phone call would have served the purpose, she smiled and said she'd come by to share some interesting news she'd heard at the day care center. One of the Beansprouts's fathers worked on a construction crew at the Laughing Horse casino and resort project.

Cleo settled beside Celeste on the cushions. "So, Mama. You'll never guess," she said lightly. "Whitehorn has another mystery."

"What kind of mystery?" Celeste turned her way. With the light of a nearby lamp falling on her mother's face, Cleo could see the signs of more sleepless nights. She hadn't noticed it earlier in the day, when her mother's delight in Jonah hid so much.

Cleo's stomach clenched with worry, but she gamely continued. "They halted construction on the resort today." She widened her eyes in mock alarm. "Because they found a skeleton."

"*What?*" Celeste's book slid off her knees and thumped to the floor. "Did you say a skeleton?"

Cleo nodded.

Her mother leaned over to pick up her book, her wavy hair hiding her face. "You mean, like an animal's, or a dinosaur or something?"

"Nope. A human skeleton. And what's more, they found a bullet lodged in one of the ribs."

Celeste didn't immediately straighten, though it still took Cleo a couple of seconds to realize her mother was frozen with...with what?

"Mama?" She put her arm around Celeste's back and

eased her to a sitting position. *Thump.* The book Celeste had retrieved fell again, out of her fingers this time, and Cleo kicked it aside and edged closer to her mother. "Mama?" She reached for Celeste's hands.

They were icy. The kind of cold that comes with shock…or terror.

Cleo pulled at the afghan tossed over the arm of the love seat and wrapped it around her mother. "What's wrong? Are you ill?"

When her mother didn't answer, Cleo jumped up. "I'm calling nine-one-one."

"No!" Celeste suddenly came to life, her gaze jumping to Cleo's face. "I'm all right, sweetie." She inhaled a shuddering breath. "Just a…just a goose…walking over my grave."

But to Cleo, Celeste looked as though she was going to be sick. "Mama—"

Her mother held up a hand. Cleo thought it was trembling. "Some tea, sweetie. I'll be fine after some hot, sweet tea."

"Are you sure?" At her mother's nod, Cleo backed toward the kitchen. "Lucky for you, tea is the one thing I don't burn." She was relieved when her mother smiled, and then even added a rusty chuckle.

The teakettle couldn't sing fast enough. Cleo checked on her mother fourteen times before the scent of steeping cinnamon and orange tea filled the kitchen and she was able to bring in a tray with the pot, two mugs, and a plate of Jasmine's heavenly tasting thumbprint cookies.

After a few sips from her mug, and one of the cookies, Celeste did appear better. Her color was back to normal and her hands seemed perfectly steady.

Cleo cradled her own mug and decided it was time to get tough with her mother. First it was the nightmares, and now this. "Mama," she said, her voice brooking no nonsense. "Mama, you must tell me what's wrong."

But another sip of tea seemed to infuse Celeste with a backbone even steelier than Cleo's. She pinned her daughter with the sharpest of gazes. "Cleo, sweetie, it's past dinner. Your baby's asleep and your husband just returned from a long trip away. But instead of being at home with him, you're visiting your mother. 'Tell me what's wrong'? I think that's my line."

Seven

Cleo stared into her mug of tea. Even though she'd come to her mother hoping Celeste would show her a way through this mess, it wasn't easy to admit to making a mistake. Especially when her family had taken her decision to marry Ethan with such aplomb. They'd been surprised, sure, but their faith in her good sense and practicality had reassured them she was making the right decision.

Instead, good sense hadn't played into her decision at all. She'd followed her heart—a heart that had done something as silly as falling in love at first sight.

Cleo didn't even know how to describe it to her mother. But one evening last January she'd wandered through the living room, her gaze on the magazine in her hand. Completely by accident, she'd smacked into Ethan, *his* gaze apparently distracted by the magazine in *his* hand. *Bump.*

Their gazes had met.

Her heart had landed at his feet.

Still without looking at her mother, Cleo now ran one finger around the rim of her mug. "Mama, why did you marry Daddy?" Cleo could barely remember her father, Ty Monroe, who had died in a car accident when she was a young child. Her memory held nothing at all of her parents' relationship.

"Not for the best reasons," Celeste said quietly.

Cleo looked up, startled. "What do you mean?"

Celeste sighed and gave a little smile. "The past just doesn't want to leave me alone."

"Oh, Mama." Cleo put out her hand, not wanting to cause her mother any discomfort. "We don't need to talk about it."

Celeste smiled again. "Maybe we do. I think it's time to shed light into some very dark corners."

"Mama…" Cleo said doubtfully.

Celeste patted Cleo's hand. "I think you need to hear this as much as I need to say it."

Cleo still had her doubts. But she set her tea on the tray and relaxed against the cushions of the love seat. "I'm listening."

Celeste took a sip from her mug. "You know about my older brother Jeremiah, about the kind of selfish, controlling man he was. After our father died, he took over the lives of us three sisters, of Blanche, Yvette and me. I don't know if it was out of a sense of protectiveness or just because he liked manipulating people."

"But, Mama, why didn't you and Aunt Yvette and Aunt Blanche break free of him?"

Celeste shook her head. "It seems like we should have, doesn't it? And Yvette did. She moved to Bozeman to get her teaching degree. But those were different times for most women, sweetie. We were expected to live under Jeremiah's rule—and his thumb—until we married."

"You told me once that you received three marriage proposals when you were in your twenties. You weren't tempted to accept one of them to get away from Jeremiah?"

Celeste smiled sadly. "Perhaps I should have. But I was waiting for…magic, I suppose."

Magic. Cleo knew all about that. It was one accidental meeting and then one heart lost. "But you didn't find it with Daddy, either?"

"I wish I could say I did, sweetie." Celeste lifted a hand to run her palm over Cleo's hair. "But as I got older, Jeremiah's reins on me became tighter and tighter. On Blanche, too."

Celeste lapsed into silence, and Cleo saw her forehead pleat, as if she were trying to figure out a puzzle or trying to remember a particularly fuzzy memory. "Then," Celeste went on, her gaze distant, "Raven disappeared. You know, Raven Hunter, the man Blanche loved and your cousin Summer's father. After Raven was gone, living with my brother became unbearable for me. Jeremiah always telling me what to do, how I should think, what I should say."

"Oh, Mama." Cleo hated the distress in her mother's voice. She couldn't imagine being treated that way by family, not when hers had always been unfailingly supportive and loving.

Celeste ran another gentle hand over Cleo's hair. "You know, that time is all so murky for me. But I *do* remember Jeremiah introducing me to Ty—your father. He was charming and he made me feel pretty and special." She smiled. "Your father was a good man, Cleo. Never doubt that. I just think he deserved more than a wife who wanted to move away from her brother more than she wanted him."

Cleo sighed. "So you think a marriage can't work without that...magic you were talking about?" And what about one-sided magic? How far could that take a marriage?

"I think a marriage takes more than magic. It takes patience and compromise and understanding." Celeste chuckled. "But I'm sure the magic makes all that compromise a little easier to swallow."

Cleo thought back to her childhood. She remembered the shape of her father's face and his smile, and then she remembered him smiling at her mother. "Daddy loved you, though, Mama. I'm certain of it."

Celeste nodded. "At first sight, he always said."

At first sight. Maybe it was a family trait. Or a family weakness. "But maybe one-sided magic is enough." Cleo spoke almost to herself.

"Well," Celeste answered, "I personally think that the magic takes two."

Cleo was unconvinced. Because what she felt was definitely magical, and Ethan fought feeling anything at all toward her.

She picked up her mug of tea, cold now, and sipped anyway. How could she have fallen in love at first sight with such a man?

A beautiful man.

A successful, hardworking man.

A man willing to sacrifice his own lifestyle and convenience for the good of his sister's orphaned son.

Maybe loving Ethan wasn't so irrational, after all. Would those first feelings of attraction have survived if he were something less? And, anyway…

Cleo looked over at her mother who regarded her with an almost pitying gaze. "You don't just stop loving someone, do you, Mama?" Some messes just couldn't be cleared away by wishing them gone. "Just because it's not convenient or it's too difficult, it just doesn't stop, does it?"

Celeste's fingers were warm against Cleo's cheek. "I don't think so, sweetie."

After realizing that she couldn't stop loving Ethan even if she wanted to, Cleo decided her best course was to live up to her reputation and be sensible and practical about her convenient marriage. But it took a toll on her to remain calm and cool around him, so she was almost grateful when a few days later he announced he had to take another trip. Though Cleo had left a napping Jonah with Ethan a couple of times and biked into town to work for a few hours, most of her days were filled with the unrelenting awkwardness between them.

The one good thing she'd managed was to dodge the terrible truth of her cooking prowess—er, lack thereof—by volunteering to taste test a bunch of recipes Jasmine was working on. Every night she and Ethan sat down to a shared silence made enjoyable only by the wonderful stuff she picked up from the B and B's kitchen every afternoon.

So her mouth was full of some sort of delicious pasta when he said he was leaving the next morning, and she merely nodded. It was a darn good show of practicality.

She was just as cool when she followed him to the front door the next day. Wearing another one of his great suits and gripping his briefcase and one of those carry-on bags that only a man would find large enough, he was inches of irresistible deal-maker. She couldn't stop herself from reaching out and brushing a nonexistent piece of lint from the right shoulder of his gray suit.

He abruptly halted, then turned around.

Caught off guard, Cleo walked right into him.

He dropped his briefcase and caught her around the waist, as if to steady her.

She wasn't going to fall. That had already happened, of course, months ago.

But instead of stepping away, Cleo looked up at Ethan. He still held her lightly, and there was a fluttering in her belly where their bodies met.

"Cleo," he started. "I wish—"

In his crib down the hall, Jonah began fussing. Cleo turned her head, then looked back at Ethan. "Nap time's over early."

"He can wait a minute." Ethan tightened his hold on her waist. "I want you to know—"

The baby's fussing turned to crying.

Cleo tried ignoring the sound, but then broke from Ethan's embrace. "I'm sorry," she said, stepping away. She called softly down the hall, "Hang in there, buddy. Mommy's coming."

And at that one word—at "mommy"—the air became thick.

Mommy.

As if in slow motion, Cleo turned her head to see what Ethan made of her instinctive word. Maybe he hadn't heard it. Maybe he would resent her assumption.

Or maybe he would burn her with the bright, blazing blue that was in his eyes.

The rest of him had gone to stone, everything except for the hot intensity of his gaze. She felt the heat on her face, on her body. It wrapped around her like a binding.

"Thank you," he said hoarsely.

The words released her from the strange spell. She hurried down the hall, not even aware that Jonah was no longer crying until she entered his darkened room to discover he'd gone back to sleep.

Maybe she should stay in the baby's room until Ethan left. But that was cowardly. Worse, it would deny her one last glimpse of Ethan, and she was too weak to deny herself that, no matter how calm and cool she struggled to be.

And she wanted to gauge again what he thought of her calling herself Jonah's mommy.

He was still standing in the small foyer, exactly as she had left him. When she reappeared, he bent to pick up his briefcase. "Everything okay?" he asked.

She nodded. "He drifted off again."

The heat was gone from Ethan's eyes. "I know you'll take good care of him."

"Of course I will."

"Goodbye, Cleo."

She smiled, and then he turned and stepped toward the door. With her feet rooted to the floor, she watched him turn the knob, and then he dropped his briefcase again and slid that improbably small carry-on off his shoulder.

The movements surprised her into retreating a step, but it didn't matter, because in milliseconds he caught up with her. "Cleo," he said, fisting his hand in the hair at the back of her head. He pulled gently, tilting up her face. "I don't want to leave you. Not without this."

And then he kissed her.

His mouth came down on hers, no softness in it whatsoever, and she opened up to him because there was nothing else but to give in to the demand of Ethan's tongue.

He filled her, hot and strong, and she leaned into his body, trying to get closer, closer, closer.

His groan was low and needy and she felt it purr against her breastbone. Cleo closed her eyes, thinking only of his indescribable taste when a shiver skittered over her spine and unmistakable passion rose again.

Only Ethan made her burn. Only Ethan could cause this sweet neediness to bubble inside her blood.

His mouth lifted off hers and she moaned, but he ignored her complaint, and pulled her head back farther so that he could kiss her neck. She felt the wet brush of his tongue below her ear and shuddered.

"Ethan," she whispered.

He came back to her mouth, biting gently at her lower lip. "I've got to get going," he said around another deep kiss.

She leaned harder against him and curled her arms around his neck. "No."

He groaned again, another purr against her breasts. "I need to make my plane."

"No," she said again.

He kissed her nose, then pulled back just enough to see her face. "If I get out of here now, it will be better for both of us."

Cleo stubbornly shook her head. "No."

"That's what you should be saying to *me*, Cleo. To what I want."

"No." She tightened her arms around his neck.

He groaned again, his expression half frustrated, half amused. "Cleo, I really, really have to leave. I hate it, I swear to God I do, but I don't have any choice."

He was right, of course. Meetings had been scheduled, appointments set. After one more delicious moment pressed against his body, she dropped her arms and sighed.

"All right." Despite how mad it made her, she felt tears sting the corners of her eyes.

To hide them, she looked down at her long skirt, as if inspecting for wrinkles. Cool and collected, right? That was what she'd promised herself to be. "Never say that I'm not sensible."

Two fingers caught her chin, tilted it up. "Oh, Cleo," he said quietly. "I could say that, and so, so much more."

With that surprising remark and one last kiss, he was gone.

But the surprises didn't end there. Before five o'clock that afternoon, a deliveryman shocked the heck out of her. Ethan had sent her another gift.

But nothing practical this time. The present was from one of her favorite shops in Bozeman. Inside a ridiculously tiny box was a heartbreakingly lovely crystal unicorn. She'd never seen anything like it. No bigger than a charm, it was strung on a delicate gold box chain.

The accompanying card wasn't in Ethan's handwriting—obviously he'd ordered it over the phone and paid a mint to have it delivered the same day—but Cleo held it against her heart anyway. Because the only thing the card said was "You."

And though she didn't believe for a minute that Ethan considered her as rare and beautiful, as delicate and light-catching as the crystal unicorn, a sensible, practical woman such as Cleo Monroe—Cleo *Redford*—appreciated the thought.

Cleo wore the unicorn every day. Later that week, she was sitting at her desk at Beansprouts, absently fingering the crystal charm when a commotion in the reception area of the day care center caught her attention. Alarmed, Cleo first scooped Jonah up from his crib in the corner of her office and then stuck her head out her door.

A gaggle of strangers was insisting on speaking with her, while a just-as-insistent Nancy refused to open the waist-high swinging gate that led into the center.

Cleo put all her toddler-management skills into her voice. "What's the problem?" she called coolly as she approached Nancy.

Before the other woman could answer, she handed Jonah to her friend and asked her to take him into the break room. Then Cleo turned to the impatient group, placing her hand firmly on the swinging gate. "I'm Cleo Kincaid Monroe. Cleo Redford. What can I do for you?"

A blonde with a helmet hairdo and a sapphire suit stepped forward. "Elaine Eaton of KMNT, Ms. Monroe. Would you mind if I brought a camera crew inside?"

Cleo blinked. "I'd mind very much. There are small children here and I don't want them to be disturbed. What's this all about?"

Another reporter stepped up, aggressive and unsmiling.

"You did say Cleo *Kincaid* Monroe?" he asked. "Niece of Jeremiah and Yvette Kincaid? Daughter of Celeste?"

Icy apprehension crawled down Cleo's back. On the desk nearby, a phone started ringing. "Celeste is my mother," she said. "Has something happened? Is she hurt?"

"What do you know about the skeleton?" asked the man.

"What?" Cleo said. Another line began ringing, and the phone's flashing lights jangled like her nerves. Skeleton? "What has happened to my mother?"

The man ignored her again. "We're looking for a comment from a Kincaid family member."

Forcing herself to stay calm, Cleo moved over to the desk and picked up the receiver. Ignoring the ringing, she punched a free line and speed-dialed the bed-and-breakfast. Busy signal.

The back of her neck as hot as the chill running down her spine was cold, Cleo turned to the group of strangers. *"Is there something wrong with my mother?"*

"As far as we know, your mother's fine," Helmet Head said, looking marginally sympathetic. "We want to know what Jeremiah Kincaid's family has to say about the skeleton."

"The skeleton?" The skeleton. The apprehension suddenly lifted and Cleo let out a shaky laugh. "This must be some mistake. You're talking about the Laughing Horse skeleton? We don't know anything."

Helmet Head lifted perfectly arched brows. "Are you sure about that?"

Cleo refused to let herself be scared again. "Of course. Now, I need to ask you people to leave—"

The aggressive man had pulled out a small notebook. "That's what you want us to print? That you don't know anything? Do you speak for your aunt and mother, too?"

Cleo stared. "I don't want you to print anything. I don't

even know why you're asking me these questions. Now, if you won't leave my property, I'm going to have to—''

"Call the sheriff?" A new voice came from behind the small crowd of reporters. "I can save you the trouble, Cleo."

Over the heads of the strangers, Cleo spied the tall, dark figure of Sheriff Rafe Rawlings, the sharp creases of his uniform and the set of his face stating he was all business. She could kiss him. "I'm having a little problem, Rafe," she called. "Maybe you could help."

With his usual commanding, unsmiling demeanor, Rafe merely half turned to hold open the Beansprouts's front door. "Ladies, gentlemen, Ms. Monroe has asked you to leave." When they scurried toward him instead of immediately departing, he held up his free hand. "And I'm only here to pick up my daughter, not to answer any questions." One more pointed look, and the group moved outside, muttering.

Rafe quickly pulled the door shut.

Breathing a sigh of relief, Cleo perched on the edge of the reception desk, then looked at her watch. "It's a little early for you to pick up Skye from the arts and crafts program. Did someone call you?"

He nodded. "Nancy, and then Jasmine."

Cleo closed her eyes. "What's going on, Rafe?"

He grimaced. "Maybe we should go somewhere private."

Apprehensive once more, Cleo unlocked the swinging gate and led the way to her office. Once inside, Rafe shut the door and they sat beside each other on the chairs in front of her desk.

Cleo swallowed. "Why were the reporters here, Rafe? How does that skeleton found on the Laughing Horse property have anything to do with us?"

"It was actually found on *Kincaid* property, Cleo," Rafe corrected. He quickly reminded her that the construction had been halted on the resort, not the casino, when the skeleton had been discovered during excavation a couple of weeks before.

Rafe gave the next details in a matter-of-fact voice. "It took a little time, but we finally tracked down some dental records. The bones belong to Raven Hunter."

Raven Hunter. The name echoed in Cleo's mind and her stomach clenched into a tight fist. "Mama's going to be very upset," she said. And her mother already *was* upset, with those nightmares continuing to plague her. "Summer, too."

She looked up at Rafe, not sure how much Kincaid family history he knew. *Raven Hunter.* "Raven Hunter was the lover of my mother's sister, Blanche. He fathered my cousin, Summer."

Rafe nodded. "And disappeared during Blanche's pregnancy, right?"

Cleo rubbed her forehead. "That's the way I always heard it. The story was that Raven ran out on Blanche after getting her pregnant, maybe paid off by my uncle, Jeremiah Kincaid, maybe just because he didn't want to be tied down."

"No one in your family ever saw him again?"

"Not that I know of." Cleo looked up at Rafe again. "What does this mean?"

"There's the bullet, Cleo," he said.

Her stomach clenched again. Right. The skeleton had been found with a bullet lodged in one rib. Someone had killed Raven Hunter. Someone had killed Aunt Blanche's lover, Summer's father.

Cleo swallowed. "You're sure, Rafe? You're sure the

bullet was the likely cause of death?'' She knew his answer, even as she asked the question.

Rafe nodded.

Cleo swallowed again. ''And the likely suspect is...?''

Rafe rubbed the back of his finger along his jaw. ''Your now-deceased uncle, Cleo. Jeremiah Kincaid.''

Her eyes widened, and her temperature seemed to drop ten degrees. Not any of the family had ever really liked the man, but to think that he'd actually *murdered* someone...

She was still trying to wrap her mind around the idea when Rafe told her he had to leave. They stood and walked toward her closed office door. Before he could get away, Cleo rose on tiptoe to kiss his cheek. ''Thanks for coming,'' she said. ''I needed a hero.''

Letting free one of his rare smiles, Rafe lightly hugged her with one arm. ''My pleasure.''

''I think I might have something to say about that.''

Cleo whipped around. Ethan stood in the doorway of her office. She hadn't heard the door open.

Maybe Rafe had, because he was out-and-out grinning now. ''This has to be the husband.''

Ethan stepped forward. ''I am. And you?''

Apparently he wasn't much impressed by uniforms, Cleo thought. She nudged him with her elbow. ''For goodness' sake. How have you missed the big shiny badge? This is the sheriff, Ethan. Rafe Rawlings.''

Rafe stuck out his hand and managed to swallow his huge grin. ''And a *good* friend of Cleo's.''

''Never doubted it,'' Ethan said, though when he shook the other man's hand it was brief. ''I'm sure you want to tell me all about it.''

Rafe's lips twitched.

Cleo shot her husband a sharp look. ''I thought you weren't coming home until tomorrow.''

Ethan dragged a possessive thumb across her mouth. "Is that why I caught you kissing someone else? You didn't expect to see me?"

Rafe was smirking at them, so Cleo decided against answering the question. That, and she was fairly preoccupied fighting the hot tremor running across her skin.

It was Rafe who spoke into the strangely charged silence. "Actually, Mr. Redford, there was some trouble—"

"Here at Beansprouts that I needed Rafe's advice on." Cleo couldn't say what made her interrupt the sheriff, but suddenly she didn't want to bare this mess for Ethan right now. She could handle it herself. "Rafe's daughter Skye attends our summer arts and crafts program."

Rafe shot her a puzzled look, but took the hint and then just as smoothly took his leave.

Ethan folded his arms across his chest and narrowed his eyes. "What's the matter, Cleo?"

She avoided his gaze by bustling over to her desk. "I'm just...tired."

"Why don't we go home, then? It's almost five."

And she usually stayed past six. But Cleo looked down at the paperwork stacked on her desk and then she looked up at the intense blue of Ethan's eyes. A little shiver tracked down her spine. She didn't know if it was because of what Rafe had told her, or because Ethan was back.

Suddenly she wanted to be home. Home with him.

"Okay," she said slowly. "Why don't you go ahead? I'll collect Jonah and be right behind you."

After Ethan left, Cleo made a quick call to Jasmine and discovered that the reporters had been at the B and B, too. But she'd gotten rid of them and Celeste seemed fine. Their mother was planning to have dinner and watch a movie over at Aunt Yvette's and Uncle Edward's house.

When Cleo arrived home from Beansprouts, Ethan was

in his room unpacking. Rather than disturb him, Cleo decided to focus on Jonah for a few minutes to avoid thinking about the skeleton and how it was connected with her family.

The last of the sun made a bright patch on the living room floor, and Cleo spread a baby quilt in its warmth. Then she put Jonah down and lay beside him, his delight in her attention and her renditions of patty-cake and This Little Piggy taking some of the chilliness out of her mood.

But then, another set of shivers skittered down her back. Cleo looked up to see Ethan watching her and the baby, and something in his eyes made her shiver again.

"You're cold," he said.

Cleo stared at his mouth, suddenly remembering the last time they'd been together in the house, suddenly remembering their last, heated kiss. Another shiver. "A little cold," she said, and it was a little white lie to gloss over the real reason for her goose bumps.

He came closer and Cleo scrambled to her feet, nervous, silly enough, to be caught lying down around him.

Ethan's jeans were faded and he wore a white T-shirt that looked soft and comfortable. "Go take a hot shower," he said. "I'll take over with Jonah."

Cleo hesitated. Not that she wasn't happy that he was going to spend some time with the baby—he needed to do that—but because despite his casual words, there was that something in his eyes. Something that made her want to run and to linger at the same time.

"Cleo?" His gaze shifted from her eyes to her mouth.

Running seemed like a really good idea. "Uh, well, thanks." She backed out in the direction of her room. "There's a bottle of formula in the fridge."

He waved his hand. "I'll take care of it." His voice hoarsened. "You go get...warm."

Naked. She thought for a second he was going to say naked.

So this time she really ran.

Though she'd taken the longest shower on record, she still felt tense when she emerged. Even more tense when she heard the doorbell ring. She jumped. Please, no more reporters.

Determined to squash the problem immediately if it was, Cleo headed down the hall in bare feet and her own jeans and T-shirt, only to find that Ethan had beat her to the door and was paying off the pizza delivery kid.

He turned around, the box in his hands. "Jonah drifted off. I put him in his crib and ordered your favorite."

Cleo tried smiling through her relief. "Oh, good."

Ethan narrowed his eyes at her again. "What's wrong, Cleo?"

"I…" She didn't want to tell him about what happened that day. Exactly why, she wasn't sure. Maybe because he was home for once and she didn't want the evening marred by talk of a thirty-year-old murder. "I'm just a little unsettled."

At her answer, he gave her another narrow-eyed look, but let it go.

In the kitchen, they polished off the pizza without much conversation. She was preoccupied keeping her thoughts free of skeletons and bullets. She had no idea what was keeping Ethan so quiet.

When they finished, they both rose to clear away the few dishes. He set the pizza box on the counter and she loaded the plates in the dishwasher.

Her gaze snagged on the kitchen windows. It was dark and for the first time the giant shapes of the pines trees surrounding their house seemed menacing. Unbidden, all that she'd learned that day rushed to the forefront of her mind. Her uncle Jeremiah had been a murderer.

Nursery rhymes and hot showers couldn't wash that knowledge away. Her whole body shuddered.

"Cleo?" Ethan put a hand on her shoulder. "Are you okay, honey?"

She swallowed. "Just…cold again."

He stepped closer and wrapped his arms around her waist, pressing his chest against her back. He was big and warm, yet even the feel of him against her couldn't dispel her disquiet.

"Talk to me, Cleo."

Ethan tightened his arms, coaxing her to lean back.

She let herself sink against him and felt his breath stir the hair at her temples. She should talk to him, she should tell him what had happened today. A murder had been uncovered and it was connected to her family. But her blood was starting to warm. If she talked about it, she might turn cold again.

Ethan's arms tightened around her. "Cleo?"

She sighed. "Have you ever felt a nightmare coming on? Like a headache? Because that's just what I'm feeling."

Ethan stilled. "That's because you've been alone too much," he said.

She leaned farther into his warmth. "You think so?"

Suddenly his hot mouth was on the side of her neck. "You don't have to have nightmares, Cleo," he said against her skin. "Let me be there for you, honey. Let me make your dreams sweet tonight."

a short journey that also took her to the forefront of his gaze. He made the trip in three short minutes.

He stood in place and hot air was sucked away from Cleo's knees. The room was all edges.

"Relax," Cleo said, hand against her midriff. "Let's eat."

"Eat, damn."

She grabbed a breath of light, could smell his charred skin around the corners.

Eight

Ethan lifted his mouth from Cleo's skin and breathed in the sweet scent of her hair. He wanted to protect her. He'd vowed he would protect her.

If he couldn't offer emotion, he could at least offer that. She laughed a little shakily. "I don't know…"

Ethan squeezed his eyes shut, trying to put out of his mind the sensation of her skin beneath his lips. "I'll just hold you, Cleo. That's all." He wanted it all, but he'd settle for watching over her sleep. It was time he gave something back.

"Oh."

A note in her voice—a touch of embarrassment?—made him open his eyes and turn her in his arms so he could search her face. "'Oh'? What does that mean?"

She looked down, her long lashes casting shadows on her flushed cheeks. "It means you don't have to go that far, Ethan. You don't need to…to share my bed."

A realization clicked in place in Ethan's brain. He stared down at Cleo—at his wife—stunned, trying to imagine how he'd made such a bad mistake. He let go of her, so mad at himself that he needed to pace around the room to ease the emotion. "Damn it, Cleo." One more turn around the too small kitchen, and then he stood in front of her again.

"Damn it."

She cocked an eyebrow, her expression wary. "I heard you the first time."

"And I think I screwed up *every* time," he said in disgust. "You didn't think— You must have realized— *Hell*." He ran a hand through his hair. "Honey. Cleo."

She swallowed. "What?"

He cupped her shoulders with his hands. "You've got to know I want you."

She shrugged, her shoulders pushing against his palms. "As a caretaker for your nephew."

His hands tightened on her. "No, Cleo. As a woman in my bed."

Her violet eyes widened. He stared into them, thinking there wasn't another color in the world the color of Cleo's eyes. How could she doubt she turned him on? What kind of man gave a woman these kinds of doubts?

A man struggling to not hurt said woman. But Ethan shrugged the little voice away and pulled Cleo against him. He whispered against her ear, feeling a shiver run through her body. "I want you, Cleo. You've got to believe that."

As if she couldn't help herself, her hips arched against his. She laughed, shakily again. "Maybe I believe that."

He caught her hips, pressing her lightly against his hard erection. "Unmistakable evidence."

"Then why—"

"Because you've given so much already." He leaned forward to kiss her forehead. "I shouldn't ask for anything else."

"Ethan..." There was a touch of humor in Cleo's voice and a smile tugged at her lips. "Something tells me you know how to give back."

There was a touch of sultriness in her voice, as well, and he smiled. "I want to."

"I want, too," she said.

And it was that honesty that did him in. Ethan could handle "I want." He could meet it, match it, satisfy it. He ran his hands up her back to cup her face, holding it at the perfect angle for a gentle, deep kiss. She tasted warm and sweet and he wanted deeper and hotter, but he admonished himself to pull back. Go slow.

When he broke away, he combed his fingers through her bewitching, wavy hair, and his fingertips snagged on a chain around her neck. Tugging gently, from beneath her shirt he pulled the unicorn he'd given her. It caught the light and sparkled, shining like Cleo's eyes.

A smile broke over his face. "You like it." He wanted to see her wearing the unicorn and nothing else.

She shivered, maybe reading the intent on his face. "I like it."

I'm going to treat her like the unicorn. As she should be treated, Ethan promised himself. Precious and fragile. He would control his impulses tonight. Unlike his father, he wouldn't let his passions overrule him. Instead, Ethan vowed to use what had always stood by him—his brains— to make Cleo happy.

He let the unicorn drop and watched it fall to rest between her breasts. His gaze lifted slowly to her face. She was flushed more deeply now, and Ethan cupped her hot cheek gently. "Tell me where you want to make love," he said quietly.

Her pupils dilated.

"Tell me where you want me to touch you first."

"Ethan—"

"Tell me where you want me to touch you second, and third."

Her skin heated beneath his hand and her tongue came out to quickly wet her lips. "Ethan."

Her mouth was ripe and wet. A heat entirely his own shot down his spine, but Ethan ignored it. This was for

Cleo. He rubbed his thumb along her cheekbone. "Embarrassed, honey?"

She ducked her head.

He ran his hands down her arms and then up beneath her breasts, to cup their weight in his palms. He ducked his head, too, so he could whisper against her ear again. "Why don't I tell you my ideas, and you can stop me if there's something you don't like or want to change."

"Ethan."

He lightly brushed his thumbs across her nipples and she shuddered. "I want to take you to my big bed. I want to undress you slowly. Piece by piece... Okay so far?"

Her lashes lifted but her gaze was languid. "Okay so far," she whispered. "But, Ethan—"

"Then I'm going to touch this pretty body of yours. Touch it, learn it, know it. Slowly."

She swayed closer. "But, Ethan—"

"Shh." He slid his hands from her breasts to cup her round bottom. "And once I know your body, honey, I'm going to please it. I'm going to please *you*."

Her hips arched, and he had to grit his teeth, willing himself to not push back. This was the time to go slow, to stay in control for Cleo. "Sound all right?" he asked.

"Ethan..." There was only an edge of purple around the black pupils of her eyes.

He clamped down on his impulses again, though his fingers tightened on the round curves they held. "You haven't told me what you think."

"I think—" Cleo reached up and tangled her fingers in his hair "—you talk too much."

His laugh died abruptly with the first electric touch of her mouth. His hold on her tightened again and she pressed herself closer in response.

Sensing she needed more, he deepened the kiss, but she

sent him reeling by sliding her tongue into his mouth and against his.

His muscles tensed and his blood burned. He pulled her tighter against him, rocking her against his erection. She slid her tongue in deeper and he sucked, tasting sweetness and heat, and his mind emptied of everything but Cleo. He needed to feel her, see her, have her.

Without breaking the kiss, he let her slide back to the floor. His hands shook as he snaked them beneath the T-shirt she wore. Her skin was smooth and hot. He quickly found her bra strap and unhooked it so he could run his palms unhindered up her spine and around her ribs and then up her sides to fill his hands—*aaah*—with her breasts.

She jerked her mouth from his, gasping for breath, and he closed his eyes, inhaling desperately. Cleo felt so good in his hands, heavy and full. Without thinking, he pulled off the annoyance of her shirt and slid the bra to the floor with one hand.

He could look his fill then, his heart slamming against his chest wall as her rosy nipples tightened.

"Ethan…"

Her hands rose, but he caught them before she could cover herself. Lacing his fingers with hers, he pushed her hands down, and then bent his head to one breast.

She smelled like flowers and tasted like sin.

She moaned, and he licked one beaded crest again, but the taste was too good, too tempting, and he sucked the nipple into his mouth.

She moaned again and the sound went to his head, making him dizzy. Somewhere along the way he dropped her hands, but it didn't matter, because she was holding his head to her body and letting him have his fill of her. He sucked at the other breast now, swirling his tongue around her nipple.

Her fingers crawled up his bare chest, beneath his shirt, inflaming him. He pushed her breasts together with his palms, wanting them both at once, wanting it all. Her nails scratched the skin of his back and he ran his tongue up her neck.

Her pulse was frantic, as needy as he felt. He took her mouth at the same moment that his hands met at the snap of her jeans. Goose bumps fanned out across her belly as he slid the denim down her body. He lifted her, and set her on the countertop wearing only a pair of silky white panties.

She grabbed at the hem of his T-shirt and he stripped it away, throwing it across the room. Then he stepped forward, pushing apart her thighs with his hips, so he could rub his chest against her damp, hard nipples.

He groaned.

She captured his head, bringing it to her for another kiss, and he met her mouth hungrily.

But the kiss, the sensation of breast to chest, still wasn't enough. There was fire inside him, fire inside her, and he wanted to touch it. Had to have it. Had to make it his.

The skin on the inside of her thighs was impossibly smooth. His fingers skimmed up it quickly, drawn toward the center of her. He reached the edge of her panties and lifted his head to gulp in a breath.

Only to see what he had done.

Impulsively, he'd bared her. In the kitchen. He had her on the counter, he had her open to him.

For his pleasure.

To satisfy him.

He'd been out of control.

Closing his eyes against the temptation of her lushness, he took in a long breath and softened his touch. "Cleo," he whispered. "Let me take you to the bedroom." Then he lifted her into his arms.

She looped her hands around his neck. He tried not to think of her breast against his chest or her breath against his ear. It soughed in and out, in a fast rhythm that almost matched the speed of his pulse.

He tried forgetting how close he'd been to sinking his fingers into her heated center, as uncontrollable as a teenager.

Now he thought only of Cleo.

His bedspread was cool against the backs of his hands as he slid her onto the mattress. He followed her down, but kept carefully to her side, thinking, *control, control, control.*

It was dark in his bedroom, and he set about learning her body all over again, this time listening for what made her breath catch. This time sensing what touch ignited goose bumps over her skin.

She moaned when he thrust his tongue in her mouth. She arched up to him when he took her nipple in his mouth. Her hands were restless along his back as he traced the delicate framework of her collarbone with his tongue.

All the while Ethan breathed Cleo in, her scent, her taste, and he fought against his darker instinct to push, to press, to possess. Tension infused her body, and his pulse quickened as she became bow-tight. But still he played and dawdled and felt damn good about his restraint.

"Ethan." Cleo's voice was breathy and she caught his hand against her breast as he played with her pretty nipple. "I—"

"Shh." He took her hand away and kissed her breast, letting his fingers trail down her abdomen. She jerked as he slid his hand beneath the elastic of her panties. He pressed his palm flat, letting her get used to this new sensation, and when she'd calmed he moved his fingers lower.

Her thighs opened wider for him, and as he slid a finger inside he lifted his head to watch her.

Her eyes closed as he found her wet heat, and then his did, too, because her body gripped him strongly, hotly. He fought the passion then, fought the need to have it, her, right that instant.

When control was back he allowed his hand to move again, sending Cleo higher. He took her to the edge—he saw it in her face, in the trembling he could feel in her muscles—and then he took his hand away.

"Please, Ethan." She reached toward him, caught her finger on a belt loop of his jeans. "Please."

"Yes, sweetheart." He shucked the rest of his clothes and rose over her, naked. "Now."

She parted her legs and he couldn't look, afraid he'd lose it. This was for her. For Cleo, first and foremost.

Hot, tight, wet. She sheathed him so completely that for a moment his mind spun. But he leashed his impulses and pulled out and slid slowly back in. She made a sound, sweet and low, and he went back to her breast to build a matching rhythm, slow and sure.

That tension built inside Cleo again, each of her breaths a little shallower than the one before. But the tension was in him, too, and with each thrust into her body he found control that much harder to keep.

"Please, Ethan."

He tilted her hips with his hands, drove deeper into her snug body, and she arched again. He kissed her, and she thrust her tongue deep.

He held control only by his fingernails. But he held on, because they were...almost...there. Cleo arched again, he angled his head deeper, and then the spasms shook her.

And him. It was a chain reaction of pleasure. They were

climaxing, and it no longer mattered who controlled whom
and who did what first and who drove whom to what.

Once he could breath again, Ethan eased off of Cleo and
gathered her into his arms. The hollow of his shoulder cradled her cheek. He smiled.

What mattered was, at last, they'd found a way to ease
the tension that had been building since the day they married. For once, he and Cleo had found an understanding.

Or so he thought. Because suddenly, into the room heated
with their passion, the sound of Cleo's three little words
rushed out. "I love you."

Cleo stared at the luminous hands of the alarm clock
beside Ethan's bed. It didn't seem as if there would be
nightmares or sweet dreams for her tonight.

Not when her mind was occupied with running over
every second of their lovemaking.

Ethan was spooned behind her, his hand heavy on her
breast. She closed her eyes, savoring the sensation, aware
of every inch where he touched her: hand, chest, his thighs
against the backs of hers.

A sweet shiver ran across her skin and her nipple tightened against the cup of Ethan's palm. His breath moved
rhythmically against her hair, so she could safely lust without his knowing about it.

Without making the mistake of saying she loved him
again.

Her eyes popped open and she stared at the clock once
more. Approximately sixty-seven minutes ago she'd uttered
the words, and then immediately, desperately, wanted to
grab them back.

What had possessed her to say them? It was all his fault.
In the first place, there was the tremendous relief of knowing Ethan was truly sexually attracted to her. But then he'd

overwhelmed her by the way he touched her, stroked her, stoked the fire of her passion for him. When her climax had nearly shaken her heart free of its moorings, the words had drifted from her heart to her mind and then out her mouth.

She couldn't be sorry they were finally in the same bed. Not only because of how good it was between them, but how good it was going to be for their marriage. Sharing a bed signaled a new intimacy that would definitely help in the building of a family.

But then again, there were still those words she'd said. The words he hadn't responded to, of course. Would a return to her own bed counterbalance them?

Too much emotion made Ethan nervous. Cleo was certain of that.

She straightened one leg and slid it across the cool expanse of sheet toward the edge of the mattress. Digging in her heel, she inched away from the heat of Ethan's body, trying not to moan as the movement dragged his palm over her bare breast.

Just as she scooted free, his arm roped her and pulled her back against his body. "Where do you think you're going?" His voice was hoarse and his breath hot against her ear.

Cleo was helpless against the shiver that rolled down her spine. "I—"

He turned her and covered her mouth with his. Cleo lost her words, her thoughts, her determination to leave his bed.

He thrust into her mouth with his tongue. His hand pulled her thigh on top of his, and he thrust into her body, already wet and soft for him. Cleo gasped, arched against his chest, and another shudder rolled down her back.

Ethan chased it with his hands, and palmed her hips to tilt her body for another delicious thrust.

Cleo moaned, then silenced herself by pressing her face

against his neck. She couldn't lose this. She couldn't lose him.

Cleo arched again as she took another thrust. She wouldn't leave his bed. She would hold on to Ethan...even if it meant holding back how she truly felt about him.

Nine

Cleo walked toward the back door of the B and B with Jonah, her mood as bright as the morning sunshine. She and the baby had woken at their usual early hour, but Ethan had slept on, either exhausted by yesterday's jet lag or by last night's lovemaking.

Her eyes narrowed as she hitched Jonah higher against her chest. Did he look a little flushed? She put her cheek against his, and he turned his head toward her, giving her what she could have sworn was a kiss. She smiled at him and he smiled back. "You angel." With a nose-to-nose nuzzle, she dismissed her little worry.

Nothing could take the sunshine out of today.

"Let's go find Auntie Jasmine," she said to Jonah. "You smile to distract her while I snitch some pastries." And if her mother insisted, Cleo thought, she'd leave Jonah with her for the morning and bring Ethan his breakfast in bed.

And if he wanted to feast on her—well, she hadn't had her fill of him yet. No matter what, she'd hurry home. She wanted to be near Ethan.

She swung open the kitchen door and sniffed appreciatively. "Scones," she whispered to Jonah. "We're in luck."

But one look at her mother, sitting at the scarred kitchen table and looking exhausted, pierced Cleo's good mood. She hurried over. "What's wrong, Mama?"

Jasmine pulled a mug out of a cabinet even as she sent Cleo a worried look. "What else? Another nightmare."

Cleo swallowed, looking from her mother to her sister, then back again. Celeste's skin looked paper-thin and pale, shadows circling her normally bright eyes. Her heart sinking, Cleo dropped into the chair beside her. "Mama, this has gone far enough. We need to do something. Can't you at least tell us what you're dreaming about?"

Jonah cooed, as if in encouragement, and Cleo's fears eased a bit when Celeste held out her arms for the baby. Celeste even smiled a little as she looked into his face and stroked his wisps of blond hair. "I'll be all right, girls. Really."

Jasmine sent Cleo another pointed look as she plopped a mug of hot coffee in front of her. "If you ask me, we can blame those damn reporters and all their questions about the skeleton."

Cleo noticed her mother stiffen. She took a fortifying gulp of Jasmine's miraculous coffee and then put all the steel she could muster into her voice. "Mama, what's bothering you? We're not going to let up until you tell us."

Celeste settled Jonah closer against her and slid her own mug of coffee toward the table's center so the baby couldn't reach it. "I don't know whether to blame the reporters or not, but I did have the nightmare again last night." She sighed, and it was a sad, weary sound. "And Blanche was in the dream."

Cleo and Jasmine exchanged glances. Their mother had never talked in detail about the nightmare before. "She, um, hasn't been in it before?"

Celeste shook her head. "No. I realize that now. Before last night it had always been the same. My brother Jeremiah…carrying someone I always assumed was my sister. But last night I knew it couldn't be Blanche."

Cleo swallowed another gulp of coffee, unsure what to say next. Should Celeste be talking of it at all? Would that only make it seem more real? But God knew that bottling it up inside her hadn't given her any relief. "How was the nightmare different last night, Mama?"

"I've always been alone, watching Jeremiah come toward me. I'm always…dreading what he holds in his arms and he's always insisting that I obey him and look at it."

An icy finger dragged down Cleo's spine and she saw Jasmine shiver, too.

"But last night…" Celeste continued. "…last night I wasn't alone. Blanche was on the shore beside me, as young and beautiful as ever, and she spoke to me."

Jasmine slipped into the chair beside Cleo. Cleo saw that her sister was trembling, and underneath the table she slipped her hand over her sister's and squeezed reassuringly. Celeste often said that Jasmine was an "old soul." Whether that was true or not, it was clear that Jasmine's soul, whatever its age, was afraid.

So was Cleo, and she suddenly longed for Ethan.

"Mama," Jasmine started, then stopped, cleared her throat, began again. "Mama, what did Aunt Blanche say to you?"

Celeste's beautiful green eyes looked off into the distance. Cleo felt that icy finger again and chills ran up through her scalp and down to her ankles.

"She told me that the past is about to rise up and greet me." Celeste's voice was reed-thin and eerie-sounding. "She told me to be careful to make the right choices."

The temperature in the kitchen dropped. Or maybe it just seemed that way. But Cleo didn't imagine the charged silence in the room. She didn't know what to say. Jasmine looked just as stunned.

Cleo's yearning for Ethan resurfaced with a force that

startled her. She was used to taking care of herself and other people. Was this what one night in his bed could do? She wasn't sure if she liked this need to have him near her.

But then, as if she'd beckoned him to her with the force of her feelings, he walked through the kitchen door. Dressed in jeans and a long-sleeved denim shirt, he looked disgruntled. Their gazes collided and his face hardened. "What's wrong?" he asked. "I woke up and you weren't there."

"I..." Cleo couldn't put her relief into words, and that worried her even more. "I came for some breakfast and...ended up chatting with Mama and Jasmine." She added a falsely casual note to her voice that made it sound as if she hadn't seen any reason to hurry home, even though their relationship had taken a new turn the night before.

"You were chatting," he repeated flatly. He didn't sound very happy.

She shrugged. "You were sleeping." Was she supposed to just start spilling the disturbing details of her mother's nightmare? She wanted to, oh, she did, but the dream was almost as scary as this new need she had for Ethan.

She could feel her mother's and Jasmine's puzzled stares. Obviously they expected her to be more open with her husband. They were the kind of family that shared problems with one another. But Cleo had never fully shared her problems with Ethan, so she avoided looking at them and offered to get him a cup of coffee.

While he served himself instead, Cleo whispered to Jasmine and her mother that they could talk about the nightmare later. For now, she just wanted to smooth over the awkward moment. Some other time, when she had better control of herself and her fears, when she didn't feel so vulnerable, she could tell Ethan all about Celeste's nightmare. About Raven's murder.

But as the awkwardness hung around the kitchen table

like a stubborn cloud, Cleo thought it might be best to get out of the B and B altogether. She stood and reached for Jonah, taking the baby out of her mother's arms. "Ready to go, Ethan?"

He stared at her over the rim of his mug. He'd taken maybe three sips of his coffee. "Now?"

She took a step toward the back door and caught sight of her aunt, uncle and cousin Frannie coming through the woods. Uh-oh. It looked like a family powwow in the making, and if it was, Ethan would know she'd been trying to keep things from him. "Now," she said firmly. "I'd like to go home now."

If she became involved in a family discussion of the past, and became scared again, she'd turn toward Ethan for sure. She didn't want to want his support and comfort that much. If she came to depend on him, it might jinx what they could eventually find together. Just as she'd jumped the gun on saying "I love you," she didn't want to jump the gun on needing Ethan.

He looked wary and puzzled and maybe even a little hurt, but she ignored him as she said a cheerful goodbye to her mother and sister. She planned on a just-as-cheerful wave to the Hannons before she and Ethan escaped to their cars.

And they almost made it. Cleo's hand was on the doorknob when Sheriff Rafe Rawlings pushed through the swinging door that led into the kitchen from the dining room. His gaze took in the family group and then he smiled a little as the doorknob was pulled from Cleo's grasp and Yvette, Edward, and Frannie filed into the kitchen.

"I'm sorry to disturb your family, Celeste," he said politely, "but I have some questions for you and Yvette."

That fingernail of fear skittered down Cleo's back again. She instinctively edged closer to Ethan, and she felt his warm palm on her shoulder. Oh, it was so easy, too easy, to lean on him.

She made herself move away. She was the capable, dependable one. "What's this about, Rafe?"

Celeste spoke for him. "It's about Raven." Her eyes roamed the faces of her family. "Get some coffee and sit down, everyone. I think we all need to hear what the sheriff has to say." Ethan moved and she pinned him with her gaze. "That means you, too, Ethan Redford."

More chairs were drawn up, more coffee poured. Cleo found herself at the table between her mother and Ethan. Jonah had drifted off for an unusually early morning nap in her arms. Rafe sat directly across the table and addressed his remarks to Celeste and Yvette, who were positioned beside each other.

"My investigation of Raven Hunter's death has brought me to Blanche and Jeremiah," he said. He reviewed the details of where and when the skeleton had been found, and the bullet, then told about the identification of the remains. As he spoke, Cleo felt Ethan's increasing attention.

"I've been talking with Jackson Hawk and wanted to verify with you what he's told me," Rafe said.

"Jackson Hawk?" Ethan asked.

Rafe answered the question matter-of-factly. "He's an attorney who lives on the Laughing Horse Reservation."

"And a friend of Raven's," Yvette added. "That much I remember."

Rafe turned his gaze her way. "What else do you recall, Yvette? Were you aware of your sister's affair with Raven?"

"Of course." Cleo's aunt nodded. "The three of us sisters were very close, and she needed our help at times to slip away from Jeremiah." Yvette reached out beside her to rub her husband's forearm. "I hadn't met Edward yet, you see, and I had never seen a love like that. It was something you could touch, how they felt about each other, and I thought it wonderfully romantic.'' A sad smile touched her lips.

Rafe circled his coffee mug with his hands and spoke carefully. ''You say that you helped her give Jeremiah the slip. Did he oppose the match?''

Yvette's eyebrows raised. ''Didn't Jackson tell you that?''

Rafe was noncommittal. ''I want to hear your impressions.''

''Jeremiah absolutely opposed the match. He was outspoken in his hatred for Raven, any Native Americans, actually, but particularly Raven.'' Yvette sighed. ''Jeremiah wasn't a tolerant or understanding man, Rafe. I don't know what fueled his hatred, but it was very, very real.''

''And you, Celeste?'' Rafe switched his gaze to Cleo's mother. ''Is that how you remember it?''

Cleo could see her mother's shoulders tense. ''It was so long ago, Rafe. I don't have much memory of those times.'' Confusion clouded her usually beautiful green eyes. ''But if Yvette says so...'' Celeste shrugged. ''I do remember Raven and Blanche, of course, and their love. But what about Raven's younger brother, Storm? He might know something.''

Rafe nodded. ''We're trying to contact him—both the sheriff's department and Jackson Hawk. But you can't think of anything else, Celeste?''

She slowly shook her head. ''I only seem to remember what came after. Of Summer, and what a beautiful little girl she was and then how glad I was to take her into my home and into my life.''

Cleo looked down at Jonah, still sleeping in her arms. She'd never doubted her mother's love for her cousin, but with Jonah to care for now she better understood how a woman could take another's child into her life and love it as her own. Without thinking, she looked over at Ethan and caught his gaze on her. There was something, some uncertainty, on his face, and it worried her. But Rafe's next question distracted Cleo.

"The night that Raven disappeared, witnesses spotted him on your brother's property. That was the last place Raven was seen. What do you both remember of that?"

Yvette spoke first. "I wasn't home. I was getting my teaching credential at that time and was in Bozeman. When I came home, Jeremiah told me he'd offered Raven money to leave Blanche, leave Whitehorn." Her face was sad again. "It seemed like something Jeremiah would do, and it made me furious. But the damage had already been done. Raven was gone and Blanche was heartbroken. I concentrated on my sister and dealt with my brother as little as possible."

She turned to her sister. "And Celeste—"

Yvette broke off and no one else spoke as they all looked at Celeste. Her hands were visibly trembling and she stared unseeing into the distance.

"Mama?" Jasmine called, her voice frightened.

Cleo gently touched her mother's shoulder. "Mama, what's wrong?"

"That night…" Celeste said. One hand shook as she reached up to rub her temple. "It all seems confused to me. Everything about that time."

"Don't think about it, then, Aunt Celeste," Frannie said hastily, obviously uncomfortable with Celeste's distress.

But Cleo's mother shook her head. "I don't think that will work, Frannie. Blanche told me so, clearly, last night."

"Blanche?" Rafe questioned quietly.

Jasmine looked at her mother, received a confirming nod,

and then turned to Rafe. "Mama has nightmares. Vivid ones that frighten her. Last night, for the first time, Blanche was in Mama's dream."

Cleo avoided Ethan's gaze. She could feel it on her, and feel his sudden understanding that she'd deliberately withheld the truth of the situation from him. Was he relieved or hurt?

"Blanche told me the past was rising up," Celeste said, her voice wavering a bit. "She warned me to make the right choices." She smiled in Frannie's direction, a wan, worn smile. "And I have a feeling not thinking about the past isn't one of the options open to me anymore, Frannie."

Ethan drove Cleo and the baby home from the B and B shortly after Rafe Rawlings left. The sheriff had obviously been unsurprised at the lack of detail Yvette and Celeste had been able to give about events thirty years earlier. Events that appeared to include a murder.

A sweep of cold had run over Ethan the night before when Cleo had whispered "I love you." It had rushed over him again this morning, colder and stronger, when he realized all that she'd been keeping from him in the past few weeks.

Guilt, remorse, and resignation coiled in his gut. He should have been there for her, and yet he doubted he could have given her the support she needed. She had her family for that, if indeed Cleo required anyone's bolstering.

Ethan braked in the driveway of their house and reached for his door handle, but Cleo put her hand on his arm. "I'm sorry. I should have told you what was going on. I don't know why..."

Ethan remembered a night months ago, the night she *had* told him something. She'd told him about her mother's nightmares then, and he'd kept on walking up the stairs, unwilling to get too close to her. Thinking it was best.

"It's okay," he said.

She swallowed. "It's just that you weren't around very much...and you didn't seem that interested in local goings-on, and..." She trailed off again.

He hadn't seemed that interested in her. Or interested enough. Damn. All along he'd been worried he hadn't anything to give Cleo. And he still continued to take, take, take. From her body. He thought of that soft "I love you" again. From her heart.

He squeezed his eyes shut. "It's all right, Cleo. You don't have to explain."

"But I do. Honestly, at first it didn't seem to have anything to do with us, with my family. But then—"

"Then those reporters showed up at Beansprouts yesterday, Cleo." Rafe had mentioned the incident and Ethan had quickly probed for the details. "Maybe I could have helped with that."

She waved away the thought. "They were gone by the time you got there. And I'd already spoken with Jasmine. Everyone was okay."

Except him. Ethan tried to force away the stupid, selfish thought, but it pierced him. Once again he'd had a chance to do something for Cleo, and failed. Once again she'd taken care of things herself.

Worry lines etched her brow and she looked over her shoulder at the baby strapped in his car seat. "Do you think Jonah is okay? He never takes a nap this long." She released her safety belt so she could lean across her seat to put her hand to his cheek. "I think he's a little warm."

But she muttered the words to herself, and Ethan was certain she wasn't soliciting his opinion. In caring for Jonah and everything else, Cleo was perfectly capable. And then there was her family. They'd rally around if necessary. It was his firsthand knowledge of their unequivocal support and caring—he'd seen it in that kitchen just this morning—that made him feel so hellishly inadequate.

And unnecessary.

"I'm heading back to Houston tonight," he said abruptly. The idea came out of nowhere, but it sounded good. Facing Cleo and his own inability to be what she needed—*someone* she needed—made him restless.

Her eyebrows shot up. "What? You just returned yesterday."

He avoided her gaze, looking out the window instead. Through the trees he glimpsed the lake, but its calm waters couldn't soothe him. "There's always something that needs to be done at the office."

He felt her looking at him. "How's the move of your headquarters coming? When do you think you'll be in Whitehorn permanently?" she asked.

His hands squeezed the steering wheel. "It's not that simple," he said. Actually, whatever had been done could be easily *un*done. Perhaps it was better if he left Cleo and Jonah to their life.

The image of his sister jumped into Ethan's mind. *I'm sorry, Della. But I'm doing the best I can here.* He knew she would want him to take care of her son. But he also felt certain she would understand why he found it so hard to become part of Jonah and Cleo's life. When he looked in the mirror, he could never duck the reflection of Jack Redford. The man had been driven by his emotions: if he was despondent he would drink, if he was angry he would yell, if he was frustrated he would hit.

Ethan had always been grateful that he didn't seem to have any emotions at all.

"I'm going to Houston," he said again. Cleo and Jonah would be better off without him. He restarted the car, still refusing to look at her. "Go ahead and get out, Cleo. I have a few errands to run before I make this next trip."

Ten

Cleo doodled on a list pad because she didn't know what else to do with herself. Ethan was still on his errands, Jonah was taking his afternoon nap, and she'd already dusted, vacuumed and scrubbed floors. Bed linens had been changed. But not one of those activities had improved her mood.

She couldn't believe Ethan was leaving again. Last night they'd made love. Today he was running from her.

At the top of her pad she'd written "Things I Should Have Known." An easy list to fill. Beside Item Ten, she'd penned " 'Fat free' was too good to be true."

And at the Item One position, of course, she'd written, "Never marry for one-sided love."

So, see, she couldn't blame it on Ethan. He had never pretended to offer her more than the building that Beansprouts was housed in—and Jonah.

Cleo crumpled her silly list and tossed it into the garbage, then wandered down the hall to Jonah's dim bedroom. Though she hadn't heard a peep from him yet, she still felt the need to check on him. He'd dozed the morning away and was still taking a full-length nap. Inhaling the sweet scent of baby, she leaned against the doorjamb and watched him sleep. Never, never could she regret Jonah in her life.

He was her love, and he could be her happiness.

All she had to do was let go of that little fantasy she'd been hoping to make a dream-come-true with Ethan.

She had to let go of Ethan.

Oh, he'd be there one way or another. Not in her bed or in their child's life, but she had no doubt he'd send regular checks and put in erratic appearances.

But they'd never be a family. She'd have to let go of him...and of that sweet dream.

The shrill ring of the phone broke into her thoughts. Cleo hurried to answer it and then wished she hadn't—because on the other end of the line was Jasmine saying, "We have a small problem."

Cleo groaned. "No. Not another problem. Not today."

"Sorry, sis, but this one actually has your name written all over it." Jasmine hauled in an audible breath. "Jonah's grandparents are here."

"What?" Cleo blinked. "Who? Where?"

"You forgot 'why?'"

Cleo squeezed the phone. *"Jasmine."*

"Okay, okay," her sister relented with a quick laugh. "At the B and B. It's those Houston grandparents you told us about. You know, the ones who precipitated your quickie marriage to Ethan."

"Jasmine," Cleo said again, then instinctively lowered her voice. "Don't call it a quickie marriage. And please tell me they're not standing right there."

"I'm in the office with the door closed. The Covingtons are enjoying tea and cookies in the living room."

The B and B living room. Cleo's stomach twisted. "What do they want?"

"To visit their grandson, they said. Ethan promised them the three of you would visit Houston in the fall, but they apparently couldn't wait. They were driving in this direction to see some friends and decided to make a short detour."

Cleo groaned. "Oh, no."

"Oh, yeah," Jasmine countered cheerfully. "And they're excited about meeting you, the paragon of all womanhood. Ethan must have painted quite a picture. You're just lucky I didn't tell them about the time you whacked off my bangs and gave me permanent-marker freckles."

"I was seven!"

"And I was three. Just remember you owe me, big sister." Jasmine's voice changed from lightly teasing to serious. "And I'm about to collect."

Beads of sweat popped out on Cleo's brow. "What?" she said warily.

"I want them to stay with you."

Cleo could only emit a little moan.

"Don't keel over on me. It's just that we're pretty full here and I don't want to put Mama under any more strain."

Cleo moaned again. Jasmine was right. If Jonah's grandparents stayed at the bed-and-breakfast Celeste would feel obligated to entertain them. She was too exhausted for that.

"I don't know where Ethan is," Cleo said desperately.

"Well, you better find him," Jasmine replied, "because the Covingtons can't wait to get to know your entire little family quite a bit better."

Your entire little family. Cleo's stomach twisted again. That was exactly what the three of them were not. She blotted her damp forehead with her wrist. "Okay, Jasmine, give them directions to our house and tell them we insist they stay with us. But can you stall them for a bit? Maybe Ethan will get home soon. We'll need a little time to get our act together."

As she hung up the phone, she almost laughed out loud at her last words. Get their act together. Oh, yeah. Everything about their marriage was an act.

And for the Covingtons, who had given up their fight for

Jonah because she'd become Ethan's bride, it better be a darn good one.

In the end, Jasmine hadn't been able to stall long enough. The first car to pull into Cleo's driveway was not Ethan's Range Rover, but an unfamiliar, expensive sedan. Cleo pasted on what felt like a sick smile, then walked outside to greet the older couple, Jonah in her arms.

Was Ethan going to be surprised when he returned.

If he returned.

At the horrible thought, she widened her smile and reached out a hand to the silver-haired woman and then her stooped but vigorous-looking husband. "I'm Cleo M— Redford," she said, pretending she hadn't almost forgotten her married name. "You must be the Covingtons."

It helped that they were truly friendly and gracious people. Once they brought their few bags inside, the three of them sat in the living room to get acquainted. To Cleo's relief, they told her almost immediately that they were happy to not have the responsibility of raising a baby at their age. They had been willing to adopt Jonah if it was best for him, though.

"But he deserves young people, a young family," Mrs. Covington said, a warm smile on her lips as she sat on the couch with Jonah in her arms.

Mr. Covington was somewhat cooler, but even he seemed to approve. "Always liked Ethan, but he's a busy man. Jonah needs a mother. And Ethan could use someone to come home to."

Mrs. Covington beamed. "It was so clear he was taken with you, Cleo, when he came to talk to us in Houston."

Cleo beamed back, hoping to conceal her panic. Oh, yeah. Ethan was so taken with her that she had no idea where he was and whether he'd be back in time for dinner.

Dinner.

Thunk. Thunk. The two syllables dropped into her consciousness like sandbags. She'd been so preoccupied with housing the Covingtons, she'd hadn't even considered *feeding* them.

Swallowing hard, she rose to her feet. "Would you excuse me for a moment?" She smiled at their immediate assent and dashed for the phone in Ethan's office, the phone farthest away from her guests.

Speed Dial No. 2 was the Big Sky B and B. She had to beg dinner off of Jasmine. No way would the grandparents leave Jonah with a woman who did what Cleo did to food.

For the second time that day a cold sweat broke out over Cleo's skin. A short conversation with her sister didn't help matters.

She hung up the phone, her heart thrumming. Even the sudden appearance of Ethan in the office didn't bring any relief.

"We're sunk," she told him.

He blinked. "We can't be. I just talked with Ned and Betsy. They like you. And I'm…sorry for leaving like that. But you covered just fine."

All the tension she'd been holding at bay rushed in. Mortified, Cleo felt tears start in her eyes and she covered her face with her hands.

"Cleo."

Shaking her head, she whirled away from him. "I'm fine," she choked.

"You're not." He pulled her toward him and turned her into his arms. "I'm sorry, honey," he said again. "I'm sorry for so many things."

Cleo didn't listen to his words. She only felt the warm comfort of his hands running down her back and his strong heartbeat against her cheek. This was what she'd wanted since going to the B and B this morning—Ethan holding her, Ethan saying it was going to be okay.

But then it struck her again. The knowledge that a hug couldn't make this immediate crisis any better. She stepped away, rubbing her cheeks with the backs of her hands. "We're still sunk," she said.

He frowned. "Cleo, what the hell are you talking about?"

"We need to make a good impression on the Covingtons, right?"

He nodded cautiously. "Right."

"Prove to them what a sweet little family we are, right?"

He nodded again. "Yes."

"And food. A family would need that, right?"

"Uh-huh." He retreated a step, as if he were afraid of what she might do next. "But we have food, Cleo, right? The refrigerator and freezer are full. The cupboards, too."

She moved closer to him and lowered her voice. "That's all for show."

His brow pleated. "Cleo? Are you all right?"

She licked her dry lips. "What would you say if I told you I can't cook, Ethan?"

"You can't cook?" he echoed stupidly.

"Unless you consider instant oatmeal in the microwave, cooking."

"What?" he said.

"I can pour from a box and add milk or pour from a can and add water. But even heating's iffy."

He took another step back. "No," he said. "I don't believe it. Not you."

She nodded. "Believe it. And I tried to cover it tonight like I've done all the other times by begging a Jasmine donation, but she doesn't have a thing for me and was on her way out."

He blinked again and she could see his mind working, going over the meals they'd shared. He blinked once more and she knew he had tallied up all the take-out and leftovers and recipes that Jasmine "desperately needed" them to taste test. His head started shaking slowly from side to side.

"I'm sorry, Ethan," Cleo whispered. "But unless it's cornflakes or chicken noodle soup, we're *Titanic*-level sunk."

He ignored her apology to attack the cuffs of his denim shirt. With quick movements, he rolled them up his strong forearms.

Cleo eyed his determined movements. "What are we going to do?"

"We're going to start being more honest with each other, Cleo."

She was afraid to ask, but she had to. "What's that mean?"

"It means, lucky for Ned and Betsy—unless they like instant oatmeal, of course—that *I* can cook."

Cleo's knees went weak. "You can cook? Really?"

"Really. How does pasta primavera sound?"

"Like music to my ears," she said, still stunned. Ethan Redford, consummate deal-maker, could *cook?* "I could kiss you."

Ethan turned toward the door. "Maybe we should start being honest about that, too," he said.

By the time the pasta primavera had been prepared and consumed, Cleo found she could relax, even with Betsy Covington keeping her company in the kitchen as she put the last of the dishes away.

Cleo hugged to herself the knowledge that, at least for tonight, she and Ethan had achieved a real partnership. As he'd made the meal, he'd smiled to himself often—she had the distinct feeling he was still bemused by her own admitted clumsiness in the kitchen—but they'd worked together well. Under his direction, she'd put together a passable green salad, though his lips had twitched at the sight of her inelegant carrot chunks.

He'd touched her, too. She shivered now, remembering it. His shoulder and hip rubbing against her to make room for himself at the countertop. A light swat on her behind to move her aside when her tippy-toe stretch still couldn't reach the water pitcher in the highest cupboard. His fingers lingering on the small of her back as he untied her apron before politely pulling out her chair.

Around the table itself, they'd been in perfect concert, too. He prompted her to tell the Covingtons tales of life at the day care center and she showed her interest in Ethan's business by following up some of Mr. Covington's questions with a couple of her own.

Now from the living room came the low murmur of the men's voices. Both men sat on the couch and Jonah's grandfather was feeding the baby his evening bottle. Mrs. Covington paused with a dish towel in her hand, peering through the kitchen doorway at the sight the three made. She smiled softly.

"Oh, look," she said.

Cleo did. Jonah was nestled in the crook of his grandfather's arm, but the baby's eyes were fixed on Ethan. They stared at each other, unblinking, and then the baby's mouth quirked around the nipple, sending a sweet, hopeful smile Ethan's way. Cleo's heart clenched. And then again, when Ethan surprised her by returning the smile to Jonah.

It was unexpected and just as sweet as the baby's, and maybe it was her imagination, but she thought she saw hopefulness in Ethan's smile, too.

Her spirits, already buoyed by the success of dinner, bubbled higher, and the words just popped out. "I love them," she said. Maybe they were going to be a family, after all. Maybe Ethan had just needed time to get used to the idea.

Betsy Covington smiled again and her gaze was warm. "That's what I came to find out. I know Ethan promised you'd visit in the fall, but I couldn't wait that long."

"I understand," Cleo said. Patience wasn't her strong suit, either. But she'd been right not to push things...push Ethan. He'd just needed time to see how things could—should—be with them. She just *knew* he wasn't going to leave again tomorrow, despite what he'd said.

"And to be honest," Betsy continued, "because of the way Ethan and Della were raised, I couldn't stop worrying. I'm surprised how well Ethan is coping with instant parenthood."

A little chill ran down Cleo's spine. She didn't know much about the way Ethan and his sister had been raised. He had been so closemouthed about it, only a few hints about growing up on the wrong side of the tracks and about his less-than-warm father.

"Ethan would do anything for Jonah," Cleo said.

"Even marry."

Cleo inhaled a sharp breath, but the other woman put out her hand. "I don't mean it as a criticism, dear, believe me. My own son failed Della and he failed his child. Any choices—and changes—Ethan has made for Jonah only deserve my praise."

The resigned hurt in Betsy Covington's face made Cleo search for a safer subject than Jonah's biological father. "You knew Della?"

"Oh, yes." She smiled sadly. "Della and my son were engaged at one time. I thought she would be his salvation. I prayed for it, because she was a wonderful person. Despite the disadvantages of her childhood, she was an engaging, optimistic young woman.''

Cleo swallowed. That was the second time the older woman had brought up Della's and Ethan's childhood. While part of Cleo didn't want to pry into her husband's past, another part thought knowing what he seemed so reluctant to speak about might cement their fragile, brand-new closeness. She swallowed again. ''Ethan doesn't talk much about…his family.''

Betsy nodded. ''Della always said her brother tried to ignore things that hurt. By refusing to acknowledge his feelings, he could protect himself.''

Cleo busied herself wiping an already-clean countertop. ''It sounds like Della knew Ethan well.''

''Oh, she did. And she adored him. He shielded her from much that went on in their household. But from what I gathered, they lived with a volatile father whose mood swings were exacerbated by drink and a mother who did nothing to help her children or herself.''

''Ah.'' Cleo's fingers gripped the sponge tighter. ''And there were…money problems.''

Betsy nodded. ''And with that in his background, too, it isn't surprising that Ethan has such a drive for making money. That's one of the things that has worried me about leaving Jonah in his care.''

Cleo turned around, surprised. The Covingtons appreciated money, too. It was obvious in the enormous solitaire on Betsy Covington's finger, in her impeccable manicure and in the sleek cut of her expensive country-club clothes. ''You're worried about Ethan's success?''

''About what he's willing to give up for it.'' Betsy looked steadily at Cleo. ''I've met men like that before. Men who only offer money and not emotion.''

Men who only offer money and not emotion. The words

dropped, each one ice-cold, into Cleo's brain. Ethan had offered her Beansprouts. He said he would always provide for her and the baby. "He wants to take care of Jonah," she said, trying to ignore the sick sense of panic rising in her belly.

"I'm certain of it," the older woman said. "But he needs you to show him how."

Cleo turned away again. Betsy Covington didn't mean Ethan needed Cleo to show him how to diaper the baby or to feed the baby, or to even play with the baby. She meant that Ethan needed Cleo to show him how to love Jonah.

And, of course, Cleo wanted Ethan to love her, too. That little balloon of happiness she'd been floating on slowly deflated. She had no idea how to make it happen.

The Covingtons didn't stay up much later than Jonah. They claimed a desire to rise early in the morning to get started on the next leg of their trip, which would take them into Canada to visit some longtime friends. After pleasant good-nights were exchanged, the older couple drifted down the hall.

With a cup and saucer in each hand, Cleo rose. Ethan immediately followed, carrying the others. In the kitchen, she placed hers on the countertop. "Go ahead and set them here," she said, not looking at him. "I'll wait for the dishwasher to finish and then unload it and put these in."

"Do it in the morning," he said. It wasn't a suggestion.

Cleo fussed with the cups and saucers, setting each one precisely in the middle of a square tile. "No. I think I'll do it tonight."

"You don't want to go to bed?"

"Mmm." Cleo turned all the cup handles in the direction of the sink and avoided the question. The issue of bed was the last of the evening's hurdles, and she wasn't even sure

Ethan realized that it loomed in front of them. The house had four bedrooms. One was used as his office. One was the master bedroom. One was Jonah's. One was the one she'd been using...and was now occupied by their guests. In the short time she'd had before their arrival she'd managed to shuffle a few of her things into Ethan's room.

Yet while she and Ethan had shared his bed last night, all the events of today hadn't made it clear that he'd welcome her back in it again.

There was all she'd held back from him about the skeleton. There was his expressed desire to leave again the next day. There was the strain of the Covingtons' visit. He knew, now, that she didn't cook.

And Cleo knew that his sister Della had thought Ethan ignored his feelings as a way of protecting himself. Betsy Covington wondered if he was the kind of man who offered money instead of emotion.

"Cleo..." Ethan's hand touched her shoulder.

Heat ribboned down her arm.

If that were true, who was going to protect her?

She refused to turn around. "What?" she asked hoarsely.

"Let's go to bed." His hand tightened on her shoulder.

There was a darkness, an intent, in his voice and in his touch that set her heart rattling in her chest. She licked her lips, stalling to get control of its wild movements. Practical, sensible Cleo couldn't be so aroused by a hand, by a voice.

"Maybe I'll, uh...maybe your office—"

"No." His other hand closed around her other shoulder.

Heat streaked down that arm and her fingertips tingled. She wasn't certain he knew what she was talking about. Wiggling her fingers to ease the strange sensation in them, she tried again. "You see, the Covingtons, uh...my room—"

"Cleo." Ethan jerked her back against him, so her shoulder blades hit the hard plane of his chest. He was hot. So hot. "Shut up."

Her eyes squeezed shut. "But the bed—"

"Our bed. We're going to—" now he hesitated "—sleep in *our* bed."

That tingling was racing around her body now. Cleo tried to think of another protest—one last attempt to protect herself—but he threw all hopes of her protest away by curving her hair behind one ear and whispering against it. "I think I missed a few spots last night."

"Missed a few spots?" she echoed stupidly, her mind distracted by the hard press of his body against her bottom.

"Like right here." He swept her hair off her nape and pressed a wet, openmouthed kiss on that surprisingly sensitive skin.

A little helpless noise made it through Cleo's tight throat.

His mouth was back at her ear again. "What was that?" His hard, big arm clamped around her middle, which was a good thing, because all the bones below her waist were ragdoll-soft. "Did you say you want me to kiss you there again?"

She wanted him to kiss her anywhere. Everywhere.

He seemed to figure out she was incapable of answering, because he stopped talking and just started kissing. The back of her neck, the side of her neck, her ear, her throat, every inch of skin he exposed as he unbuttoned her blouse.

As he pulled the sides open, Cleo's eyes drifted open. They were in his bedroom. On his bed.

She couldn't remember the journey from kitchen to mattress.

And when he bent over her to wet with his tongue the silky material of her bra, right over her nipple, she didn't care. Sensible, practical Cleo decided that some details were extraneous.

And some details were delicious.

Ethan explored her body with excruciating slowness. When she tried to reach for him, he firmly placed each hand on one side of the wide pillow beneath her head. "Hold here, honey," he said, and then bent to her skin again, to run his mouth over each of her ribs, to circle her navel with his tongue, to stroke his fingers from hipbone to hipbone.

"Ethan," she whispered, his name coming out more like a moan.

But he wasn't swayed by the plea in her voice, and only settled himself alongside her. He was still completely dressed, and the scratch of his clothes against her skin was erotic.

"Ethan," she tried again, and lifted a hand toward his chest.

He caught it and pulled it back to the pillow. "Hold here," he commanded once more.

She obeyed, because then he sucked her nipple into his mouth and she couldn't do anything but ride the ripples of pleasure that slid down her body, heating her center. Her legs moved restlessly, and Ethan immediately insinuated one hand between them.

They instinctively parted, and then he was between her thighs, his shoulders pressing against the sensitive skin inside them. Cleo gripped the corners of the pillow. "You're still wearing your clothes," she said desperately.

He was looking at her. Cleo's body suffused with a new degree of heat. The silvery moonlight was beaming through their window, making it easy for her to see him. See Ethan, fully dressed, fully between her splayed thighs, looking at her.

Then he shuddered. Cleo saw it roll down his spine, felt his fingers tighten on her hips.

She closed her eyes, even more desperate now. "Ethan. Please. Make love to me."

His fingers tightened again, but he didn't move. "I am, Cleo." And then he bent his mouth to that hot, melting, most intimate spot on her body.

Oh. Cleo jerked. Ethan licked again. Cleo jerked again, her body nearly rising off the bed.

He lifted his head for just a moment. "Hold on," he said.

But she didn't know if he was talking to her or to himself, because when he bent to kiss her again he tightened his grip on her hips and tilted her body. His mouth found her once more, a sweet, sweet spot, and Cleo squeezed the pillow corners to keep herself from shooting straight into the moonlit night and a mind-blowing climax.

But Ethan wanted it all. He wouldn't stop, didn't seem to want to stop. Cleo couldn't catch her breath. Her nipples tightened, swirling into harder points. Desperately close and determined to tell him to stop, she looked down once more.

And just then, Ethan traced one hand down her hip to slide two fingers inside her.

Cleo died.

They used to call it that, the little death, and Cleo understood it now, because her body spasmed and her mind spun free from reality and heaven was certainly the moon-gilded Ethan as he quickly shed his clothes and joined their bodies.

Finally, when both their breathing had quieted, Cleo allowed herself to stroke his hair. Her fingers drifted through it slowly, and she gloried in the freedom to touch him. From the beginning, she had always wanted so much to touch him. Satisfaction and happiness welled up inside her.

She was free to touch him. He was her husband. He was hers.

She spoke without thinking. "Ethan, I—"

His hand quickly covered her mouth. "Shh."

Cleo froze. She wouldn't have believed his sated body could move so quickly, but it must have been an almost reflex that made him stifle her with such speed.

An instinctive reflex.

To protect himself from what she'd been about to say.

Her eyes squeezed tightly shut. She made herself breathe. Then she puckered her lips and kissed away his silencing fingers.

And *then* she stared into the moonlit darkness and listened to the man she loved breathe a sigh of relief when she didn't tell him so.

Eleven

Standing in the front doorway, Cleo lifted her hand for one more wave to the departing Covingtons, then slid a look at Ethan. "How do you think the visit went?"

His brows rose in surprise. "Fine." His lips twitched. "And your coffee and bagels and cream cheese weren't even half bad this morning."

Cleo looked away. Making breakfast had been her excuse for rising earlier than usual. When she'd opened her eyes and met Ethan's across the pillow this morning, she'd been desperate for a reason to escape.

He didn't want her love.

He didn't want her to need him.

And lying beside him in bed, she thought it might be too easy for him to see that she *did* love him, that she *did* need him. Wildly.

But he'd married her because she was sensible, practical and capable. He'd married her because she was a woman who could handle herself and the adorable baby he'd brought into her life.

As if she'd woken him by her thoughts, in his crib down the hall, Jonah started to cry. Cleo turned quickly, frowning. Usually Jonah took at least an hour's nap in the morning, but she'd put him down only fifteen minutes before.

"Cleo."

Ethan's voice made her pause. "Hmm?" She turned and directed her gaze in the vicinity of his left shoulder, not trusting herself to look at his face without giving her feelings away.

"I just wanted you to know I'm taking a late afternoon plane."

Cleo's heart dipped, and she swallowed. "Okay." Before her expression could give away her disappointment, she turned back toward Jonah's room.

"Cleo."

She slowed, but didn't turn around this time. "What?"

"Are you going to be okay...with the baby?"

His hesitation asked her more. Was she going to be okay with the baby *and* with the limits he was putting on their relationship? No.

But Cleo had her pride. And she was that practical, sensible, capable woman he had married. "Of course," she said, continuing on to Jonah's room. If she wasn't okay now, well, then, she would be. She'd find a way to live with half a marriage. Somehow.

Jonah's face was flushed and he didn't immediately stop crying when she picked him up. A niggle of unease rolled down Cleo's spine. He was usually such an easygoing baby.

She went through the checklist. His diaper was dry and his tummy was full. The worry getting stronger now, she shifted him in her arms and put his cheek against hers. He was hot.

To the tune of his fretting, she carried him into the adjoining bathroom to retrieve the thermometer. Blessing the inventor who thought up something so simple as taking a temperature via the ear, she quickly checked Jonah's.

Well over 98.6.

Clamping down on a strange nervousness—at Beansprouts they handled kids with temperatures weekly!—Cleo reached for the infant pain-reliever drops. Squinting at the dosage while she tried to soothe the baby, Cleo considered calling Ethan in to help.

But he'd hired—no, married—her for her experience. She could do this, even though she suddenly realized that she was not quite as calm and cool as when a Beansprouts's kid was sick or injured. "Oh, Jonah," she whispered, putting down the drops to run her hand over his wispy hair. "You're mine now, and I want to make you feel better so badly."

With new resolve, Cleo unwrapped the tamper-proof bottle of medication and filled the dropper with the proper dosage.

Jonah batted her hand away, though, and the dropper fell into the sink. "Okay, okay," she whispered, shifting the baby to her other shoulder. She fished the dropper out, cleaned it, then sucked medicine inside it again, all the while trying not to worry over Jonah's unhappy snuffling.

This time she was ready for his hands. She avoided their reach, and quickly squeezed the medication into his mouth. He blinked, hiccuped, and then some of the sticky red stuff dribbled out of his mouth and onto her sleeve.

Cleo stared down in dismay at the stain on her sleeve, trying to judge how much he'd actually swallowed. But then Jonah started crying again, harder now, and Cleo gave up. Her hair was damp, her hands sticky, and her uneasiness was back, big-time.

She gently cradled Jonah against her, as much for his comfort as for her own. "It's okay, baby," she whispered over and over. She paced the room, patting his back and crooning.

"Okay, okay, okay." That's what she'd promised Ethan. She would be okay. Jonah would be okay. *Please.*

Whether it was thanks to the medicine or thanks to her pacing, in a few minutes Jonah dropped off again. Cleo carefully put him back in his crib, but she stood over it, watching him sleep.

"Is everything all right?" a low voice suddenly asked in her ear.

Cleo jumped and goose bumps trickled down her back. "You scared me," she whispered accusingly.

Ethan was watching Jonah. "He's quiet now. I came to see if you needed help earlier, but you were walking back and forth and he looked ready to sleep. I didn't want to disturb him."

"He's a little warm," she said, continuing to watch Ethan watch Jonah. There was something on his face, a yearning, maybe, that she'd never detected before.

His hand reached out, but stopped short of touching the baby's blond hair. He minutely adjusted the light blanket covering the baby. "Is it something to be concerned about?"

Cleo didn't want it to be. "No. I'm sure it's nothing," she said, keeping her voice very low. "He could be teething. I gave him some medicine, though."

"Good." His gaze stayed fixed on the baby.

"He looks like you," Cleo found herself saying. She'd noticed it before, but had never expressed it to Ethan. "Not just the coloring, but the shape of his eyes and his mouth."

"You think so?" Ethan's lips quirked in an almost smile. "Della and I looked quite a bit alike, so maybe it's not so surprising."

He hadn't mentioned his sister in a long time. But Della had been on Cleo's mind a lot, especially since Mrs. Covington had talked about her. "Is that who Jonah gets his sunny disposition from, Della?"

Ethan shot her a glance. "Well, I don't think you could claim that about me, could you?"

Cleo shifted her gaze to the baby again. "Oh, I don't know. You can be very charming. But you know that."

"Charming." Ethan's voice held humor as he ran a slow finger down Cleo's cheek. "I like that."

Her face heated. "It's the deal-maker in you, don't you think?"

"Maybe." The amusement left his voice. "Though that makes me sound shallow."

Cleo shook her head. "You're not shallow, Ethan. Never that. But...contained, I guess is the word." He had walls around him that she wasn't sure could ever be breached. Or that *she* could breach, anyway. Maybe some other woman.

Ethan cleared his throat. "Della used to tell me I was a cold fish."

Cleo couldn't help herself. "Well, *that* I know is not true."

His gaze jumped to hers. She raised her eyebrows, meeting the incredible blue without flinching.

He shook his head, then chuckled. "You surprise me sometimes."

Cleo let it go at that. But maybe that was what she needed to do more often. Surprise him.

After a few more moments Ethan wandered away to complete his packing and make a few phone calls. Without acknowledging how worried she was, Cleo remained by the baby's bedside. When he woke up thirty minutes later, Cleo instantly put down her book and rose from the rocking chair.

He was hardly fretting at all; as a matter of fact he appeared more listless than she'd ever seen him. Cleo took the baby in her arms, and knew instantly that his temperature had risen.

She swallowed a bubble of panic. She forced down the instant urge to call out for Ethan.

He would be leaving for the long drive to the airport shortly. She would just call the pediatrician, make an appointment and get her fears calmed by a professional.

Keeping her arms protectively around Jonah, she headed for the kitchen and her address book.

But her fears were escalated instead of soothed when the nurse who answered the phone insisted Cleo come in immediately. High temperatures for infants under a year old could be particularly dangerous, the woman explained.

Cleo felt strangled. She could hardly get out enough breath to finish the phone call. "Ethan!" she called.

His brow furrowed, he appeared in the kitchen. "What's the matter?"

Cleo opened her mouth, then closed it. He was wearing one of his deal-maker suits and, as usual, it added another layer to that protective wall of his. Mentally forcing down her panic, she spoke again, more quietly. "I just wanted you to know I'm taking Jonah to the doctor. His fever seems to be getting worse."

Ethan frowned. "I don't like the sound of that."

Cleo wanted to scream that she didn't, either, but there wasn't any reason to worry Ethan. That was her job, to calmly, practically, capably, handle these kinds of minor crises. That's why he'd married her. "It'll be okay," she said firmly.

His gaze raked her face, and she struggled to keep it composed. "You're sure?"

Cleo's stomach was flip-flopping with nervousness, but she refused to let him see it. "I'm sure," she said. "I'll just put a few things in the diaper bag and be on my way."

In Jonah's room, she had to put the baby in the crib to restock the bag with diapers and an extra outfit. She breathed deeply of the baby-powder scent of the room, trying to calm herself, but when she couldn't seem to unzip the bag, Cleo realized her hands were shaking. Shaking hard.

She bit down on her lower lip, scolding herself. She was good in emergencies, darn it. Everybody said so. It had always been so.

At the sound of Jonah's little whimper, she rushed over and picked him up again. But she'd never had her own child. His overheated skin and listless gaze scared the heck out of her.

She'd never had her own sick child.

Only by admonishing herself to focus, could Cleo get herself and the baby ready. With Jonah in her arms and the diaper bag slung over her shoulder, she hurried down the hall to the kitchen. "Keys," she said softly to the baby. "We just have to find my keys and then we can get you some help, sweetheart. Mommy's going to take very good care of you."

Cleo's keys were missing from their convenient little hook. Her stomach roiled as she tried to think of where they could be. In another panic, she whirled.

To face Ethan. There was a tight expression on his face. "I'll drive you," he said.

Drive her! She almost sank to the floor with gratefulness. But no. A capable, practical woman wouldn't need to be driven to a doctor's appointment. "I'll be fine," she said. Of course she would be.

His mouth tightened. "For God's sake, for once—" He stopped, his voice quieting. "Cleo, you're shaking all over. I'm not letting you drive...our son."

Our son. Cleo wanted to think about those words, but her worry was taking over again. Ethan steered her toward the door and she realized he was right. Her whole body was trembling, and continued to tremble for the entire drive to the doctor's office.

In the back of Ethan's Range Rover, Cleo sat next to Jonah's car seat, so that she could stroke the baby's arm, his hand, his hair. "I love you," she whispered.

She prayed, too.

Ethan hated hospitals. He hated the smells and the lights and the quiet soles on the nurses' shoes. The last time he'd been in one was to say goodbye to his sister.

And now his sister's son was in another antiseptic, bright and too quiet hospital room.

It had all happened so damn quickly. He and Cleo had taken Jonah into the pediatrician's examining room. The nurse had taken his temperature. Then the doctor had hurried in and quite calmly, matter-of-factly, told them to drive to the hospital. He would call ahead so they would be ready for Jonah.

When babies had temperatures as high as Jonah's, the pediatrician had explained it could be a sign of a bacterial infection that could lead to…Ethan couldn't even wrap his mind around what could happen.

Once at the hospital, some of Jonah's spinal fluid had been immediately drawn. Now they would have to wait for the results. The cultures that would specify the seriousness of the illness would take three days to develop. In the meantime, Jonah would remain in the hospital and be treated with antibiotics in case it was bacterial. The only comforting thing to remember was that this practice was standard.

The walls of the hospital room were painted cream and green. The linoleum floor was a darker green. Jonah appeared small and fragile lying in a stainless-steel crib.

"It looks like a cage," Ethan muttered. When Cleo didn't respond, he turned his head toward her. A green rocking chair sat to one side of the crib. She had slid into it earlier, but she wasn't rocking. Perched on the edge of the seat, she stared in front of her, unseeing.

Something cold and sharp pierced Ethan's chest. "Cleo?"

Her eyes flickered, and then she focused on him. "What?"

Her eyes were like amethyst crystals. For a moment he imagined he could look clear through them, straight into her soul, straight into—

He shook himself. "Do you want me to call someone? Your mother or your sister?"

Her eyes were unfocused again, but she managed to shake her head. "Not now. Not yet."

"God," he muttered, looking away from her face. "It's cold in here." But even colder was the chill in his blood. Cleo was still shaking, finely trembling all over, and watching her was almost worse than watching Jonah.

With a smothered oath, he shrugged out of his suit jacket and strode over to drop it around Cleo's fragile shoulders. When she didn't move, he tugged up the collar and brought the edges close together. "There," he said firmly.

There. He'd done what he could for her now. Provided for her.

With two strides he crossed the small room and stood beside the narrow window, staring out over the parking lot and into a small slice of the Montana sky. He tried to focus on his current project. He tried to dredge up the list of calls he knew he needed to make.

He tried damn hard to detach himself from the scene behind him. The child in the hospital crib. The woman in the rocking chair.

Instead, he turned around. Instead, he watched them for hours, as day darkened into night. Nurses and doctors bustled in and out. Jonah woke up, Cleo fed him a bottle, Jonah went back to sleep, Cleo went back to staring in front of her. And trembling.

Always trembling.

He didn't know exactly what time it was, but it was fully dark when Cleo finally looked at him. "It's late," she said, and there was surprise in her voice.

Ethan left his place by the window and approached her. "Do you need something? We haven't eaten." He hadn't even thought about it. "Can I—"

Cleo shook her head. "I'm not hungry."

"What about coffee?" Hell, he wanted to do *something*.

Jonah whimpered. Cleo's head whipped around and they both rushed to the crib. When the baby saw them bending over him, his mouth moved into a little smile.

Another cold and sharp pain stabbed Ethan's chest.

Cleo took him up in her arms. "What a good boy," she said. She put her cheek against his hair. "Mommy's good boy."

Ethan looked away. He didn't know why. As Cleo murmured to the baby, he retreated to his spot by the window. More time passed and Jonah must have fallen asleep again because Cleo put him down in the crib.

A nurse came in on her quiet shoes and checked on the baby, then someone else brought in a narrow cot. "For the mama," the man said with a quick smile. On its middle were stacked a thin pillow and a mint-green blanket.

Cleo looked over at Ethan, then slipped his jacket off her shoulders. At some point she'd put her arms through the sleeves and rolled them up. Now she unfolded them, sending him a small, apologetic smile. "Here," she said, holding it out to him. "Thank you."

It wasn't any warmer in the hospital room. At least it wasn't to him. "Keep it," he said.

She shook her head. "I'm going to use the blanket." She pointed at the cot. "Why don't you go on home?"

Go on home. That was a good idea. He could go into his office. Fire up the laptop. Do some work. Send some faxes. Check his e-mail.

Anything to forget about Jonah in his stainless-steel cage and Cleo, with her amethyst-crystal eyes and her shivering body. He opened his mouth. "No" came out.

Her brows came together. "Why not? You could get some rest."

A very definite no. Hell. The last thing he'd be able to do was go to that bed they'd shared the past two nights and sleep.

A feathery shiver tickled his spine as he remembered the sensation of Cleo's skin against his palms, of sinking into her hot, still climaxing body. He wanted to touch her, taste her again.

He wouldn't go back to that bed until she was there beside him.

"I'll stay right here," he said.

"I can handle it," she said defensively.

Ethan frowned. What did she mean, she could handle it? Hell, he *wanted* her to handle it. He worked best when emotions were at a minimum and, take it from him, hospitals weren't the kinds of places that minimized emotions. But maybe it was because he couldn't get Della out of his mind, or maybe it was because he knew Cleo's eyes would haunt him if he left her here. "I won't be in your way."

She turned away from him wearily, and they retreated to their separate corners. He shifted against the ugly green vinyl chair beneath the window. Cleo curled up on the cot.

Hours went by and neither of them spoke. Jonah slept, thank God. And then so did Cleo.

It was well after midnight when, restless, Ethan found

the controls to the television in the corner of the room. He
turned it in his direction then thumbed it on—no volume.
The flickering images offered him a flat, sterile kind of
company.

During the third-in-a-row rerun of episodes of the "I
Love Lucy" show, Jonah whimpered. Ethan immediately
looked toward Cleo. She didn't move. The baby whimpered
again, louder, and Ethan pushed to his feet.

Cleo had looked exhausted *before* they arrived at the hospital. If he could quiet the baby, he guess he'd give it a try.

Over the side of the crib, he peered at Jonah's face. The
baby was looking in the other direction, his eyes open. Then
his face screwed up, readying itself for another wail.
"Champ," Ethan whispered softly. "Over here, champ."

Jonah's head rolled on the mattress and his expression
eased.

"That's right," Ethan whispered. "I'm here, champ."
Champ. Where the hell had that come from? He'd completely forgotten the pet name Della had called her son.

Jonah whimpered again. Apparently a few words in the
night wasn't enough to comfort him. Casting a quick glance
to make sure that Cleo was still undisturbed, Ethan scooped
Jonah up into his arms. Jonah blinked. Ethan blinked back.

"That's right, champ. The guys are going to handle this
one. We're going to let Cleo sleep."

With quiet footsteps he retreated to the window. The two
of them looked out on that slice of sky. Ethan counted the
stars in their little rectangle of darkness. "Five," he whispered to the baby. "There are five twinkling stars." His
gaze snagged on the baby's face and his wide-eyed expression.

He looks like Della. Cleo had said Jonah resembled him,
but she hadn't known his sister. Thinking of Della, he felt
another stab of that cold pain pierce him, and Ethan sucked

in a breath. But the pain didn't subside and he couldn't seem to sidestep it.

He stared down into the baby's face. "Your mama was special," he whispered. "And I still can't believe she's gone. I always watched out for her, always."

Ethan glanced up at those five twinkling stars. Maybe it was Della's turn now. He gathered the baby closer and squeezed shut his eyes. *Watch over him, sis. Watch over Cleo, too.*

Watch over the three of us.

Ethan breathed easier after that. Jonah fell asleep against his chest, and he reluctantly laid him back in his crib, thinking the baby might have a more comfortable rest. Soon after, Cleo stirred, and through slitted eyelids he watched her get up to check on the baby.

She stood by the baby's crib for almost an hour. Ethan thought about telling her to lie back down. He thought about joining her. But instead he watched her. Her hands gripped the top rail of the crib and she took in long breaths.

His chest ached again, damn it. Ethan tried avoiding the hurt by avoiding the sight of Cleo. He closed his eyes.

Watch over her, he told Della again.

Suddenly it was morning.

He blinked, stretched, his muscles as stiff as an over-baked pretzel. Jonah slept.

Cleo was in the rocker again. Somehow, in the hours since he'd last looked at her, she'd turned even more fragile. Shadows darkened her eyes. He knew if he touched her she'd still be shaking and cold.

That unfamiliar pain twisted inside him again. He rose and walked toward her. "Cleo—"

"You're awake." She popped up, her movements jerky. "Will you watch Jonah? I'll be right back."

He stared at her. She was talking fast, moving fast, clearly fueled by nerves. "Of course."

"The doctor should be here in an hour or so. The nurse just checked Jonah. No change."

No, all the changes were to Cleo. Her cheekbones poked against skin almost translucent with weariness. No doubt, with the exception of that brief nap, she hadn't slept the rest of the night. On her way to the door she halted at the cot and frowned. With another jerky movement, she snatched up the blanket, shook it out, then folded it into a precise square.

Ethan stared at her. The blanket had already been folded into a precise square. Cleo was strung so tight he could practically hear her tendons humming.

"Cleo—"

But he was speaking to her back, and then the door.

She must have run downstairs and then back up, she was back in such short order. In one palm she cradled two cups of coffee, a bag from the hospital gift shop in the other.

"Here," she said, shoving the coffees in his direction.

He grabbed both, fairly sure that worry was the only stimulant she needed right now.

She dropped the bag onto the seat of the rocking chair. Out came a teddy bear. Three books. A toy airplane. A build-it-yourself model of a race car. Ethan squinted. He thought the age level said over eight.

More stuff came out of the bag and she arranged it around the room. The only thing she put near the baby was the soft teddy bear, and even that took eleven tries for her to find exactly the right location and pose.

Then she swung around and found him with the coffees. Before he could protest, she grabbed one and a napkin he'd found on the room's tiny table. The coffee went down in one gulp.

She tossed the cup into the trash, then took the napkin and blotted her hands. Next, she used the napkin to wipe down the small table. Then the arms of the rocking chair.

Ethan set his coffee cup down. "Cleo," he said softly.

She pretended she didn't hear him. Or maybe she just couldn't stop her frenetic cleaning.

"Cleo." He approached her, and still she bustled around the room.

With a sigh, he grabbed her by the upper arms. "Cleo," he said, shaking her gently. "Stop. You need to stop, honey."

She looked up at him, the woman who had become his wife. There were so many things in the amethyst facets of her eyes. Worry, fear, love for the child that he'd come to her with.

That pain tore through his chest, no small stab, but a huge hole. Then something swelled to fill it, something like a heart, and it kept getting bigger.

Cleo's mouth trembled. "I'm scared," she whispered brokenly.

A lump rose in Ethan's throat. His chest hurt, his throat hurt, he never knew there was this much pain in all the world. "I know, honey." He pulled her against his chest.

She broke down then, sobbing against him. He held her tightly, feeling the tension drain from her. "I'm so scared," she said again.

Ethan stared out the window as he stroked her hair. The five stars were gone and it was another sunny day in Montana. He leaned his cheek against the top of her head, breathing through the pain that came in beats now, beats that matched the thudding rhythm of the heart he'd forgotten he had.

The sun was climbing. Its brightness stung his eyes and he blinked away the irritating tears.

Twelve

Later that morning, Ethan made a phone call to enlist the help of Cleo's mother and sister. They arrived at the hospital around noon and, after much coaxing, were able to drag Cleo away for lunch.

Leaving Ethan with a baby that suddenly seemed better. The nurse had said his temperature was down a degree, which only seemed to make Jonah cranky. Ethan took him up into his arms and the two of them paced around the room, inspecting anything the least bit noteworthy.

To the tune of the baby's whimpers, they examined their minute view from the window and the box holding the car model. When neither distracted Jonah, Ethan "flew" the plane over to the crib and retrieved the soft teddy bear. He settled the stuffed toy against Jonah's chest and the baby stopped his fractious wriggling and smiled.

Ethan felt like a million bucks.

He sank into the rocking chair with Jonah and the teddy bear. One foot flat on the floor, he rocked the three of them in a soothing rhythm. At first it seemed that Jonah might protest again, but then Ethan started talking too. He told Jonah about the day he was born. He told him how sad he'd been when Della died. He told him about the vow he'd made at his sister's side. That no one he loved would ever be taken from him again.

He stared down, into his nephew's—his son's—wide

blue eyes. "That's right. I love you, champ." He swallowed. "I love you, son."

Jonah's hand reached out and patted Ethan's chin. "That's why I came back to Cleo," he continued. "I wanted the best for you. For us."

The door squeaked as it was pushed open and Ethan lifted his head. Cleo stood framed in the doorway, her mother and sister standing behind her. Her eyes widened. "Is everything okay?"

He nodded, his foot still gently rocking the chair back and forth. "Fine."

She stepped into the room, and his heart clenched. The lunch hadn't made her look any less tired or less fragile. "Do you want me to hold him?" she said hesitantly.

He didn't. But suddenly he realized that Cleo needed to hold the baby herself. It would comfort her, as strangely, it had comforted him.

He stopped rocking the chair. "Come here," he said, rising from it.

She dashed forward and he gently transferred the baby and the teddy into her arms. Then, just as gently, he pushed her into the rocking chair. From the cot, he fetched the mint-green blanket and unfolded it. Hunkering beside the chair, he carefully tucked the soft fabric around Cleo and Jonah.

With a sigh, she closed her eyes and laid her head against the back of the chair. Ethan stroked her hair off her forehead, then put his hand on the arm of the chair. He pushed, setting it to a very slight rocking.

Celeste spoke quietly from the doorway. "Would you like to go get something to eat now, Ethan?"

He shook his head, his gaze not leaving the faces of the mother and child.

His wife and his child.

As long as they were in the hospital, he wasn't going to leave their sides. He'd always wanted to provide for them, but now they needed something else, too.

They needed his love.

After one more backward look at the baby, Cleo shut Jonah's bedroom door. She rested her forehead on the wood, inhaling a long breath. The past three days were finally over. Jonah was home, and while he was still recovering from a virus, a serious bacterial infection had been ruled out.

A few more days and he'd be completely recovered.

Cleo shivered. She might be able to convince herself the entire episode had been a nightmare, if it wasn't for the chill she couldn't seem to shake and the smell of antiseptic that had found its way into the fiber of her clothes.

She walked into her room and pulled out some fresh clothing and headed for a hot shower. Oh, how she wished she could pretend it had all been a dream. But the truth was, she'd fallen apart. She, who was always so calm in an emergency, who was always so practical under pressure, had cracked.

And Ethan had picked up all the pieces.

He'd picked up Jonah, too.

Under the hot spray of the shower, she remembered walking in on them in the rocking chair that second day. While he'd surrendered the baby readily enough when she'd asked, for the next forty-eight hours Ethan had held the baby as much as she did. He'd also asked intelligent, calm questions of the doctors and the nurses.

He'd brought her tea and soup and wrapped her in blankets when he sensed she couldn't get warm.

The practical, capable, sensible person in that scary, sterile room had been Ethan. In that crisis, he hadn't needed her.

She'd failed him.

Cleo stepped out of the shower, dried off, then pulled on her clothes. She sat on the bed to tie her shoes and thought about just crawling under the covers and going to sleep herself. The sheets were fresh—changed in the hours between the Covingtons's leaving and their departure for the hospital—and maybe in sleep she could avoid the knowledge that was pounding like a bad toothache in her brain.

She'd failed Ethan.

With a sigh, she pushed to her feet. She didn't want to be a coward, too.

In the kitchen she stared at the contents of the cupboards and thought about heating some soup for their dinner. Ethan was in his office, she could hear his printer humming away and his fingers clicking at the keyboard. With another sigh, she turned away from the pantry and looked idly through the small tower of mail and the three-day stack of newspapers.

Three days' worth of front pages focused on Raven's skeleton, his obvious murder and what it would mean to Lyle Brooks's Laughing Horse project. The name Jeremiah Kincaid caught her eye several times.

The past will rise up to meet you. That was the warning Aunt Blanche had sent to her mother in her nightmare. Cleo shivered.

"Are you all right?" Ethan's voice sounded from the entrance to the kitchen.

Cleo looked up, then ducked her head. His golden hair was dark and wet and he smelled like soap. He'd exchanged the deal-maker suit he'd been wearing for three days for a pair of jeans and a sweatshirt, the sleeves pushed up to expose his powerful forearms. She wanted him more than she wanted to be happy.

Because it didn't seem that both could coexist.

"Cleo," he said sharply. "What's going on?"

She gestured vaguely at the newspaper in front of her. "Just catching up on the latest Whitehorn news."

His gaze flicked to the paper, then back to her face. "A sick baby can put a thirty-year-old murder into a little perspective, don't you think?"

"I suppose."

He came forward. "It puts a lot of things into perspective." His fingertips stroked her cheek. "Cleo, honey—"

The phone rang.

Ethan frowned when she stepped away to reach for it. "Let it ring," he said.

Cleo didn't. The person on the other end was Ethan's secretary in Houston. He frowned again as she handed him the receiver.

Hearing one side of the call wasn't easy to avoid, but was easy to understand. Ethan had put his business—*all* his business—on hold for the next few weeks. Though it appeared his secretary was having trouble appeasing some of his clients, Ethan was adamant. He was going to be in Montana spending time with his wife and child.

Cleo shivered again. She didn't blame him for not trusting her anymore, but that feeling of failure rose once more. He'd married her because she could care for Jonah.

The receiver clicked against its cradle. She smelled the delicious fragrance of Ethan as he approached her. His hand ran down the back of her hair. "Now. Where were we?" he said softly.

Cleo knew what she had to do. Had known it from the moment she'd fallen apart in his arms in the hospital room. She whirled to face him. "I won't contest our divorce," she said. Quietly. Firmly. She couldn't believe her voice hadn't broken.

His jaw dropped. "What?"

Cleo swallowed, holding on to her control by just a thread. "I know what kind of marriage we were supposed to have."

His eyes narrowed. "What kind is that?"

"We had a deal. You're very good at arranging those, and I agreed to it."

There was heat in his slitted blue eyes. "I am very good at deals. Maybe too good."

"No!" Cleo wasn't about to lay the blame at Ethan's door. "I went into our marriage with my eyes wide open. I knew that you wanted someone who could keep custody of Jonah for you."

His mouth twisted. "I said something to that effect, didn't I?"

Cleo nodded. "You were completely honest."

"About that—"

"And I want you to know that I was being honest, too. I really thought I could make Jonah a great mother. I am—was—always practical and capable. It's just…just—"

"This time it was your child."

She blinked. He understood. Seeing Jonah in the hospital had made her feel helpless and frustrated, and so very, very afraid.

"Cleo, I didn't like it any more than you did. Seeing Jonah in that hospital crib and thinking something might happen to him was like losing Della all over again."

She looked away. "But you didn't turn into Miss Clean and Tidy." He'd remained calm while her excess nervousness had surfaced in the oddest ways. At one point Ethan had bodily restrained her from remaking the cot for a fifth time. And then there was her small obsession with stacking in alphabetical order the magazines her mother had brought her. *Vanity Fair* always before *Vogue*.

He grinned faintly. *"Mrs.* Clean and Tidy Redford."

Her brows drew together.

That faint grin again. "Just a little name the nurses had for you."

Mrs. Redford. The hospital staff had called her that for three days and she'd felt a fraud each time she'd heard it. She met his gaze squarely. "I'm not holding up to my side of our deal, Ethan. You wanted to continue with your life, your business, while I was supposed to be the caretaker for Jonah."

He shifted uncomfortably. "That's not exactly—"

"You knew I'd fall for Jonah, and I have." She sucked in a breath. "But you deserve to have the kind of wife you wanted. The kind of wife you thought you were getting when we made our deal."

"I wish you'd stop calling it that," he muttered.

Tears stung her eyes. She was going to lose them both, the baby she loved, the man she loved. "So I'll make it easy for us to get a divorce. I'm sure with a little research you or your secretary can find the quickest, simplest manner." A thought struck her. "Maybe because it's been so short a time we could have it annulled."

His jaw was tight and blue fire jumped in Ethan's eyes. "We *have* shared a bed," he said tightly. "Or maybe you've forgotten that?"

At the lethal tone in his voice, Cleo backed up a step. "No, of course not." She'd never forget. All her life she'd remember the hard planes of Ethan's body. Of having him beside her, against her, *inside* her.

"Good." He strode closer.

Cleo stepped away again, the backs of her thighs hitting

the edge of the kitchen table. Her heart fluttered at that searing blue in Ethan's eyes. She swallowed. "Ethan—"

He cut her off. "I wish—"

The doorbell rang.

He swore.

Ignoring Ethan's "I wish for once we wouldn't be interrupted," she ran to answer it.

Facing whoever was at the door had to be easier than facing Ethan as they worked out the details of their divorce.

It was her buddy Gil. Cleo was so relieved to see a familiar, friendly face at this moment that she cried out his name with gratitude and immediately stepped into his welcoming embrace.

The past three days had been hell, but watching his wife step into another man's arms—*again*—moments after bringing up divorce stoked Ethan's temper.

"Gil!" Cleo's voice was light and sweet and no one would never know that she'd just torn out his newly discovered heart and fandangoed all over it.

He stood behind her, grim.

Gil squeezed her tight, then pushed her away to kiss her on each cheek, and then lightly on her lips.

Ethan folded his arms across his chest.

The other man blithely ignored him, his eyes only for Cleo. "I heard you were having a rough time and came by to see if there was anything I could do."

Rough time? Ethan wondered if she was going around Whitehorn complaining about their marriage. Hinting at divorce. God knew that would certainly bring dozens of Cleo's ex-consorts out of the woodwork.

She was beaming up at this one. "I haven't seen you in ages," she gushed. "How have you been?"

Ethan's chest ached. She'd never gushed over him.

"Great. I'm in town visiting Mom and Dad. Had to check on my best girl."

That was it. Ethan stepped forward.

The man's deceptively friendly brown eyes met Ethan's over Cleo's head. "You must be Ethan," he said, his smile too friendly.

Ethan bared his teeth. "The husband."

The man's mouth went instantly serious, but Ethan swore there were a few twitches at the corners. He kept his arm curled around Cleo as he held out a hand to shake Ethan's. "Gil Grayson."

As all the rest of the men who adored Cleo, this one didn't appear as afraid of Ethan as he should have. Ethan squeezed.

Gil winced.

Cleo frowned. "Ethan, this is a very old friend of mine." She dragged her old friend over the threshold and into their living room, leaving Ethan to trail behind. "Come sit down, Gil," she said.

They shared the couch.

Ethan shared a menacing look with Gil.

Gil looked as if he wanted to laugh again.

Ethan cleared his throat. "So, you're an old friend of Cleo's?"

His wife was staring at him, her expression puzzled. What did she think? That he wouldn't care that her beautiful curves and her full lips had been so close to another man?

Gil shot a look at Cleo. "One of the oldest, I think."

"He knocked me down on my very first day in school," she explained, her amethyst eyes warming.

The other man flicked a long finger on Cleo's nose. "Because you had the cutest little braids. I had to get your attention somehow."

She laughed. "So that was it. The braids. Maybe I shouldn't have gotten rid of them."

Gil had a dimple, Ethan realized with disgust. It poked a hole in his cheek when he smiled ever-so-charmingly at Cleo. "You don't need braids to get my attention, sweetheart."

She nodded in agreement, still amused. "No, you're right. You noticed me for more practical reasons. Like math homework? Biology assignments? Tell Ethan that without me you wouldn't have made it through high school."

Gil looked up at Ethan, his face serious. "Without Cleo I wouldn't have made it through high school. I wouldn't have *gone* to school."

Cleo's brows snapped together. "Oh, stop."

Gil covered one of her hands with his. "It's true, Cleo. I was on a downhill slide. But you dragged me to the top of the hill with you every day."

Cleo appeared unconvinced. "That's nice of you to say, Gil, but—"

"It's true," he said implacably. "That's why when Mom told me things had been hairy for you lately, I thought I better check in. Maybe this time *you* need me."

Oh, no, buster. That was all that Ethan was going to take. No way was he just going to stand here while another man offered to be what his wife needed.

He stepped forward, that fire inside him heating up. *"I'll* be taking care of Cleo."

Gil's brows rose. "Yeah?"

Ethan stared pointedly at the man's hand, the hand that was still touching Cleo's. *"Yeah."*

"Stop being so silly," Cleo said.

To him.

Ethan stared back at her. "What?"

"Stop being so silly," she said again. "Why would you be rude to Gil?"

Ethan took a calming breath and explained to her slowly, rationally, "Because I'm your husband and I'll be damned if I'm going to let one of your lovesick swains waltz into *our* house and claim he's going to take care of you."

Cleo's forehead wrinkled. "What lovesick swains are you talking about?"

"Let's see." Ethan ticked them off on his fingers. "There was John and Jeremy and Stuart," he said, naming all the men he'd met in Whitehorn that couldn't wait to get their hands on Cleo. "And now there's Gil."

"None of those men is the least lovesick for me." She appealed to her brown-eyed "old friend." "Right, Gil?" But she didn't wait for him to agree with her. "Ethan, you know me. I'm the practical, sensible girl who's friends with all the guys. None of them ever really *wanted* me."

Ethan's eyes widened as he listened to his adorable, practical, sensible, capable but featherheaded wife. Only when it came to men, of course, but a featherhead all the same. "Cleo—"

Gil cleared his throat. "I think I might be able to help out here."

Ethan crossed his arms over his chest and narrowed his gaze at the other man. "I'm a little suspicious of your help," he said.

"Ethan!"

"He's right, Cleo," Gil said.

The featherhead scrunched her face up again. "About what?"

Both Ethan and Gil sighed.

Gil spoke first. "We all loved you, Cleo. Wanted you." He shrugged. "All those men Ethan mentioned, and some others besides."

She made another face. "I introduced at least half of those men Ethan named to their wives."

"Whom they only fell in love with after getting over you. After finally accepting the fact that you weren't going to give your heart to them."

She was staring at Gil, speechless.

"Really, Cleo. We used to joke about having our own club. 'Those Who Have Loved and Lost Cleo.'"

She shook her head. "No."

"And there are some of us, including me, who haven't ever gotten over—"

"Thank you, I believe she's heard enough." Ethan dragged Gil up from the couch by the elbow. As much as he was grateful to the guy for getting Cleo's attention at last, he wasn't feeling so kind as to let him try another round of "Take Me, I'm Yours."

Ethan steered Gil to the door. "I owe you," he muttered.

Gil dug his feet in once they reached the front door. "I mean what I was trying to say." His brown eyes went hard. "I'll be watching to see if you screw up."

Ethan looked at his wife, still sitting stunned and beautiful on the couch. "Don't hold your breath, friend. I love her more than you and anyone else in your little club. And she's never going to forget it."

The door closed behind Gil with a satisfying snap. Just to be on the safe side, Ethan turned the lock. Then he approached Cleo.

And found his feelings for her were rising in a big lump in his throat. He knelt on the floor in front of her. "Cleo," he said, his voice hoarse. "Do you understand now?"

She laughed a little shakily. "I don't know."

He stroked back her hair with his hand, aware he was trembling, just as she had been in the hospital. "No man has ever wanted you because you're practical or sensible or any of those things. They haven't wanted to just be your friend. They've only *settled* for being your friend.''

A flush rose on her cheeks and he wanted to kiss them and her nose and her forehead and her lips and everywhere else he could reach.

''*You* wanted me because I'm practical and sensible. You said so,'' she pointed out.

Ethan groaned. ''I'm an ass, Cleo.'' Maybe he didn't deserve her. ''I was trying to come up with some plausible explanation for why I crossed five states to marry myself a convenient wife.''

She lifted a hand toward him, but brought it back to her lap without touching him. ''Is there an implausible explanation?''

He sucked in a breath. Maybe she wasn't such a featherhead when it came to men. Because that was the biggest, most pointed question she could have asked.

The one he'd ducked and dodged for the three months they'd been apart and the two months they'd been married.

He stared straight into her amethyst eyes. ''I fell in love with you, Cleo. Instantly, I think.''

When he confessed that to her, he'd imagined a dozen reactions, but not the one she had. Cleo recoiled from him and looked as if he'd slapped her. ''What?'' she whispered.

He swallowed. ''Last January. At the bed-and-breakfast. Do you remember how we met?''

''We bumped into each other,'' she said, as if the words were dragged from her.

''I looked down at you, at this curvy, warm, beautiful, amethyst-eyed witch and I thought someone had dropped something on my head. I was dizzy.''

She didn't respond.

''And not one day went by after that I didn't hope to catch a glimpse of you, or talk to you. When I had to go back to Houston I had arguments with myself every day. I had to force my hand off the phone a dozen times.''

She bit her lip. ''Why didn't you want to love me?''

Oh, God. The hurt in her voice twisted Ethan's heart. How could he have done this? How could he have caused pain to this woman?

And then he realized the most horrible truth of all. He could lose her. He could love her, and he could lose her.

He might find himself part of Gil's club, after all.

''Cleo,'' he said hastily, his brain spinning and whirling as it did at the conference table. What's the best way to present his case? What does the adversary want to hear? What words would best persuade her?

His mind went blank.

And from somewhere else, the truth arose. ''It's easier not to love, Cleo. You can't get hurt—with a fist or with words. I thought that was the best way to live. And, hell, I was a success in anyone's eyes, including my own.''

He raked his hand through his hair. ''And then when I felt that...*thing* for you, I thought I was wrong to pursue you. You were a woman with heart, obviously, and I had managed to squeeze mine to nothing. I thought I didn't have the emotions to offer you.''

''And then came Jonah.''

He nodded. ''And he desperately needed someone who had emotions, who had love. I instantly thought of you. I *wanted* you, all the while still telling myself that it was for Jonah's sake. All the while still thinking that what was beating inside me wouldn't be enough for you.''

She reached out, and her fingertips touched his chest. He felt them through the thick material of his sweatshirt and he couldn't read their meaning, or what was written on her face. ''What changed?'' she whispered.

''I didn't think you or Jonah really needed me, Cleo,''

he said, his voice hoarse with honesty. "But in the hospital, I was able to comfort you, and comfort him. Not just provide for you both, you understand. You needed me. And I was there."

There was something in her eyes that was giving him hope, giving him strength. He caught her hand against his chest and flattened her palm over his heart. "It's bigger because of you, Cleo."

She threw herself at him.

He was unprepared, so they both crashed to the living room floor and his head hit the hardwood. The shooting pain didn't stop him from sinking his fingers into her hair and angling her face for his kiss.

She threw herself into that, too, but when they both came up for air, her eyes were worried. "Did I hurt you?"

He shook his head. "I was afraid you might, but then you came into my arms."

Her delectable lips pursed. "Your head, silly. Did you hurt your head?"

"I have no idea. I think you better take me to bed and check me out. Thoroughly."

Her lips twitched. But then her face sobered. "You love me?"

"I do. I will. I'll vow it all over again in front of a thousand people if you want me to. Particularly in front of that large fan club of yours. I want them to know some man has finally and forever leashed Cleo."

She wrinkled her nose. "'Leashed'?"

He smiled. "You're a menace to men, honey. It's the least I could do."

She pursed her lips again. He could tell the featherhead still didn't quite understand how many hearts she'd broken. But he was damn glad his wasn't one of them. A little doubt lingered in her eyes. "Are you sure you don't mind that I'm not so practical, so…"

"Capable?" he supplied.

She nodded, and he swiftly exchanged places with her so she was on the bottom and he was on top. He insinuated his hips into the warm notch of her thighs. "Mmm," he said, savoring the sensation. "I don't mind at all. I have big plans to keep you busy with some very impractical, very sexy activities."

She smiled dreamily up at him and linked her hands around his neck to pull him down for another kiss. "Is that so?"

He resisted, just long enough to get in the last word. "Oh, yeah. And I'm going to make sure you're incapable of speech for long nights of our long, happy marriage."

Ethan let himself be drawn down to her mouth. And then he took her to their bedroom where they made love.

When it was all over, he was the one made incapable of speech. But when she was able to whisper "I love you" and he only mouthed the words in return, he knew by her stunning smile that she understood.

*   *   *   *   *

And the Winner—Weds!

Robin Wells

To Ken—the winner of my heart

One

"What do you think of Summer's hair?"

Frannie Hannon pulled her eyes away from the computer screen and swiveled around in the wooden office chair to see her two gorgeous cousins, Jasmine and Summer, standing in front of the front desk of the Big Sky Bed & Breakfast. Summer's long, dark hair fell in a tousled cascade of curls to her shoulders, where it lay in dramatic contrast against the red silk of her short chic dress.

"Give me your honest opinion, Frannie." Summer ran a hand through the loose waves in her normally straight hair. "Do you think Gavin will think curls look good on me?"

Frannie pushed her tortoiseshell glasses higher up on her nose, a dry smile curving the corners of her lips. "Your husband would think you looked gorgeous if you shaved your head and painted your skull green. And the annoying thing about it is, he'd be right."

It was the absolute truth. With her beautiful Native American features, deep chocolate eyes and wide, expressive mouth, Summer Nighthawk was breathtaking. But then, so was Jasmine Monroe, with her close-cropped dark hair, delicate features and creamy pale skin. Either woman's face or figure could stop traffic and a man's heart at fifty paces.

All mine could stop is a clock, Frannie thought ruefully. A familiar twinge of inferiority tweaked at her heart. She'd grown up here in Whitehorn, Montana, with Summer, Jasmine and Jasmine's equally gorgeous sister, Cleo, and she viewed them more as sisters than as cousins. Their mothers, in fact, *were* sisters. Frannie's mom, Yvette, and Jasmine's and Cleo's mom, Celeste, ran a bed-and-breakfast in the rambling arts and crafts-style manor house. Summer's mother, Blanche, had died shortly after Summer's birth, so Celeste and Yvette had raised their sister's daughter as one of their own.

The four cousins had all grown up together. They'd spent summers splashing in the waters of Blue Mirror Lake and winters tobogganing down the foothills of the Crazy Mountains. They'd shared their dreams and their secrets, their toys and their clothes. They were family in every sense of the word, and yet sometimes, when Frannie looked at her cousins, she found it hard to believe she'd come from the same gene pool.

Times like now. Summer was so dark and exotic, Jasmine so fair and fragile. Next to them, Frannie always felt like a little brown mouse.

Well, not little, exactly, she thought ruefully. Tall and gawky was more like it. At five-foot, nine-inches, Frannie's height was the only exceptional thing about her. There was nothing special about her light brown hair except its unruly nature, which was why Frannie kept it clamped back in a tight ponytail. Her skin was clear and fair, but her features were unremarkable. Her eyes were an okay shade of hazel, but she kept them hidden behind her large, tortoiseshell-framed glasses. Oh, she had her own unique characteristics, of course—her nose was faintly freckled, her figure was on the scrawny side, and she grew incredibly clumsy whenever she was nervous—but overall, she was drab, colorless and nondescript.

Which suited her just fine, Frannie reminded herself. It was better to fade into the background than to stick out and be ridiculed. In fact, she deliberately cultivated an inconspicuous look. She dressed to blend in, wearing brown or beige suits for her job at the Whitehorn Savings and Loan, and jeans and shapeless sweaters, like the baggy gray one she was wearing now, on evenings and weekends.

When it came to her appearance, Frannie didn't kid herself. She was plain, and she knew it. She'd made peace with that fact years ago, and now, at twenty-six, she knew there was no point in pretending to be something she wasn't.

"So what do you think?" Jasmine prompted. She waved her hand toward Summer's hair as if she were Vanna White pointing to a grand prize. "Am I a maestro with a curling iron, or what?"

"You are the Queen of Coif." Frannie leaned back in the rolling chair and gazed approvingly at Summer. "You look great. But what's the special occasion? You and Gavin haven't been married long enough to be celebrating an anniversary."

Summer lifted a shoulder. "No occasion. Just a Saturday night date with my husband."

"Who's baby-sitting?" Frannie asked. "Isn't it the nanny's night off?"

"She switched to accommodate our schedules. It isn't often Gavin and I are off on the same Saturday night." The nanny took wonderful care of their toddler Alyssa.

"So where are you going?"

"To dinner at the country club—if he ever finishes up at the hospital. I told him I'd change here instead of driving all the way home." Summer sighed. "I love living in the country, but as many hours as we spend at work, sometimes I think we just ought to live in a room at the hospital."

Frannie nodded sympathetically. Gavin was a general surgeon at the Whitehorn Hospital, the same place where

Summer practiced as an immunologist. Both of them spent most of their waking hours there or at the clinic on the reservation. Since their home was twenty miles away, Summer often used the bed-and-breakfast to change clothes, wait for Gavin, or simply relax between shifts.

"So if there's no special occasion, what's with the snazzy dress and new hairstyle?" Frannie asked.

Summer shrugged. "I just think it's good for a husband to see his wife looking different every now and then. I want to keep the magic in my marriage."

Jasmine and Frannie looked at each other, then simultaneously burst into laughter.

Summer put her hands on her hips and eyed them indignantly. "And what, pray tell, is so funny about that?"

"Summer, your entire life is magic," Jasmine said.

"Yeah," Frannie seconded. "You're beautiful, you have a fantastic career, a beautiful daughter, and you're married to a successful surgeon who worships the ground you walk on."

Summer's hands fell to her sides. "Well, you know the old saying—familiarity breeds contempt. I don't want Gavin to get bored with me."

Jasmine rolled her eyes. "As if that could ever happen."

"Yeah, Summer. Gavin's not fickle like Jasmine here." Frannie grinned at her pixie-faced cousin. Jasmine was hotly pursued by all the local bachelors, but she had yet to get seriously interested in any of them. "Who's the lucky guy you're going out with tonight?"

Jasmine looked down at her neatly buffed nails. "Bill Richards. You know—one of the architectural engineers of the new resort and casino. He stayed here a few weeks ago."

"Oh, I remember him! Broad shoulders, dark hair..."

Summer frowned. "But I thought he left town when the construction halted."

The construction of a casino on the Laughing Horse Reservation and a resort on adjacent private land was the biggest thing to ever hit Whitehorn. The development was supposed to boost the local economy, become a major revenue source for the Northern Cheyenne tribe, and create several hundred jobs for the citizens of Whitehorn. The ground had barely been broken for the project, however, when a skeleton with a bullet in its rib had been unearthed at the construction site.

And it wasn't just any old skeleton, either. Dental records had revealed that the remains belonged to Summer's father, Raven Hunter. Fortunately—well, it wasn't exactly fortunate, Frannie mentally amended, but in view of the discovery of his body, it certainly made the situation less emotionally painful— Summer had never known her father.

The police were conducting a murder investigation, and to the distress of the citizens of Whitehorn, the construction project had been put on hold until the investigation was completed. Rumor had it that the police probe could take months. If it lasted until the onset of winter weather, the grand opening could be delayed for a full year.

"I thought the engineers weren't going to return until construction resumed," Frannie remarked.

Jasmine nodded. "Evidently it has. When Bill called to ask me out, he said they've decided to build the resort's sports complex first. It's being built further to the east, on Garrett Kincaid's property."

"So the project is back on track," Summer said. "Well, that's good news for Whitehorn's economy."

"Not to mention Whitehorn's single women." Jasmine gave a mischievous smile. "The town's probably filling up right now with hunky engineers and contractors and heavy-equipment operators.''

"That's right." Summer's gaze fastened on Frannie, one eyebrow arching in mock reproach. "But in order for a gal to meet any of them, she'd have to get out there and mingle."

Frannie winced, knowing she was in for another round of the old familiar lecture.

Jasmine quickly picked up on Summer's theme. "Are you going out tonight, Frannie, or are you going to hole up here like you usually do?"

Frannie swiveled her chair back to face the computer. "The books are a mess. You know how hopeless Aunt Celeste is with finances, and she's been doing all the purchasing since Mom's been gone."

"But it's Saturday night," Summer scolded. "Don't you know all work and no play makes you a dull girl?"

Frannie made a face. "I'm already dull. It's too late to worry about it."

Summer wagged a finger at her. "It's never too late to get a life, Frannie. You need to go out and meet some men."

"It's not as if they're eagerly lining up for an introduction."

"That's because you're always hiding away here," Jasmine insisted.

"That's right." Summer nodded. "You'll never meet anyone if you don't get out and circulate."

"You two do enough circulating for all of us." Desperate for a change of subject, Frannie glanced at her watch. "Speaking of circulating, when are your guys arriving?"

"Gavin should be here any minute."

Jasmine glanced at the grandfather clock in the entryway alcove, then clasped a hand to the lapels of her white terry-cloth robe. "Oh, dear. Bill will be here in ten minutes and I'm not even dressed! Summer, come help me figure out what to wear."

"Okay—if you'll let me borrow your new necklace."

"Deal."

Frannie heaved a sigh of relief as her cousins scurried upstairs to Jasmine's room in the back wing of the house. She knew they meant well, but she hated it when they tried to coax her into social situations. The few times she'd allowed them to drag her to the local nightspots, she'd sat on the sidelines as man after man ignored her.

Her cousins refused to accept it, but Frannie knew it was a fact: she didn't have what it took to interest a handsome, successful, desirable man—not for any length of time, anyway. The best she could hope for was a kindhearted geek, and she had yet to meet one who held the least bit of appeal.

She was better off sticking with the one thing she knew she was good at: numbers. Numbers could always be counted on. There was no guesswork, no wondering if the results would be worth the effort, no question about how things would turn out. Numbers didn't care if they were gussied up in colors and fancy fonts or set down in plain black and white. Unlike men, numbers were solid and reliable and trustworthy.

She plucked a yellow slip of paper off the top of the stack of receipts in front of her, determined to get her mind back on bookkeeping. She'd been managing the books for the Big Sky Bed & Breakfast since she was fifteen, but she still found it a challenge. Aunt Celeste's unorthodox way of operating kept it that way.

She stared at the receipt in her hand and frowned. Whitehorn Cleaners. Was this a bill for laundering business linens or Aunt Celeste's personal clothing? Lately Aunt Celeste had been even more careless than usual about labeling the receipts. With a sigh, Frannie placed the receipt in the growing stack of items she needed to ask her aunt about and reached for another.

She was inputting information from an itemized grocery list when the bell over the heavy oak front door jangled. Since Summer had said her husband was due any minute, Frannie assumed he'd arrived. "Come on in, Gavin," she called. She heard the door open, but didn't bother to turn around. "Summer's getting ready. She'll be out here in a moment."

"Well, now," said an unfamiliar voice. "I thought summer was already here, seeing as it's the end of June."

It was a low, deep throb of a voice, smoky and unrelentingly masculine. Something about it made the hair on the back of Frannie's neck stand up, as if she'd just entered an electric force field.

She jerked around to find two men standing just inside the doorway. The one on the right was middle-aged and stout, clad in denim overalls, a red plaid shirt and brown work boots. His gray hair was sparse and closely shorn, and he had a face as round and friendly as a pumpkin pie.

But the other one… Frannie tried to swallow, but her mouth was suddenly so dry she felt as if her tongue had melded to the top of her mouth.

The other one… *My, oh, my.*

He was obviously the owner of that seductive voice. Tall, lean, and muscular, he wore jeans and cowboy boots, and held a battered, buff-colored Stetson hat in his hand. Frannie wasn't sure if it was his deep tan or his denim shirt that made his eyes look so blue, but they seemed to jump out of his handsome face like blue flames, blue flames that licked at her very soul. There was a strange heat in his gaze—the heat, Frannie realized with a jolt, of sexual awareness.

He was looking at her in the way a man looks at a woman. Well, of course he was, she thought distractedly—after all, she *was* a woman, and he was most definitely a man. What surprised her was that he was looking at her as if she were a *desirable* woman. His mouth was curved into a small, amused smile, and Frannie realized he was waiting for her to speak.

She started to scramble to her feet, and tipped her chair over in the process. She leaned to pick it up, caught her foot on a chair roller, and toppled into the overturned chair face-first, leaving her bottom in the air.

"Hey, are you all right?" The handsome man quickly rounded the desk and took her arm, helping her pull herself upright.

His hand was warm, and the warmth spread rapidly through her body, causing her cheeks to burn. Frannie smoothed her sweater, embarrassed at her awkwardness. "I, uh, I'm fine. I was, uh, expecting someone else."

"Sorry to disappoint you, ma'am." His low, smoky voice managed to make the word "ma'am" sound like a caress.

His hand was still on her upper arm. Frannie felt as tongue-tied as a schoolgirl. "Oh, I'm not disappointed." The moment she said it, she wanted to bite her tongue. Why did she always manage to say and do the most awkward things whenever she was around a handsome man?

The corners of his mouth curved up further. "Well, good." He dropped his hand and stepped back.

Frannie was certain she'd never met him before, yet something about him seemed strangely familiar. "Do I know you?"

"I don't believe I've had the pleasure. I'm sure I would have remembered."

Frannie gave a wry grin. "Not necessarily. I don't always make such a memorable first impression."

The man laughed, and a fresh tug of attraction pulled at Frannie's chest. Did he look at every woman that way, as if he found her attractive and fascinating? He no doubt did. Most women probably just weren't as susceptible to it as she was. It was probably some kind of subliminal body-language come-on that she ought to know better than to fall for, but she knew no such thing. Whatever he was doing, it was working. Oh, yes, it was definitely working.

She tried to pull her thoughts out of the fog and search her mind for a reason the man looked so familiar. Maybe he was a movie star or a TV actor.

Maybe, she thought as she watched him circle back around the front desk, he was just the man of her dreams. Aunt Celeste believed that dreams were gateways to the soul, that they held clues to both the past and the future.

What on earth was the matter with her? There was no way a man such as this was going to be a part of her future. She was still staring, she realized abruptly.

She pulled her eyes away and tugged at the bottom of her sweater again. "Thanks for the help. Sorry about the klutz attack."

"I'm sorry we startled you."

Frannie was relieved to hear Summer's high heels click on the hardwood floor as she entered the foyer. "Gavin, is that you?" Summer appeared in the doorway, her arms high, her hands behind her neck as she fastened what Frannie recognized as Jasmine's new necklace.

Summer stopped in her tracks, immediately dropping her arms. "Oh, I'm sorry," she said with a smile. "I was expecting my husband." She stepped forward and stuck out her hand. "Welcome to the Big Sky Bed & Breakfast. I'm Summer Nighthawk."

"Nice to meet you, ma'am." The tall handsome man shook her hand. "I'm Austin Parker, and this here's Tommy Deshaw."

Summer shook hands with both men, then cast a quizzical look at the younger one. "Austin Parker—the race car driver?"

The man smiled sheepishly. "Afraid so."

"My husband is one of your biggest fans." Summer's smile widened. "We'd heard you'd bought some land around here."

"Yes, ma'am. The old Givens ranch."

"That place has a huge house. Do you have a large family?"

"No, ma'am. I'm not married."

"No?" Summer gestured to Frannie. "Well, neither is Frannie here."

Frannie longed to crawl under the front desk.

"I take it you two have met?" Summer continued.

"Yes, ma'am. But we hadn't quite gotten around to introductions." He treated Frannie to a blinding smile.

Frannie had no choice but to reach out her hand. "F— Frannie Hannon." Good grief, she could barely say her own name! It was a good thing she'd managed to spit it out before he touched her, because when his large, warm hand closed around hers, the ability to speak deserted her along with all coherent thought. She felt a sense of both relief and loss when he loosened his grip.

She turned and shook hands with Tommy. The older man smiled warmly. "It's a pleasure, ma'am."

"Frannie, Austin Parker is the hottest ticket on the NASCAR circuit," Summer said.

"How...nice."

"Tommy here's the really hot ticket," Austin said, gesturing to his companion. "He's my pit crew chief, so he's the one who really runs the show. The crew's what keeps a driver on the road.''

"We're delighted to have both of you here.'' Summer's smile included both men. "What can we do for you two gentlemen?''

"I'd like to book a room for Tommy for the next few days, if you've got one available.'' Austin shifted his hat to his other hand. "He's going to be overhauling the engine on my car. I intended for him to stay out at my ranch, but I'm havin' the place renovated and all the guest rooms are a wreck. Do you happen to have any vacancies?''

"As a matter of fact, we're nearly empty this evening.'' Summer smiled at Tommy. "We'd be delighted to have you stay with us. Right, Frannie?''

Frannie smiled wanly, edging her way back to the computer. That gleam in Summer's eye meant she was up to her old matchmaking tricks, and Frannie wanted no part of it. Trying to interest Austin in her would be like trying to interest a yacht owner in a rowboat. Turning, Frannie picked up a handful of receipts and lowered herself back into the wooden swivel chair.

"Frannie, would you like to handle the check-in?'' Summer prompted.

Frannie froze. "I—I, uh…oh, gee, I really need to get these numbers into the computer. Since Gavin's not here yet, could you go ahead and take care of it?''

Summer had no choice but to graciously nod. "Why, sure.'' She pulled a large leather book out from under the desk, opened it and angled it toward Tommy. "If you'd just sign in here, Mr. Deshaw.''

The look she shot Frannie told her she was in for a lecture as soon as Summer got her alone. Frannie fervently hoped Gavin showed up before that happened.

* * *

Frannie had no such luck. Austin had no sooner said his goodbyes and Tommy Deshaw headed to his room than Summer grabbed the back of Frannie's chair and spun her around to face her. Frannie could tell from the way her cousin's lips were pressed in a thin tight line that she was thoroughly exasperated.

"What's the big idea?" Summer demanded.

"Of what?"

"Of ignoring the most eligible bachelor to hit Whitehorn since my Gavin, that's what."

"Oh, Summer, a man like that's not going to be interested in the likes of me."

"Not if you turn your back to him and act rude!"

"I wasn't acting rude. I was acting busy. Which, it just so happens, I am."

Frannie was relieved to see Jasmine saunter into the front foyer, wearing a striking black pantsuit. Frannie seized on the opportunity to change the subject. "Jasmine, you look great."

"Thanks. What's going on?"

Summer pointed at Frannie. "A wonderful specimen of manhood just walked in here, and our cuz wouldn't even talk to him."

"I didn't have anything to say!" Frannie protested.

"You don't have to *say* anything, Frannie," Summer said. "You just have to *talk*."

"Oh. Thanks for the clarification," Frannie said dryly.

Jasmine laughed. "You know what she means, Frannie. Make small talk. Be pleasant. Show you're accessible."

"Let him know you're interested," Summer added. "Smile. Flirt."

"That's easy for you two to say. I don't know how to do any of that."

"Well, then, it's high time you learned. Jasmine and I can teach you."

Jasmine nodded vigorously.

"Oh, no." Frannie held up her hands, palms out. "No way. No, thanks."

Jasmine's flawless forehead creased in a frown. "Why not?"

"Because it wouldn't work. Besides, I'd feel like an idiot."

"No, you wouldn't. Not for long, anyway." Jasmine circled the front desk and stopped in front of Frannie, her hands on her hips. "Think about it, Frannie. Isn't it better to feel a little silly for a little while than to feel lonely forever?"

Lonely forever—was that what they thought she was destined to be? A sharp little knife of pain sliced into Frannie's heart. "There are worse things than being lonely," she mumbled.

Such as being humiliated. And heartbroken. And feeling like a pathetic fool.

Summer's dark eyes filled with sympathy. "Just because you had a bad experience with one guy in college is no reason to shy away from all other men for the rest of your life."

It wasn't just a bad experience, Frannie thought, it was an amputation of part of her soul. Joe had not only betrayed her; he'd emotionally maimed her. He'd stripped her of her self-confidence and her ability to trust anyone.

Frannie pushed back her chair and rose, wrapping her arms around herself. "I'm not shying away. I'm just minding my own business, living my own life."

"Frannie, you're practically a recluse," Jasmine said softly.

"I'm not!"

"Yes, you are," Summer affirmed. "You never go to any parties or social events. You go to work at the bank, then you come home and work here. And if an attractive man happens to come within a mile of you, you duck your head and avoid making eye contact."

"And then there's the matter of how you dress," Jasmine added gently. "You're hiding all of your best qualities. You have a great figure, but no one would ever know it under the clothes you wear. You have beautiful eyes, but instead of wearing your contact lenses, you hide behind your glasses. I'd love to have thick, curly hair like yours, but instead of making the most of it, you keep it skinned back in a ponytail or a tight little bun."

Frannie was surprised to find herself blinking back tears. "Sorry I'm such an embarrassment to you."

"Oh, Frannie, that's not what we're saying!" Jasmine stepped forward and embraced her in a hug. "We love you and want you to have all the good things in life, that's all."

"That's right. We want you to be happy." Summer placed a hand on Frannie's back and gave her a consoling pat. "I didn't mean to hurt you. I was just trying to jar a little sense into you, that's all."

Frannie sniffed and wiped her eyes, then pulled away. Summer gave her another pat on the back, then pulled herself onto one edge of the computer workstation. "I don't think you realize it, Frannie, but when it comes to men, you're your own worst enemy. You'll never meet anyone if you don't stop hiding."

"I'm not deliberately hiding. I'm just...I don't know. Being self-protective, maybe." Frannie turned away and stared at the large stone fireplace in the living room across the foyer. She took a ragged breath. "If I had one-tenth of the good looks you two have, things would be different.

But I don't. I don't want to set myself up for rejection again, that's all.''

"You've got everything we've got," Summer said.

"And in some places, more." Jasmine looked down at her own petite chest in such an amusingly wistful way that Frannie had to smile.

"I'm plain as mud," Frannie said bluntly.

"You're not!" Summer said. "You just need a little polishing up."

"That's right." Jasmine nodded. "And attitude."

Frannie gave a tight smile. "Oh, I've got plenty of that."

"Boy, do you ever!" Jasmine grinned. "But that's not the kind of attitude I mean. You need to project more self-assurance."

"Jasmine's right," Summer said. "Your outlook and expectations become a self-fulfilling prophecy. If you think you're unattractive and don't expect anyone to approach you, you're going to act in ways that will make men keep their distance. But if you act confident and look your best and expect men to be attracted to you, that's exactly what will happen."

Frannie wished she could believe them. Something about that race car driver had stirred up longings she'd all but forgotten she could feel. She heaved a sigh. "You make it sound so easy. Too bad it isn't."

"Well, how about giving us a chance to prove that it is?"

If she had any sense, she'd say no right away. But the memory of Austin's touch was too fresh on her mind. "What have you got in mind?" Frannie asked.

Summer grinned. "I just thought of the perfect occasion to prove to you that a makeover of your appearance and attitude can make over your love life."

"And what might that be?" Frannie asked skeptically.

"Yeah, what is it?" Jasmine asked.

Summer paused dramatically. "The Whitehorn Ball. It's the hospital's big annual fund-raiser, and all of the staff is expected to be there. There's this new doctor in radiology. He's single, he doesn't know anyone in town and he doesn't have a date."

Panic welled up in Frannie's chest. "Oh, no. Not a blind date."

Summer raised her hand in a calming gesture. "Just hear me out. The dance is three weeks away. That's plenty of time for Jasmine and me to make you over and give you some pointers."

"Oh, Summer, I don't think this is a good idea...." Frannie began.

"It's not a good idea. It's a *great* one," Jasmine said excitedly. She clasped her hands together. "We could triple date."

"But—"

"But what?"

"But it's a formal dance," Frannie protested.

"So? That makes it all the more fun. We'll turn you into Cinderella for the ball."

"But—" Frannie swallowed around a lump in her throat. "But I was supposed to go to a formal dance with Joe the night after...after..."

"After you found out what a heel he was," Summer finished for her.

Frannie nodded.

Her gaze was soft and warm. "That was what? Five years ago?"

"Six."

Summer gently placed her hands on Frannie's shoulders. "Can you look me straight in the eye and honestly tell me you don't ever want to go to a formal dance again the rest of your life?''

Did she really want to limit her life in that way? Frannie sighed. "I guess not."

"Well, then, it's high time you got back in the saddle."

"But the idea makes me so—so *uncomfortable*."

"Frannie, sometimes we have to move outside our comfort zone in order to move forward. We have to face our fears in order to get over them." Summer's tone was calm and authoritative, the tone that Frannie secretly called her doctor's voice. "This is a great opportunity for you to put the past behind you, once and for all, and start a new chapter in your life."

Jasmine nodded earnestly.

"Besides," Summer continued, "what have you got to lose? It's just one night out of your life. For just one night, try things our way. If you don't like the results, you can always go back to the way things are now."

A car pulled up in the drive and killed its engine. The hum of another engine rapidly followed. A wave of relief washed through Frannie. "Sounds like both of your dates are here. Too bad we'll have to discontinue this fascinating discussion."

Summer rose and straightened her skirt, her lips curved in a smile. "Don't worry. We'll continue it later. In the meantime, will you promise to just think about it?"

It would be a disaster. She was awful at making small talk. She would make a fool of herself. She was nuts to even consider it.

But she *was* considering it. Heaven help her, she was. Meeting that race car driver had made her realize how much she longed for male companionship. More than anything, she wanted a husband and a family.

Her cousins were right, Frannie thought ruefully. She

wasn't likely to meet any prospective mates sitting at home
in front of the computer.

Frannie sighed and reluctantly nodded. "Okay. I'll think
about it."

Two

Frannie thought of little else for the rest of the evening. She was still thinking about it the next morning when she strode into the large sun-filled kitchen, where Aunt Celeste was fussing over the stove.

Frannie smoothed a wayward strand of hair back into the tight bun she'd coiled at her crown, thinking how different her own drab coloring was from her vivid aunt's. A natural redhead, Celeste had russet hair that became progressively brighter over the years as she fought off the signs of aging. Her current shade was called Autumn Flame, and she'd evidently taken the theme to heart, because she was dressed in a loose yellow shirt over a filmy orange and yellow gypsy-style skirt.

"Ouch!" Celeste dropped a heavy skillet back onto the stove with a loud clatter, then stuck her index finger into her mouth and dashed to the sink, her bangle bracelets jangling.

Frannie hurried forward. "Are you all right?"

Celeste flipped on the faucet and stuck her right hand under the running water. "Depends on your definition of 'all right.' That's the second time I've burned myself this morning, and the third skillet of scrambled eggs I've nearly ruined."

"Where's Jasmine?" Jasmine normally did all the cooking at the B and B.

"That nice young man she went out with last night came

by and wanted to take her fishing this morning,'' Celeste said. ''I told her to go ahead, that I'd enjoy taking a turn in the kitchen. I didn't know I was going to be all thumbs this morning.''

Frannie frowned. Aunt Celeste might be less than careful when it came to bookkeeping and paperwork, but she was usually the very picture of efficiency in the kitchen. Celeste's personality was as warm as her hair color, and she was just as nurturing as she was warm. She loved cooking and baking, and was as comfortable around the stove as Frannie was around the computer.

Frannie stepped closer. Her aunt's complexion seemed paler than usual this morning, and the delicate skin under her eyes was etched with deep blue shadows.

''Are you feeling ill?''

Celeste brushed a strand of hair away from her forehead with her left hand and sighed. ''I'm fine, dear. Just tired. I didn't sleep well again last night. I kept having those awful dreams.''

Celeste had been plagued by nightmares for the past two weeks. All of them involved members of her family, and most of them centered on her sister, Blanche. In one particularly vivid dream, Blanche had warned that the past was about to rise up and greet her. She'd also cautioned Celeste be careful to make the right choices.

''Have you had any more dreams about Blanche?'' Frannie asked.

''All of them seem to involve her.'' Celeste stared out the kitchen window at the forest. ''A couple of them last night were about my brother, Jeremiah. He was angry— horribly angry—but I don't know why or at whom or what was going on. Another time I woke up with my heart racing, and I'd been dreaming about Blanche. I could see her in the distance.''

Celeste shut off the faucet and reached for a paper towel. "She was trying to tell me something, but for the life of me, I couldn't understand what it was. She was too far away. I could see her lips moving, but I couldn't hear what she was saying."

Frannie reached for a clean cloth and filled it with ice. She gave it to her aunt. "You've been having a lot of bad dreams lately."

Celeste put the ice pack on her injured finger. "Just about every night. I'm sure it's a sign."

"Of what?"

"I don't know. Blanche keeps trying to tell me something. I keep thinking back to the dream where she told me the past was about to rise up. Something's about to happen. And whatever it is, it's important."

Celeste was a deeply spiritual person, but she harbored some odd notions about dreams and ghosts and the afterlife. She'd lived in Louisiana for a year with her late husband, and she'd brought back some strange beliefs from the bayou.

"Sometimes a dream is just a dream," Frannie commented.

"And sometimes it's not." Celeste shook her head. "You know, dreams are nothing to dismiss lightly. Sometimes they contain messages from the other side. The problem is, the messages are often hard to read." Celeste inspected her finger. "They're like smoke signals—they can drift away before you get a chance to understand them."

An acrid odor reached Frannie's nose. She sniffed, then looked at Celeste in alarm. "Speaking of smoke, is something burning?"

"Oh, dear!" Celeste dashed across the kitchen, grabbed an oven mitt and yanked open the oven door, then reached inside. "Ouch!" she exclaimed, waving her hand.

"Did you burn yourself again?"

"Yes, dadblast it! Frannie, come and take these cinnamon rolls out of the oven before they burn to a crisp."

Frannie patted her aunt's back. "Why don't you go sit down and relax? I'll get breakfast for our guests this morning. We only have three, don't we? Mr. Deshaw and that nice couple from Washington?"

"Four. Mr. Deshaw's friend came by to pick him up, and I invited him to stay for breakfast. I believe Mr. Deshaw said he's a race car driver, of all things."

Frannie's heart unaccountably picked up speed. She pulled on the oven mitt her aunt had abandoned and retrieved the burned rolls from the oven.

"The couple ate an hour ago. They're out on the lake in the rowboat, fishing."

"Well, then, I'll get breakfast for the gentlemen."

"Why, thank you, dear." Celeste smiled at her niece. "I believe I'll take you up on that offer."

"Are you serving breakfast on the back porch?"

Celeste nodded. "It was too beautiful a morning to stay inside. Since the rolls are burned, why don't you make some toast? You can serve it with the scrambled eggs. I made enough to serve an army."

Celeste made her way upstairs and Frannie bustled around the kitchen. In a matter of minutes she'd prepared two attractive plates garnished with sliced cantaloupe and fresh strawberries. She loaded them onto an antique silver tray, her stomach fluttering nervously. Taking a deep breath, she headed out of the kitchen, through the den and onto the screened-in back porch.

The porch overlooked Blue Mirror Lake and Frannie usually found the view breathtaking, but she was too distracted by the sight of the tall, handsome man to notice the scenery this morning. Austin was settled in a rustic twig chair at a wooden table, deep in conversation with Tommy, and he looked even more handsome than she remembered. Her pulse fluttered wildly when he looked up at her and smiled.

He rose as she approached the table. "Good mornin'. May I help you with that?" He gestured toward the tray.

Frannie hesitated, completely flustered. She wasn't accustomed to guests standing and offering to help when she tried to serve them. "Oh, no. Please take your seat." She lifted a hand from the tray and gestured toward his chair.

She immediately knew she'd made a mistake. The tray tipped and the plates slid. She watched in horror as they headed toward him, as if in slow motion. Trying to correct the slant of the tray, she jerked it upward, but overcompensated.

"Oh, no!" Frannie gasped. A plate of scrambled eggs hit Austin full in the face, then landed back on the tray with a loud clatter.

Frannie stared, too aghast to move. Scrambled eggs dripped from his forehead, from his eyebrows, from his nose. "Oh, I'm so sorry!"

Austin ran his fingers across his eyes, clearing a path through the yellow blobs. Setting the tray quickly on the table, Frannie grabbed a blue cloth napkin and handed it to him. He used it like a washcloth, completely covering his face and wiping the egg away.

Frannie watched helplessly, dying a thousand deaths. "I'm so very, very sorry! Are you all right?"

He pulled the napkin away and opened his eyes. "Fine." Turning the napkin, he took another swab at his forehead. The corners of his mouth turned up in a wry grin.

"It's not the first time I've had egg on my face, is it, Tommy?"

The large man across the table slapped his knee and chortled. "No, sirree. But usually you're the one that put it there."

"I'm *so* sorry," Frannie repeated. She grabbed another napkin and began dabbing at his shirt. His chest beneath the blue cotton knit was disconcertingly hard and warm. "Oh, dear, you've got it on your jeans, too." She lifted the napkin, ready to attack his crotch, then froze as she realized what she was about to do.

His hand closed over hers, stopping her. The heat from his hand radiated up her arm, through her shoulder and straight through her chest. She stared up into blue, blue eyes.

His grin was blinding. "I think I'd better take over the clean-up operation."

"I'm so sorry," she repeated, her voice a low, mortified whisper.

"It's all right. It's no big deal." Releasing her hand, he took the napkin from her and brushed off his lap. "Looks like you took a bit of a hit yourself." He reached out and brushed a blob of egg from her cheek.

The intimacy of the touch sent a shock wave curling through her. She jumped away as if he'd gigged her with a cattle prod, only to immediately realize the absurdity of her reaction.

"I didn't mean to startle you."

"You didn't," she lied.

"Well, there's a little more egg right…" He reached out his hand again. Once more she reflexively jumped back. Something about this man's touch made her feel hot and bothered and breathless.

"I'm, uh, ticklish," she lamely explained, vigorously rubbing her cheeks. "Is my face clean now?"

He seemed to be looking at something over her head. He

pulled his eyes down to meet her gaze. "Your face? Uh, yeah."

"Good. Well, I'll...I'll go fix you another plate, then come back and clean all this up."

She fled to the kitchen, feeling as awkward as a three-legged chair. Quickly she made more toast, sliced more melon and plated up two more servings of eggs.

"Here you go," she said a few minutes later as she hurried back to the porch. She set down his breakfast and backed away from the table, unreasonably worried about getting too close to Austin. "I'll just go get a broom and dustpan and—" She stopped short and stared at the spotless wooden floor. "You cleaned it all up!"

Austin shrugged. "We found a roll of paper towels by the serving bar in the corner."

Frannie frowned in dismay. "But you're guests, and I'm the one who made the mess, and—"

Austin waved away her objections. "We're used to cleanin' up crank cases and oil pan spills. This was nothing."

"That's right." Tommy smiled, his widely spaced teeth giving his round face the appearance of a friendly jack-o'-lantern.

But it was Austin's amused expression that held her gaze. He was looking at her in such a strange way, as if he found her intensely interesting.

Frannie felt her pulse race. She was used to being ignored by men, not treated as an object of endless fascination—especially not by the likes of Austin Parker. She was drab and colorless and average. She certainly wasn't dressed to rate any undue attention; she was just wearing a faded brown sweatshirt and loose-fitting khakis. She wasn't wearing any makeup, her hair was wound in a bun at her crown, and her glasses were firmly in place on top of her nose. Austin's intense scrutiny rattled her down to her toenails.

"Well, uh, thanks for the help. Can I get you anything else?"

"I think we're all set."

She beat a hasty retreat to the kitchen, where she tried to drown out her clamoring thoughts by loading the dishwasher and vigorously mopping the floor. She was nearly finished when Austin stuck his head inside the door fifteen minutes later. "Breakfast was delicious. Thanks. And give my thanks to your aunt."

She heard the men's footsteps retreat down the hall, then heard the front door close behind them. She leaned against the kitchen wall and inhaled a deep breath, her hand on her stomach.

Thank goodness they were gone. Austin made her feel as if her lungs were too small to draw enough air. And the way he looked at her! His gaze went so...so *deep,* as if he were seeing things in her that no one else had ever seen.

"You're being ridiculous," she muttered to herself. Instead of standing around mooning over an unattainable man, she needed to march herself back to the computer and finish the bookkeeping. She started through the dining room on her way to do just that, then jerked to a halt as she caught sight of her reflection in the mirrored china cabinet.

"Oh, dear," she murmured.

There in the mirror, staring back at her from between plates of flowered Franciscan china, was the reason Austin had regarded her with such fascination: a giant glob of scrambled egg was perched atop her head like a yellow rubber tiara, supported by the bun she'd pulled her hair into that morning.

"Great. Just great."

Striding back into the kitchen, she held her head over the

sink and dislodged the enormous lump of egg. She pulled a paper towel off the holder and rubbed her hair, heaving a sigh of disgust. Austin was the sexiest man she'd ever set eyes on, and what did she do? She acted like a hopelessly tongue-tied klutz, so skittish that the poor guy didn't dare tell her that the top of her head looked the inside of an egg salad sandwich.

Summer and Jasmine would never have been behaved so clumsily. They would have known how to talk and behave and flirt. Summer and Jasmine never would have thrown a plate of eggs in a guest's face in the first place, and they certainly wouldn't have ended up walking around all morning looking as if an airborne goose had just used them for target practice.

Maybe she should take them up on their offer to make her over. She had no expectations of being as glamorous as her cousins, but maybe, just maybe, she could gain a little of their self-assurance. Maybe Summer was right. Maybe if she quit feeling like such a nerd, she'd stop acting like one.

"What the heck," she muttered, heading upstairs to wash her hair for the second time that day. It was worth a try. When Jasmine got home, Frannie would tell her she'd agreed to the makeover.

Frannie was still burning with mortification over the egg incident when the bell over the front door jangled thirty minutes later. She looked up from the computer to see a tall man in a tan uniform stroll into the foyer, accompanied by an attractive blond woman dressed in jeans and a white cotton shirt with a large black tote bag over her shoulder.

Frannie rose from her seat and smiled. "Sheriff Rawlings, good morning!"

Rafe Rawlings's rugged face creased in a friendly smile.

"Good mornin', Frannie. I'd like you to meet my new detective, Gretchen Neal."

Frannie stepped forward and shook the blonde's hand. "Nice to meet you." The woman's handshake was as sturdy as her tall, athletic build. With her milky skin, light blond hair and blue eyes, she reminded Frannie of the movie star Gwyneth Paltrow.

"Gretchen just moved here from Elk Springs," Sheriff Rawlings said. "But before that, she worked on the police force in one of the toughest neighborhoods in Miami. We're lucky to have someone with her experience join our force."

"We sure are. Can I offer you two breakfast?"

"No, thanks. I'm afraid we're here on business today, Frannie."

Frannie raised her brows in surprise.

Rafe's dark eyes grew serious. "Gretchen's heading up the investigation into Raven Hunter's death. I need someone who can devote one hundred percent of their time to the case, and Gretchen's got the background to handle it."

"I...see." Although she didn't. Not really. That still didn't explain why they were here on a Sunday morning. "Do you have any other suspects? Other than Uncle Jeremiah?"

"No one." The sheriff adjusted his holster, his expression uneasy. He cleared his throat. "We're still investigating your uncle."

Frannie nodded slowly. Her mother's brother had died before Frannie was old enough to remember him, but she'd heard plenty of tales about him. According to her mother, Jeremiah had been cold-hearted, bigotted and controlling. Based on what she'd heard about him, Frannie wasn't at all surprised that he was a suspect. Jeremiah's hatred of Raven Hunter was well known.

"We'd like to talk to your mom and your aunt again, to

see if they remember anything else about the night Raven disappeared,'' Rafe said gently.

"I'm afraid Mom's in Minnesota. Dad's mother just had hip replacement surgery, and so Mom and Dad went to stay with her for a while while she recovers."

"When will they get back?" Gretchen asked, pulling a small notebook out of her tote bag.

"I don't know exactly. But I can give you a phone number where you can reach them."

"Thanks. I can take her statement over the phone."

Rafe glanced at Gretchen. "And if need be, we can get the police in Minnesota to take a deposition from them."

Frannie rounded the front desk, flipped through a Rolodex file and located the number. She wrote it on a slip of white paper. "Here it is." She handed the number to Gretchen. "I'm afraid Mom won't be much help to you, though. As she told Rafe, she was in Bozeman when Raven disappeared."

Gretchen tucked the number into a pocket of her folder. "Well, we'll give her a call and get an official statement."

"What about Celeste?" the sheriff asked, leaning on the front desk. "Is she around?"

"Yes. She's upstairs, resting."

Rafe's brow pulled together. "I thought she was always up at the crack of dawn."

"She usually is. But she hasn't been herself lately. She hasn't slept well for the last couple of weeks."

The sheriff glanced at Gretchen. "That's about how long it's been since we found Raven's skeleton."

Gretchen nodded, then turned to Frannie. "Could I talk to your aunt?"

"Of course." Frannie motioned toward to the large silver coffee urn that sat on a sideboard in the hall, next to a stack of cups, spoons and cloth napkins. They always kept it filled in the mornings for the convenience of their guests. "Help yourselves to some coffee. I'll go get her and we'll join you in the living room."

Frannie climbed the winding staircase, headed down the long hall, then turned right at the end, where it intersected a shorter hallway. She stopped at the second door and knocked softly. "Aunt Celeste?"

"Come in, dear."

She found Celeste sitting in a rocker by the window, her eyes closed. Frannie paused. She was used to seeing her aunt bustling around the house, full of energy and vitality, tending to everyone else's needs. It was disturbing, seeing her so still in the middle of the day.

"Aunt Celeste?" She hesitantly stepped into the room, closing the door behind her. "Rafe and a new detective are here. They want to ask you some more questions about the night Raven disappeared."

Celeste opened her eyes and gave a long, deep sigh that sounded as if it came from the depths of her soul. "Fine. I'll talk to them." She got up from the rocker. "But I've already told Rafe what I know."

The forlorn, troubled look on Celeste's face touched Frannie's heart.

At least Rafe was an old family friend, she thought as she followed her aunt downstairs. That should make the interview process easier on Celeste.

The sheriff stood as they entered the room.

Celeste mustered a warm, hospitable smile and kissed him on the cheek. "Hello, Rafe, dear. It's good to see you again."

"It's a pleasure to see you, too, ma'am."

"How are your lovely wife and child?"

The lawman's face softened. "Raeanne's just fine. And Skye keeps us plenty busy."

Celeste smiled. "I bet she does. You'll have to bring her by."

"I'll do that." Rafe turned and gestured to Gretchen. "Celeste, I'd like you to meet Gretchen Neal, my newest detective. Gretchen, this is Celeste Monroe."

Celeste nodded. "It's a pleasure." She shook Gretchen's hand, then waved her palm toward one of two mission-style sofas that faced each other in front of the massive stone fireplace. "Please have a seat."

Rafe and Gretchen lowered themselves onto one of the sofas. Frannie sat beside Celeste on the opposite one, across the heavy oak coffee table.

Rafe leaned forward, resting his forearms on his thighs. "I suppose Frannie told you I've put Gretchen in charge of the investigation into Raven Hunter's death."

"Yes."

"I'm sorry, Celeste, but she'd like to ask you some questions you and I have already discussed."

Gretchen pulled a small tape recorder out of her black leather tote bag. "Do you mind if I record our conversation?"

Celeste looked questioningly at Frannie, her green eyes round. Frannie nodded encouragingly.

"I—I suppose that would be all right," Celeste conceded.

Gretchen punched a button on the machine and placed it on the coffee table, then opened her notebook and pulled out a pen. "Let's start at the beginning, then, Mrs. Monroe. Would you please describe the relationship between your brother Jeremiah and Raven Hunter?"

Celeste eyed her warily. "What do you mean?"

"Were they friendly? Did they get along?"

Celeste wound her fingers together in her lap and stared down at them. "No. Not at all."

"Why not?"

Celeste took a deep breath and exhaled it in a sigh. "My sister Blanche was in love with Raven. She wanted to marry him, but Jeremiah wouldn't hear of it."

"Why not?"

"Well..." Celeste looked at Rafe pleadingly. "I hate to speak ill of the dead. We don't know if they can hear us."

Rafe's eyes were sympathetic, but his tone was firm. "You need to tell us everything you know, Celeste. We need all of the facts."

Celeste nodded, her lips pressed tightly together. She took another deep breath. "Well, I'm afraid Jeremiah was something of a racist. He didn't want a Kincaid from our side of the family to marry an Indian. And Raven, of course, was Cheyenne."

"Did Raven and Jeremiah have an argument about it?"

"Oh, many. Jeremiah forbade Blanche to see Raven."

"Did Blanche routinely do what Jeremiah told her to do?"

"Oh, yes, indeed. We all did—me, Blanche, and Yvette. After our parents died, Jeremiah ran the family. He was very strong-willed."

"You and your sisters lived with Jeremiah at that time?"

"Yes. In the old house."

Rafe turned to Gretchen. "Garrett's Kincaid's place now. It was boarded up for years until he moved in a couple years ago."

Gretchen jotted the information down in her notebook, then looked at Celeste. "Did your brother own a gun, Mrs. Monroe?"

Celeste's fingers tensed in her lap. "Yes. He had a whole collection."

"Did he have a pistol in his gun collection?"

"Several."

"Where did he keep that gun collection?"

"In his study. He had a glass case built into the wall for it. He was very proud of it."

"What happened to those guns?"

"I—I don't know. I imagine they're all still in the house."

Gretchen and Rafe exchanged another look, and Gretchen scribbled another notation. At length she looked back up at Celeste. "I'd like to get back to the topic of Blanche and Raven. Did Blanche follow Jeremiah's orders to stay away from Raven?"

The older woman stared down at her hands. "No." She shifted uneasily and plucked at the fabric of her skirt. "She continued to see him. And she became pregnant with his child." Her eyes took on a gentler look. "With Summer."

"What was Jeremiah's reaction to that?"

"Oh, my." Celeste's fingers twisted and untwisted the fabric. Her forehead creased in a frown. "Oh, dear. I—I really don't remember. I know he was upset. I know Blanche and Raven planned to run away and elope. But my...my memory about those days is all kind of a blur."

"Do you remember when Blanche told him she was pregnant?"

Celeste shook her head. "Blanche didn't want to tell him. She kept putting it off. But as time went on, it became impossible to hide her condition. And when Jeremiah found out, he—" Celeste broke off.

"He what?"

Celeste pressed the back of her hand to her forehead. "I'm not really sure. Everything about that time gets all jumbled up in my mind."

Gretchen leaned forward. "This is really important, Mrs. Monroe."

"I—I'm afraid I'm getting a terrible headache. Everything is all mixed up and confused."

"Take your time, Celeste," Rafe said soothingly. "Do you remember anything at all about that time?"

Celeste leaned her head back against the sofa and wound the fabric of her skirt around her index finger. "Let me see... Well, I remember Summer's birth. I was there, you know, when Blanche gave birth. And I was there when she died of complications, a week afterward." Celeste grew silent. "I promised her that Yvette and I would raise her baby. Jeremiah didn't want us to, but we did."

"You and Yvette did a fine job of that," Rafe said softly.

Celeste smiled. "We did, didn't we?"

"Yes, indeed. And I'm sure Gavin agrees." Rafe returned her grin. After a companionable silence, he pressed forward. "Do you remember anything about Jeremiah's reaction to Blanche's pregnancy?"

"No. But I remember something Blanche told me about it after Raven was gone."

"What?" Gretchen took over the questioning.

"She said that Jeremiah tried to pay Raven to leave town."

"Did she think Raven took the money and left?"

"Oh, no. Raven had told her about the offer. He said at first he thought it would be best if he accepted it—that Blanche and the baby would have a better life without him. But when push came to shove, he couldn't do it. He couldn't break Blanche's heart like that. He loved her— everyone knew that. He told her he was going to give back the money...."

"So he'd taken the money?" Gretchen asked.

Celeste massaged her right temple. Her eyes looked dazed and confused, and her face had grown pale. "I—I guess. I don't know. I—I really can't remember."

Gretchen glanced at the sheriff.

"Do you remember the night Raven disappeared?" Rafe asked.

Celeste shook her head.

"When was the last time you saw Raven?" Gretchen asked.

"I—I don't know. I'm all confused. And my head…" Celeste pressed her palm against her forehead.

Frannie noted with alarm that Celeste's hand was trembling. She put an arm around the older woman. "She hasn't been sleeping well," she said apologetically to Rafe and Gretchen. "I think she needs to go back upstairs and lie down."

"Yes. I think I should. I—I'm sorry I can't be more help," Celeste said weakly.

Gretchen and Rafe exchanged a meaningful glance, then both simultaneously rose from the sofa. Celeste and Frannie rose, as well.

"Thank you for your time, Mrs. Monroe," Gretchen said. "I hope you get to feeling better."

"Me, too." Rafe studied the older woman, his dark eyes thoughtful. "Give me a call if you remember anything you think might help us, all right?"

"I will."

"I'll see our visitors out, Aunt Celeste," Frannie said. "You go on upstairs."

"All right. Goodbye." Celeste shuffled from the room, looking old and wan.

Rafe gazed after her for a long moment, then turned to Frannie. "Thanks for the coffee."

"You're more than welcome." Frannie smiled at Gretchen. "It was nice meeting you, Gretchen."

"Nice meeting you, too."

"Good luck with your investigation."

"Thanks. With a thirty-year-old murder case, we're likely to need it." Gretchen tucked her pen and notebook into her tote bag, then looked at Frannie. "Has your aunt ever told you anything about that night?"

Frannie shook her head. "She never talks about Jeremiah."

"Doesn't that strike you as odd?"

Frannie lifted her shoulders. "Celeste is very superstitious. She used to live in Baton Rouge, and she picked up a lot of Cajun beliefs about spirits and such. She's probably afraid Jeremiah will hear her talking about him. My mom said all of them were afraid of Jeremiah. He evidently had quite a temper."

"Hmm," Gretchen murmured. "Well, I'm sorry if we upset your aunt."

Rafe followed the detective out the front door, then paused on the porch. He turned to Frannie. "Have a good day. And thanks for your time."

"Any time."

The sheriff paused, his hand on the door. "We'll probably need to come back and question Celeste again."

"I understand."

Frannie leaned against the door as soon as she closed it behind the sheriff. Aunt Celeste was one of the kindest, warmest, most helpful women she'd ever known. She was a natural-born nurturer, and she'd always been open and straightforward.

Her reluctance to talk about Jeremiah and her inability to recall the events surrounding Raven's death struck Frannie as highly unusual. The sheriff and his new investigator seemed to think so, too. There was more to the story than Celeste was telling, and Frannie couldn't help but wonder what it was.

Three

Frannie looked up from a stack of loan applications late the next morning to see a familiar figure in a white physician's coat approach her desk at the Whitehorn Savings and Loan. "Summer! What brings you here?"

"You do." Summer sat in the armchair across from the desk and grinned at her cousin. "Jasmine tells me you've agreed to let us give you a makeover."

Frannie shifted uneasily in her desk chair. She'd told Jasmine yesterday that she'd go along with Summer's plan, but now she was having second thoughts. "Well, I've been thinking about that, and—"

"Oh, no," Summer broke in, lifting her hands in a stop gesture. "We're not going to let you back out now. I've already told Kyle that his date with you is confirmed."

"Confirmed!" Frannie's eyebrows flew up. "What do you mean, confirmed?"

Summer's mouth curved into a small smile. "Gavin and I ran into Kyle at the country club Saturday night, and I asked if he'd be interested in having me fix him up with you for the dance. He seemed quite eager."

Probably because he thinks I look like you. Frannie eyed her cousin suspiciously. "Saturday night? But how did you know I'd agree?"

Summer didn't even pretend to look apologetic. "I didn't." She reached into her pocket and pulled out a newspaper clipping. "Anyway, here's your first assignment."

"Assignment?"

Summer nodded. "Jasmine and I are going to give you assignments, and you're going to follow them exactly."

Oh, dear, what had she let herself in for? Summer's take-charge attitude and sense of initiative had served her well—it had helped her work her way through medical school, and she'd used it to see her husband through a difficult episode when he'd been falsely accused of a crime—but sometimes Summer could make Frannie feel as if she'd been hit by a steamroller. She eyed her cousin warily. "What kind of assignments?"

Summer handed Frannie the clipping. Frannie glanced down at it, then looked up quizzically. "This is an ad for Kiss of Dew makeup and skin care products."

Summer nodded. "A representative is giving free facials and makeup lessons at Kaylor's Drug Store today. I want you to go on your lunch hour."

Summer read the clipping more closely. "It says you have to call and schedule an appointment."

"I've already done it for you. I know you take a late lunch, so your appointment is set for one."

"Summer, I usually eat *lunch* on my lunch hour."

"As a physician, I'm fully aware of your nutritional needs." Summer took out a packaged sandwich from her purse. "That's why I brought you this from the hospital vending machine."

Frannie sighed as Summer set the sandwich on her desk. "You're a real piece of work, Summer. You know that, don't you?"

Summer flashed a blinding smile. "So I hear." She glanced at her watch and rose from the chair. "I have to get to the clinic. I'll stop by the Big Sky on my way home this evening to see how your makeup looks." She hoisted her large purse on her shoulder and raised a hand as she walked away. "Ta-ta!"

Frannie watched her go, a sinking feeling in her stomach. Why had she ever agreed to this silly plan? She'd be better off taking an assertiveness training class—or lessons in basket weaving or tea cozy knitting or trapeze flying. Then, at least, she'd stand a ghost of a chance of succeeding.

"We need the smoothest skin possible under our foundation, so we're going to start with this lovely kiwi avocado skin mask."

The Kiss of Dew cosmetics representative evidently spoke of everything in terms of "we." She'd already told Frannie that "we" had beautiful skin. All the same, she'd spent the past five minutes preparing it for a beautifying skin treatment.

Frannie winced as the stocky middle-aged woman poured a mound of green slime into her palm and picked up a cotton ball. "Is this really necessary?"

The heavily made-up lady nodded, jiggling her well-powdered multiple chins. "Oh, yes. Absolutely. Why, it's part of our Essential Exfolliants and Emollients Kiss Kollection."

Frannie glanced at the bottle and wondered if it was merely a coincidence that the initials spelled out EEEKK. That was certainly her reaction to the prospect of having the green goo slathered all over her face.

Especially in such a public setting, Frannie thought morosely. Right in the drugstore window.

Oh, well. Frannie had already endured having her face cleaned and swabbed with two different potions while passersby stopped and gawked. Wearing the green goop couldn't be too much more humiliating. Folding her arm under the black cosmetics cape, she closed her eyes and resigned herself to the inevitable.

The woman began dabbing the cold, gooey substance on her face. "There. Doesn't that feel refreshing?"

It felt like having a mixture of gelatin and undiluted pea soup globbed on her skin. Frannie pulled her lips into an expression simulating a smile and tried not to cringe as the woman smeared the thick paste across her forehead, over her nose, on her cheeks and down her chin.

"There! We're all done." The woman held a mirror up to Frannie's face.

She looked as if she'd just stepped off a space shuttle from Mars. The only parts of her face that weren't vivid green were her eyelids and her lips.

"Now all we have to do is sit and wait fifteen minutes while the mask works its magic," the woman said perkily, batting her false eyelashes. "Then we'll sponge it off and apply your makeup."

Great. Fifteen minutes of sitting in the front window of Kaylor's, looking like Swamp Thing. The only good thing about it was that nobody would be likely to recognize her under all that gunk.

Frannie pulled on her eyeglasses and stared out at Main Street, noting that there seemed to be more traffic than usual. Three yellow dump trucks cruised slowly past in single file, heading toward the resort and casino construction site.

She was following their progress when a small black-and-white object on the sidewalk across the street caught her eye. It was a dog, Frannie realized—an adorable, tiny dog with a puglike face and long, fluffy hair, probably a Shih Tzu. As Frannie watched in horror, the little dog wandered into the street and narrowly missed being hit by a passing blue van. The animal headed back to the curb, but a white Chevy cruised by, forcing the dog into the center of the road. Turning, the little dog skulked down the yellow line in the middle of the street, its tail tucked between its legs.

Frannie tensed. The dog was in front of the drugstore window now, directly in her line of vision. Judging from the rhinestone-studded collar and red bow, it was obviously someone's pampered pet.

The little animal timidly started across the street again, heading right into the path of a red sports coupe. Frannie gasped as the driver swerved and honked. She didn't realize she'd shut her eyes until she opened them a second later to see the little dog cowering in the street, its tail tucked, as the red car zoomed past.

Before she had time to consider her actions, Frannie flew off the stool, dashed through the drugstore and ran out the door. She stood on the sidewalk for a second, scanning the street for the little dog, then spotted it standing in the middle of the eastbound lane. The creature's big brown eyes gazed at her pleadingly as it cringed in the road, directly in the path of a sleek black Jaguar rapidly barreling toward it.

"Stop!" Frannie yelled, waving her arms and stepping toward the road. The car showed no signs of slowing. The driver honked, but continued to speed toward the little dog.

"Don't hit the dog!" Frannie screamed. The driver either didn't hear or didn't care.

There was no time to waste. Frannie dashed into the street, the black plastic cape flapping wildly around her. She threw herself headlong at the little dog, clutched it to her chest and rolled onto the pavement, praying she was rolling out of harm's way.

She heard the squeal of brakes and smelled the burn of rubber. When she opened her eyes, she was facedown on the pavement, so close to the concrete that the pebbles in it looked like boulders.

She slowly lifted her gaze to see the bumper of the Jaguar less than a foot away. It was a good thing she was lying down. Otherwise, she surely would have fainted.

The driver's door jerked open, and an angry man climbed out. His face was so mottled with rage that it took her moment realize that it was Lyle Brooks, the owner of the Whitehorn-based construction company building the resort and casino.

"What the hell do you think you're doing, running in front of my car like that?" Lyle demanded.

Frannie gazed down at the black and white dog wriggling in her arms. "I was saving this dog."

"To hell with the dog! He's not big enough to have caused any damage to my car. You, on the other hand, are a different story. Do you have any idea what it would have done to my insurance premiums to have an accident like that?"

Frannie gasped. She knew who Lyle was—his picture had been in all the papers when he won the contract for the casino and resort—but she'd never met him before, even though he was a distant Kincaid cousin. She'd heard he was callous and hard-hearted, but she'd always figured the stories were exaggerated. She was beginning to think differently.

"Your insurance premiums wouldn't have been nearly as high as your court costs and bail bond," said a low male voice from behind her, a familiar smoky voice, full of unfamiliar, barely controlled anger. "I saw the whole thing, and it looked to me like you were speeding. And I'd testify to that in a court of law."

Frannie turned to see Austin Parker behind her, his eyes narrowed and his lips set in a hard, ungiving line.

* * *

The woman on the pavement stared up at him, her strangely familiar hazel eyes huge in her bright green face. Under any other circumstances Austin was sure he'd be amused, but what he'd just witnessed left him too shaken and angry to feel any sense of humor.

"Are you all right?" he asked.

"Yes."

He reached down a hand and helped her up. The moment he touched her, he knew why she looked familiar. This was the woman from the bed-and-breakfast—the one who'd fallen over her chair when he first met her, then spilled egg all over both of them. He peered at her curiously.

"Frannie?"

"Yes?"

How the devil had her face gotten in that condition? "You didn't just try to serve someone something green, did you?"

She looked at him blankly, then pulled her hand away to get a better grip on the dog, who was licking her cheek with gusto. Comprehension dawned. "Oh. N-no. I was having a facial."

Austin turned back toward the driver of the Jaguar, a feeling of distaste rising in his throat. Even if he hadn't just seen the man nearly run down a helpless animal with what looked like cold-blooded deliberation, he was certain he would have disliked him on sight. His lips were set in what looked like perpetual disdain, and he had a foppish, overly groomed look that spoke of self-absorption. His perfectly combed hair was so heavily moussed and gelled that the wind lifted it as a single unit. He wore a Rolex watch on his left wrist and a pinky ring on each hand. A gold chain was visible at the open neck of his custom-made shirt.

Austin looked him dead in the eye. "Looked to me like you were aiming for that dog."

"It had no business being on the street." Lyle glared at Frannie. "And the same goes for you."

Austin took a menacing step forward. "Well, now, I believe you have that all wrong. Frannie here has as much right as anyone to be anywhere she pleases. You're the one who was out of line. You owe Frannie an apology, and I'd like to hear you make it."

"I'll do no such thing. I had the right of way. I was driving along, minding my own business, when she recklessly threw herself in front of my car."

"There's no such thing as 'your own business' when you're behind the wheel of a car," Austin said sharply.

The man stared at him coldly. "I know who you are. You're that racing hotshot that just moved here, aren't you?" He pulled himself up to his full height, but Austin still towered over him. The man puffed out his chest and scowled. "Maybe you don't know who you're dealing with here. I'm Lyle Brooks, the owner of one of the biggest construction companies in Montana, and I don't need lessons in how to drive a car."

Austin glared at the man. "Well, then, maybe you need lessons in how to read street signs, because you were clearly exceeding the speed limit. You were racing down Main Street as if it were the final lap at Winslow, and I'll have no problem telling that to the police."

"The police?" Lyle's eyebrows shot up. His brow furrowed, and his eyes widened in apprehension. "Hey, now, there wasn't an accident. There's no reason to get the law involved."

Austin took another step forward, enjoying the fact that it forced Lyle to back up. "Not if you apologize to Miss Hannon."

The man's eyes narrowed.

Austin rubbed his chin. "If you have a problem with that,

well, then, I'm afraid I'll have a problem letting this matter go without filing a report. And Miss Hannon, here, is likely to want to press charges for reckless endangerment.''

Frannie looked at him wide-eyed. Austin was pretty certain she'd never do any such thing, but he was thankful she kept silent.

''If we all stand here blocking traffic much longer, the police are likely to show up whether we want them to or not,'' Austin added.

Lyle's eyes were small, hate-filled slits. With an impatient sigh, he turned toward Frannie. ''Sorry.''

He hardly sounded sincere, but Austin decided not to push it. He watched the man stalk back to his expensive car, climb in and peel rubber as he drove away.

''What a charmer,'' Austin muttered. He looked at Frannie, and the absurdity of her green face made him smile. ''We'd better get out of the street.''

He took her arm, started to the sidewalk, only to realize she was limping. ''Are you hurt?''

She winced in pain. ''I think I skinned my knee.''

''I've got a first-aid kit in my car. Let's get you to that bench on the sidewalk, then I'll go get it.''

They'd made it to the sidewalk and had nearly reached the bench when an elderly woman rushed up to Frannie, all out of breath. ''Snook'ems!'' Her wrinkled face beaming, she clasped her hands to her chest. ''Oh, you found my Snooky-Wook'ems! Oh, how can I thank you?''

The fur ball in Frannie's arms thumped its tail madly. Frannie passed the dog to the woman's outstretched arms.

The woman joyfully kissed the animal on its wet black nose. ''I've been looking everywhere for her.'' The little dog nearly knocked off the woman's glasses in its effusive expression of delight. ''Where did you find my angel?''

"Wandering around in the middle of the street," Frannie said.

"Oh, dear! I'm glad she wasn't hit by a car. I don't know what I'd do without my Snooky-Wook'ems!"

Austin fixed her with a stern look. "You'd better keep her on a leash, then. Frannie risked her life to save your dog."

"Oh, my! Oh, I'm so sorry!" The woman's gray eyes were round and earnest behind her thick trifocals. "I left Snooky in my car while I ran into the drugstore to get my heart medicine. I put the window down so she wouldn't get hot, and well, she must have jumped right out." The woman held the little dog up to her face and spoke in a high-pitched, babyish voice. "You were a naughty girl, weren't you, Snook'ems? You gave Mommy quite a scare."

"Scared me pretty good, too," Frannie said dryly.

They weren't the only ones, Austin thought. His heart had nearly jumped out of his chest when he'd seen a woman—Frannie—dive in front of that car.

"I don't know how to thank you, dear." The woman kissed the dog again, then turned to Frannie. She peered over the top of her thick lenses. "It just goes to show, you can't judge a person by the way they look. I never knew you punk rockers cared about animals. "

"Punk rocker?" Frannie's eyes were shocked. " I'm not a punk rocker!"

Austin leaned toward the old woman conspiratorially. "She's very sensitive about her skin condition. I keep telling her its nothing to be ashamed of. Anyone can pick up a fungal condition."

The old woman's eyes flew wide. "You mean, that's fungus? Is it contagious?"

Austin nodded somberly. "I'm afraid so. The only antidote is to cover your entire body in peanut butter for twenty-four hours immediately after exposure.''

"Oh, dear!''

"I suggest that you and Snooky go right home and get started.''

Wearing a look of horror, the woman hurried down the sidewalk, clutching the little dog to her ample chest.

Frannie convulsed in a fit of laughter. It took her a minute to regain her ability to speak. "You're as naughty as Snook'ems,'' she finally gasped.

Austin grinned. "Served the old biddy right.''

She grinned at him, her smile so warm and bright he practically reached for his sunglasses. A jolt of attraction zapped through him despite her green face.

He cleared his throat, disconcerted. "Let's take a look at your knee.'' He gestured to a wooden bench under the green-and-white-striped drugstore awning. Frannie sat down, lifted the cape and pulled up the long tan skirt of her gabardine suit to reveal long slender calves.

Her right knee was scraped and bleeding. Austin felt a rush of empathy. "You sit right there, and I'll go get my first-aid kit.''

"Okay. Thanks.'' He could feel Frannie's eyes on him as he sprinted across the street. Opening the door of his black pickup, he pulled out a box from under the seat, then strode back across the street.

She looked so ridiculous, sitting on that wooden bench in that ridiculous cape, with that goofy green face and those enormous eyeglasses. Something inside of him went warm and oddly mushy.

"Are you okay?'' He squatted in front of her and opened the box.

"Yes. But you might as well go ahead and say it.''

"Say what?''

"What you're thinking. That it was stupid of me to run out in the street like that."

Austin pulled out a cotton pad and squirted it with disinfectant. "Why do you think that's what I'm thinking?"

"Because it *was* stupid. I acted before I thought. But that little dog looked so scared and helpless, and that car was coming so fast. I knew if I was going to try to help it, I had to act fast."

"Well, I gotta say, you nearly gave me a heart attack."

"I did?"

Austin nodded. "I was just coming out of the automotive store when I saw you flying across the street. You looked like Batman, swooping into the street in that cape."

He was glad to see that he'd made her grin.

"I didn't see the dog at first, but I heard you yell, and I saw the Jag speeding toward you. When I saw you take a tumble right in front of it, well, my heart was in my throat."

"It was?"

"Dang right. No one knows better than me the damage an automobile can inflict on the human body."

"I'm sorry. I'm not usually so reckless."

Something about the chagrin on her green face made him smile. "Hey, I said you scared me. I didn't say I wouldn't have done the same thing."

Her hazel eyes fixed on him in a way that made him forget all about her green face.

"Come to think of it, I *have* done the same thing," Austin found himself saying. "I nearly got trampled by a stallion once, trying to get a sick colt out of a herd back when I was breaking horses."

"You used to break horses?"

He grinned. "Well, it's debatable who got broken more, the horses or me." He set the bottle of disinfectant on the sidewalk and lifted the soaked pad. "This is likely to sting, but I need to clean the wound."

"Okay."

He dabbed at her left knee. She bit her lip, but didn't cry out. Once again he felt that odd, mushy feeling.

"Did you work with horses here in Montana?" she asked.

He shrugged. "Among other places. My father never stayed in one place for long."

"Because of his job?"

Austin gave wry smile. "Not really. Because of his lifestyle."

Frannie tilted her head quizzically, and looked at him, really looked at him, in a way he hadn't been looked at in a long time. She wasn't just looking at him; she seemed to be really seeing him.

"What do you mean?" she asked.

Austin lifted his shoulders. "He didn't want to put down any roots, didn't want to get attached to anyone or anything." Including me, Austin thought bitterly. "We moved a lot."

"What did he do?"

"He was a ranch hand. Had a real talent with cattle. Me, I always preferred horses."

"Is that what you're raising on your ranch?"

Austin nodded. Why was he telling her all this? It wasn't like him to gab about his personal life with someone he'd just met. It must be that sincere way she looked at him, as if she were somehow connecting with him.

Austin picked up a Band-Aid strip and peeled the paper away. He gently set it on her knee, covering the wound, then found himself oddly reluctant to take his hand from her leg.

It was a very nice leg. Her skin was warm and smooth

and lightly tanned. Her calves were well-shaped and slender. It was a shame that a woman with legs like that would hide them under such a long skirt.

"There." He pressed down the edges of the Band-Aid strip, then pulled back his hands. He had the oddest urge to bend down and kiss her knee.

But that made no sense—no sense at all. He clicked the metal box of bandages closed and straightened.

She stood, as well. "Thanks. I really appreciate your help."

"My pleasure."

His gaze fell to her lips. They were moist and pink, and they stood out in sharp contrast to the green on the rest of her face. In fact, she seemed to be all eyes and lips. Beautiful hazel eyes. Plump, luscious-looking lips—lips that parted slightly as he stared at them. A rush of heat coursed through him. How he'd like to press his mouth to those lips, to draw that pouty bottom one into his mouth, to slide his tongue right between her lips....

The inappropriateness of his thoughts jarred him. He shifted the first-aid kit to his other hand. "Well, I'd better get back to the ranch. Tommy needs these parts for the car."

"And I'd better get back inside and get this goop off my face."

"Right." Austin nodded curtly. "Well, see you later."

"Okay." Those tempting lips curved into a smile. "And thanks. For the first aid, and for stepping in with Lyle." Her hair had come loose from the low ponytail she wore, and she brushed a stray strand behind her ear.

"My pleasure." But it was pleasure of an entirely different kind that he was thinking about as he watched her turn and scurry back into the drugstore.

I must have taken one too many knocks to the head in

race collisions, Austin thought as he strode to his car. Why else would a woman covered in a shapeless plastic cape who looked as if she'd fallen face-first into a bowl of puréed spinach turn him on more than any woman had in a long, long time?

Lyle Brooks gunned the engine of his expensive car as he tore down the dirt road leading to the resort construction site, still fuming over his near accident in town.

Who the hell did Austin Parker think he was, telling him what to do? He might be a hotshot on the NASCAR circuit, but that didn't mean he was anyone here in Whitehorn.

Around here, Lyle thought heatedly, *he* was the hotshot. After all, he was the owner of the construction company building the resort and casino, the biggest thing to ever hit this one-horse town. The complex was going to put White-horn on the map. Even more importantly, it was going to make Lyle richer and more powerful than ever.

Lyle braked as he approached the construction trailer, pulling into the spot directly in front of the door. His fore-man had suggested that they reserve the spot for the hand-icapped, but Lyle hadn't cared for the idea. It was *his* con-struction company, by damn. If anyone was going to get the best parking spot, it was going to be him. He wanted the best out of life, whether it was parking spots or cars or cigars or women. He wanted it, he deserved it, and he in-tended to see that he got it.

Slamming the door of the Jag, he strode up the wooden steps into the luxury trailer to find his secretary, Pam, on the phone. "Oh, he just walked in, sir," the attractive blonde said into the receiver. "Just a moment." Pam punched a button and looked up. "It's your grandfather."

So the old goat finally decided to call me back, Lyle thought. He'd been trying to reach Garrett Kincaid all morning, but all he'd got was the old man's answering machine. Lyle didn't know why his grandfather didn't just get a cell phone. Garrett said he didn't need one, but Lyle was certain he was just being stubborn. It was awfully hard to get the old man to change his mind about anything once his mind was made up about it.

But Lyle was working on it. Oh, yes, he was working on it. "I'll take the call in my office," he said, stalking past the secretary and closing the door.

He lowered himself into the tall cordovan leather chair. It was a custom-made chair Lyle had ordered from a furniture company in North Carolina, stately and large, with an extra-high back. Even with the two-inch lifts in his shoes, Lyle was only five-foot-nine, and he liked to make an imposing impression.

He picked up the phone and punched the button, forcing a warmth he didn't feel into his voice. "Hello, Granddad. Thanks for calling me back."

"What can I do for you today, Lyle?"

"I was, er, wondering if you've given any more thought to what we were discussing yesterday."

He heard his grandfather sigh. "Lyle, we've been all through that, and you know how I feel about the matter. That land is reserved for Gabriel, and I'm not going to swap it for yours. There's no point in discussing it further."

"I'm not asking for a straight trade. I'm willing to offer a considerable amount of money in addition to my land. For the sake of fairness, I don't see why you can't at least consider the possibility of selling it to me."

"I've been more than fair with you, Lyle." Garrett's voice was as hard as steel. "It's my land, and I'll do what I damn well please with it."

"But two years ago, you didn't even know about Larry's brood of bastards!"

"I won't have you talking about your cousins that way." The steel in Garrett's voice sounded razor-sharp.

"Cousins." Lyle spit the word out, derision dripping from his voice. "I don't understand how you can consider those illegitimate whelps as family." As far as Lyle was concerned, they were nothing but unfortunate reminders of his uncle Larry's philandering ways.

"Because that's what they are, whether you like it or not." Garrett's voice cut sharply through the phone line. "They're Larry's sons. They're as much my blood as you are, and I suggest you start accepting that fact."

Lyle stared out the window at the Crazy Mountains, their tops rugged and craggy above the timberline. They looked just like his grandfather sounded, tough and indomitable and unmoving. No, his grandfather was tougher than the mountains, Lyle thought ruefully. If a mountain was in his way, he could always blast through it with dynamite. With his grandfather, he'd have to find a way around.

The old man was completely intractable when it came to this topic. Ever since he discovered two years ago that his late son, Larry, had fathered seven illegitimate children, Garrett had refused to listen to reason. The old man had not only welcomed the bastards into the bosom of the family, but given them all large chunks of the Kincaid ranch, as well. Land that should have been split three ways—between Lyle and his two legitimate cousins, Melanie and Collin—was now going to be split among the bastards.

And that wasn't even the worst of it. The piece of land the old man had given Lyle was a worthless parcel abutting the Laughing Horse Reservation up north. The land the resort was being constructed upon, however, was being saved for Gabriel Reilly Baxter, Larry's youngest illegitimate child who'd been adopted by Jordan Baxter. Adding insult to injury was the fact that the little bastard was probably still in diapers.

Lyle's grandfather refused to see the injustice of it all. Lyle had tried to reason with the old man. He'd tried wheedling and logic. He'd even had his mother intercede on his behalf. She'd manage to convince Garrett to give Lyle an extra piece of the Whitehorn property, but it had been more of that useless tract next to the reservation. He'd even offered to buy the land the resort would be built on from the stubborn old mule. The only concession he'd gotten was that Garrett had agreed to let him represent the land in negotiations with the Indians, and he'd made sure that Lyle's construction company got the contract to build the casino and resort.

"You've gotten a huge real estate commission from acting as my agent, and you stand to make a fortune from this building contract," Garrett had told him. "You're making out a like a fat cat on this deal."

That was true. Lyle had also made a few under-the-table deals his grandfather didn't know about that would make him plenty more money once the complex was completed. But that wasn't enough. Lyle wanted more.

Lyle wanted it all.

But it was clear he wasn't going to get it from his grandfather. Not this way. Not today.

He took a deep breath and forced a conciliatory tone to his voice. "You're right, Granddad. It's your land, and you're free to do as you wish."

"Well, I'm glad you're finally starting to see reason."

It wasn't so much reason as the writing on the wall, Lyle thought dourly, turning his Mont Blanc pen in his hand. The harder he pushed, the deeper the old man dug in his heels.

"I know you don't share my view of things, but I want to put the past behind us. All of us," Garrett continued.

Lyle sighed. His grandfather was getting on his soap box again. This might take all day.

"This family has been divided too long," Garrett was saying. "I want us all to make peace and get along. I want us to be a real family." There was a long pause. Lyle realized his grandfather was waiting for him to say something.

"We *are* a real family, Granddad."

"No, we're not. Want me to tell you what a real family's like?"

As if I could stop you. "Sure, Granddad."

"Well, son, in a real family, the members look out for the best interests of each other and not just for themselves."

"I see." Lyle saw, all right. He saw that the old man had just slapped him on the wrist, and he didn't appreciate it, not one little bit. Gritting his teeth, he forced a pleasant tone into his voice. "That's a good definition."

"Glad you think so. Guess that means I won't be hearin' any more nonsense from you about tryin' to get your hands on Gabriel's property, then."

Lyle's fist clenched around the phone, but he carefully kept his tone light. "I only want what's best for the family, Granddad."

"Good to hear it. Well, you have a nice day." The phone clicked in Lyle's ear.

Lyle slammed down the receiver, pushed back his chair and rose to his feet. Muttering a low oath, he shoved his hands into his pockets and strode to the large window that looked out at the mountains behind him.

Damn, but the old man was a stubborn cuss! It had been a tactical error to keep pushing for him to trade the land. Instead of trying to convince his granddad to give him that property, he should have been working harder to convince the Indians to move the resort site up north to his land.

He'd tried to get them to move the whole project—the resort and the casino—to the north earlier, but it was a hard sell. The casino had to be built on Indian land for legal reasons. The land that abutted Lyle's property was so mountainous and rocky that it would take a small fortune to just level it enough to lay a foundation. The land adjacent to Gabriel's property was already level. Since the Indians wanted to locate the resort as close as possible to the casino, they'd naturally selected Gabriel's property instead of Lyle's.

When the construction project was halted after the discovery of a skeleton, Lyle had tried again to convince the Indians to move the resort site to his land, but they'd stuck with their original decision. The tribe's lawyer, Jackson Hawk, had suggested that Lyle's company begin construction on the resort's pool and sports complex while they waited for the murder investigation to be completed. Lyle couldn't argue with the logic of the suggestion. In fact, his company had dynamited a forty-five-foot hole for the sports complex foundation just yesterday, and workmen were clearing away the debris now.

Maybe he'd tried the wrong approach, Lyle thought now, staring out at the mountains. Since he couldn't outsmart the Indians with logic, maybe he should have tried appealing to their superstitious nature. He probably could have frightened them away with stories about a horrible curse.

Lyle's dark thoughts were interrupted by a knock on the door. "Who's there?" he growled.

"Peter Cook," came the answer.

"Who?"

"Pete Cook. I operate one of the earth movers."

Where the hell was his secretary? At lunch, Lyle supposed. Heaving a sigh, he strode back to his desk and lowered himself into his massive chair. Damn, but he hated having to deal with all the daily headaches of the construction business. The way he saw it, he shouldn't have to. His role was to figure out the money-making angles. The day-to-day work was the problem of his construction foreman.

Lyle picked up a stack of papers. "You're supposed to report to Hank," he called.

"He went into town to get a part for a broken backhoe. Besides, this is somethin' I think you might want to know about person'lly."

Hell. Lyle rubbed his chin and sighed. "Come on in."

A man about Lyle's height stepped into the room. Clad in jeans and a dirty gray T-shirt, the thin, middle-aged man held an orange hard hat in one hand and what looked like a chunk of rock in the other.

"Yes?"

"Sorry to bust in on ya like this, Mr. Brooks, but I found somethin' just now at the construction site that I thought you'd want to know about."

Lyle closed his eyes and rubbed his forehead. "I hope it's not another damn skeleton."

"No, it's not that."

"Well, then, what is it?"

Peter's neck moved as he swallowed. "I'm no expert, but I hit somethin' that looks an awful lot like a vein of sapphire."

Sapphire! Lyle's pulse began to race. He'd heard rumors about a sapphire vein hidden in the mountains, but he'd always thought it was nothing more than an old prospector's tall tale. He leaned back in his chair and gave the man his full attention. "Where?"

"At the south end of the project, about forty feet down. I've brought you a piece of it."

Peter handed him the rock. Lyle turned it in his hand. The back of it looked like ordinary granite, but a thick vein of deep blue shot through the center. Excitement mounted in Lyle's chest.

Don't give away your hand, he cautioned himself. Play it cool. "Hmm. Well, it's interesting, but I don't know that it's sapphire."

"I don't, either. But I know a little about stones— I like to collect 'em—and this darn sure looks like the real thing. These hills are rumored to have a sapphire vein in them somewhere, and, well, I just figured you'd want to know."

Lyle nodded, trying to remain calm. "You did the right thing, bringing this to me. I'll send it off and have it analyzed." Lyle's mind worked fast. He turned the chunk of rock in his hand, then looked up at the older man. "Does anyone else know about this?"

Peter shook his head. "I just found it, and I came right here."

"And you didn't tell anyone else?"

"No one else was around. The rest of the crew is at lunch. No one knows but you and me."

"Good. Let's keep it that way." Lyle rose from his chair and circled his desk. He placed his hand on the man's shoulder. "After all, you don't want to have to share your finder's fee, do you, Pete?"

The man's brow knit quizzically. "Finder's fee?"

"Sure. If this is real sapphire, why, you should get a nice chunk of change for being the first to spot it."

Pete's face lit up. "What kind of money are we talking about?"

Lyle raised his shoulders. "I don't know. Depends on whether or not this is real and how much there is of it."

The man's eyes lit in a way that told Lyle he had him

in the palm of his hand. "But if it's real, I'll get some money?"

Lyle nodded. "Absolutely. I'll see to it personally. Provided you don't tell anyone just yet." Lyle turned the rock in his hand. "I'll get this tested. In the meantime, don't breathe a word of this to anyone." He looked at Pete closely. "No one. No girlfriends, no buddies, no bartenders. Not even your wife, if you've got one."

"I won't tell a soul," Peter promised.

"Good." Lyle strode across the lush burgundy carpet to the door of his office. Pete followed. "We're going to shut down the digging operation for the day."

"What'll I tell the foreman when he gets back?"

"Tell him I came out and told you to stop. Something about not having the right permits. Have him come see me. I'll tell him we have a paperwork hassle to straighten out before we can proceed." Lyle pulled his lips back in a smile. "Don't you worry about a thing. Not a thing, except keeping your mouth shut."

Lyle could practically see the dollar signs in the man's eyes. The poor fool was probably buying a new double-wide trailer in his mind's eye right now.

Pete touched his fingers to his forehead in a snappy salute. "Don't you worry, Mr. Brooks. I'll be quiet as a mouse."

Lyle closed the fist of his left hand possessively around the rock and extended his right hand to the construction worker. "I'm counting on it, Pete. I'm counting on it."

Lyle waited until the foreman returned, then took the rock into Whitehorn and over-nighted it to a mineralogist in Seattle. He didn't dare send it to anyone within the state; he didn't want to risk word getting around that sapphire had been discovered near Whitehorn. To further insure secrecy, he even enclosed a note saying that he'd found the stone in North Dakota.

If this really was a sapphire vein, Lyle intended to keep it to himself—all to himself.

He was at his desk signing payroll checks the next morning when his phone intercom crackled. "Mr. Jasper with Seattle Mineral Testing is on the line," Pam said.

"All right. Thanks." Lyle's hand was shaking when he picked up the phone. "This is Lyle Brooks."

"Andy Jasper here," said a cordial voice. "I have some interesting news for you."

"You do?"

"Yes. That specimen you submitted for analysis—it's sapphire, all right. High-quality stuff, too. Top notch."

Lyle tamped down the urge to let out a whoop of victory. "What's it worth?"

"Well, the gem in that rock would retail for around fifteen or twenty thousand dollars, depending on how it was cut."

Fifteen or twenty thousand, for a rock small enough to hold in his hand—and there was whole mountain of the stuff, just sitting out there! Lyle's heart pounded like a jackhammer. He fought to keep his voice calm. "Is that a fact?"

"Yes, sir."

"Any guess how much sapphire's likely to be at the site where I found that?"

"Well, it's anyone's guess. But usually these gems run in veins. When conditions are right for creating some of the stone, they're right for creating a lot of it. Judging from the size of the gem in this rock, I'd say that most likely, you've stumbled onto quite a windfall."

Lyle swallowed, his mouth dry.

"You say you found this on your vacation property in North Dakota?" Mr. Jasper asked.

Lyle immediately grew wary. "Uh, yeah. That's right."

"Well, I'd say you're a mighty lucky man." Mr. Jasper chuckled. "You don't happen to want a partner, do you?"

"No. I'm afraid I don't."

"Well, I knew you were anxious for the report. Do you want me to send the rock back to you by special courier?"

"No. I don't want to call undue attention to it. Just insure it and send it back by overnight mail." Lyle gave the man his home address, then switched the phone to his other ear. "And, Mr. Jasper, I trust you'll adhere to your company's confidentiality policy."

"Oh, yes, sir."

"You'd better. Because if you leak anything to anyone about this, my lawyers will be on you like ticks on a blood-hound."

Lyle hung up the phone, then rose from his chair and pumped his fist victoriously in the air. He was sitting on a dad-blasted gold mine!

Or rather, Gabriel Reilly Baxter was. The thought made his exuberant mood sputter and die.

Lyle knotted his hands into fists. "Well, not for long," he muttered. His mind churning, he paced the floor in front of his office window.

If he could get the Indians to move the resort site to his property up north, his grandfather would probably agree to the property swap. After all, the old man's only concern was insuring that his precious bastard grandchild had a valuable piece of real estate.

Lyle's face broke into a smile. Oh, this was ingenious. Why, Lyle would look downright generous if he gave his little cousin the more valuable land! His sudden big-heartedness might be a little hard to explain, though. He'd have to come up with a story about how he was sentimentally attached to this particular piece of property. Granddad had always been a sucker for an emotional story.

Lyle smacked a fist into the palm of his hand. Oh, but he was brilliant! He grinned broadly as he stared out the window. Just think—a whole mountain of sapphires sitting out there, and only he knew about them.

He—and Peter Cook. Frowning, Lyle rubbed his jaw. He couldn't let a small-time wage earner like Cook interfere with his plans. No, sir.

Cook was an obstacle that could easily be eliminated. All it took was the guts to do it. And the sooner he did it, the better.

Striding to his desk, he picked up a piece of notepaper and scrawled a note:

Pete—
I have news about that rock you found. Meet me at the construction site tonight at 10:00 p.m. and I'll fill you in. Tell no one.

Lyle signed his name with a flourish, then riffled through the paycheck envelopes on his desk until he found the one marked Peter Cook. He stuffed the note inside, licked the flap and sealed it closed.

He was smarter than all of them, Lyle thought smugly. Smart enough to know exactly what he wanted and smart enough to figure out how to get it. And no one—not his grandfather, not his bastard cousin, and certainly no one the likes of Peter Cook—was going to stand in his way.

Four

"So how's it going?"

Frannie looked up from the container of yogurt she was eating to see her pixie-faced cousin lowering herself into one of the chairs across from her desk at the Whitehorn Savings and Loan.

"What are you doing here, Jasmine?"

"I came downtown to pick up a few things for Mom at the drugstore, and I thought I'd stop in and see how you're doing."

"I'm doing fine."

"I didn't mean *you*. I meant the flirting. How's it going?"

The flirting, Frannie groaned. That was today's assignment from Summer and Jasmine. Wearing her contacts, which she hated, and mascara, which she loathed, she'd been instructed to make eye contact with a man and give him "the treatment"—whatever that was. And it didn't end there. She had to wear these blasted four-inch heels that looked like radio towers. All designed to make her legs look shapely.

Frannie tossed the empty yogurt container into the wastebasket, avoiding her cousin's eyes. "I thought I didn't have to report back to you two until tonight."

Jasmine folded her arms across her chest and eyed her accusingly. "You haven't tried it, have you?"

"Not yet." Frannie straightened a pad of forms on the

corner of her desk. "I happen to be on the payroll here to work, not to pick up men."

Jasmine glanced at her watch. "I thought you were on your lunch hour."

"Well, I technically am, but I have a lot of work to do, so—"

"So come on." Jasmine rose and motioned for Frannie to follow her.

"Where are we going?"

"To the ladies' room to put on more mascara. Then you're going to march back to your desk and give the eye treatment to the next man who walks in here."

"Ah, Jasmine, I don't think I can bat my eyelashes like Summer said."

Jasmine eyed her sternly. "You agreed to let us make you over, and this is an important part of the process."

There was no point in arguing with Jasmine when she got that determined look in her eye. With a sigh, Frannie rose and followed her cousin.

She returned to her desk a few minutes later, her eyelids feeling unnaturally heavy. "I think you overdid the mascara," she grumbled to Jasmine.

"With the lighting in here, it takes more makeup to do the job. But don't worry. You look great." Jasmine smiled at her. "Now, I want you to give the eye treatment to the next man who walks through that door. I'm going to go stand on the other side of the lobby and watch."

Frannie knew Jasmine was as tenacious as a bulldog. Unless she wanted her cousin standing around watching her all afternoon, she'd have no choice but to go ahead and get it over with. Frannie heaved a sigh. "All right. The very next man who walks through the door—provided he's not old enough to be my grandfather, someone I work with or a man I know is married."

"I know you'll be great." Jasmine flashed an encouraging smile, then sauntered to the far side of the lobby.

With her luck, Frannie thought, the next man to walk through that door would look and smell like Sasquatch.

Her shoulders tensed as the door opened. A blue-haired old lady in a lavender dress toddled in. Frannie was just inhaling a breath of relief when the door opened again and Austin Parker strode into the lobby.

Great. Just great. Frannie cast a desperate look across the room to see Jasmine nod her head in Austin's direction.

Oh, dear. Why did she have to practice this silly technique on *him?* He no doubt already thought she was mentally deranged. With a last desperate glance at Jasmine, Frannie took a deep breath and looked directly at Austin. To her surprise, he looked back and smiled.

Frannie's pulse pounded in her throat. She glanced away, only to see Jasmine wildly blinking her eyes in a silent command. Frannie gulped, turned her gaze back to Austin and blinked rapidly.

Oh my stars—it was working! Austin was heading to her desk. Frannie frantically busied herself, gathering pieces of paper on her desk into a senseless pile.

"Good afternoon, Frannie."

"G-good afternoon."

"I hardly recognized you without your glasses."

Frannie continued to collect the papers into a haphazard stack. "Sometimes I wear my contacts."

"Well, you look very nice. Are they new?"

"No. I've had them for a while."

"Oh."

Behind Austin, Frannie saw Jasmine point to her eye. Frannie looked up at Austin and repeatedly blinked.

He frowned. "Do you have something in your eye?"

"What?"

"I notice you keep blinking."

"Oh. No. I'm okay." Oh, dear, just as she'd feared. The blinking made her look like a nutcase. To make matters worse, she suddenly did, indeed, have something in her eye. All that blinking seemed to have dislodged a fleck of mascara, and it hurt like the dickens. She blinked some more, trying to get it out.

"Well, good." Austin looked her uncertainly, the way one might look at a dog suspected of having rabies. "I came by to open a savings account. Can you help me with that, or do you only handle loans?"

She closed the afflicted eye, wanting to ease the pain, only to realize in horror that it must look as if she was winking at him. "I—I do it all." Oh, heavens, that hadn't come out right. It sounded alarmingly suggestive. "I mean, I can handle anything. I mean, everything."

Her eye was twitching now. This was going from bad to worse. "I—I'll do anything you want."

Austin studied her, his brow furrowed. To her distress, Frannie realized that now her eyes were watering. Not just watering—gushing.

Through the wet blur, she saw Austin lean across her desk. She couldn't make out the expression on his face, but his voice was concerned. "Have I said something to upset you?"

"Of…of course not." Frannie tried to act normal, but it was hard, what with her eye twitching and her face feeling like Niagara Falls. She could barely see him through the haze of tears. She did her best to sound nonchalant. "Why would you think a thing like that?"

She couldn't see well enough to be sure, but she thought his lips quirked upward in a grin. "No reason. Except I'm not really used to having bankers cry when I try to open a savings account."

It was time to cut her losses and run. Frannie rose from her chair. "I—I'm sorry. I seem to have something in my eye, after all. If you'll excuse me for a moment, I'll be right back." She rounded her desk, wobbling on her unnaturally high heels.

Austin moved to steady her. "Are you all right?"

"I'm..."

Oh, dear, she was losing it—her poise, her vision, but worst of all, her balance. She tried hard to regain it. "I'm..."

She toppled forward and grasped at Austin, pushing him into the chair. She fell hard on top of him. The next thing she knew, she was perched atop his lap. "...I'm fine," she finished weakly.

"Fine" didn't begin to describe it. His thighs were hard and warm beneath hers, and his chest was solid under her hand. She could feel his heartbeat through the cotton of his burgundy sports shirt. Her face was pressed to his cheek, which smelled deliciously of soap and shaving cream, and his freshly shaven skin against hers sent goose bumps skittering all over her.

One of his hands rested on her arm, the other on her hip. "Are you okay?" he asked.

Her voice didn't seem to work. She numbly nodded.

"My goodness, Frannie—what's going on?" asked a deep, raspy voice.

Frannie abruptly looked up. Her vision was cloudy, but she could make out the heavy jowls of the bank manager over Austin's shoulder. She struggled to sit upright, her face burning heat. "I—I lost my balance and fell."

"On a *customer?*"

Frannie nodded. Clearly nonplussed, the large man looked at Austin. "Well! I don't know what happened here, but on behalf of the Whitehorn Savings and Loan, I'd like to apologize for—''

"No apology needed," Austin said quickly. "I happen to like a bank with friendly, personal service." He tightened his grip on Frannie's hip and angled a smile down at her. "Why, the last place I opened a savings account, all I got was a toaster."

Frannie couldn't help it. The ridiculousness of the situation, the banker's befuddlement and the outrageousness of the remark made her burst into laughter. Even with her tear-impaired vision, she could tell that Austin was grinning at her.

The bank manager looked from her to Austin, his lips stretched in an uncertain smile. Recognition suddenly poured over his face. "Say, you're that race car driver, aren't you?"

Austin nodded. "Austin Parker." He stuck out his right hand, his left one still firmly planted on Frannie's hip.

The banker pumped his hand. "I'm a big fan. Here, let me get Miss Hannon off your lap."

"No hurry." Austin's fingers surreptitiously caressed her hip.

Heat flared through Frannie. Her face flaming, she took the bank manager's proffered hand and rapidly struggled to her feet.

But the banker's attention was focused on Austin. "Tell me about that car you drive. Does it have a V-8 engine?"

"Well, it's a converted Chevy Monte Carlo, and..."

While the two men talked cars, Frannie circled back behind her desk, pulled her lens case out of her purse and quickly removed her contacts. Oh, that felt so much better! She rubbed her eyes in relief. Her near-sightedness allowed her to see things at close range, but she could no longer tell if Jasmine was still watching from across the room.

"…So now my pit crew chief is at my ranch, fine-tuning the transmission," Austin was saying.

"He's here in Whitehorn?"

Austin nodded. "He's staying at the Big Sky. That's where I met Frannie."

"Oh, so you and Miss Hannon had previously met?"

"Oh, sure." Austin smiled at Frannie. "We're old friends. In fact, I decided to move my savings account to your bank because of Frannie."

The banker's face creased in a pleased smile. He nodded at Frannie approvingly. "Frannie is one of our finest employees. Our satellite office in Billings has been trying to hire her away from us for years, but fortunately for us, she's too fond of Whitehorn to move. I'm sure she'll take good care of you."

Austin gave Frannie a slow grin. "That's what I'm banking on."

His eyes were warm, and Frannie felt a jolt of sexual awareness as she met his gaze. The bank manager waddled off, and Frannie looked down at her lap, nervously twining her fingers together. "That was kind of you."

"What?"

"Telling him I'm the reason you're opening an account here."

"You are."

"Oh, come on." Frannie opened her file drawer, trying hard to hide her racing pulse. "You didn't even know I worked here."

"Not at first. But after you landed in my lap like that, well…" He lifted his shoulders. "Where else am I going get a dividend like that?"

The fact that he was being so nice about her clumsiness only increased her embarrassment. "I'm usually not such a klutz, but my cousin talked me into wearing her shoes to-day, and I'm not used to high heels, and, well..."

"What are you apologizing for? I liked it."

Even without her contacts or glasses, she could see an unmistakable light in his eyes. He was flirting with her! Her palms began to sweat, and she suddenly felt as unsure as a twelve-year-old girl.

Which was ridiculous, she sternly told herself. A man like Austin probably flirted with every woman he met. She'd be an idiot to think he meant anything by it. She'd treat him as if he were any other customer, she decided. In fact, she probably ought to redouble her efforts to appear professional, considering how unprofessionally she'd acted when he'd first come in. All the same, her face began to burn.

Austin watched her cheeks flame and grinned. Lord, but she was a mess! Black streaks of mascara ran from her eyes to her chin, and her eyes were ringed like a raccoon's. And now the rest of her face was turning as red as a Stop sign.

For reasons he couldn't begin to fathom, he felt a stir of arousal. He shifted on the chair. "Do you, uh, still need to go fix your eyes?"

She shook her head. "I took my contacts out while you were talking to my boss."

"Oh." He started to tell her about the condition of her makeup, then changed his mind. If she knew it looked like an eighteen-wheeler had laid rubber all over her face, she'd want to go to the rest room to clean up, and he didn't want her to leave.

His lips curved in a grin. "You know, you look different every time I see you."

She rummaged through her file drawer and gave a dry smile. "That's because I don't have egg or green stuff on my face today."

He rubbed his chin, trying to repress his smile. She was going to die of embarrassment when she discovered what she *did* have on her face, but Austin wouldn't be the one to tell her.

Frannie plucked a sheet of pink paper out of a file folder and handed it to him. "If you're interested in opening a savings account, you'll want to look over this form."

I'd much rather look over yours. The thought surprised him. Racing fans and groupies were constantly throwing themselves at him, but Austin hadn't had much interest in women lately.

Heck, he hadn't had much interest in *anything* lately. The past few months, he'd been feeling burned out and restless. Which was one reason he'd bought the ranch. He used to have a passion for horses, used to dream of one day owning a ranch like the kind he'd worked on in his youth. As so many of the dreams that he'd achieved, though, the ranch hadn't lived up to his expectations. He still felt as if something were missing, as if some essential key to satisfaction was eluding him.

"That sheet explains the different type of accounts we offer." Frannie tapped her pen on the desk. "I'll need you to fill out an application, once you decide what you want."

Oh, I already know what I want.

He rubbed his jaw and frowned at the wayward thought. After a long, slumbering hiatus, why had his libido suddenly decided to return with such force? And why on earth had it settled on this unlikely woman who seemed to specialize in wearing the mess du jour?

Part of it had to do with the way she'd felt in his lap, he decided. She was hiding one heck of a shapely body under that baggy tan suit. Her bottom was firm and round, her waist was small, and the breast she'd unknowingly pressed against his arm had felt surprisingly full and lush.

He realized she was waiting for him to select an account. He pointed his finger to the top listing. "I'll take this one."

"Fine." She slid a yellow paper in front of him. "Here's the application."

There was something about the way she acted so stiff and professional, as if she were wary of him, that turned him on, too. He was accustomed to women throwing themselves at him. At every race, there were beautiful, Barbie-doll-shaped women scheming to meet him. Some of them bluffed their way through racetrack security, some approached him in bars and restaurants, some even stalked him to his hotel room. He thought he'd seen it all—but he'd never seen anything quite like Frannie Hannon.

"Do you need a pen?"

He realized he was staring at her, gazing deep into her black-ringed eyes. "Yes."

She handed him the pen in her hand. His fingers deliberately brushed hers as he took it. She pulled back, cleared her throat and spun toward her computer so abruptly that she nearly hurled herself out of her swivel chair.

Austin grinned. No, sirree. He'd never met anyone quite like Frannie.

He quickly filled out the form while she pulled a program up on the computer. When he finished, she entered the information into her computer, printed out a paper and handed it to him.

"I need you to check this over and make sure all the information is correct, then sign it."

"All right." He glanced over the page, scrawled his name on the line at the bottom and pushed the paper across the desk toward her.

Frannie opened a side drawer and pulled out a small packet. "That takes care of the paperwork. Here's your account number and passbook, along with some checks and deposit slips. How much would you like to deposit?''

Austin rubbed his chin. ''Oh, I don't know. About a hundred grand, I guess.''

Frannie's blackened eyes widened. ''You want to deposit one hundred thousand dollars?''

Austin nodded. ''If that's all right.''

''Well, yes, of course. But most people would want to put that kind of money in one of our higher interest-bearing accounts.''

Shucks, honey, if my interest were much higher, I'd have a hard time walking out of here.

Austin ran a hand down his face. Good grief, what was the matter with him? Hell. He ought to just ask her out and be done with it. Once he got to know her and the newness wore off, he was sure he'd lose interest, just like always.

He opened his mouth, ready to ask what she was doing Saturday night, but she was leaning across her desk, her ridiculously streaked face frowning with seriousness.

''It's your decision, of course.'' Her eyes were earnest in that burglar's mask of mascara. ''But we have some excellent rates on our C.D.s. You really ought to consider a long-term investment.''

''I'm not much for long-term arrangements.'' *But I bet she is,* came a wayward voice from inside his head. The thought hit him like a splash of cold water.

Hell, he had no business getting involved with a woman like Frannie. He wasn't a long-term kind of guy, and it didn't take a call to the Psychic Hotline to figure out that a buttoned down, serious-eyed gal like Frannie wasn't one-night-stand material. In fact, it was a pretty sure bet that she didn't take anything—including dating—lightly. Which was exactly the reason he needed to keep his mouth shut, leave the lady alone and haul his tail out of there.

"Long-term investments pay the highest returns," Frannie insisted.

He shoved back his chair. "Sorry, but that's not my style. I prefer to take my chances in the stock market. This account is just to have some money handy in case I need it." He pulled a checkbook out of his pocket and rapidly filled out a check. Pushing it across the desk, he rose to his feet. "It's been nice doing business with you. Stay out of traffic and don't rescue any more dogs, you hear?"

And stay off of men's laps, unless you want to deal with the consequences.

The annoying thing was, he wasn't altogether sure she didn't. She sure sent out a lot of mixed signals. He turned and strode out of the bank, wanting to put some distance between them before he was tempted to try to figure out exactly what her signals meant.

Five

"I looked like I'd gone six rounds with Mike Tyson," Frannie moaned that evening after work as she sat at the kitchen table of the B & B with Summer and Jasmine. She stared down at her glass of iced tea. "When I looked in the restroom mirror, I wanted to sink right through the floor."

"Well," Jasmine said defensively, "I tried to signal you to wipe your face."

"Without my contacts or glasses, I can't see across the room. Why didn't you come over and tell me?"

Jasmine lifted her shoulders and grinned sheepishly. "I didn't want to interrupt you and Austin. He was staring at you as if you were the most fascinating creature he'd ever seen."

"Creature's the word for it," Frannie mumbled.

Jasmine grinned. "Well, I told you about your makeup as soon as he left."

Frannie squeezed a slice of lemon into her glass. "I just wish you'd come over and told me when things first started going downhill."

"You mean when *you* went downhill—into Austin's lap?" Jasmine asked.

Summer snorted.

Jasmine grinned impishly. "Gee, I thought that was when things really started to pick up."

Both cousins snickered and Frannie shot them a disgusted look. "I'm glad you're both amused."

Jasmine reached out and patted her hand. "Oh, come on, Frannie. You've got to admit, it was awfully funny."

"Depends on your perspective," Frannie replied. "I'd be a lot more inclined to laugh if I weren't dying of embarrassment."

Summer raised her hands in a placating gesture. "Well, it seems to me that we're overlooking the really important thing here."

"Oh? And what's that?" Frannie asked.

"That the flirting technique was successful. Austin came over when you made eye contact. We just need to send you out to practice it some more."

Frannie shook her head. "Oh, no. I'm through with making a fool of myself in public."

Jasmine and Summer looked at each other and frowned.

"Well, then, we'll just have to coach you in private," Summer said decisively. "That's how beauty contestants do it." At Frannie's inquisitive look, she explained, "A lot of contestants have behind-the-scene coaches who work with them on their posture and facial expressions and body language."

"Let me see if I've got this straight." Frannie looked from Summer to Jasmine, then back again. "You two would be my coaches?"

Summer and Jasmine both nodded.

"And as my coaches, you'd criticize everything I do, every minute that I'm awake?"

"Pretty much," Summer admitted.

"Oh, gee. Excuse me if I'm not jumping up and down with enthusiasm."

Jasmine laughed. "I know it sounds unpleasant, but Summer's right. The key to sending out the right vibes to a man is body language."

"And what's wrong with my body language?" Frannie asked.

Jasmine looked at her, her eyes narrowing thoughtfully. "Well, right now, for example, you're slumping in your chair and wearing a woe-is-me expression. Your body is saying 'Go away. Leave me alone.'"

"So can't you guys take a hint?"

Jasmine went on, undaunted. "You send out signals that tell men to keep their distance. Instead of crossing your arms and looking all shut down and inaccessible, you ought to sit up, lift your head and smile."

Frannie shifted uneasily. "I don't want to be a phony."

"This isn't about being phony. It's about being smart." Summer's voice was matter-of-fact. "It's about being your best self. If you become aware of what you're doing, you can start behaving the way you want, instead of just acting out of habit."

Frannie hated to admit it, but Summer's words made sense.

"You agreed to this whole makeover idea in the first place because you wanted to be more confident," Jasmine chimed in. "Well, the key to feeling more confident is to start acting as if you already are."

"I don't know…"

"Well, I do," Summer said adamantly. "I wouldn't be married to Gavin right now if I hadn't changed my ways."

It was true, Frannie realized. Summer had made a deliberate effort to change her studious, bookworm persona, and it definitely had paid off. Frannie was now so used to thinking of Summer as charming and gorgeous that it was hard to remember how she used to hide her beauty.

Of course, Frannie thought, Summer's beauty had been there all along. All she'd had to do was let it shine.

Was the same thing possible for her? A ray of hopefulness lit up her heart. She couldn't expect to be a raving beauty like Summer, of course, but maybe she could stop being such a plain little mouse.

"We're right, and you know it," Jasmine said.

The bell over the front door jangled. Frannie pushed back her chair, relieved at the interruption. "I'll get it. That's probably the couple with reservations for tonight."

Jasmine glanced at her watch. "Oh, dear, look at the time! I need to run by the dry cleaner's before they close."

"And I'd better get home," Summer said, rising from her chair.

"You all get going, then. I'll go take care of the guests."

"Stand up straight and pull up your chin," Jasmine called.

Frannie made a face as her cousins headed out the kitchen door, but she did straighten her back as she pattered barefoot across the waxed wood floor to the entry foyer.

Instead of the elderly couple she was expecting, Frannie found Whitehorn's newest police detective standing at the front desk.

"Gretchen, hello. It's nice to see you again."

The attractive blonde smiled. "Good to see you, too."

"How's the investigation going?"

"We're making a little progress, thanks to your aunt." Gretchen tucked a strand of blond hair behind her ear. "Actually, much as I hate to upset her, I wondered if I might speak to her again and see if she's recalled anything further."

Frannie's stomach tightened uneasily. The previous visit by the sheriff and Gretchen had left her aunt more troubled than ever. Celeste's nightmares had worsened, and she'd grown even more distracted and jittery.

All the same, Frannie couldn't very well refuse the detective's request. "She's on the porch with some guests. I'll

go and get her.'' Frannie gestured toward the front room.
"Why don't you wait in the parlor?''

Gretchen placed her hand on Frannie's arm as she turned
to go. "Before you go, let me ask you something.''

Frannie hesitated. "Sure.''

Gretchen's expression was warm and concerned. "How
is your aunt's memory? In general, I mean. Does she usually have trouble recalling things?''

"Not usually, no.''

Gretchen looked at her thoughtfully. "You know, sometimes people repress memories that are extremely traumatic.
I can't help but wonder if your aunt has blocked something
out that is just too awful to face.''

Frannie had been wondering the same thing. And if the
memory was so terrible that Celeste had buried it for thirty
years, how would she deal with it if it resurfaced now?

Five minutes later Celeste clutched the upholstered arm
of the leather chair in the parlor and told herself to breathe.
Sometimes she forgot to do it automatically. She had to
concentrate, to consciously make an effort, just to take in
air. It was a feeling she often got in her dreams—those dark,
swirling, awful dreams that tangled her up like sea grass,
holding her down, winding around her. The harder she
struggled to get free, the more tightly bound she became.

She looked over to the matching armchair, and Frannie
gave her a reassuring smile.

The detective seated on the sofa leaned forward. It was
the same one who had come the other day with Rafe—the
pretty young woman with the shiny hair and the intelligent
eyes, the woman who looked far too nice to be investigating
something as dark and evil as murder.

"Tell me, Mrs. Monroe,'' the detective said, "have you

remembered anything further about the night Raven disappeared?''

"No. I..." Celeste made herself take another breath, then briefly closed her eyes. She felt as if she were floating down a river, floating away, away from herself. And yet part of her was standing on the riverbank, watching. She opened her eyes and reminded herself to exhale. "It was all a very long time ago."

Why couldn't she remember? Why was that time so fuzzy and gray in her memory? A whole piece of her life was missing. She'd tried and tried to remember it, but it only brought headaches and a sad sense of shame. She ought to be able to do better than this.

She saw the look Gretchen shot Frannie. The lady policeman thought she should be able to do better, too. Inadequacy, heavy and smothering, wrapped around her like a thousand grasping tentacles.

"We followed your advice and went out to the old Kincaid mansion yesterday. We found two guns in Jeremiah's collection that could have been used in the shooting," Gretchen said. "It's looking more and more like Jeremiah was the murderer."

"No," Celeste breathed.

The detective's brows shot up. Celeste found herself as surprised as the blond woman looked.

"You don't think he did it?" Gretchen asked.

"No."

"Why not?"

Celeste didn't know. She was bewildered at her own response. "I—I just don't feel right about Jeremiah being blamed for this," she mumbled.

"The evidence all points to him, Mrs. Monroe. He disliked Raven and didn't want his sister to marry him, so he had a motive. And now it looks like he owned the murder weapon." Gretchen's eyes settled on Celeste, warm and understanding. "It's always hard for family members to accept that someone they knew and loved was capable of murder."

Oh, Jeremiah was capable, all right—Celeste had no trouble believing that. Yet somehow, the whole thing just didn't seem right. It was like a piece in a jigsaw puzzle that had the right shape and the right color, but just didn't fit.

The room felt as if it had started spinning. That sometimes happened in her dreams, too—the room would spin faster and faster, like the ballerina in the music box she'd owned as a child. She'd loved that shiny wooden box, loved its lilting music, loved to watch the beautiful, twirling, porcelain ballerina. Her parents had given her that box, and when she was ten years old, she liked to think of them smiling down from heaven as she danced to its music, danced a private pas de deux with the ballerina, just for them.

Jeremiah had smashed that box against the wall in a fit of anger one afternoon, because the music had interrupted his viewing of a football game.

Celeste closed her eyes and gripped the arm of her chair as the room spun faster and faster.

"Mrs. Monroe?"

She opened her eyes to find Gretchen looking at her quizzically. "If you remember anything, please give me a call." She pulled a card out of her black bag and held it out to Celeste. "Anything—even something small, something you might think couldn't possibly be significant—might be a help."

Celeste nodded. "All right." She cautiously let go of the chair arm long enough to take the small white card, then gripped it again.

"What happens now?" Frannie asked the detective.

"Well, we wait for the ballistics report on the guns," Gretchen said. "And we're trying to locate Raven's brother, Storm Hunter, to see if he can shed any light on the events of that night."

"Where is he?"

"We don't know. Jackson Hawk, the attorney for the Laughing Horse Reservation, is helping us look for him."

"So you're in a holding pattern for a while."

"On this case." Gretchen tucked a strand of hair behind her ear. "But I've got plenty to keep me busy. Another body was found at the resort construction site this morning."

"Another body!" Frannie gasped.

The words echoed in Celeste's head, circling around and around, making her feel as if she were trapped inside a bad dream. Another body, another body, another body...

Gretchen nodded grimly. "This one's recent. It appears to be an accident or suicide."

"Who was it?" Frannie asked.

"A heavy equipment operator named Peter Cook. He evidently fell to his death."

Another death, Celeste thought. So much death. It was everywhere—hiding, lurking, biding its time, just waiting to strike. Life was so short. So short and so precious.

And yet she'd lost a part of hers. There was a void in her memory, a missing part of her life.

Frannie rose and saw the investigator out. Celeste leaned her head back against the chair and closed her eyes, listening to the creak of the door opening, the murmur of soft goodbyes, the thud of the door closing. Soft footsteps told her Frannie had returned to the room. With an effort, she opened her eyes.

"Are you all right?" Frannie asked.

"Yes. But that detective's on the wrong track."

"What do you mean?"

"I don't know." Celeste rose from the chair. She was tired, so very tired, yet she could no longer sit still. "But I feel it in here." She touched her chest. "It just doesn't seem right that Jeremiah should take all the blame for this."

Frannie put a hand on Celeste's arm. "Like Gretchen said, I'm sure it's hard to accept that your brother could do such a horrible thing. But the evidence all points to Jeremiah, Aunt Celeste."

"The evidence is only physical." Celeste brushed a strand of hair from her forehead. A need, a compulsion, was growing inside her. She needed to do something. She could no longer sit idly by. She needed to take some action. "Sometimes things aren't as they seem. I've got a feeling— a strong feeling—that there's more to this than meets the eye."

And I intend to do a little investigating of my own, she suddenly decided. The truth was there, somewhere inside her. It was swirling around in her dreams, skirting the edges of her nightmares.

What was that line from the Bible? "The truth shall make you free"—that was it.

She needed freedom. She needed truth. She needed to reclaim her memory—for the sake of Blanche, the sake of Jeremiah, the sake of Raven.

But most of all, she thought with a twinge of desperation, for the sake of her own sanity.

Six

"Oh, Frannie, you look like a princess!" Summer finally found a moment at the festive, elegant Whitehorn Ball to speak with Frannie and Jasmine.

"I *feel* like a princess." Frannie touched the fabric of her sleek red gown that her cousins had helped her find in a marathon shopping expedition in Bozeman. Her hair, thanks to a new stylist, was swept up into a tousle of loose, elegant curls.

In the past week, her cousins had put her through the equivalent of beauty boot camp. They'd taught her how to apply makeup, drilled her on posture and body language, and made her walk in heels for hours. They'd helped her pick out shoes, a matching purse, and face-flattering rhinestone earrings. They'd insisted she get a manicure and pedicure. They'd even made her select a new perfume.

And it had paid off. Frannie looked better than she'd ever dreamed possible. "Is this really me?"

"It's you, all right." Summer beamed like a proud mother. "I wish that slug Joe who dumped you in college could see you now."

Joe. For years, the mention of his name had conjured up the image of his face, complete with painful details such as the cowlick in his hair, the paleness of his lashes, the cleft in his chin. Most painfully of all, it reminded her of the way he'd dumped her for her college roommate.

For the first time, Frannie realized she couldn't recall

exactly what Joe looked like. Her stomach didn't knot at the thought of him, she didn't ache with loneliness, and his memory didn't stir up the old, awful feelings of inferiority that used to grip her like a bad cold whenever he came to mind.

He'd lost his power to hurt her. She was over him. Her lips curved in an enormous grin.

"Kyle seems floored," Summer said.

"Kyle?"

"Your date," Summer said dryly.

Frannie blushed. She knew it was silly, but throughout this whole night the man she kept thinking about was Austin. She couldn't seem to get him off her mind. She kept thinking about the way he'd come to her rescue with Lyle, the way he'd gently bandaged her knee, the way he'd felt when she'd fallen in his lap. The smell of him, the warmth of him, the feel of his hand on her hip—the thought of it sent hot shivers racing all over her body.

Summer leaned across the linen-draped bistro table in the dimly lit hall. "So what do you think of Kyle?"

Frannie saw the tuxedoed back of her date disappear into the crowd as he and Gavin and Jasmine's date headed to the bar to refresh her and Summer's drinks. "He's very nice."

"Uh-oh." Summer looked at her closely. "I hear a 'but' in your voice. But what?"

Frannie hesitated.

"But you don't find him attractive?" Jasmine prompted.

"No, he's very nice-looking. But…" Frannie's voice trailed off.

But he's not Austin. It was ridiculous and Frannie knew it, but she couldn't help it. "Kyle's very nice," she said, "but I just don't feel any chemistry."

"Well, that's certainly not the case on his part," Summer

said. "He hasn't taken his eyes off you." Summer looked around and smiled. "But, then, neither have most of the men in this room. You're the belle of the ball." She looked out of the corner of her eye and lowered her voice. "Don't look now, but here comes another admirer."

Frannie glanced up to see a stocky man with a brown mustache standing behind her chair. The man nervously cleared his throat. "Would you like to dance?"

"Go ahead," Summer urged. "I'm sure Kyle won't mind."

Frannie rose and smiled. She *did* feel like the belle of the ball. She felt attractive and feminine and sought-after. Instead of wasting the evening mooning over someone unattainable like Austin Parker, she told herself, she ought be enjoying the attention of all the men who *were* interested in her.

Her cousins were right, she decided as she stepped onto the dance floor. It didn't hurt to live a little.

It didn't hurt a bit, she thought when the orchestra played its last song two hours later as she danced with Kyle. "Is it already over?"

Someone turned up the lights. Kyle looked at her, his pale eyes shining hopefully in his even paler face. "It doesn't have to be. We could go somewhere else."

"Oh, let's!" Frannie looked around the table. "I still feel like dancing. Why don't we all go to the Hot T?"

Summer and Jasmine exchanged amused glances. Frannie smiled sheepishly, realizing that the suggestion was completely out of character. But she *felt* out of character tonight. Just for tonight, she felt as if she were living a fairy tale.

"That's a great idea," Jasmine said.

Summer turned to her husband. "I think that sounds like fun, don't you, Gavin?"

Gavin glanced longingly at Summer and sighed, then smiled gamely. "Whatever you say, sweetheart."

Loud country-western music spilled out of the wooden door into the night air as Frannie followed Summer into the Hot T honky-tonk thirty minutes later. It took a moment for Frannie's eyes to adjust to the dim lighting. When they did, she saw that several couples in the casually clad crowd were wearing formal attire. Evidently a few other people attending the ball had decided to prolong the evening.

"There's an empty table against the wall." Gavin had to shout to be heard above the music and the noisy crowd. He steered Summer toward it. Jasmine and her date followed, and Frannie and Kyle brought up the rear. His hand was on the small of her back when Frannie suddenly froze in her tracks.

"Is something wrong?" Kyle asked.

Just that my heart stopped beating for a moment, and now it's going a thousand beats a minute. "I—I'm fine," Frannie managed to say.

"You look like you've seen a ghost."

He's not a ghost, but he's been haunting me all the same. There, on the far side of the tavern, stood Austin, as handsome as the devil in jeans and a Western-cut blue shirt. He was leaning against the pine-paneled wall, his head inclined politely, smiling at a busty blonde in tight jeans and an even tighter halter top who was talking to him in an animated fashion. He looked over as Frannie stared at him, and his gaze collided with hers like a semitrailer in a head-on crash.

Frannie couldn't breathe. She couldn't move. She could only stare as Austin stared back.

"Frannie?" Kyle asked, his forehead wrinkled with concern. "Are you feeling all right?"

"Huh? Oh, yes." Frannie knew she should pull her eyes away from Austin, but she couldn't seem to make herself. As she watched, Austin's lips curved in a sexy smile, and he lifted his can of beer in a silent salute. Frannie unfurled her fingers in a weak wave, then hurried to the table to join Summer and Jasmine, feeling oddly shell-shocked.

Kyle pulled out a chair and Frannie lowered herself into it, letting the conversation at the table buzz around her. The waitress came and took their order. Frannie tried not to look at Austin, but she seemed unable to help herself. She watched the blonde hand him a piece of paper. She saw him scribble something on it, then hand it back to her. Probably a phone number, Frannie thought. A hot poker of jealousy burned in her chest.

Kyle leaned toward her, blocking her view. "I think I can handle this song, if you'd like to dance."

Frannie realized the band was playing a slow ballad. After urging everyone to continue the evening because she felt like dancing, she couldn't very well refuse. "Sure."

She rose from the chair and let Kyle lead her to the dance floor, but she was no longer interested in dancing. She was only interested in the tall man across the room with the vivid blue eyes that seemed to follow her every move.

"Say, aren't those two of the gals from the bed-and-breakfast?" Tommy Deshaw angled his bottle of beer toward the table with Summer and Jasmine.

Austin took a swig of his beer. "Yep."

"Wow, they sure look swell. Musta been some kinda fancy shindig somewhere in town tonight. I wonder where their cousin is. You know—the one who threw egg on your face and tumbled into your lap at the bank and nearly got killed savin' a dog in traffic." Tommy chuckled and shook his head.

"She's out on the dance floor."

"She is?" Tommy craned his head. "Where?"

"There. In the red dress."

"That's her? *That's* Little Miss Hap?" Tommy stared, bug-eyed, then let out a low, appreciative whistle. "I wouldn' have recognized her. Man, she sure cleans up nice."

"No kidding."

"Wonder who she's dancin' with?"

Austin was wondering the same thing. He didn't like the way the man's hand rested on her waist, or the goofy grin on his face as he looked down at her. He didn't like the man at all, for no other reason than the fact that he was dancing with Frannie.

"I don't know who it is right now," Austin said, thrusting his beer into Tommy's hand, "but it's about to be me." Striding purposefully onto the dance floor, Austin dodged his way through the crowd and tapped the tuxedo-clad man on the shoulder.

Frannie's dance partner turned around, his expression startled. Austin looked past him to Frannie. Her eyes were wide, her lips slightly parted.

"Mind if I cut in?"

"Well, uh…"

Before the man could form a response, Austin swept Frannie into his arms and guided her to the far side of the dance floor. "Hey, there."

"Hey, yourself."

It was there again, that sharp, electric attraction he'd felt when she'd landed on his lap that day at the bank—an attraction so keen that everything else receded into the fuzzy distance, everything but the warmth of her skin and the glow of her eyes.

The scent of her perfume invaded his senses, curling around him like a magic spell. "You look gorgeous."

Frannie's lips curved up. Austin found himself staring at them in fascination, wondering how they would feel under his.

"You're just saying that because I don't have any goo on my face. Or do I? Maybe I should go check."

Austin tightened his hold on her. Damn, but she felt good—warm and soft and silk-covered. The desire to get closer pulled at him like undertow. "I don't want you to go anywhere."

He heard the little hitch in her breath, felt her fingers clutch at his back, and it struck him as intensely erotic, the kind of response she might make during lovemaking. Arousal, strong and hot, flamed within him. He moved his hand low along her spine, aligning her body more closely with his.

She sighed and shifted, pressing her breasts against his chest.

Oh, criminy. This was torture—hot, sweet torture. He swallowed, his mouth suddenly dry, and searched for something to say, for something, anything, to divert his attention from the entirely inappropriate response his body was having to her. "So what's the special occasion?"

"Hmm?" Her eyes held a dark, desire-dazed look. A fresh flash of heat flared inside him. So she felt it, too.

"You're all dressed up."

"Oh. We went to the Whitehorn Ball. It's an annual benefit for the hospital."

"Who's your date?"

"Kyle Johnson."

"Are you two serious?"

"Oh, no." Frannie's hair brushed his cheek as she shook

her head. "He's a blind date my cousin fixed me up with. They're both doctors."

An irrational sense of relief filled his chest. "Well, it's good to know there's a doctor in the house." *Because the way you're affecting me, sweetheart, I'm likely to need one before this dance is over.*

"So what about you?" she asked. "Who are you with?"

The warm weight of her breasts against his chest made it impossible to think coherently. "Tommy."

She lifted one eyebrow. "I meant, the woman."

"What woman?"

She pulled back and looked at him archly, as if she thought he was trying to pull a fast one. "The blonde you were talking to when I came in."

"Oh, her. I don't even know her name. She just wanted an autograph."

"An autograph," Frannie repeated softly. "Do a lot of people ask for one?"

Austin lifted a shoulder. "A lot more than I'd like."

Frannie's eyes rested on him. "Sounds like you're not all that comfortable with your celebrity status."

He lifted a shoulder. "I don't like folks to make a big fuss."

"You don't like being the center of attention?"

"Not unless it's from someone I want attention from." He pulled her closer. "Like you."

He wasn't sure, but he thought he felt a shiver pass through her. He definitely heard her sigh, because he felt the warmth of her breath on his neck. She rested her cheek against his chin and let him rock her to the music, which ended all too soon.

He reluctantly pulled back as the last note faded and the crowd applauded.

"I'll walk you back to your table," Austin said.

* * *

Frannie could tell by the tight look on Kyle's face that he wasn't happy to see Austin accompany her back to the table, but he was too much of a gentleman to make an issue of it. With a forced smile, Kyle stood and pulled out her chair as she and Austin approached.

Austin stuck his hand out to Kyle. "Thanks for letting me cut in on you out there. I'm Austin Parker."

"So I've heard." Kyle gestured to Gavin. "Seems you've got a big fan here."

Gavin was immediately on his feet, his hand outstretched. "Gavin Nighthawk. Around here I'm better known as Summer's husband." Gavin grabbed an extra chair from the next table. "Please, have a seat and join us."

"Well, all right, if you'll let me buy you a round."

Austin sat between Frannie and Gavin. Kyle placed his arm territorially around the back of Frannie's chair.

"I saw the TV coverage of your race in Atlanta," Gavin said, leaning forward. "Man, that was something, the way you pulled into the lead at the last moment."

The conversation was off and running as if a checkered flag had been dropped. Frannie was relieved, because she felt far too rattled to speak.

Never in her life had she felt anything like the surge of attraction she'd felt in Austin's arms on the dance floor. He made her feel weak-kneed and foggy-headed and incredibly, meltingly aroused. Even now, it was hard not to gravitate toward him, like metal shavings to a magnet.

Frannie realized she was actually leaning toward Austin. She started to straighten, but as she pulled away, the hard, warm weight of his thigh against hers under the table made her freeze. The next thing she knew, his hand rested on her leg, just above her knee. Shock waves of pleasure rolled through her. The secret, unexpected intimacy was like forbidden fruit, delicious and irresistible.

She suddenly realized Kyle's hand had slid from the back of her chair to her neck.

"I got shortchanged on that last dance," he said. "Don't you think you owe me another?"

On the other side of her body, Austin gave her leg a little squeeze. A shiver of pleasure coursed through Fannie. It was hard to act normal as she turned to Kyle and forced a smile. "Sure. And I'm ready to pay up."

Austin's hand slipped slowly off her leg as she rose. She could still feel the heat of his hand as she stepped into Kyle's arms and let him lead her in a two-step. She couldn't help but compare the difference in the way it felt, dancing with the two men. She tried to make casual conversation, but her eyes kept drifting to the table. Austin was watching her, his eyes licking over her like blue flames.

The other two couples were on the dance floor when Kyle and Frannie returned to the table. The prospect of sitting alone between Kyle and Austin made her palms begin to sweat. With a quick, "Excuse me," she grabbed her small beaded bag and fled to the safety of the ladies' room.

She hid out until she heard the song end. Hoping that either Summer or Jasmine would have returned to the table, she stepped out of the restroom door—and ran smack into Austin.

Her heart pounded hard as he took her arm and began steering her toward the wall. "What are you doing?"

"I need to talk to you for a minute."

"I—I really ought to get back to the table."

He stopped at the end of the small hallway that housed the restrooms. "It's okay. The doc's outside, returning a call from his answering service." Austin placed his hands on her upper arms. His fingers were warm, his touch gentle, yet Frannie felt as if he left a burning trail of heat as his fingers slid down her bare skin. "Look, I know you're here

with him tonight, so I won't try to horn in, but I want to
take you out. What are you doing tomorrow night?''

Frannie's heart pounded hard. Something about Austin
scared her to death. The way she responded to him was so
out of character, so strongly emotional, so completely il-
logical. "I don't know…"

What she didn't know, she realized, was *herself* when
she was around him. He brought out a side of her she'd
never known, a sensual side so intense and compelling that
she couldn't trust her own judgment.

"Well, then, I'll tell you what you're doing." He trailed
the back of his curved finger gently down her cheek.
"You're having dinner with me at the Lakeside Inn. I'll
pick you up at seven." His finger continued its erotic path,
trailing down to her mouth. He gently traced the outline of
her bottom lip, then gave a slow smile and walked away.

Frannie leaned against the wall, both terrified and
thrilled. How in the world was she supposed to hold her
own against a man like Austin?

Seven

Jasmine leaned over the front desk the next evening and tapped her wristwatch. "Frannie, it's ten minutes until seven. Why on earth aren't you dressed?"

Frannie glanced up from the stack of receipts she was sorting, then looked down at her jeans. "I *am* dressed," she said calmly.

Jasmine rolled her eyes. "You know what I mean. Dressed for your date with Austin."

Frannie turned back to the receipts. "I'm as a dressed as I'm going to get."

"Are you out of your *mind?* You're wearing your oldest jeans and a baggy gray sweater, you don't have on a lick of makeup, and you're hiding behind your glasses again."

"This is me. This is how I am. If Austin doesn't like it, well, that's just too bad." She entered the information from a pink receipt into the computer, trying to act more confident than she felt. "Besides, I'm not sure I'm going."

"Of course you're going!" Circling the front desk, Jasmine charged toward her.

"I never said I would. Austin didn't actually ask." Frannie clicked the computer mouse, pretending not to notice that her cousin had pulled up a stool, plopped herself at her elbow and was staring at her in disbelief.

"And why on earth wouldn't you? What possible objection could you have to Austin Parker?" Jasmine placed her hands on her hips and frowned indignantly. "Is he too nice, too charming, too famous, too wealthy or too good-looking?"

"Yes."

"*Yes?*" Jasmine's voice was an incredulous shout.

Frannie raised her finger to her mouth. "Keep it down, Jasmine. You'll disturb the guests and Aunt Celeste."

"What's with you, Frannie?" Jasmine grabbed the arms of Frannie's chair and swiveled her around to face her. "Summer and I spent a lot of time making you over so you'd have some confidence and get a social life, and it worked better than any of us dreamed. The sexiest man ever to hit the state of Montana asked you out, and now you're telling me you don't think you're going to go?"

"That's just it. Last night wasn't me." Frannie's hand swept from her glasses to her jeans. "*This* is me."

"That was you last night, too." Jasmine's eyes flashed hotly, and her voice held a hard edge of insistence. "The only difference is, last night you were making an effort."

Frannie sighed. "Don't you see, Jasmine? I can't sustain that kind of effort, that kind of illusion, for long. I'm not a graceful, glamorous, outgoing person. I'm a shy, awkward, number-crunching bookworm. And sooner or later, any man who spends any time around me will discover that. And when he does, he's bound to dump me for someone more exciting. I think it'll hurt a whole lot less if it happens sooner rather than later."

Jasmine placed a hand on Frannie's arm, her brow creased in concern. "Oh, Frannie, I can't believe how you underestimate yourself! You're letting one bad experience warp your outlook."

Maybe so, Frannie thought, but it was the self-protective thing to do. A man such as Austin Parker was not going to be interested in someone like her for long. And judging from the intensity of emotions he stirred inside her, he had the potential to break her heart ten times worse than Joe ever did.

The loud chime of the doorbell broke her thoughts. Both Frannie and Jasmine turned in the direction of the front door.

"That must be Austin. Everyone else just walks in," Jasmine said. "Aren't you going to answer it?"

Obviously Jasmine had no intention of doing so. Frannie took a deep, steadying breath and rose from the computer. Despite her determination not to fuss with her appearance, she couldn't keep from tugging at her sweater and smoothing her ponytail as she walked to the door.

The sight of the tall, handsome man standing on the porch hit her like a blow to the solar plexus, knocking most the air out of her. "Hi."

"Hi." He grinned, revealing a dimple on his right cheek. "May I come in?"

Frannie realized she was just standing there, staring at him. She stepped back out of the way. "Of course."

He waved a greeting to Jasmine, who was standing behind the front desk, then settled his gaze back on Frannie. "Am I early?"

Frannie hoped she didn't look as nervous as she felt. Her heart was pounding and her palms were damp. "No. I think you're right on time."

"Great." He shoved a hand into the pocket of his khaki slacks. "So, are you ready?"

Was he asking because he didn't think she was? Frannie tugged at the sleeve of her sweater and eyed him suspiciously. "I never actually said I'd go out with you, you know. You didn't exactly ask."

He grinned. "That's because I didn't want to give you an opportunity to say no."

Good heavens, but he had sexy eyes. It was hard to think when he turned them on her that way.

He flashed that dimple again. "If you want to just stay here, though, that's fine with me. We could order in a pizza, and just sit and talk."

Frannie pushed her glasses up higher on her nose, trying to decide what to make of him. Was he suggesting that they stay in because he didn't want to be seen in public with her? Maybe he thought being seen with someone so ordinary would be bad for his image, as Joe had thought all those years ago. The thought roused a stubborn streak within her.

"No. Since you're here, we might as well go ahead and go out."

"Okay." He looked at her curiously, then gestured toward the door. "Well, then, shall we?"

"You two have a good time," Jasmine called.

Frannie stiffly walked beside Austin out the door and across the porch. Part of her was thrilled to be with him, but another part, a self-protective part, was scared to death and wary. What on earth would they talk about?

He led her to a black pickup truck parked in the drive, and she seized on it as a topic of conversation. "I thought you'd be in a racy red sports car," she said as he opened the passenger door.

He lifted his shoulders. "I get my fill of racing on the track. This is a lot more practical for running a ranch." Slamming the door closed, he circled the truck and climbed in the driver's seat. Frannie half expected him to lay rubber as he backed out of the drive, but he drove slowly and carefully.

Frannie felt a disconcerting pull of attraction as she glanced at his profile. She was curious about him, curious why he'd moved here. "Tell me about your ranch. You said you raise horses?"

He nodded. "Quarter horses."

"I would have expected a race car driver to raise Thoroughbreds."

"Nah. Too temperamental. Quarter horses are big, strong and smart. When they race, they run on a straightaway. It's the horse that wins or loses a race, not the skill of the jockey."

"How many do you have?"

"Just six right now. Three brood mares, two foals and a stallion. I'm trying to start a breeding operation. When I retire from racing, I'll expand it into a training facility."

Frannie looked at him in surprise. "You're thinking about retiring from racing?"

Austin shrugged. "Every driver thinks about it, and sooner or later, most of them do. I've told myself a dozen times that I'll quit after the next race. But then there's another one, and, well…" He lifted his shoulders. "I know the smart thing to do is to quit while I'm ahead, but so far I just haven't been able to bring myself to do it. I love the challenge of the sport. I'm beginning to think I probably won't quit until I'm too old to handle the pressure."

"The pressure must be pretty intense. It's an awfully dangerous sport, isn't it?"

His head bobbed in a single nod. "One mistake out there and it's all over."

"Aren't you afraid?"

"Nah. Not for myself. I've got nothing to lose."

"Right," Frannie said dryly. "Just your life."

"Well, yeah, I suppose there's that." Austin shot her a rakish grin. "Or my mind. A few more head injuries, and there won't be enough brain cells left to worry with."

Frannie felt a surge of alarm. "You've been injured?"

"Oh, sure. I don't think there's a serious racer out there that hasn't hit the wall or had a bad crash or two. It happens."

"Doesn't that worry you when you get behind the wheel?"

Austin shook his head. "Once I strap on that helmet, there's no room for worry. There's no room for thinking about anything but driving. It takes total concentration. That's the thing I like best about it, I guess."

"But while you're concentrating, you still have to be aware of the risks."

"Well, sure, but I don't dwell on them. Like I said, I've got nothing to lose—no family to worry about, no wife, no kids. Aside from my pit crew, no one in the world is depending on me. And my crew could find other jobs in a heartbeat if something happened to me."

The flat, matter-of-fact tone of his voice sent a chill up Frannie's arms. "I can't believe you can talk about your life like that."

"Like what?"

"Like it's expendable."

Austin shrugged. "Well, I guess it is. It's of no value to anyone but me. And I like it that way."

She knew she shouldn't ask, but she couldn't help herself. "Why?"

"I don't have to worry about hurting anyone else."

"You could hurt another racer."

Austin nodded solemnly. "Yeah. But I try to look at it this way—out on the track, it's an even playing field. Everyone knows the odds. Everyone's taking the same risks. So I just show up and do my best, and so far, my luck's held out."

"Sounds like an awfully lonely life."

"It's all I've ever known. Besides, having nothing to lose gives me a winning edge."

Frannie gazed at him, trying to fathom the emptiness of a life that wasn't connected to anyone else's in any profound kind of way. "I can't imagine living that way."

Austin shrugged. "It's easy when you're accustomed to it."

Frannie gazed at him. "What happened to your family?"

"I never had much of one. I was an only child, and my mother left when I was six."

"What do you mean, left?"

"Left. Went away."

Something hard in his tone of voice warned Frannie not pursue the line of questioning. She decided to take another tack. "What about your dad?"

"He died when I was sixteen." Austin squirmed on his seat and cut a glance at Frannie. "So tell me about your family. Do your parents live at the Big Sky?"

It was an obvious ploy to change the subject, but Frannie decided to go along with it. Maybe she could get him to tell her more about his family later. "No. My folks have a house about a mile from the bed-and-breakfast, but right now they're out of town. My dad's mom had hip replacement surgery, and they're in Minnesota helping her get back on her feet."

"Do you have any brothers or sisters?"

"One older brother. David's with the F.B.I. in Atlanta. And I have three cousins who seem like sisters."

"I've met Summer and Jasmine."

Frannie nodded. "And the other one is Cleo. She runs the day care center in town. She just got married, so she's off on an extended honeymoon with her new husband and his little boy."

Austin shot her an interested glance as he turned the truck

onto a side road. "Must be nice, having a large family. What are your parents like?"

Frannie grinned. "A couple of overgrown kids."

"Yeah?" Austin's eyes were amused. "In what way?"

"Oh, they're outgoing and fun-loving and free-spirited." Frannie smiled. "Sometimes I used to feel like our roles were reversed, like I was the parent and they were the children. They were always trying to get me to go out and have fun. I've always been kind of quiet and reserved and serious."

"What line of work are they in?"

"Dad is an architect, and Mom helps Aunt Celeste run the B and B. Despite their careers, though, they're both really spontaneous and adventurous. They're a perfect match. They have a really close, loving marriage—the kind I hope to have some day."

"How did you come to live at the B and B?"

"I spent so much time there when I was growing up that it felt like a second home. In fact, I started doing bookkeeping for the place when I was fifteen. After I graduated from college, Celeste offered me free room and board in exchange for continuing to keep the books. I didn't like living alone and I was spending all my free time there anyway, so it was a perfect solution."

"It's a grand old house. Has it been in your family long?"

"Quite a while. Aunt Celeste and her late husband bought it before any of the kids were born. She and Mom ran it, figuring it'd be a good way to earn a living while raising a family—which it was. In addition to their own children, Aunt Celeste and Mom raised Summer, their late sister's child."

"Sounds like your family is awfully close."

Frannie grinned. "We are. We're like a big wooly blanket—large, close-knit and warm."

"When I was a kid, I used to like to pretend I had a family like that," Austin said. "I never could really picture it, though."

The wistfulness in his voice struck a chord within Frannie, a chord that reverberated right to her very soul.

The pickup slid to a halt, and Frannie was surprised to realize that they'd already arrived at the restaurant. "Stay put," Austin said. "I'll come around and get your door."

Frannie watched him circle the truck, a single word echoing in her head: *lonely.* For all of his success, Austin Parker was a deeply lonely man.

And he seemed to prefer it that way. What was it he'd said? *Having nothing to lose gives me a winning edge.*

She walked beside him across the parking lot, wondering why she was so attracted to a man who'd clearly stated he didn't want a deep relationship. And why was she so talkative around him? She was usually closedmouthed and bashful around people she didn't know well, yet she'd talked a blue streak on the drive to the restaurant.

They were thoroughly unsuited for each other, complete opposites. She wanted a home and family, and he wanted the freedom of being unattached. He belonged to an exciting world of fame and fast cars, while she craved anonymity and quiet.

So why did she feel more drawn to this man than to anyone she'd ever met?

The restaurant hostess seated them beside a window overlooking a portion of Blue Mirror Lake. The water was calm and dark, and the sky held a slight cast of purple as the sun sank into the horizon.

"What a wonderful view," Frannie sighed.

"I was thinking the same thing." She looked up to find Austin's gaze fastened on her face.

Frannie felt her skin heat, and she suddenly wished she'd taken more pains with her appearance. The amazing thing was that Austin seemed to think she was just fine the way she was. He was looking at her with a light in his eye, with real interest, as if he saw beyond her glasses, beyond her casual clothes, beyond her skin.

A warm shiver chased over her.

"Tell me about yourself, Frannie. Have you always lived in Whitehorn?"

Frannie nodded. "Except when I went away to college."

"Where did you go?"

"Montana State University in Bozeman." Frannie looked at him. "How about you?"

Austin shook his head. "After my old man died, I had to go to work to support myself. I didn't even finish high school. I took correspondence courses and earned my high school diploma, but college wasn't in the cards for me. I've always admired people with a lot of education." He leveled his eyes at her, and she felt another thrill of attraction. "What did you major in?"

"Mathematical sciences and literature. I had a double major."

Austin let out a soft whistle and shook his head. "You must be a real brain."

Frannie shrugged. "I've just always loved math and reading."

"Lots of folks love reading—I'm one of them—but I don't know that I've ever heard anyone say they loved math before."

Frannie smiled. "I know. I've always been something of an oddball. My parents used to fuss at me about it."

"How?"

"Oh, when I was a kid, they were always pushing me to get my head out of my books and go outside and play. When I was a teenager, my mother lectured me about not being sociable enough."

"You seem pretty sociable to me."

It was true. Around him, she even *felt* sociable. It was odd, how he made her feel both unsettled and at ease. She shrugged her shoulders. "I've always found it hard to make small talk. I never much saw the point in it. I guess I like my connections with people to be deep instead of plentiful."

"I was kind of a loner, too. But I can't say that I enjoyed math."

"People think math is hard, but it's not, not really. It can be fun, like doing puzzles or riddles. In fact, I've always wanted to write children's books that illustrate that."

"So why don't you?"

"Actually, I have." Frannie twisted the napkin in her lap, immediately embarrassed. Why had she told him that? No one else knew about the stack of papers stuffed in her bedside drawer.

"You've written some books?"

"Well, they're not books, exactly. I mean, they're not published. They're just some pages I've written down."

"What are they about?"

"Oh, nothing. I mean, they're silly."

Austin regarded her solemnly. "I promise not to laugh."

"Well, actually, they're supposed to be funny."

"Then I'll laugh like a hyena."

Why had she ever opened her big mouth? Now she had to tell him or appear rude. "Well, they're a series of stories about a baby kangaroo. He and his koala bear buddy make up games about numbers and fractions and percentages, games that the reader can play along with."

"Are they illustrated?"

Frannie nodded, her face growing warm. "I'm no great artist, but I can draw cartoon figures. Like I said, the books are pretty silly."

"Are they finished?"

"As finished as I can make them. I have three of them."

"Have you sent them to any publishers?"

Frannie shook her head.

"Why not?"

"Oh, I'd be embarrassed. They're really not all that good."

"How do you know?"

"Well, they're just something I've been playing around with. I'm not a professional."

"No one is when they first start out. Everyone has to begin somewhere." Austin leaned forward. "What's the worst that can happen if you send it to a publishing house?"

Frannie shrugged her shoulders.

"They can tell you no, that's what. And then you could turn around and put those manuscripts right back in the mail and send them somewhere else."

Frannie gave a sardonic smile. "So another publishing house can tell me no, too?"

"Maybe. But then again, they might just tell you yes." Austin leaned back in his chair. "In order to have a chance of winning the race, Frannie, you've got to show up at the track."

"But what if every children's book publisher in the country tells me no?"

"Well, then, you use all the information you've gained and you try again. You write another book." Austin looked at her intently. "What do you have to lose, except a few dollars on postage?"

Frannie felt her chest tighten. "My dream," she said softly. "I could lose my dream."

"But by not taking action, you're losing the chance of ever making it a reality."

There was no arguing with his logic. Still, a part of Frannie resisted. "It's just…" She took a deep breath and slowly let it out. Her finger toyed with a loose thread on the tablecloth. "I hate to be rejected."

Austin's hand covered hers, enveloping her with warmth. "Everyone does. And sooner or later, everyone is."

An edge to his voice made her look up. His smile had faded, and his eyes held an intensity she hadn't seen before.

"You sound like you've had personal experience with rejection," she said softly.

"I have."

"By whom?"

"Oh, no one important." His mouth quirked into a mirthless smile. "Just my mother."

Frannie's heart turned in her chest. She wanted to ask him more, but he cut her off by picking up her menu and handing it to her. "The waiter is heading our way. We'd better decide what we're going to eat."

They'd just placed their order when Austin waved at someone in the doorway. Frannie turned to see a familiar man with handsome Native American features walking toward their table. "Hi, Austin," the man said, extending his hand. "How's it going?"

Austin stood and shook the man's hand. "Great. Frannie, this is Jackson Hawk, the attorney for the Laughing Horse Reservation."

"We know each other," Frannie said, shaking the man's hand. "Jackson is a good friend of Gavin's."

"Nice to see you, Frannie."

"Good to see you, too." Frannie looked from Jackson

o Austin, then back again. "How do you two happen to know each other?"

"Austin came to the reservation and spoke to our boys' club last week." Jackson turned to Austin. "I can't thank you enough, either. You made a big impression on some kids who were veering off in the wrong direction."

Austin shrugged modestly. "Glad I could help."

Frannie looked at him, her heart growing warm. The more she learned about him, the more she found to like. And it scared her to death.

"What did Austin talk about?" she found herself asking Jackson.

"The importance of hard work and goal-setting," Jackson replied. "He gave a really inspiring speech."

Frannie grinned. "Why, that's the very same speech he was just giving me!"

Austin laughed, but he shifted uncomfortably.

Jackson smiled. "The kids listened to him in a way they won't listen to other adults. Austin's a great role model."

Austin gazed at the tabletop. It was funny, Frannie mused, the praise seemed to embarrass him. Who would have guessed that a man in such a high-profile profession would be so modest and unassuming?

"Are you meeting someone here?" Austin asked Jackson, as if he were eager to change the topic.

Jackson nodded. "Lyle Brooks. To discuss some business."

"On a Sunday night?"

Jackson nodded and heaved a sigh. "Afraid so. Lyle is the contractor building the casino and resort, and he wants to talk about moving the location to a piece of land he owns further north."

"I've met the illustrious Mr. Brooks," Austin said. "He left me with a bad taste in my mouth."

Jackson's lips tilted in a dry smile. "He seems to have that effect on people."

Austin's brow pulled into a frown. "You say he wants to move the site? I thought he'd already begun construction on the resort."

"He has. He's blasted and cleared a forty-five-foot-deep construction pit."

Frannie leaned forward. "That's what the equipment operator fell into, isn't it?"

Jackson nodded somberly. "It's a real tragedy, and it's bringing a lot of unfavorable publicity to the project. That's what Lyle says he wants to talk about. Because of that man's death and an old skeleton that was found earlier on a nearby site, he thinks the land is cursed. He says it'll bring the tribe bad luck if we build there."

"Won't it be expensive to move the site now?" Austin asked.

Jackson's head bobbed again. "That's the oddest part. Lyle said he'd absorb the cost for any extra work involved. Says it won't cost the tribe a penny." Jackson shook his head. "I don't know what he's up to, but he tried to wring every last nickel out of us when he negotiated the contract. It's hard to believe he's suddenly willing to swallow tens of thousands of dollars out of the goodness of his heart."

"From what I saw of the man, it's hard to believe he even *has* a heart," Austin remarked. "He didn't strike me as the kind of person likely to look out for anyone's interests but his own."

Jackson grinned. "I'd say you're a shrewd judge of character, Austin." He winked at Frannie. "Not to mention of women." Jackson glanced toward the restaurant entrance. "There's Lyle now. I'll steer him toward the bar and see if a little bourbon will flush out his real motives." He gave a little salute. "You two enjoy your dinner."

Frannie watched Jackson head across the room. "I wonder what Lyle is really up to."

"My guess is it's some kind of scheme to pad his pockets."

"Well, I hope he's more careful in his business dealings than he is at driving."

"I don't think our little encounter with Lyle was a matter of carelessness. I think he was acting with cold-blooded deliberation."

"What do you mean?"

"It looked to me like he was deliberately aiming for that dog."

Frannie's eyes widened. "Why would he do a thing like that?"

Austin shrugged. "For the sport of it. Some men have no conscience." He leaned across the table. "I gotta tell you, you scared me to death when you dashed out in front of his car."

A wave of warmth rushed through her. *Don't take it personally,* she warned herself. Austin was the kind of man who would be concerned about anyone in harm's way. For some reason, though, the realization didn't kill the tenderness that was taking root inside of her.

"I guess it was a pretty foolish stunt," Frannie conceded.

"You *guess?*"

"Oh, all right," she said grudgingly. "It was."

"No kidding." Austin's eyes warmed her as they slid over her face. The hint of a smile curved his lips. "But you know what else it was? One of the kindest, bravest things I've ever seen." He reached out and covered her hand with his. His thumb moved over the tops of her knuckles, leaving a trail of heat that raced straight up her arm into her chest.

Frannie gazed at Austin, and his gaze held hers, just as surely as his fingers did. Her eyes dropped to his lips. What would it be like to kiss a man like Austin, she wondered. A man so thoughtful and sexy and...

"Here you go," the waiter said, interrupting her thoughts as he set down their salads.

Here I go, all right, Frannie thought grimly. Jumping in too deep, too fast. She had no business letting Austin touch her, physically or emotionally. There was no future in a relationship with a man who was not only out of her league, but not interested in commitment.

She pulled back her hand, but it was too late. The heat of his touch had already burned its way inside of her.

The sky was deep blue, almost black, when Austin opened the door from the restaurant for Frannie an hour and a half later.

"That was delicious," she said.

Austin nodded. "The best meal I've had in weeks." The best conversation, too, he thought. They'd talked about music and work and movies, about politics and racing and art. He'd found Frannie bright and witty and amusing. He smiled as she stepped out the door. "The company was good, too."

"You're just saying that because I let you do most of the talking."

"Ow!" Austin placed a hand over his heart, as if he'd been shot. "Well, that's what you get for telling me you wanted to know all about racing."

"But I did. And it was fascinating." She reached out and touched his arm, her lips curved in a smile. "I was teasing you just now."

You've been teasing me all night, Austin thought. Her whole buttoned-down appearance was a tease. All evening long, he'd been itching to take off her glasses, to loosen her hair, to touch the lovely body he knew was hidden under her bulky sweater. "Do you want to go somewhere else? To a movie, or maybe out for a drink?"

She shook her head. "I have to be at the bank early in the morning. I'd better be getting back."

But Austin didn't want the evening to end. Not yet. "It's such a beautiful night. Why don't we walk down by the lake? I saw a path earlier."

"All right."

He led her to the edge of the parking lot, where a trail headed through the forest toward the lake. He fell into step beside her. About a hundred yards from the restaurant, the path twisted to follow the shoreline, and the restaurant was obscured by the trees. The sounds of the night enfolded them. A soft breeze rustled the leaves overhead, stirring the water just enough to make little lapping sounds against shore. A bullfrog croaked, and a chorus of crickets sang backup.

Frannie wrapped her arms around herself and gazed out at the night. "It's so beautiful here."

"Seems like we're miles away from the rest of the world."

Frannie nodded. "It's so unspoiled. Just think—we're looking at exactly the same view Indians saw centuries ago."

"Not exactly the same," Austin found himself saying. "Nothing stays the same for long."

Frannie looked at him curiously.

"Everything is always in a state of change." It was a fact he knew all too well, a fact he'd learned as a boy. And because nothing lasted forever, it was best to not get attached to people or to places or to things. "Better to move on while things are good than to hang around and wait for them to turn sour," his father used to say. So every few months, Austin would stuff all his belongings into his small, brown duffel bag and leave whatever place had come to feel like home. He used to look out the back window of his father's old truck and cry as they drove away. By the age of ten, he'd learned it hurt less to never look back.

"If you mean the seasons, well, yes, of course," Frannie was saying, "But the basic landscape is the same."

"Nah. Even that has changed. I'm sure there have been floods and fires. A bolt of lightning hits a tree, then—zap!" He snapped his fingers. "An entire forest is burned down."

"Yes, but given enough time, it grows back just as it was. It won't be exactly the same—not tree for tree, not exactly identical—but the basic character of the land is the same."

Austin looked at Frannie. "Like you, huh?"

"What do you mean?"

"Well, you're the same person with the same character, but every time I see you, you look different."

Frannie shot him a teasing smile. "That's because some days I wear an egg beret, and other days my face is green, and sometimes I have raccoon rings around my eyes...."

"...And sometimes you're so drop-dead gorgeous you nearly stop my heart." He turned toward her and lifted her hand. It felt small and warm, and the softness of it wrapped around him like a spell. "I had trouble sleeping last night, and it was all your fault. I just lay there, picturing the way you looked in that red dress."

Frannie's smile faded. She stepped back and pulled away her hand. "Last night wasn't me." She made a sweeping gesture toward herself. "*This* is me."

Her mood had abruptly darkened. He tried to lighten things up. "So who was the girl I danced with last night? Your secret twin?"

Frannie's spine straightened. Her eyes grew serious, her mouth unsmiling. "That was an illusion my cousins created. They wanted to make me over for the evening and I let them, but this is the real me. This is how I usually am."

She sounded so defensive, so prickly. Combative, almost. Austin frowned, wondering what he'd done to cause her reaction.

"I, uh, get the feeling I said something wrong." He rubbed his chin. "I was just saying you looked great last night. I didn't mean to offend you."

She seemed offended nonetheless. "Well, don't get the idea I'm that way all the time."

Austin's frown deepened, along with his confusion. "What do you mean, 'that way'? Attractive?"

Her eyes flashed. Her chin tilted up defiantly. "If your idea of attractive is someone who's all made up and manicured and teetering around on high heels, well, then, yes, that's what I mean."

What was with her? She acted as if he'd insulted her, when he'd been trying to give her a compliment. "Hey, I don't think it takes any of that stuff to make a woman attractive."

"Hmm." She arched a disapproving eyebrow. "Well, that figures."

What had he done now? He stared at her blankly. "What figures?"

"That you'd prefer the natural beauty type."

He was damned if he did and damned if he didn't. He pulled his brow into a hard scowl. "What's that supposed to mean?"

She pulled herself so straight and taut she looked in danger of snapping in two. "Well, you obviously prefer the kind of woman who wakes up in the morning looking fresh as a daisy without so much as brushing her teeth. Believe me, there aren't very many women who can pull that off."

He'd obviously said something to upset her, but he was

damned if he knew what it was. The infuriating part was that she seemed determined not to tell him. "What in blue blazes are you talking about?"

She blew out a huffy breath. "There's no point in pursuing this conversation. I'd like for you to take me home." She turned and started up the trail.

"Sorry. No can do."

She whipped around and glared at him, her eyebrows high. "You won't take me home?"

Austin took two steps forward, stopping just inches from her. "I'm not taking you anywhere until you tell me what the hell is going on."

"Nothing's going on!"

Austin's frustration had built to the point that by all rights, steam should be shooting from his ears. He stuck his face close to hers and scowled. "Damn straight. And I want to know why not."

Now she was staring at him as if *he* were the one who'd lost his mind. "What do you mean, why not?"

"I brought you out here to kiss you, and we're arguing instead. And I want to know why."

He wanted to kiss her? The concept made Frannie's head spin. She realized she was staring at him, slack-jawed, and abruptly closed her mouth. "We're...we're not arguing," she finally stammered.

"Well, we're damn sure not kissing!"

They glared at each other, each breathing hard.

Austin raised both his hands. "Okay. If you say we're not arguing, I won't argue with you about whether or not we're arguing. But would you mind telling me just what the hell it is we're supposedly discussing?"

He wanted to kiss her because he'd liked the way she looked last night, she reminded herself. He was attracted to a bunch of cosmetics, not to her. "Your male chauvinism."

Austin's fingers clenched, then unclenched at his sides. His voice was low and calm, but that probably had something to do with the fact that he was speaking through gritted teeth. "Perhaps it would help if you told me exactly how I'm chauvinistic."

"You said I looked beautiful last night."

"And that somehow makes me chauvinistic." He rubbed his head, shaking it at the same time. "Well, at the risk of offending you further, I've got to admit, sweetheart, I still don't know what I did wrong."

"Last night was smoke and mirrors. This is me." Frannie gestured toward herself. "The real me. I'm sorry to disappoint you, but this is what I look like without all the artifice."

Comprehension broke over his face. "And you think I was just attracted to the trappings?" His eyes glittered with something far more dangerous than his earlier anger. "Well, now, Frannie girl, you've got it all wrong."

"No, I don't."

"Oh, yes, you do." His voice was low and silky, and it made her breath catch in her throat. He took a step toward her. "Besides, it looks to me like you've still got a little artifice going there. "

Frannie nervously backed up. "What are you talking about?"

"Well, something artificial seems to be holding your hair back." He took two steps forward, invading her personal space, then reached behind her head and pulled the clip out of her hair. Her hair tumbled around her shoulders. His fingers sifted through it, arranging it on her shoulders. A shiver of pleasure shot through her. "There. That's better. Much more natural."

He inched even closer, until she could feel his breath on her face. "And about those glasses— I'm sure you weren't born with them. If you're going to be without any artifice, we'd better get rid of them, too." His fingers brushed her temple as he gently removed them. "Hmm. Well, now, look at that."

He was so close she could smell the faint scent of his shaving cream. It smelled clean and intoxicatingly masculine. "Look at what?" Her voice was a hoarse whisper.

"You. Now you look exactly like the woman I fantasized about last night."

He'd fantasized about her? Frannie's heart pounded hard against her ribs as he slid her glasses into his back pocket, then placed both hands on her upper arms. His touch was warm and electric. He shifted closer until his nose was less than an inch from hers and she could see the facets in his blue, blue eyes.

"Your eyes are incredible," he murmured. "So beautiful, so talkative. They're talking to me right now."

Frannie swallowed, her mouth dry.

"Can you see at close range?"

The ability to speak had deserted her. She nodded, her head bobbing as jerkily as a cork on a fishing line.

"Good. Because I want you to see how very, very much I want to kiss you. Right now. Just the way you look, at this very moment."

His eyes were hot and hungry, and she melted under the warmth of his gaze. Her skin ached to be touched. Her lips ached to be kissed. Her fingers ached to feel his skin. Oh, mercy, she was aching all over. Aching of want, of need, of impatience.

He moved with exquisite, torturous slowness. Slowly, slowly, his hands slid up her arms, to her shoulders. Slowly, slowly—oh, he was killing her with his slowness!—his face moved nearer, his eyes heavy-lidded but still open, still looking straight into hers. The first brush of his lips on hers was soft, as soft as butterfly wings, a soft taunt of a kiss. He pulled back, still gazing into her eyes, then resettled his lips over hers, deepening and expanding the kiss. When he took her bottom lip into his mouth and softly suckled it, she was shocked to hear a moan escape from her throat, shocked to feel her arms reach up to encircle his neck. And then she was lost, swept up like Dorothy from The Wizard of Oz in the tornado, transported to another time and place. The world disappeared, gravity lost its power, and her grip on reality grew weaker and fainter and increasingly insignificant.

"Wow, Frannie," Austin murmured some time later. He pulled back and looked at her, his eyes glazed, and his breathing labored. "Where did you learn to kiss like that?"

"I think you just taught me," she whispered.

"Well, then, come back to class." Lowering his head, he pulled her close and reclaimed her mouth.

Eight

The moon shone through the pickup windshield as Austin drove down the tree-lined road an hour later.

"It's hard to tell without my glasses," Frannie said, "but I think you're about to drive past the house."

Sure enough, the truck's headlights gleamed on a wooden clapboard sign that marked the long drive leading to the Big Sky Bed & Breakfast. Austin braked harder than he'd intended, causing the tires to screech. He glanced over at her and grinned. "Sorry. Guess my mind is still on other things."

Like that amazing, incredible kiss.

Austin had kissed a lot of women, but he'd never felt anything like the high-voltage heat he'd felt with Frannie. It was good thing they hadn't been standing in water at the time or they probably would have electrocuted each other.

He'd never gotten so carried away in a public setting that he'd forgotten about time and place and decorum. If another couple hadn't wandered down the path, he would have made love to Frannie right there in the leaves. As it was, he'd had her sweater halfway off when they were interrupted.

After the startled couple beat a hasty retreat, Frannie had pulled away, straightened her clothes and asked Austin to take her home. He'd been aching to take her back to his ranch, but he hadn't wanted to pressure her.

Hell, who was he kidding? He would have been willing

to apply all kinds of pressure if he'd thought it stood half a chance of working, but he'd figured it would do no good. Especially after they got back to the truck when he sat down and heard a loud snap.

Her eyeglasses. In his back pocket. He'd broken them to smithereens.

"I'm really sorry about breaking your glasses," he told her now for the umpteenth time as he turned into the driveway of the Big Sky.

"Don't worry about it. It was an accident."

The pickup reached the end of the long drive. Austin flipped off the engine and turned toward Frannie. A light shone from the porch, dimly illuminating her face. He reached out a hand and sifted it through her hair. It was silky and soft and sweet-scented, and it aroused a fresh burst of desire. "When can I see you again?"

She brushed a strand of hair out of her face, her eyes downcast. "I don't know if that's a good idea."

"It's a great idea." He reached out and cupped her chin, urging her to look at him. "There's so much chemistry between you and me that we should probably wear rubber gloves when we touch."

He was glad to see he'd made her smile. "I know."

"So?"

"So that's why I'm not sure it's a good idea."

Oh, no. She wasn't going to start another one of those conversations where he didn't know what the heck she was talking about, was she? "I'm not following you."

"We're awfully different."

"Sure. But in a lot of ways, we're a lot alike. We're both loners, we share similar tastes in music and movies, we make each other laugh, and we're incredibly physically attracted."

"We want different things out of life."

The only thing I want right now is you. Austin sucked in a deep breath, then let it out. What he was dealing with here was a case of stubbornness. He knew a thing or two about stubbornness. Next to a woman, the most stubborn creature on the planet was a horse, and he'd had plenty of practice with stubborn horses. The best way to deal with a balky horse, he'd learned, was to walk away before the creature dug in its heels. That left the door open to try a different approach at a later date.

"Well, it's late. I'd better get you inside. Sit tight and I'll get the door for you." He strode around the truck, opened her door and helped her down. "I intend to pay for your eyeglasses," he said as he walked her to the porch.

"That's very kind, but it's not necessary."

"But I want to."

Frannie grinned. "I really don't want to have to explain to my optician how they happened to be in your back pocket."

Austin grinned back. "Well, then, let me know how much they cost and I'll reimburse you."

"That's not necessary." She hurried up the porch steps and stopped, her hand on the door. "Thanks for dinner. I had a wonderful time."

"Me, too." Austin stepped toward her, intending to give her another kiss.

She stopped him by opening the door. "Good night," she said softly.

"Good night." Austin watched her slip inside and close the door behind her. With a sigh, he turned and walked back to his truck.

There was a warmth about Frannie that drew him like a moth to a flame. She was amusing and independent one minute, shy and defensive the next. She was sassy and sexy and smart as a whip, and he was determined to see her again.

Frannie sat bolt upright in bed and looked around the darkened room. She thought she'd heard a blood-curdling scream, but the only sounds in the quiet bedroom were the pounding of her pulse and the rustling of the leaves in the tall oak outside the window.

She must have been dreaming, she told herself, brushing the hair out of her face. A scream sure seemed out place among the dream fragments she remembered—dreams of Austin's face and hands and lips, dreams of his kisses and caresses. There was plenty of material in that dream to make her heart race, but none of it seemed connected to a scream.

Austin was turning her life upside down, she thought with a sigh, leaning back against the pillow propped against the mahogany headboard. Just thinking about the kisses they'd shared made her hot and restless. Throwing off the covers, she glanced at her bedside clock. Two in the morning. She'd be a wreck if she didn't get some shut-eye. She'd already stayed up far too late, reliving every luscious detail of the evening.

Punching her pillow, she lay back down. But she'd no sooner closed her eyes than another ear-splitting scream ripped through the air.

Aunt Celeste! The scream was coming from her room.

Grabbing her robe from the foot of the bed, Frannie dashed out the door and across the hall to her aunt's room.

The dim glow of a night-light revealed Celeste curled in a fetal position in the middle of her double bed. Frannie reached out and touched her. "Aunt Celeste?"

The older woman grabbed her hand as if it were a lifeline. "Oh, Frannie. Is that you?"

"Yes. Are you all right?"

Jasmine darted into the room, her white nightgown floating around her. "Mom? What's wrong?" Flipping on a bedside lamp, she helped Celeste sit up. The older woman's cheeks were wet and her hands trembled as she tried to brush away her tears.

"What happened?" Jasmine asked.

"I—I had a dream. Oh, girls, it was so awful!"

Jasmine and Frannie exchanged a worried look. Jasmine sat on the bed and put her arms around Celeste, hugging her for a long moment. Frannie fetched a tissue from the nightstand and handed it to Celeste. Her aunt took it and wiped her eyes.

"I'm sorry I awakened you. Oh, I hope I didn't disturb the guests."

"I doubt if they can hear anything from this wing of the house," Frannie reassured her.

"Do you want to talk about it?" Jasmine asked. "When I was a little girl, you used to tell me it helped to talk about nightmares."

Celeste took a deep breath and shuddered. "This was more than a nightmare. It was like a vision. It was so...so vivid. So real!"

"It was just a dream," Jasmine said soothingly. Celeste took another deep breath and dabbed at her eyes.

"What was it about?" Frannie urged.

Celeste leaned over to her nightstand and lit a white candle. It was her ritual after any of these nightmares. Her aunt rubbed some bergamot oil into her left hand, from a skeleton-shaped vial she'd brought back from Louisiana. Then, when she'd finished, she replied, "It was like a dream within a dream. I was in the house—you know, the one Yvette and Blanche and Jeremiah and I lived in."

"The old Kincaid mansion," Frannie prompted.

Celeste nodded. "I was in my old bedroom, in bed, in the middle of the night, and it started storming. Oh, it was a horrible storm! The thunder boomed like it was right overhead, and the lightning lit up the sky outside the window like it was high noon. And then I saw Blanche sitting at the foot of my bed, and she was like the ghost of Christmas past. She said she was going to show me something. And then she was gone, and I thought I heard Jeremiah yelling in another part of the house. So I went downstairs, and—" Celeste's voice broke.

"And what?" Jasmine urged.

"And there was an intruder—a big man—and he was fighting Jeremiah. I walked into the room, and he had Jeremiah pinned to the floor. And then the fighting turned into the storm, and then the storm was inside the house. And the next thing I knew…" Her voice trailed away and she covered her face with her hands.

"What?"

Celeste's hands moved to the side of her face. "Lightning struck the room and there was a horrible thunderclap, and then it was raining blood. Blood was everywhere. And I started screaming, and…" She inhaled a ragged breath. "And I guess that's when I woke up."

"How horrible," Jasmine murmured, rubbing Celeste's arms. "But it was just a dream. You're awake now and we're with you, and everything is nice and safe."

"But it was so real—and so awful!"

"No wonder it woke you," Frannie remarked. "A dream like that would wake the dead."

Celeste's gaze rested on her. Her eyes grew large. "I almost feel like that's what's happening."

A shiver coursed through Frannie. She should have thought before she'd spoken, given her aunt's frail mental state. "I didn't mean that literally. It was just a thoughtless remark, just an expression."

Celeste nodded, her eyes somber. "I know, dear. But I can't help thinking that Blanche is trying to help me get my memory back. I think that's what all these dreams are about. But they're in some sort of code, and I don't know how to break it." Celeste's expression grew determined. "Not yet, anyway. But I intend to. I intend to do a little investigating of my own."

Jasmine exchanged a long, worried look with Frannie. She patted Celeste's shoulder and gave her an encouraging smile. "Well, the thing we need to investigate right now is how we can help you get back to sleep. Would you like for me to make you some warm milk?"

Celeste squeezed her hand. "No thanks, dear. I feel much calmer after talking about it. I think I'll just watch a little television here in my room until I get drowsy again. You two go on back to bed. I'm sorry I woke you."

Frannie and Jasmine kissed Celeste good-night, then headed out the door. Frannie pulled it closed behind her.

"I'm worried about her," Jasmine whispered. "She hasn't been herself lately."

"Maybe she needs to see a psychologist," Frannie suggested.

"I tried to talk her into that. She refused. She said this is a spiritual quest. She said it needs to unfold as it's meant to, in its own time and its own way."

Frannie sighed. Her aunt had been heavily influenced by the bayou beliefs she'd picked up the year she and her late husband had lived in Louisiana, and she had a deeply spiritual nature. She wasn't a bit surprised that she would insist on letting things take a natural course. "You know, Jasmine, I'm growing more and more convinced that she heard or saw something traumatic the night Raven disappeared—

something so awful that she's subconsciously blocked it out.''

Jasmine nodded. ''I think so, too. I think even Mom has come to believe that. Otherwise, why would she want to be doing any investigating? But the whole idea worries me.''

''Why?'' Frannie asked.

''She says she wants to get her memory back, but I think a part of her is still afraid to face whatever happened.'' Jasmine pulled Frannie further down the hall, away from Celeste's room, and lowered her voice. ''Mom doesn't know it, but I discussed all this with a psychiatrist that Summer recommended.''

''And?''

''And the doctor said that if Mom doesn't want professional help, it won't do any good for us to push her into it. We need to let her deal with this at her own pace.''

''How can we help?''

Jasmine sighed. ''The doctor said we need to keep doing what we're doing now—support her, encourage her to talk and hold her hand in the middle of the night.''

It didn't seem like much, but it made sense. Frannie nodded.

Jasmine gave a big yawn and stretched. ''Right now, though, I think the best thing we can do is to go back to bed and get some sleep.'' She looked at Frannie and grinned. ''Unless you want to sit up and tell me all about your date with Austin. I'm dying to hear about it.''

''No, thanks.''

''Must have been some dinner. I was already asleep by the time you got home.''

''Go to bed.'' Smiling, Frannie turned her cousin by the shoulders and pointed her down the hall.

''Only if you promise to tell me everything—and I mean everything—at breakfast.''

"Okay." Frannie headed back to her bedroom, making a mental note to grab a fast-food breakfast on her way to work.

Frannie hoped to sneak out of the house the next morning without seeing Jasmine, but before she'd even finished dressing, she heard a soft rap on the door. She turned to see Jasmine slip inside her room.

Frannie finished buttoning the top of her black linen skirt and grinned at her cousin, one eyebrow arched reproachfully. "Most people wait to hear the magic words, 'come in.'"

"Sorry, Frannie. I'm too excited."

She looked it. The petite brunette was practically vibrating with excitement.

Frannie turned to her closet and pulled her suit jacket off a clothes hanger. "About what?"

"You've got a visitor." She paused melodramatically. "Austin."

Frannie was chagrined at how hard her heart began pounding. "At this hour? It's seven-fifteen in the morning!"

Jasmine nodded, grinning widely.

"What does he want?"

"He said he wants to see you."

Frannie tried hard to remain calm, but her hand shook as she picked up her hairbrush. She reached for an elastic band to pull her hair back, then changed her mind. What the heck. He'd liked her hair down. She'd wear it that way.

Jasmine's gaze raked her over from head to toe. "You look great. You're wearing your contacts. Frannie, you've even got on a little makeup!" Jasmine beamed, then narrowed her eyes suspiciously. "Did you know he was coming by this morning?"

"No."

Jasmine looked less than fully convinced. "So what happened last night?"

"We went to dinner at the Lakeside Inn."

"And?"

"And then he brought me home." Frannie fastened on small gold hoop earrings.

"That was it? No kissing?"

Frannie's palms started to sweat at the memory. She reached for her purse. "I'd better get downstairs. It's rude to keep him waiting."

"Oh, he's fine. He's drinking a cup of coffee." Jasmine peered at her closely as Frannie walked past her and opened the door. "You *did* kiss him! Oh, this is so exciting!"

"Shh! Don't broadcast it to the entire house!" Hoisting her purse over her shoulder, Frannie hurried down the stairs, Jasmine close on her heels.

Austin was waiting in the vestibule, wearing jeans and cowboy boots, his dark hair slightly damp, as if he were fresh from a shower. A hint of dark hair peeked out the unbuttoned neck of his denim shirt. The sheer masculinity of him made Frannie's breath catch in her throat.

"Good mornin', Frannie."

She fiddled nervously with the strap of her purse. "Good morning."

His mouth curved into a slow smile. "At the risk of somehow insulting you, I think you look mighty nice this morning."

Frannie could feel her cousin's curious gaze practically burning a hole in her. "Uh...thank you."

"It occurred to me that you might need a ride to work or to the optometrist's office."

Jasmine poked her head around Frannie's shoulder. "Why would she need that?"

Frannie suppressed the urge to strangle her.

Austin seemed unperturbed by Jasmine's flagrant eavesdropping. "Well, I accidently broke Frannie's glasses last night."

Jasmine's eyebrows rose. "While she was wearing them?"

"No. I'm afraid I sat on them."

Jasmine looked at Frannie, no doubt wondering why she'd taken off her glasses in the first place. Frannie could practically see her cousin's mind putting two and two together and coming up with five. Jasmine's face creased into a knowing grin.

"Don't you need to do something in the kitchen?" Frannie asked her.

"What?"

Frannie eyed her sternly.

Jasmine sighed. "Oh, sure. Nice seeing you, Austin." She gave Frannie a sly smile as she sauntered off.

Austin grinned at Frannie. "I was afraid you wouldn't be able to see well enough to drive without your glasses."

"That's very thoughtful of you." And it was, Frannie thought. Surprisingly thoughtful. A feeling of warmth flooded her chest. "But I'm wearing my contact lenses."

"Oh. Great." He gave a relieved smile. "Well, as long as I'm here, can I take you to breakfast?"

It had been awfully nice of him to drive all this way just to give her a ride, and she didn't want to appear ungrateful. Besides, she reasoned, if she stayed here, she'd be subjected to the third degree from Jasmine. Those were both valid reasons for saying yes—reasons that had nothing to do with the fact she was dying to spend more time with him.

"That sounds terrific."

With a little wave to Jasmine, who was watching with

undisguised fascination, Frannie walked through the door Austin held open.

"You really do look nice this morning," he said as they walked down the porch.

"So do you."

Austin laughed as he opened the passenger door on his pickup. "You must not be able to see very well with those contacts."

"Actually, I can see better with them than with my glasses."

Austin shot her a puzzled look, then walked around the truck and climbed in. "So why don't you wear them more often?"

Frannie shrugged. "I'm more comfortable in the glasses, I guess."

"The contacts hurt, huh?"

"No. I'm just more at ease in the glasses. I feel more— I don't know—relaxed or something."

"Why?"

Why, indeed. Why had she opened her big mouth? Why was it that every time she was around Austin, she found herself saying something she had no intention of saying?

She gazed out the window as he backed out of the drive. "I guess I feel all exposed in my contacts. Kind of undressed and naked."

"I like your naked face." Austin shot her a wicked grin. "Wouldn't mind seeing the rest of you that way, either."

Frannie hated the way her face burned. She wished she were more at ease with sexual banter, wished she could take it more in stride the way other women did.

Austin didn't miss a trick. "Hey, I didn't mean to embarrass you. That was a crude and pathetic attempt at humor. Sorry."

I'm the one who's sorry. Sorry I get so nervous and tongue-tied around you.

He glanced over at her as he braked at a Stop sign. "Guess I need to brush up on my social skills. The talk at ranches and racetracks isn't as high-brow as what I'm sure you're used to hearing at the bank."

Frannie seized the opportunity to change the topic. "Speaking of ranches and racetracks, how did you get from horse ranching to car racing?"

"Natural progression, I guess. I've always liked speed and power, always liked taking on a challenge. The wilder and meaner the horses were, the more I liked taming them. And like most teenage boys, I also loved cars."

"How old were you when you started racing?"

"Seventeen. It was a year after my old man died. I was working at a ranch in east Texas, and the boss hired a new foreman who was into amateur drag racing. He invited me to the track one day and, well, I got hooked right from the get-go. I started spending all my free time at the track, helping him fine-tune his car, and sometimes he'd let me take a turn in it when no one was around."

She loved the way his face lit up as he talked about it. "I take it you liked that."

"Are you kidding? I loved it. When I was eighteen, he had a streak of wins, and he qualified for the championship finals in Oklahoma City. He got some sponsors to pay the way, and two other guys and I went with him to serve as his pit crew. Then, just two hours before the race, he got sick, really sick. Seems he'd eaten a bad turkey sandwich and gotten a big ol' case of food poisoning."

"Oh, no!"

"Oh, yes. And it was bad. He ended up in the hospital and everything. Well, the sponsors were in a pickle. They'd paid the entry fee and painted his car with their logo and coughed up a whole lot of cash for the trip, and they weren't too happy about pouring all that money out and not even having the car in the race. So I offered to drive, and they took me up on it. I guess they figured it was better than nothing. The car would at least be in the race, and they'd get some exposure for their money."

"So what happened?"

"Well, I won."

Frannie liked the modest, simple way he said it. "And everyone was surprised."

"No one more than me. The next thing I knew, folks were calling me to drive their cars, and then sponsors started making offers, then I got my own car, and then I moved from drag racing to the NASCAR circuit. And, well, here I am."

"I'm sure that's an understated version of things."

"It's a pretty fair summary." He parked outside the Hip Hop Café. "Is this okay?"

"Great. They make the best pancakes in the county."

Austin watched Frannie pour cream into her cup, then add a teaspoon of sugar. Even her smallest gesture fascinated him, from the way she held the spoon to the precise way she stirred her coffee. Without a doubt, she was the most fascinating woman he'd ever met in his life.

He wasn't sure what it was about her, exactly, that held him so in thrall. Maybe it was the novelty of her buttoned-down appearance. Maybe it was her forthright way of speaking, or her unexpected dry sense of humor. Maybe it was all of those things, combined with a soft, understated beauty that seemed to grow more pronounced every time her saw her.

And then, of course, there was the memory of that kiss. He couldn't remember ever responding so intensely to someone on a first kiss. She hadn't seemed exactly immune to him, either. There had been more heat in that kiss than in his car's radiator after fifty laps. Whatever it was that drew people together—chemistry or pheromones or vibrations or whatever—the two of them had it in spades.

He rested his forearms on the green Formica-topped table and watched her take a sip of coffee. Lucky cup, he thought absently. It got to feel the press of her lips.

"How come a great gal like you isn't spoken for?"

Frannie set down her cup and lifted her shoulders. "Mr. Right just hasn't come along."

"Had any close calls with Mr. Wrong?"

"One. When I was in college."

"What was he like?"

Frannie's eyes grew somber, but her mouth twisted into a wry smile. "That depends."

"On what?"

"On whether you're asking what I thought he was like at first, or what I'd found out about him by the time we broke up."

"I'd like to know both."

Frannie sighed. "Well, when I met him, I thought he was wonderful. A few months later, I'd learned he was a lower life form than plankton."

She had a real way with words. Austin grinned. "What happened?"

Frannie toyed with the handle of her coffee cup. "He dumped me for my college roommate."

Austin shook his head. "What an idiot."

Frannie raised an eyebrow, her mouth pulled into a small grin that was half amused, half sad. "You wouldn't say that if you'd seen my roommate."

"Yes, I would. I've seen you."

Frannie stared down at her coffee cup, nonplussed.

"Well, Ginger transferred to the university the second semester of my junior year. She was the blond, busty, golden-girl type. A dead ringer for Pamela Anderson."

Austin reached out and covered her hand. The contact of skin on skin caused a rush of heat to shoot up his arm. He saw her eyes grow wide, saw her pupils dilate, and knew she felt it, too. "Well, you're better than any old dead ringer. You're one of a kind. A real original. Not a second-hand version of anyone."

She kept her eyes down, but he saw her swallow, saw the corners of her mouth form a faint smile. He ran his thumb over her knuckles. "So this guy—he really hurt you, huh?" he asked softly.

Frannie shrugged, but her eyes remained downcast. "I'm over it."

"Are you?"

"Yes."

"Prove it."

Frannie looked up, her eyes wary. "And just how do you propose I do that?"

"Say you'll spend Saturday with me."

"Oh, Austin…"

He leaned forward. "I'm going to be hitting the road Sunday, and I'll be gone for about three weeks. I have races every weekend, and my sponsors have me booked with appearances in between. Saturday is the only day I'll have off for nearly a month, and I'd like to spend it with you, at my ranch. We can go horseback riding. I'll even cook for you." He squeezed her hand and smiled. "If you say no, I'm going to figure you're not really over this guy."

Her eyes were full of reproach. "I don't have to prove anything to you."

His hand tightened over hers. "No. But maybe you need to prove something to yourself."

Frannie's fingers tensed inside his palm. She looked at him, and he could see the wariness in her eyes. "Austin, I don't think this is too wise...."

Austin grinned. "I've never been accused of being too wise."

"You and I... We're complete opposites."

"Then I guess what they say about opposites attracting is true."

A waitress in a green-and-white-striped apron appeared at their table with two plates of pancakes. Austin reluctantly turned loose of Frannie's hand.

Don't give her a chance to say no, he reminded himself. Instead of pressing the issue, he needed to figure out a way around her resistance.

Nine

Frannie was searching through a file cabinet behind her desk at the bank later that day when she heard a familiar voice. "Hi, Frannie. Ready to go?"

Startled, Frannie straightened and turned to see Austin standing in front of her desk. "Go? Go where?"

His smile warmed the air around her by at least twenty degrees. "On a picnic. I've got two boxes of fried chicken in my car, and I'm taking you to the park."

Frannie shook her head. "I can't. I'm supposed to have lunch with a customer who wants to discuss investment options. My boss set it up."

"I know." Austin's smiled widened. "Pretty clever on my part, don't you think?"

She stared at him blankly. "You mean..."

He nodded. "Yep. I'm your client."

A surge of alarm rushed through Frannie.

"Come on," Austin urged. "Let's go. Boss's orders."

Frannie frowned. She didn't like the feeling of being set up. "Austin, this is entirely inappropriate."

"Now, why is that? I have an account at this bank. Aren't I entitled to a little personal service?"

"Probably not the kind of service *you* have in mind. Besides, Mr. Billings is going to expect me to come back with a piece of business."

"And you will. You can tell him you talked me into investing another hundred grand in C.D.s."

"I thought you didn't make safe investments. You said the stock market was a lot more exciting."

Austin leaned across the desk and gave her a sexy smile. "Frannie, Wall Street doesn't have anything nearly as exciting as the assets this bank has going for it."

He was manipulating her, pulling her strings like a puppeteer. And just like a puppet, she was responding. She fought against it. "Now wait just a minute. Just because you're going to put more money into this bank doesn't mean I'm going to…to—"

His lazy grin grew wicked and sexy. "To what? Engage in customer relations?"

"Exactly."

"Ah, Frannie, I'm not asking for anything inappropriate. All I want is a little of your time, and your boss was kind enough to allow me to have it."

Frannie put her hand on her hip. "Austin, if you've already decided to make the investment, then we can do the paperwork right now and forget about lunch."

"Did I say I'd already made the decision?" His eyes grew round and innocent. "Oh, gee, I'm sorry if I gave that impression. I'm afraid you'll have to talk me into it. Over lunch." He flashed a devilish grin.

Frannie felt her resistance crumbling. The more time she spent around Austin, the more it eroded. She would have none left at all if she were exposed to much more of his charm. She decided to play the guilt card. "What I really need to do with my lunch hour is pick out some new glasses."

"Okay. We'll take care of that together, then we'll go on our picnic."

"That will take too much time."

"Oh, don't worry about that. Your boss expects it to be a long lunch."

Frannie tensed. "What, exactly, did you tell him?"

"Just that I trust your judgment and want your financial advice, and that I have a very complicated portfolio to discuss. I told him it might take two or three hours."

It was useless to fight against his appeal. He was incorrigibly charming, relentlessly persistent. He could charm the raisin out of a cookie—and the heart out of Frannie's own chest.

Which was exactly why she was worried.

Frannie shot Austin an irritated glare as they left the optical shop. "You knew I didn't want you to do that."

"Do what?" Austin flashed that annoyingly innocent look again as he opened the passenger door to his pickup for her.

"Pay for my eyeglasses." She'd practically created a scene, trying to pay for them herself. But Austin had been quick on the draw with his American Express card. The staff had been smitten at having a celebrity in their midst and had been more than happy to let him have his way.

Austin climbed into the driver's seat, checked the rearview mirror, then carefully pulled the pickup out of the parking spot. "Now, Frannie, I was responsible for breaking your glasses, and I felt really bad about it. You don't want me to go around lugging a big old load of guilt, do you?"

It was maddening, how impossible he was to argue with. Frannie shook her head and sighed.

"Besides," Austin said, a mischievous grin curving his lips. "Maybe now you'll think of me every time you put them on."

That's exactly what I'm afraid of, Frannie thought ruefully. Austin was getting too close, too fast. And she was going to end up getting hurt. She twisted around on the leather seat to confront him. "Look, Austin, I don't like the way you're trying to take over my life."

"I'm not trying to take it over." His mouth was smiling, but his eyes were serious. "I just want to share a little of it with you."

Of all the things he could have said, why did he have to say that? The one thing she wanted more than anything else was to share her life with someone—someone she could laugh with and confide in, someone to have and to hold and to love. Someone warm and bright and funny. Someone just like Austin.

The thought sent a dart of terror zinging through her. Oh, dear heavens, was she falling in love with him? No. She couldn't be. She wouldn't let herself. It would be a terrible mistake. Falling in love with Austin was a guaranteed ticket to a heartache. She was looking for forever, and he wasn't in the market for commitment.

He'd said he wanted to share a little of her life, Frannie reminded herself. The operative word in the statement was *little*. A little of her life, for a little while.

To her chagrin, she realized Austin was braking in front of the city park. He killed the engine and grinned over at her. "If you'll bring the chicken, I'll get the blanket and drinks out of the back of the truck."

Before she knew it, he'd led her to a secluded spot by the duck pond. He'd evidently scouted the park before coming to the bank, because he led her without hesitation to a spot too private to be stumbled upon by accident. A thick stand of red cedar shielded the site from the west and north, and a sprawling caragana bush provided privacy to the east. Even the view of the pond was partially blocked by a flowering potentilla shrub.

Frannie helped Austin spread a large blanket on the

ground, then sank beside him, gazing out at a narrow stretch of pond, feeling hidden from the world.

"This is a beautiful park," Austin remarked. "Is the pond natural, or did the city build it?"

"It's actually an old quarry," Franny said. "It gets really deep just a few feet from shore."

"That must be why the water looks so blue."

Frannie leaned back on her elbows, enjoying the view. Through the yellow-flowered branches, she watched a toddler in a pink jumpsuit giddily throw pieces of bread to three white ducks across the pond. The child looked to be about two years old. Frannie could see the child's mother sitting on a nearby bench, a newborn baby in her arms, calling encouragement to the child. The woman's hair was the same shade of deep gold as the little girl's. Lucky woman, Frannie thought wistfully—two beautiful children. She probably had a husband who adored her, too. That was what Frannie longed for—a family of her own, a life filled with love.

It was not the kind of life she was likely to ever have with Austin.

Why was she having such inappropriate thoughts about Austin? She needed to stop it, and stop it immediately. Frannie sighed.

Austin heard her. "What are you thinking?"

Frannie gazed up at the overhanging branch of a blue spruce and stared through the deep green needles at a deep blue sky. "About what a gorgeous day it is," she lied.

Austin nodded. "Summers in this part of Montana are about as perfect as weather can get. I'm not a big fan of oppressive heat. I remember a summer in southern Louisiana when I thought I was going to parboil. And I spent more than a few summers in Texas and Oklahoma where I dry-roasted."

Frannie looked over at him. "You've lived a lot of places."

"More than my share."

She was curious about his family, curious why he seemed so reluctant to talk about them. "You said the other day that your dad started moving when your mother left."

"Yeah." Austin unzipped the padded red cooler and pulled out a soft drink. He popped the top and handed it to Frannie.

Her fingers closed around the cold can. "Where did she go?"

"She took off with another guy." A pop top hissed as Austin opened another can of soda. He took a long drink. "She'd always had a dream about making it big as a country-western star. She wanted to go to Nashville, and he evidently promised to take her there."

"So she just up and left you?"

"Yeah."

Frannie sat stock-still, stunned by the concept. The idea of abandoning a child was as alien to her as the concept of life on Mars. "What was she like?"

Austin shrugged. "My memory of her is kind of hazy. She wasn't like other kids' moms. I mean, she didn't cook or clean, and she wasn't much on playing with me or taking me places. She didn't even want me to call her Mom when Dad wasn't around."

"Why not?"

"She said it was bad for her image. She wanted me to call her Daisy." Austin took a long swig of soft drink and leaned back on his elbows. "That was her stage name."

"Was she talented?"

"Who knows? I thought she was, but I was just a child." He gazed out at the pond. "I don't remember hearing people talk too much about her talent, but everyone always raved about her beauty. She had long blond hair and big blue eyes, and she looked like a movie star.''

"What else do you remember about her?"

Austin stretched out his legs. "She loved having an audience. She sang and played guitar in bars every chance she got, whether she got paid or not. She and my father had a lot of arguments over it.''

He picked a rock off the ground beside the blanket and absently turned it in his palm. "My dad was working two jobs, trying to give her all the things she wanted. While he was working, she'd go to the bars. Some nights she'd take me with her. I'd just sit in the corner and pretend I was invisible. I got pretty good at it. Sometimes I believed I really was.''

Austin expertly skimmed the stone on the water, making it skip three times. The toddler across the pond watched with wide-eyed delight.

"Daisy was a big dreamer. She loved to talk about what life would be like when she made it big. She said we'd have a big white-columned house like in *Gone With the Wind,* and it would have a big swimming pool. She said we'd invite all the neighborhood kids over for swimming parties. We'd serve ice cream and soda pop." Austin's mouth twisted into a tight smile. "I used to believe her.''

Frannie's heart turned in her chest. "Oh, Austin," she whispered.

"The night she left, she told me she had to go away so she could become a big star. She said she'd come back for me and when she did, we'd live together in that big white-columned house. I clung to her and cried. I told her I didn't care about the house. I just wanted her.''

He picked up another rock. "She pried my hands from her neck, and she walked away. The man was waiting for her outside. I could hear his car engine running when she opened the door.'' A nerve worked in Austin's cheek. ''I remember the way that door sounded when it closed behind her. It made a real empty, hollow sound. It seemed like I could feel it in the pit of my stomach.''

The lump in Frannie's throat made it hard to speak. ''Did you ever see her again?''

Austin shook his head. ''We got word less than a year later that she'd died in a car accident.'' Austin threw another stone. ''Right after that, we moved. And we just kept moving. Dad never wanted to put down any roots. Said life was easier if you never got too attached to anyone or anything.''

The story explained so much about this man. ''Is that what you think, too?'' she asked softly.

Austin shrugged. ''It sure makes it easier to do what I do for a living.''

''But you've bought a ranch. You must want some roots.''

''Oh, yeah. I've always wanted a place with some permanence, a place I could go back to.'' Austin rolled his eyes. ''Disgustingly typical, isn't it? People always want what they've never had. In my case, that's a home.''

And love. It sounded like he'd never had love. Did he want that, too? Frannie gazed at his profile, her heart twisting. If he did, he wasn't likely to ever admit it, even to himself. His brief experience with love had hurt too much.

''What was your father like?'' she asked.

Austin lifted a shoulder. ''The tall, silent type. After Mom left, he got to where he hardly spoke at all. He took it hard. He tried to be a good dad, but I don't think he knew much about raising kids. He did the best he could.''

What a sad, lonely childhood he'd had. Frannie reached out and touched his arm. ''Austin, I'm so sorry.''

"Hey, there's nothing to be sorry about. That was all a long time ago. It's water under the bridge."

But Frannie wasn't so sure. Abandonment by a mother—that wasn't the kind of thing a person was likely to ever get over. And from what he'd just told her about his father, his dad had been too deeply wounded to take up the slack. She couldn't imagine the kind of pain Austin must have felt. Must still feel in many ways.

Austin straightened and smiled. "Hey, I'm starved. Let's dig into that chicken."

Frannie passed him a box, and the conversation drifted to lighter topics. They were finishing their chicken and discussing a mystery novel they'd both read when a loud splash sounded across the water. Frannie looked through the veil of leaves and flowers to see a flash of pink flailing in the dark water.

"The baby!" She jumped up from the blanket and headed to the pond, but Austin was ahead of her, kicking off his shoes and diving in. Frannie looked for the child's mother. She saw the blond woman standing by a baby carriage several feet away from the pond, her face a mask of terror.

"Emily!" the woman called. She placed the infant in the stroller and raced toward the pond, her expression panicked, her blond hair flying behind her. "Emily!"

The mother jumped into the water and disappeared beneath the surface just as Austin reached the drowning child. Frannie's heart pounded hard as she watched him turn the toddler onto her back, put his arm around her and swim for shore. Just then, Frannie saw the mother bob to the surface in the same spot she'd disappeared, only to sink once more back under the water. Oh, dear heavens, now the mother was in trouble, too!

Without stopping to think, Frannie plunged into the cold

water. It felt like ice, and it tasted like algae. Frannie kicked off her shoes and plowed through it, reaching the flailing woman just as Austin reached the shore with the toddler.

The woman was gasping and sputtering, her eyes wide with terror. "My baby!" The woman went under again, then resurfaced. "Help my baby!"

Frannie gulped a breath as she treaded water. "She's being helped. Let me help you."

The woman sank again. Frannie dove down to the spot she'd last seen the woman and brought her to the surface. The woman's arms whirled like a windmill. Her sneakered feet kicked Frannie in the stomach. "Can't swim," she spluttered.

Frannie spat out a mouthful of water, trying to remember the lifesaving training she'd taken as a teenager. "Put your arms around my neck. I'll take you to shore."

The woman frantically grabbed at Frannie's head, nearly drowning them both.

"Stop trying to swim," Frannie ordered. "Put your arms around my neck and just hang on."

The woman grabbed at her again. Frannie struggled to keep her head above water. "I can't help you if you're fighting me. Let me get you to your children."

The mention of her children seemed to calm the woman, and Frannie managed to haul her the few yards to shore. Austin reached them just as Frannie's feet touched bottom. Holding the toddler in one arm, he extended his other hand to pull Frannie and the woman ashore.

Gasping, Frannie helped the woman to her feet. The woman staggered forward, then reached for her bawling daughter, who was sobbing into Austin's neck.

The child grabbed her mother, and the woman clutched her as if she'd never let her go. "Emily," she murmured over and over. "Oh, Emily."

Austin hauled Frannie against his chest, his arms tight around her. "Are you okay?" he murmured.

"Yes. Is the child?"

"She's fine."

The mother looked up, her eyes filled with tears, her voice thick with emotion. "Thank you. I don't know how to thank you. Both of you."

"We're glad you're okay." Austin ran a hand down his face, rubbing the water from his eyes. "Your girl didn't lose consciousness, but she swallowed a lot of water. It would probably be a good idea to get her checked out by a doctor."

The woman nodded. Her face was streaming with tears and pond water, and her eyes were full of gratitude. "I don't know how to thank you. I looked away for a moment while I changed the baby's diaper, and the next thing I knew, Emily was in the water."

"I'm glad we were here to help."

"How can I ever thank you?"

"You just did. Do you need a ride home?"

"Oh, thank you, but no. We live just a block away." After more effusive thanks, the woman and her dripping daughter traipsed toward home, pushing the baby carriage.

Austin looked down at Frannie. "Are you sure you're all right?"

Frannie nodded.

Austin's gaze latched on to hers. His eyes held a warm light that made it hard for Frannie to breathe. "You're really something, Frannie. A real-life hero."

"I was about to say the same about you. You saved that baby's life. You got to her in nothing flat."

"I didn't even see the mother, I was so focussed on getting to the child." His teeth gleamed as he smiled. "You handled that like a pro. Did you used to be a lifeguard or something?''

Frannie shyly grinned and nodded. ''Or something. My dad made my brother and me take lifesaving training. He said that if we were going to live near a lake, we needed to know what to do in an emergency.''

''Your dad sounds like a smart guy.''

Frannie ruefully looked down at her sopping clothes. ''I wonder what he'd say I should do about this.''

''If he's as smart as I think he is, he'd probably say you should go home and change clothes.'' Austin tightened his hand around her arm. ''Come on, let's go gather up our stuff.''

They trudged around the grassy bank of the pond, back toward the heavy foliage that hid their picnic blanket.

''How am I going to explain showing up at the bank dressed in different clothes, after an extended business lunch with you?''

''Hmm. Guess I've put you in a compromising position, haven't I?'' Austin rubbed his chin. ''Well, maybe you should just take the rest of the day off.''

Frannie lifted her eyebrows. ''I go off to lunch with you, then call to say I'm not coming back?''

''I see what you mean.'' He suddenly snapped his fingers. ''You could say you caught a sudden cold.'' He pulled her close to his side and ran his hand up and down her arm, causing Frannie to shiver. ''You *are* cold, aren't you?''

She was actually growing quite warm, but she wasn't about to tell him that.

''On the other hand, honesty is usually the best policy,'' he continued. ''Why don't you just tell them the truth?''

''That our business lunch was a picnic in the park? It doesn't sound very businesslike.''

''Nonsense. We can discuss business here just as well as

we could in a restaurant. But if it'll make you feel better, I'm perfectly willing to sit down and discuss investments now.''

"That still won't explain why I changed clothes. And an explanation about getting wet during a lifesaving maneuver is going to sound pretty fishy."

"Not as fishy as we smell."

Frannie gave him a playful push. "Thanks a bunch, Austin. You're really helping a lot here."

"I pride myself on being helpful."

Frannie couldn't help but smile.

"Maybe I should pour a can of soft drink all over you," Austin suggested with a mischievous smile. "That way you can say I spilled a drink on your clothes and you needed to go home and change."

"Well, that's more plausible than the truth, but it's still going to look suspicious."

Austin stopped and lifted a branch of a red cedar tree. "Here's our blanket. You nearly walked right past it."

Frannie stepped into the secluded area and plopped down onto the blanket. "Face it, Austin. Whatever I say, people are going to think you and I are fooling around."

"Well, if that's what they're going to think anyway..."

Before Frannie knew it, he was beside her on the blanket, pulling her into his arms, his mouth slanting over hers. The kiss was playful at first, but it rapidly deepened into something more, something lusty and hungry and primal. A surge of heat pulsed through her as his lips mated with hers. His mouth was hot and demanding, his body warm beneath the wet cotton of his shirt. The feel of his masculine, muscular body stirred an urgent need to get closer. Frannie's arms wound around his neck and she pulled him down until he was lying on top of her on the blanket.

He rained kisses everywhere—her neck, her ear, her

jaw—then returned again to her mouth, deepening the kiss. Frannie clutched at him, drowning in sensation, drowning just as surely as either of the victims they'd just rescued. She felt the weight of his body over hers, felt the warmth of his hand cupping her bottom, felt the hard length of his arousal pressed intimately against her. She moaned and arched against him, wanting more.

His hand moved up the inside of her thigh, pushing up her skirt and warming her skin. Heat shot through every muscle, every pore, every molecule of her being. The heat melted away all reason, all sense of time and place, leaving her with only a fierce, aching need.

His mouth slid down her neck to her chest, to her breast. He took her taut nipple in his mouth, through the silk of her blouse and the satin of her bra. The pressure was exquisite, but she wanted more. She longed for the feel of skin on skin.

She reached up and began unbuttoning her blouse, giving him access. One button, two buttons, three buttons…

A woman's voice broke the heady spell. "They came from over here somewhere."

Austin pulled back and looked at Frannie. Twigs snapped and leaves crunched. Someone—several someones—were coming.

Austin put his finger to his lips, then rapidly helped her refasten her buttons.

"Maybe they've already left," said a man's deep voice.

Austin pulled down Frannie's skirt and helped her sit up. Adjusting his khakis, he cleared his throat and slowly rose to his feet. "Are you looking for someone?"

Frannie saw the woman she'd rescued point to Austin. "That's him! That's the man who saved Emily. And there's the lady who saved me."

Frannie scrambled to her feet, self-consciously straight-

ening her skirt. The woman had changed into a long denim
umper over a white T-shirt, and she was still pushing the
baby carriage. She held the toddler, who was now wearing
a yellow playsuit with Sesame Street characters on the
front. Both of them still had wet hair.

Behind the woman stood two men. The tall one had a
large camera dangling from a thick strap around his neck,
and the other one was carrying a notepad.

The shorter man stepped up and stuck out his hand.
"Hello. I'm Hugh Miller with the *Whitehorn Journal.* I
understand you two just saved my wife and little girl."

Austin shook the man's hand. Hugh's face broke into an
enormous smile. "Say, aren't you Austin Parker, the race
car driver?"

Austin nodded.

"Oh, wow! This story is going to be huge! Do you mind
if we get some pictures? Maybe of you holding Emily, and
the lady here with my wife?"

Austin gave Frannie an apologetic smile. "Well, at least
you won't have to worry about anyone not believing why
you needed to change clothes," he murmured under his
breath. "Now you'll have documentation."

But Frannie was too busy reeling from the impact of that
kiss to worry about awkward explanations. It was alarming,
how quickly and thoroughly Austin could turn her from a
clear-headed, sensible loan officer into a panting, lovelorn
vixen.

"Oh, dear," said the woman, gazing at Frannie's bare
feet. "You've lost your shoes!"

She was afraid she'd lost far more than a pair of pumps,
Frannie through ruefully. Somewhere between the rescue
and the kiss, she'd completely lost her heart.

Ten

Summer walked into the kitchen of the bed-and-breakfast the next morning, carrying a stack of newspapers. She kissed Aunt Celeste's cheek, then plopped the papers onto the kitchen table and hugged Frannie. "I'm so proud of you!" She gave her a tight squeeze, then stepped back and beamed. "Imagine—our Frannie is a real, live, honest-to-goodness, front-page, news-making hero! She's famous!"

Frannie winced and hunkered down over her bowl of cereal. "The paper made entirely too much out of it."

Over at the stove, Jasmine grinned. "No, it didn't. You saved someone's life."

"Doctors like Summer save people's lives everyday," Frannie said.

Aunt Celeste smiled at Frannie. "Yes, but most doctors don't have the most popular race car driver in the country with them when they do it."

"And most of them don't rescue the wife and child of the local paper's news editor," Jasmine added as she turned out the last pancake onto a plate. She walked over and looked at the newspaper spread on the table.

Summer seated herself at the kitchen table. "I stopped by a newsstand to pick up some extra copies on the way here, and the story has evidently been picked up by a wire service. That picture of you and Austin with the baby and her mother is in just about every newspaper in the country!"

Celeste grinned. "You know what they say—everyone in the world will be famous for fifteen minutes. This is your time in the limelight."

"Great," Frannie said dryly. "My fifteen minutes of fame arrive, and I'm dripping wet."

"Oh, hey, get a load of this!" Jasmine looked up from her copy of the *Whitehorn Journal,* her eyes sparkling. "It says you're Austin's girlfriend!"

Frannie's heart pounded hard. "That just goes to show you can't believe everything you read."

"It says you were having a romantic picnic in the park when the accident occurred," Jasmine read.

"It was a business lunch," Frannie corrected.

Jasmine's gaze said she wasn't buying that for a moment. "Oh, come on! A picnic?"

"In the park?" Summer asked.

Celeste raised a questioning eyebrow. "Just the two of you?"

Frannie sighed. This was exactly the reaction she was likely to get from the staff at the savings and loan. She'd called the bank yesterday afternoon to explain that she needed to take the rest of the day off, but Mr. Billings had been in a meeting, so she'd left a message with his secretary. She wasn't looking forward to all the questions she was going to face this morning.

She glanced at her watch and sighed. It was time to head in and face the music. Her chair screeched on the wooden floor as she pushed back from the table. "I'd love to sit around and chat some more, but I've got to get to work."

"Not so fast!" Jasmine said. "I want to know about this romantic picnic."

"There's nothing to know." Frannie picked up her empty cereal bowl and carried it to the sink.

"Sure there is. Was it?"

"Was it what?"

"Romantic."

All three women turned and regarded her curiously. Frannie felt her face flame.

Jasmine and Summer looked at each other and smiled triumphantly. "It was!" they said in unison. They smacked their palms in the air in a high-five.

"You two leave Frannie alone," Aunt Celeste scolded. "Jasmine, you need to take those pancakes out to our guests."

Jasmine moved to comply. Summer glanced at her watch. "And I'm due at the hospital. I'd better get going, too." She rose and smiled at Frannie. "I just had to stop by to congratulate Whitehorn's newest heroine."

Frannie shot her aunt a grateful look as her cousins left the room. She rinsed her cereal bowl and placed it in the dishwasher, then glanced at Celeste. "I heard you up in the night. Were you having more dreams?"

The older woman nodded, her face solemn. "I dreamed Blanche visited me again."

A shiver chased up Frannie's arms. "Was it the same dream?"

Celeste shook her head. "Raven was with her. They were both sitting on the end of my bed and Blanche was trying to tell me something again, but this time I could understand what she was saying."

"What was it?"

"To look to the past. That old faces and old places would help jog my memory."

The chill on Frannie's arms moved to her spine. "What do you think that meant?"

"I don't know. But since Blanche has come to visit me a few times, I thought I'd return the favor."

"How?"

"I plan to visit the cemetery this morning."

The cemetery held the graves of both Blanche and Jeremiah. Given her aunt's fragile mental state, Frannie wasn't sure it was wise. What if she had a flashback and it was more than she could handle? Frannie's brows knit in a worried frown. "Are you sure you're up to that?"

Celeste nodded. "A part of my life is missing, and I want to get it back. I think Blanche is trying to show me the way."

"I don't think you should go alone."

Aunt Celeste smiled. "That's just what Jasmine said. She offered to go with me."

"Well, I hope you took her up on the offer."

"I did. We're going after all the guests finish breakfast."

"Good luck," Frannie said, kissing her aunt on the cheek. She lifted her purse from the back of the oak chair and slung the strap over her shoulder.

"You, too." Celeste smiled as Frannie headed to the door. "Enjoy your fifteen minutes of fame."

Frannie grimaced. "I think I'd enjoy a tooth extraction more."

Make that an unsedated tooth extraction, Frannie thought an hour later. She hated being the center of attention, and she found herself just that. She forced her mouth into a smile as Mr. Billings droned on about her bravery during an impromptu speech in the middle of the bank lobby following the weekly meeting of the bank's board of directors.

"...And since Frannie's brave actions yesterday exemplify this bank's commitment and dedication to the community, the board of directors has authorized me to give her this certificate of commendation." He handed Frannie an official-looking document. "Furthermore, Frannie, the board wants to usc your picture and story in a new advertising campaign to promote the high standard of service we offer here at Whitehorn Savings and Loan.'' Mr. Billings turned and shook her hand. ''On behalf of all of us, thank you for representing us so well.''

All of the bank staff broke into applause.

''Would you like to say a few words?'' Mr. Billings asked.

A feeling of panic grabbed Frannie's stomach and squeezed it like a vise. She longed to just sink right through the floor. ''I'm…I'm not good at speaking in public,'' she murmured to Mr. Billings.

''Oh, come on.''

The panic escalated to terror. She couldn't. It was impossible. The last time she'd tried speaking in public…

The memory sent a surge of fear pulsing through her. She fought to tamp it down. ''No, really. I—I—''

To Frannie's relief, Mr. Billings's secretary whispered something in his ear, causing him to change the focus of his attention. Smiling broadly, he raised his hands to quiet the crowd. ''I've just learned that the Mayor of Whitehorn plans to present an award to Frannie and Mr. Parker tomorrow, and that a TV camera crew will be in town to film it for a segment of the show 'Celebrity Spotlight.'''

Another round of applause greeted Frannie. Frannie felt her face burn.

''What do you think of that, Frannie?'' Mr. Billings asked.

''I'm not a celebrity,'' she muttered.

''You are now.'' Mr. Billings beamed and patted her on the back.

Everyone else seemed to want to pat her on the back, too, or to shake her hand or to offer congratulations. It seemed to take forever for the crowd to disperse. When it finally did, she saw Austin seated in a chair in front of her desk, grinning at her. She would have thought she'd exhausted all of her emotion reserves, but her heart gave a wild, erratic little jump at the sight of him.

Trying hard not to let him see the effect he had on her, she walked to her desk, sank into her chair and gave him what she hoped was a calm smile. "How did you get in here without being carried on the shoulders of your adoring fans?"

"They were too preoccupied with you." And it was no wonder, Austin thought. She was adorable with her cheeks all rosy, her eyes as wide and bashful as a deer's. She was so different from the women he routinely met. Most of them were attracted to his fame. If it ever disappeared, so would they.

Not so with Frannie. She was shy and retiring and seemed to actively dislike the spotlight. He couldn't help but notice how pale she'd grown when Mr. Billings had asked her to say a few words. She wasn't ego-driven or self-involved, he reflected. She was low-key and warm and caring, and those were among the things he loved about her.

Loved? The thought alarmed him. No, that was the wrong word. He meant liked. Her unassuming demeanor was one of the things he *liked* about her, along with her soft shiny hair and gray-green eyes and that slim, shapely body she kept covered up like a race car under a tarp.

"It's ridiculous, all the fuss everyone is making," she was saying.

"Well, when a story involves the wife and child of a newspaper editor, it tends to get blown out of proportion." He eased himself out of the chair and perched on the edge of her desk. "Which is why I came by."

"What do you mean?"

"Seems the camera crew that Mr. Billings just mentioned

wants to tape more than just the mayor's award. They want to do a whole segment of their show about us.''

"Us?"

Austin nodded. "My chief sponsor, SeaBreeze Detergent, is thrilled about all the publicity our rescue is getting. They contacted the show and urged them to do a story. Under the terms of my contract, I'm supposed to cooperate.''

"Well, fine, but leave me out of it.''

"Hey, I'm not going on the air and taking all the credit. I won't do it without you.''

"No.'' Frannie shook her head. "No way. I hate public speaking.''

He reached across the desk and placed his hand over hers. "It won't be that bad.''

"I—I can't speak in front of a crowd. I—I freeze.''

"There won't be a crowd. It won't be like making a speech. It'll just be talking to a reporter, just like you're talking to me now.'' He lifted her hand from the desk. "Please, Frannie?''

He could see her reluctance, see the difficulty she had saying yes. He turned her hand over and stroked her palm. "Please?''

She sighed. "They're not going to ask me to stage a reenactment, are they?''

He laughed, an irrational sense of delight sweeping through him at the thought that she was doing this for him, despite her misgivings. "You won't have to get in the pond. I promise.''

"Well…'' She pushed a swath of hair behind her ear and sighed. "You're very hard to say no to, do you know that?'' Her lips curved up in a small smile that he found incredibly seductive.

"Glad to hear that.'' He squeezed her hand and returned

her grin. "Since I'm on roll, I might as well go ahead and ask you for another favor."

"What?"

"Well, I have a new computer, and I don't know anything about setting it up. I'm wanting to get it up and running before I leave town, but I don't know anyone who's computer literate besides you." He gave her his most pleading gaze. "Would you come out to the ranch and help me get it set up on Saturday?"

Frannie sighed. "It seems to be my day for saying yes to you."

Austin smiled wolfishly. "Then maybe I should keep asking questions until I get to some really interesting ones."

Frannie grinned. "Maybe you should get the heck out of here and let me catch up on my work."

"All right. My agent arranged for the camera crew to come to my ranch early in the morning. I'll bring them here afterward—if you think that'll be all right with Mr. Billings, that is."

"Are you kidding? If it'll give the bank any publicity, it'll put Mr. Billings in seventh heaven."

"Well, then, I'll see you tomorrow. And on Saturday." He reluctantly turned loose of her hand as he rose from her desk. "And to pay you back for helping me out, I'll treat you to a horseback ride and a steak dinner."

He left the bank before she could voice an objection, pleased that his ploy had worked. He'd figured she'd have a hard time turning down a plea for help. Now all he had to do was buy a computer.

Frannie squinted against the afternoon sun as the female reporter angled the microphone toward her face. "How would you describe your relationship with Mr. Parker?"

Frannie shot Austin a look that reminded him of a horse

about to rear and run. "He's a...a friend. And a client of the bank where I work."

"Is that all?"

Austin stepped up, putting his arm around Frannie. "Our personal relationship is just that. Personal. And we intend to keep it that way."

The reporter's bright red lips curved in a knowing smile. She turned her attention back to Frannie. "I don't know if you're aware of it, but Austin was just voted the sexiest man in racing by female race fans. What do you have to say about that?"

Austin held his breath. He cared a lot more about Frannie's opinion than the public's.

He was relieved to see her smile. "Well, his fans obviously have excellent taste."

The reporter laughed, and the field producer signaled for the cameraman to turn off the camera.

"Good," the producer said. "We'll shoot the mayor's award, and then we'll be finished."

About time, Austin thought. It had been a long day. The TV crew had arrived at his ranch at seven that morning and had shot footage of his race car, his horses and home. Next they'd gone to the bank. As Frannie had predicted, her boss had been overjoyed at the publicity. The next stop had been the scene of the rescue, where the woman they'd saved, her child and her husband had all effusively thanked Austin and Frannie on camera. And now they were waiting outside city hall, where a large crowd had gathered in front of a portable stage.

"Here comes the mayor now," the producer said, raising his voice to be heard over the loud patriotic music of the Whitehorn High School band.

Mayor Ellis Montgomery, a tall, portly man with a self-important attitude, strode toward them. After a round of greetings and introductions, the producer asked, "What's the agenda for the ceremony?"

"Well, I'll make a few remarks, then I'll present the awards. After that, we'll ask Mr. Parker and Miss Hannon to each say a few words."

Frannie shook her head. "Oh, no. I can't."

"Oh, sure you can," the mayor said.

"No. You don't understand. I can't. Really. I—I freeze up in front of a crowd, and…"

"Oh, nonsense. You only have to say a few words."

Austin had never seen Frannie so pale. He put an arm around her and felt her tremble, and felt a surge of anger at the mayor's insensitivity. It took an effort to keep his voice even when he spoke. "You know, I don't much feel like talking, either, Mayor. Why don't you handle all the speaking duties, and Frannie and I will just come up and accept the paperwork."

The mayor immediately backed down. "Well, of course, if that's the way you want it. I just thought, with the cameras and all…"

"That's how we want it."

"Well, of course," the mayor sputtered.

Austin looked at Frannie and a surge of protectiveness shot through him, a fierce protectiveness he'd never felt before in his life. Her eyes were wide, her cheeks colorless, and her teeth were practically chattering. She looked scared to death—scared beyond mere bashfulness or stage fright. It was the look of a driver getting back into a car after a painful crash, the look of someone who'd had first-hand experience with terror.

Something in her past had hurt her, and hurt her deeply. He didn't know what it was, but he intended to find out. For reasons he didn't understand, it was important that she tell him, that she trust him, that she need him, because…

Because what? Oh, no, he was going soft in the head, having such mushy thoughts about a woman. He'd never needed anybody, and he'd sure as heck never wanted anybody to need him. He liked Frannie and he wanted to help her, that was all. The only reason he thought about her day and night was that he had a raging case of the hots for her. It was a perfectly normal, perfectly natural case of hormones. He was making a big deal out of nothing.

The mayor mopped his brow. "Well, if you two are ready, I guess we'll get things underway."

Austin glanced down at Frannie and was hit by a fresh wave of emotion, warm and unexpectedly sweet. It socked him right in the midsection and felt suspiciously like tenderness.

It wasn't, of course. He didn't feel things like that. He didn't allow himself to. It was attraction—plain, pure, physical attraction, that was all.

"You ready?"

Her eyes were still wide and terrified, but she smiled bravely. "I am if you are."

"I've been ready for quite a while." And he wasn't just talking about the awards presentation, he thought grimly. He was more than ready to do something about this insane, obsessive attraction he felt for Frannie. It was unnatural, wanting someone so much and not being able to satisfy the craving. Playing the gentleman for this length of time had left him so addled he scarcely knew himself anymore.

He'd always been able to separate his emotions from his physical needs, and he was certain he'd be able to again. Once his relationship with Frannie progressed to the physical level, his emotions would surely settle down and he'd once again be able to think about something besides Frannie's smile, Frannie's scent, Frannie's voice, Frannie's touch and Frannie's sweet, sweet taste.

Eleven

Jasmine held up two padded satin hangers. "Which is better, the yellow dress or the green one?"

Frannie studied the dresses, her head propped on her hands as she sprawled on Jasmine's bed. It was Thursday evening, and she was trying to help her cousin decide what to wear to a wedding in Billings that weekend. "I don't know. Why don't you try them on?"

Jasmine had started to do just that when the phone rang.

"I wonder which of your many admirers this is," Frannie teased.

"It's just as likely to be one of yours," Jasmine replied from somewhere under the green dress. "You've had several men ask you out since the dance, but you've turned them all down." Jasmine's head reappeared at the neckhole. "Not that I blame you. No one can compare to Austin. Maybe that's him now."

Frannie's heart pounded at the thought. She reached for the telephone and lifted the receiver. "Hello?"

"Well, hi there, kiddo. How are you?"

"David!" Frannie sat up, startled to hear the unmistakable voice of her older brother. She swung her feet off the bed, her mouth pulling into a wide smile. "Long time, no hear! I'm great. How are you?"

"Proud as punch to have a hero for a little sister."

Frannie felt her face heat. "You saw that photo, I take it." Over the past few days Frannie had received phone calls from her parents and several distant friends who'd seen the picture of her and Austin in their local newspapers.

"Yep. In the *Atlanta Constitution*. Could have knocked me over with a feather. How the heck did you get involved with the likes of Austin Parker?"

A wave of apprehension shot through Frannie. "We're not involved."

"Uh-huh. Right." David's tone was more than a little dubious.

"And what do you mean, 'the likes of'?"

"Well, he's not the average, run-of-the-mill guy I expect to be dating my sister. But for the record, you have my complete approval."

"You know Austin?"

"Not personally, but I've heard about him. And after I saw that picture of you with him in the paper, I ran a little background check on him."

"A background check? You're kidding."

"Hey, you're the only little sister I've got. Anyway, he seems like a straight-up kind of guy. Everyone I talked to says he's as nice as they come. Runs a clean race, never tries any funny stuff with his car, pays his taxes, doesn't have any kind of a criminal record. Far as I can tell, the guy has never even gotten a traffic violation."

Frannie remembered how carefully Austin drove his pickup and smiled. "I'm not surprised."

"Yeah, well, he gets my seal of approval."

"He's just a friend."

"Yeah. Sure."

"He is!"

"Uh-huh. Hey, kiddo, what's with all the deaths on the casino construction site? I've been following the case about Raven, and I saw an article in the paper the other day that another body had been found at the construction site."

"Yes. They don't think the two deaths are related, though. They think the second one was an accident or suicide."

"Hmm. Pretty strange coincidence. Is Uncle Jeremiah still a prime suspect in Raven's death?"

"Yes. A couple of the pistols at the old house could be the murder weapon. They're running tests on them now."

"So how's Aunt Celeste taking all this?"

Frannie sighed. "Not too well. She's been questioned several times, but she can't seem to remember anything. She draws a blank about the night Raven disappeared. The detective in charge of the case thinks she might have blocked something out of her mind."

"Hmm. This is even more intriguing than I thought. Look, Frannie, I have some vacation time coming in soon. I thought I'd use it to come visit and take the opportunity to look into this whole situation while I'm there."

"It would be wonderful to see you."

"Well, you'll have that privilege in just a few weeks."

"Great!"

"Well, I just wanted to call and tell you I'm glad your lifesaving training didn't go to waste."

Frannie grinned at the phone.

"I'm proud of you, kiddo."

Frannie coiled the cord around her finger. "It wasn't that big a deal. The lady was just yards from the shore."

"Yeah, but if you can't swim, a yard is the same as a mile. Especially in an old quarry."

"Well, I'm glad I could help. But I didn't do anything that special. Anyone would have done the same thing in that situation."

"You're overestimating the human species. In my line of work, I see plenty of people who wouldn't have lifted a finger. Anyway, I'm awfully proud of you, sis."

Frannie felt her throat thicken with emotion. "Thanks."

"And not that it makes any difference, but Austin gets a thumbs-up from me."

"We're just friends," Frannie said.

"Right. Whatever you say." She could practically see his sardonic smile. "See you soon, sis."

"Okay. I'll look forward to your visit."

"David's coming for a visit?" Jasmine asked as Frannie hung up the phone.

Frannie nodded. "He's intrigued by all the news reports about a mystery in his hometown."

"Good. Your folks will be thrilled to see him, and Mom will, too. Maybe he can help get her mind off ghosts and nightmares and murders."

"Maybe." Frannie watched Jasmine as she looked at herself in the mirror. "I'm hoping this wedding in Billings will do the same thing. I'm glad you're going with her."

"Oh, I love weddings. You can meet the cutest men at them. Are you sure you don't want to come with us? Mom said her friend invited all of us."

"I can't. I've got plans."

"With Austin?" Jasmine fixed her with a keen gaze.

Frannie shrugged and looked away. "He needs some help setting up a new computer."

Jasmine's eyes twinkled. "A likely story."

Frannie threw up her hands. "Why does no one believe there's nothing going on with Austin and me?"

"Because it's obvious that something is. Anyone who's seen the two of you together can feel it in the air."

"He asked for help, and I told him I'd help. That's all there is to it."

Jasmine smiled at her. "Well, if your help requires you to stay overnight, you won't have to answer to me or to Mom. We're spending the night in Billings, and Mom is putting the No Vacancy sign on the door of the bed-and-breakfast for the weekend.''

''Don't be ridiculous, Jasmine. Things aren't like that with Austin.''

Jasmine's eyes narrowed as her lips curled into a knowing, catlike smile. ''Maybe not yet. But I can't wait to get an update on Sunday.''

Saturday dawned bright and clear, a perfect day for an outing. The bed-and-breakfast's three guests checked out early, and Celeste turned the sign on the front door to Closed as soon as Tommy and the elderly couple's cars left the driveway.

Frannie stood in the foyer with Celeste as Jasmine lugged two suitcases down the front stairs. ''Are you only taking one bag, Mom?''

''Yes. It's just an overnight trip.'' Celeste turned to Frannie. ''Are you sure you don't want to come with us?''

''I'm sure.''

''She's got better things to do than go to a wedding,'' Jasmine volunteered. ''She's spending the day with Austin.''

Celeste smiled and patted Frannie's arm. ''How nice. I really like that young man.''

Jasmine grinned. ''Frannie does, too, but she won't admit it.''

Celeste looked at her watch and moved toward the door. ''Come on, Jasmine. If we want to get there by noon, we'd better get started.''

Frannie helped Celeste carry her bag to the car. ''You two enjoy yourselves.'' A change of scenery ought to do Celeste good, Frannie thought.

She watched them drive off, then climbed into her white Camry and drove to Austin's ranch. He'd wanted to come pick her up, but Frannie had wanted the independence of having her own transportation. It gave her a sense of control, and heaven only knew she needed as much of that as she could muster whenever she was around Austin.

He'd given her detailed instructions, and she found her way easily. She turned onto a gravel road off a two-lane highway, traveled two miles, then came to a large stone entry gate. Above it hung an iron sign proclaiming The Range.

Austin had a home on the range. Smiling at his sense of humor, Frannie turned her car onto the narrow gravel drive. The road wound around a densely forested hill, then took two more turns before a house came into view. It was a large, rambling, one-story house made of rock and natural wood that blended in with its surroundings. It had a deep, covered porch supported by large cedar beams, and the tall, multiple windows were all framed in rough-hewn wood.

Not a white column anywhere in sight, Frannie noted. She had secretly wondered if Austin's house would resemble the one his mother used to promise him. It made sense that it wouldn't, she thought as she pulled the car into the circular drive. That house had been his mother's dream. Austin was the kind of man who would have dreams of his own.

She braked and turned off the engine, still looking at the house. It suited him, she thought, unfastening her seat belt. Like him, it was rugged and handsome and larger than life.

Austin stepped out of the heavy wood entry as she shut the car door. Her heart seemed to slam in her chest, as well, as he walked toward her. "Did you have any trouble finding your way?"

"No. You gave excellent directions."

He gave her a friendly peck on the cheek. Frannie inhaled

the faint scent of shaving cream and soap, and found it strangely hard to breathe.

"Good," he said, casually looping an arm around her shoulders. "Well, I hope you can do the same on my computer."

Her short leather boots clattered on the wooden porch. He held the front door for her, and she walked into an enormous room filled with oversize pine furniture, colorful Navajo rugs, Native American pottery and artwork. A massive stone fireplace sat against one wall. The back of the room was largely glass and looked out over an immense outdoor pool.

"This is beautiful," Frannie breathed, looking around.

"Thanks. I like it."

"I remember you saying you were in the process of remodeling. Is this room part of that?"

Austin shook his head. "No. Just the bedrooms. The family that lived here before me had four daughters. All of the bedrooms except for the master one had flowered wallpaper, pink carpeting and dainty little chandelier-type light fixtures. Since most of my guests will be members of my pit crew, well, it just didn't seem fitting somehow."

Frannie grinned. "It *is* kind of hard to picture Tommy sleeping in a room with pink carpeting."

Austin grinned. "Yeah. He might start showing up for breakfast in a lacy pink robe and curlers. I couldn't risk that."

Frannie laughed.

"You want some coffee?"

"Sounds good." Frannie followed him through the living room into a large sunlit kitchen with hardwood flooring, granite countertops and custom-made pine cabinetry. Best of all, there was another fireplace in the kitchen, next to a large old farm table. "What a wonderful kitchen! It must be a real pleasure to cook in here."

"I'm afraid I really wouldn't know."

"You don't cook?"

He pulled two brown mugs down from the cabinet and gave a sheepish smile. "My culinary skills don't extend much beyond steaks and salad, but I've got those down to an art. I'll show you tonight."

What else was he planning to show her tonight? The thought sent a shiver running through her. His fingers brushed hers as she accepted a mug of coffee from him. Sexual awareness hung thick in the air, giving it an electric charge. Frannie looked around nervously, wanting to break the tension. "So where is your computer?"

He waved his hand toward a room across the living area. "In the study."

Frannie followed him through a pair of open French doors into a well-lit, pine-paneled room lined with bookcases. A large old desk stood in the center of the room, and piled in the center of it was a brand new computer, its cords still wound and wrapped with wire. Its empty box sat on the floor.

"I started to try to assemble it, then figured I'd just wait for you. I figured it would be easier for you to start from scratch than to undo my mistakes."

"This won't take long," Frannie said. She got busy and ten minutes later, the computer was assembled. She turned it on, watched the screen flicker, then studied the menu. "It's loaded with software. Which do you want me to show you how to use?"

Austin stood behind her and gazed at the screen. "I don't know. Something that'll let me keep track of my finances, I guess."

Frannie seated herself in the cordovan leather chair behind the desk and clicked an icon for an accounting program. Austin pulled up a matching chair and scooted it close beside Frannie's.

It was hard to concentrate on the computer screen with him sitting so close to her. His shoulder was several inches from hers, but she could practically feel the heat emanating from his body. She forced herself to focus on the program and carefully explained it to him.

"That's all there is to it." Frannie slid the mouse and pad over to him. "Here. Try it for yourself."

He hesitated, and it occurred to her that he might not know anything at all about computers. "Do you know how to use a mouse?"

"Why don't you show me?"

His hand looked intimidatingly masculine. Tanned and large, with a smattering of dark hair across the top, it completely covered the mouse. A wayward thought rushed through her mind. What would it feel like to have that hand on her body, moving across her skin?

But this was not the time for erotic conjecture. Taking a deep breath, she placed her palm on top of his hand. A shock wave of sensation flashed through her, making her stomach tighten. He seemed to feel it, too, because his long fingers curled around the mouse.

She forced her thoughts back to the computer. "Have you ever used a computer before?"

"Yes. This is a different type, though."

"Well, the mouse is for moving the cursor." She clicked it and guided his hand. He leaned forward, his face close to her hair. She heard him inhale deeply, as if he were smelling her shampoo. There it was again—that incredible awareness, that tension that stretched like a high wire between them. She pulled back. "You try it."

He guided the cursor across the screen.

"Very good. Now, see if you can open the program."

He hit the wrong icon. "Oops."

"Try again."

"I think I need some more help."

Frannie moved her hand back over his. He leaned in close again, so close she could feel his breath on her neck "That's better," he murmured. He cut her a sideways glance as she helped him guide the mouse. "I guess you took all kinds of computer courses in college."

"A few."

"I've always wished I had more formal education." He clicked the mouse, and the program opened.

Frannie looked at him. "It's never too late to go to college."

"Maybe I will someday."

"What would you study?"

"I don't know. Literature, science, history. All the stuff that an educated person knows. I'd just like to feel more educated."

As famous and successful as he was, he had an inferiority complex about his education. The realization touched her "You know, being educated isn't really a matter of having a college diploma. It's a matter of having knowledge and knowing how to use it. It seems to me that you know an awful lot about a lot of topics."

"I'd like to know more."

"About any particular topic?"

"There's one that's really got my interest."

"What?"

His gaze latched onto hers and wouldn't let go. "You."

Frannie swallowed, her throat suddenly dry. She stared at him for what must have been several seconds. She should change the subject, she should move, she should do anything but sit here and stare at him, letting the heat between hem intensify. She should, but she didn't. Instead she found herself asking in a voice so low she could barely recognize it as her own, "What do you want to know?"

"Everything."

The air was charged with an almost palpable tension. Frannie tried to pretend it wasn't. "There's not much to know."

"Sure there is."

Pull back. Pull back, or it will be too late. Oh, dear Lord, maybe it already was. She swallowed hard. "Ask me one question and I'll answer it. Then we'll get back to the computer."

"All right." He reached up and touched her face, his finger soft as a feather. "What are you thinking right now?"

"Well, uh, I, uh..." *I'm thinking how much I want to kiss you. I'm thinking that your mouth is the sexiest, most sensual thing in the world. I'm remembering how it felt on mine and thinking about how much I want to feel it again. I'm thinking that I've fallen head over heels for you, that I have no defenses against you, that I want to feel your arms around me, your hands upon me, your skin against mine. I'm thinking that fighting something I want so desperately is impossible. I'm thinking that if I had a shred of an instinct for self-preservation, I'd stand up and leave right now.*

She jerked her gaze back to the computer and forced a lightness she didn't feel into her voice. "I'm thinking that I should probably show you the word processing program next."

Austin let out a long sigh, then rubbed his jaw. "Frannie, I've got to admit something."

"What?"

"Well, don't hate me for this, but I already know how to use a computer."

"You do?"

He nodded, his expression contrite. "I already have one. It's a different type, and I'm no great whiz at it, but I already know how to do the basic stuff."

Frannie stared at him. "So why did you act like you needed my help?"

"Well, I did need some help in setting this one up. And I've never used an accounting program before."

Frannie didn't like the feeling of having been duped. "If you're familiar with computers, you could have figured it out yourself."

"I know." Austin's chest rose and fell as he inhaled and expelled a deep breath. His gaze was direct and remorseful. "The truth is, I didn't think you'd come if I just invited you to spend the day with me. Knowing what a nice person you are, though, I figured you wouldn't be able to turn down a plea for help."

She knew she should be angry, should feel some measure of outrage, but she couldn't seem to muster any. "Let me see if I've got this straight. You deliberately took advantage of my good nature?"

"Pretty much." His blue eyes were doleful. "I guess I wouldn't blame you if you decided to leave."

If she had any sense, she would. It was obvious where all of this was headed. The attraction between them was clearly out of control. The problem was, her feelings for him were out of control, as well. She was head over heels in love with him.

She loved him. The realization broke over her like a freshly cracked egg, pouring slowly down around her, revealing the bright yellow center of truth.

She loved him. She could suddenly see it, could suddenly

see it with sparkling clarity. She could also see that she was kidding herself, trying to keep from getting involved with him. She was already involved. It might not be wise, but it was too late for wisdom.

"Please don't leave," he murmured.

How could she? How could she leave, with the discovery that she loved him fresh on her heart? She'd waited all these years to feel this way about a man. She might never get another chance to experience real, heartfelt love. She couldn't leave. Not now.

Besides, he was going to do the leaving for both of them. He was going leave tomorrow.

Frannie looked into his blue, blue eyes.

"Don't leave," he whispered again.

Her mouth pulled into a soft smile. "I won't. I intend to stay and make an honest man of you."

One dark eyebrow lifted quizzically.

"You promised me a horseback ride and tour of your ranch, and I'm going to hold you to it."

His eyes sparkled as he grinned. "I also promised you a steak dinner."

"Well, then, I'll hold you to that, too."

"I'd rather just hold *you*." There was no mistaking his meaning. His gaze deepened and darkened, and ran caressingly over her face.

Frannie strove for a light tone, but her voice came out so low and soft, she was afraid she sounded like Mae West. "Pay off your promises, and then we'll see."

But it was no longer a matter a question of "if," Frannie thought. It was merely a question of when, where and how.

Twelve

Frannie walked beside Austin as they strolled down a path through the woods for about a quarter mile. The dense forest around the house had given way to rolling pastureland. He'd taken her hand as they'd left the house, and he was still holding it. Frannie reveled in the sensation. All of her senses seemed heightened, and the world somehow seemed more intense—the sky looked bluer, the pines smelled crisper, the sun felt warmer. She felt as if she could stroll hand-in-hand with Austin forever.

As they rounded a bend in the path, a large rusty-red outbuilding loomed ahead. Austin gestured toward it. "There's my shop."

"Your shop? I thought you were going to show me the garage where you keep your race cars."

Austin grinned. "It's one and the same."

"It looks like an old-fashioned barn," Frannie commented as they approached the building. She looked out over the rolling pastureland, where two similar buildings sat on separate hills. "In fact, it looks like you have three old-time barns."

"Glad you think so. It's supposed to look that way." Austin pulled out a set of keys and unlocked the wide, sliding door of the building. "When I bought the place, I had to build a shop and a stable, but I didn't want them to be eyesores. The architect suggested that we keep them all in the same style as the existing barn."

"It looks great," Frannie commented. "Like something from a postcard."

Smiling, Austin rolled up the door to reveal am enormous automotive garage.

He flipped on bright overhead lights as they stepped inside.

Frannie looked around and marveled. It was larger and better equipped than any service station garage she'd ever seen—and definitely cleaner. "This looks more like an operating room than a garage," she murmured.

It was true. The shop had two car lifts and all kinds of computerized testing equipment, and all of it gleamed as brightly as Aunt Celeste's freshly polished silver. So did the tools lined up on the shelves and in the rolling toolboxes. Even the concrete floor looked as if it had just been pressure-washed.

She turned to Austin in amazement. "I've never seen a garage so spotless!"

Austin grinned. "I like a clean shop."

Two low-slung, red-and-yellow race cars covered with decals and logos sat at the back of the shop. Frannie headed toward them. "You have two race cars?"

"Actually, I have four. These two are for use on short and intermediate tracks—tracks that are just a half mile to two miles. The other two are for use on superspeedways—tracks that are two and a half miles around."

"Where are they now?"

"On their way to a studio in New York City. Tommy and another member of the crew left yesterday to haul them out there."

"Why are they going to a studio?"

"I'm supposed to shoot a TV ad for SeaBreeze on Monday. Then the cars and I are scheduled to make an appearance at a big automotive show in New Jersey. After that

I'll do some appearances in Philadelphia, then I'll head to Atlanta on Thursday for a qualifying race on Friday."

Frannie shook her head. "I had no idea there was so much involved in racing."

"There's a lot that goes into it."

"I guess you don't just drive the cars to the racetracks, huh?"

Austin grinned. "Nope. I have a special truck for hauling them." He pointed to a large empty spot at the back of the garage. "It's usually parked there. And the motor home is parked beside it."

Frannie's eyes widened. "You have a motor home?"

"Yep. It's home base when we're at a track."

"Is that where you sleep?"

"Sometimes. I usually stay in a hotel and let the crew stay in the motor home."

Frannie looked around, trying to absorb it all. She pointed to eight immense, shiny motors. "What are those?"

"Extra engines."

"You change them out?"

Austin nodded. "After every race."

Frannie shook her head at the incredible expense of it all. A truck, a motor home, extra engines… It was mind-boggling. "It's amazing, what it takes to operate one race car."

"It's a pretty pricey enterprise," Austin agreed. "That's why we have sponsors."

"SeaBreeze Detergent pays for all this?"

"Well, they're my main sponsor. I also have a soft drink company and a tire chain. Sponsorship's the name of the game."

Frannie looked at the decals that covered the cars. "How does a sponsorship work?"

Austin grinned. "It's pretty simple. A company pays me

a huge amount of money, and I let them put their logo on my car and clothes. I also agree to do a certain number of public appcarances and ads for their product. That's what SeaBreeze was holding over my head about that TV show.''

Frannie had no idea that racing was so involved. "Can I get a closer look at the cars?"

"Sure."

He walked with her to the far end of the garage. Frannie stared as they neared the vehicles. "They don't have any doors!"

Austin nodded, his face creased in a huge grin. "It makes them more streamlined. We crawl in and out through the windows.''

Frannie leaned down and peered through the window. "There's no passenger seat, either!"

Austin smiled. "Nope. That's where we put the primary and secondary ignition systems.''

Frannie gazed at the sparse interior. It looked stripped down, just dials and controls and foot pedals. "They don't exactly look like luxury vehicles."

"They're strictly built for speed," Austin agreed.

"What about safety?" Frannie asked.

"Oh, there are lots of safety features." He leaned in beside her and pointed to the black dashboard. "The gauges are all extra large and easy to read. And we have a built in fire extinguishing system, padded roll bars and a shock-resistant seat.''

"How fast do you drive?"

"About two hundred miles per hour."

Frannie felt as if he were talking at that speed as he explained about engine components, using foreign words such as "bulkhead" and "crankshaft" and "bearing bosses." Frannie didn't understand half of what he was talking about, but she loved the way his eyes shone as he talked about the cars.

"Do you keep track of all the publicity you get?" she finally asked.

"Yep." Austin led her to the side of the garage, pulled open a large drawer and extracted an enormous black folder that looked something like an artist's portfolio. Placing it flat on a workbench, he unzipped it to reveal large, plastic pages with laminated newspaper articles inside. "My publicist sends me these. There are some great shots of the cars in action."

Frannie thumbed through the pages, less interested in the cars than the photos that clearly showed Austin. The book was full of them. Austin in a one-piece scarlet racing suit, holding his helmet. Austin seated inside the car. Austin holding a trophy. Austin standing between two gorgeous girls, each one kissing his cheek.

An unfamiliar flash of jealousy stabbed through Frannie as she gazed at the photo. "I guess you have a lot of fans."

Austin nodded amiably. "We've got our share."

Frannie pointed to the photo of the two women. "Looks like some of them are pretty enthusiastic."

Austin grinned. "I guess you could say that."

"Do you have a lot of women fans?"

Austin nodded and shifted his stance. "There are quite a few ladies who follow the races."

"Like groupies follow rock bands?"

"Sort of."

"Do women throw themselves at you?"

Austin rubbed his chin. "Some of them can be pretty persistent." He took a step toward her, his eyes warm. "But, hey, Frannie, you've got nothing to worry about."

Frannie's heart pounded hard. Were her thoughts so transparent that he could read them?

He lifted a strand of her hair and twirled it around his finger. "I have no interest in being a notch on some bimbo's bedpost."

The statement was so blunt and outrageous that Frannie couldn't help but laugh.

"It's true," Austin said, and his eyes looked as though he meant it. "I did my share of cattin' around a few years ago, but not anymore. It's not worth the risk, physically or financially."

"What about emotionally?"

"That has never been an issue."

At least he was honest, Frannie thought. She wondered if his emotions would be involved as far as she was concerned. He probably wouldn't want them to be.

Frannie swallowed around an unexpected lump in her throat. She didn't want to ruin today by worrying about tomorrow. She loved him, and she wanted to experience that love to the fullest.

She flipped another plastic page, and saw a photo of Austin pouring champagne over the heads of five smiling men. "Your crew?"

Austin nodded and grinned. "They're the best in the business. Those guys do all the real work. I just do the fun part."

"The risking-your-life part," Frannie reminded him.

"Yeah, but still, I just sit behind the wheel and drive. Those guys change out the tires, gas up the engine and service anything else that needs it in just sixteen seconds flat."

"Sixteen *seconds?*"

Austin nodded. "Amazing, isn't it?"

"I'll say." Frannie flipped through more pages. "What actually happens at a race?"

"Well, on Fridays, we have the qualifying rounds. The

top finalists in that are the only ones who get to enter the real race. Along with the actual racing, there's a lot of mandatory schmoozing that goes on. The sponsors bring their top clients, and we have to mingle with them at dinners and parties and what-not.''

"Do you do something special before the race to psyche yourself up?"

Austin shook his head. "This is the only sport where the participants don't get much time to mentally prepare. There's usually a big sponsorship breakfast, then photos beside the cars and last-minute schmoozing with the sponsors.'' He closed the portfolio and zipped it. "There is a drivers's prayer meeting, though, right before the race. I always go to that.''

"Do you pray to win?"

"Nah. I pray that nothing I do ends up hurting another person. That's my worst fear about racing.'' He put the portfolio back in the drawer, then turned back to Frannie. "And I pray to drive my best so I don't let my team down. That's it.''

Frannie's heart opened like a morning glory at dawn. She loved him, all right. How could she not?

"You said you've been in some accidents.''

Austin nodded. "It happens.''

"An accident at two hundred miles an hour must be pretty serious.''

He gave a short nod, then looked away and shifted his stance. "Hey, what do you say we head back to the house, pack a lunch, then saddle up a couple of horses?''

He didn't want anyone to care, she reminded herself, just as *he* didn't want to care. He'd told her as much. His detachment was his winner's edge. If she didn't want to drive him away, she couldn't let him know how deeply she'd grown to care about him.

* * *

"Whoa, there, Charlie Horse." Frannie pulled on the reins and leaned back in the saddle as the large roan gelding hurried toward the corral.

Austin watched her hair gleam in the last rays of sunlight and grinned. He couldn't remember when he'd spent a more enjoyable day. He and Frannie had ridden up a winding mountain trail and picnicked on a flat ledge that offered an expansive view of the ranch. They'd laughed and joked and talked, then talked some more. He didn't know when he'd talked more freely, or enjoyed a woman's company more. They'd covered anything and everything—everything, that was, except the incredible sexual attraction sizzling between them.

Jumping down from his mount, Austin tethered his horse to the fence, then turned to help Frannie dismount. She didn't really need the help—he'd been pleased to discover she was an experienced horsewoman. All the same, Austin wanted to be there to catch her as she climbed off her horse, simply because he wanted the excuse of feeling her warm, soft body against his.

He was acting like a schoolboy, he thought ruefully, trying to find sneaky little ways of getting close to her. He'd wanted to kiss her all day, but he'd restrained himself, afraid he'd scare her off if he came on too strong. He needed to take his time. If he were smart, he'd let her make the first move.

He'd never known waiting could be so hard. He couldn't remember ever wanting a woman as much as he wanted Frannie.

Austin put his hands on her waist as she swung her leg over the horse and jumped down. The scent of her soft perfume filled his nostrils for a sweet, short moment, then she pulled back and rubbed her leg.

"I haven't been on a horse in a while, and I'm starting

to feel it," Frannie said, massaging her calf. "I think Char-lie Horse has given me one."

"I've got just the cure for that. A long soak in the hot tub."

Frannie's eyes grew large and round. "I—I didn't bring a swimsuit."

"That's okay. Tommy bought me half a dozen women's swimsuits as a housewarming present."

He enjoyed the way Frannie's mouth fell open. "Why?"

"He said I needed to be prepared if company dropped by."

"Yes, but half a dozen?"

Austin uncinched the saddle on Frannie's horse and hauled it off the animal's back. "I'm afraid he's got some warped fantasies about bachelor life." Austin shot her a grin. "He said he didn't know what size to get, so he ended up buying every size the store carried." Austin grinned at the memory. "He said it was his proudest moment. The salesladies were all whispering behind his back that he must have a harem."

The vision of the stocky, grizzled man surrounded by a bevy of bathing beauties made Frannie laugh. "So have any been worn?"

"You'll be the first."

Frannie slid the saddle blanket off her horse's back and draped it over the corral fence. She turned and did the same with the blanket from Austin's mount as he removed the saddle, then picked up the blankets and headed for the tack room. He followed her with the saddles.

"Where are your curry brushes?" she asked, putting away the blankets.

"Over there." He indicated a shelf off to the side. Fran-nie picked up two of them and headed back to the horses.

Austin followed, trading out the horses's bridles for soft harnesses while Frannie groomed the horse she'd ridden.

He liked the way she just pitched in and helped. He liked the way she talked to the horse in low, soothing tones and brushed its coat in long, smooth strokes. Heck, he liked everything about her. And the more he was around her, the more he found to like.

He realized he was standing there like an idiot, watching her do all the work. He picked up the second brush and quickly groomed his own mount, finishing just as she did.

"Let's give these fellas some oats and put them out to pasture," he said.

He led the horses through a gate on the far side of the corral, unhitched the lead ropes and turned them loose. They ambled over to the water trough. Austin grabbed a bag of oats from inside the stable and poured it into two feed buckets. The horses eagerly trotted over and were soon head-down in the feed.

Frannie followed Austin back to the stable as he put the oats away. "Who takes care of the horses while you're gone?"

"I have a husband and wife caretaker team. They're terrific. She cleans the house, and he sees to the grounds and horses."

Austin and Frannie returned to the tack room to put away the brushes and hang up the bridles. Austin locked the door as they left, then turned to Frannie.

"How's your leg? Can you walk back to the house?"

"Oh, sure. It's just a little stiff, that's all."

Austin stifled his disappointment. He'd been hoping she'd need to be carried. "Well, a soak in the tub should fix that right up."

"Considering that I now smell like Charlie Horse, a soak is probably a good idea."

The thought of Frannie in a swimsuit made Austin break a sweat. He was already in hot water where she was concerned, and he wasn't anywhere near the hot tub.

The sun was setting behind the mountain ridge out the west window as Frannie stood in the yellow guest room, holding the can of beer Austin had handed her as they'd passed through the kitchen. She gazed at the assortment of tiny bikinis in the dresser drawer in dismay. "Oh, dear," she murmured, lifting out a tiny white thong.

Austin had guided her to the guest room and told her where to find the swimsuits. He'd shown her where the towels were kept, and pointed out the adjacent bathroom. He'd told her everything she needed to know, except that Tommy's taste in ladies' bathing suits ran from skimpy to barely there.

Frannie pulled out a hot pink bikini top and stared at it. The bra cups were approximately the size of her head. Oh, dear, she certainly hoped these sizes didn't indicate Austin's usual taste in women, or he was going to be sorely disappointed.

Frannie took a long swig of beer, then pawed through the drawer until she found a black string bikini that appeared to be her size. It was far more daring than anything she'd ever worn—just two little triangles of fabric up top, and a scant amount of cloth on the bottom that tied together at the hips. The only good thing about it was that at least it wasn't a thong.

Taking another long draught of beer for courage, Frannie scrambled out of her clothes and into the swimsuit. It took two more long sips before she worked up the nerve to look at herself in the mirror.

"Oh, my," she murmured. It was a shock, seeing herself

so scantily clad. And the really shocking thing was, she looked...great.

She turned to one side and then the other, staring at her image. Maybe the beer was blurring her vision—after all, she wasn't much of a drinker. Or maybe it was her new haircut, or the fact she was wearing her contacts. Whatever it was, she sure didn't look like the plain Jane she'd always assumed herself to be.

She looked attractive. And desirable. Seductive, even.

The thought sent a rush of heat coursing through her. Oh, dear. What would Austin think? She was too shy to just stroll out there in front of him, wearing only this! It was scantier than her most daring underwear. Looking around, she grabbed her denim shirt and put it on over the bikini, buttoning it nearly to the neck. Rapidly swallowing the rest of her beer, she took a deep breath and headed down the hallway.

She found Austin standing in the kitchen, wearing a pair of blue swim trunks. Her mouth went dry at the sight of his shirtless chest. Good heavens, his body was even better than she'd imagined. His biceps were large, his pectorals well-defined, his chest covered with dark hair that narrowed to an enticing line that disappeared into his waistband.

She suddenly realized she was gawking at him. She pulled her eyes away from his chest to find him gazing at her with amusement. "Want another beer?"

She probably shouldn't, Frannie thought. She was already feeling a little tipsy from the first one, but it was helping to take the edge off her nervousness. "Sure," she said.

Austin popped the top on the can and handed it to her, his eyes on her legs. He glanced up, his gaze appreciative. Frannie fiddled self-consciously with the top button of her shirt, feeling practically naked.

He picked up a stack of towels he'd placed on the kitchen counter, then led the way through the French doors of the living room out onto the deck. He'd turned on the whirlpool as soon as they'd headed back to the house, and now steam was rising in the cool twilight air.

He set the towels on a padded chaise longue. "Can I take your shirt?"

She folded her arms across her chest, feeling as skittish as a colt. "I—I think I'll keep it on for a while. It's starting to get chilly."

"The tub is heated," he pointed out.

"I'll wear it anyway."

Austin looked at her as if he were wondering if she was wearing anything under it. "Didn't you find a swimsuit that fit?"

"Yes. If those tiny scraps of fabric actually qualify as swimsuits."

Austin grinned. "I'm afraid Tommy belongs to the less-is-more school of thinking when it comes to women's apparel."

"What about you?"

His grin deepened. "It depends on who's doing the wearing."

A shiver chased through her. He seemed to notice. "Let's get in the water where it's nice and warm." He stepped into the tub and held out his hand. She gingerly took it and stepped in with him.

The water was warm, very warm, and turbulent. Just as he made her feel inside.

Austin stepped down further, then motioned to the ledge. "Have a seat."

She sat where a water jet bubbled against her back. With water covering her up to the chest, she felt herself relax. "Oh, this feels great."

Austin held out his hands. "Give me your sore leg."

Frannie turned sideways and gingerly placed her calf in his lap. His thigh felt hard and muscular, and his fingers on her skin sent quivers of heat racing up her leg. She nervously took another long pull on her beer.

He gently kneaded her muscle. "You have beautiful legs."

"Thanks. Yours are pretty nice, too."

Mortified at what she'd just said, she took another long drink. Austin laughed. "Frannie, are you getting tipsy?"

"I'm getting a bit of a buzz," she admitted. "I'm not much of a drinker."

"Well, now is not the time to turn into one." Austin took her beer and placed it on the deck, out of her reach, then shifted closer so that both of her thighs now rested on top of his. "I want you to know exactly what you're doing tonight."

"What am I going to do?"

"Darned if I know." He slowly massaged her calf, his fingers both strong and gentle. "But I want you to be in complete control of your faculties."

It was hard to be in control of her faculties around him—especially when she was wearing practically nothing under her shirt, and his hands were rubbing her leg so erotically. Yet he said he wanted her to be.

"You're a really different kind of guy," she found herself saying.

"What do you mean?"

"Oh, I don't know—decent. Straightforward. Honest."

"That hasn't been your experience with men?"

Frannie leaned her head back against the side of the tub and rolled her eyes. "Ha!"

"Tell me about the guy from college."

"He was a jerk. End of story."

"So how did you meet him?"

She hadn't talked about Joe in a long while. There were parts of the story she'd never talked about at all. Maybe it was the beer, maybe it was the deepening twilight, maybe it was just Austin. Whatever the reason, she found the words just spilling out. "Joe was in my junior calculus class. He was having trouble with the course, and he asked if I'd help him." Frannie stared up at the sky, at the enormous orange moon hanging low over the mountains. "One thing kind of led to another. I was crazy about him. I thought he was The One." Frannie gave Austin a wry smile. "And then I got a new roommate."

Austin's eyes looked silver in the moonlight. "The Pamela Anderson look-alike."

Frannie nodded. "She was new to Montana, and she didn't know anybody on campus. I invited her to go out with Joe and me a few times because I didn't want to leave her sitting alone in the dorm room. Like an idiot, I missed out on all the signals that anything was brewing between them."

Austin's hand continued to rub her calf. The muscle didn't hurt anymore, but she decided not to tell him just yet. His fingers felt delicious, and she didn't want him to stop. "Anyway, about that time, a professor talked me into running for class treasurer. He said it would look good on my résumé. All of the candidates had to make a speech to the junior class the day of the homecoming ball. I was nervous about it, but I had it all prepared. I'd practiced and practiced and practically knew it by heart."

The memories were getting uncomfortable now. She took a deep breath. Seeming to sense her anxiety, Austin shifted closer and started rubbing her neck.

"What happened?"

"Right before I was supposed to give the speech, I went

to lunch with a friend at a pizza place. The restaurant had high-backed booths where you couldn't see who was seated behind you. Anyway, my friend went to the rest-room, and while she was gone, I heard a familiar voice from the booth behind me.''

''Let me guess. Joe and Pamela.''

Frannie gave a mirthless smile. ''No. That would have been a lot easier.'' She leaned her head back as Austin's fingers massaged her neck. ''It was Joe, all right, but he was with a new pledge to his fraternity. Each upperclass-man was assigned a freshman fraternity member that he was supposed to mentor—sort of a big brother, little brother arrangement.''

''I get the picture.''

''Anyway, Joe was talking to his plebe, giving him the lowdown on life, as if he were some kind of all-knowing, experienced man of the world. It probably would have been funny, listening to him, if the topic hadn't hit so close to home. Joe was explaining that women are like currency. 'You use them to get what you want,' Joe said. 'Take Fran-nie, for example. I used her to get through a couple of tough math classes.'''

''What a jerk,'' Austin muttered.

''Oh, it gets better. This freshman—I think his name was Nathan—said something like, 'I thought you and Frannie were kind of serious.' Joe laughed and said I didn't know it yet, but we were seriously finished. He'd already found my replacement.''

''Man.''

Frannie's mouth twisted into a wry smile. ''Joe said he was ready to trade up. He said being seen with a beautiful woman was a status symbol, like driving a fancy car, and if a guy wanted to be looked up to by his peers, he'd better find—and I quote—'a real show dog.'''

"Ah, honey." Austin's voice poured over her like a balm. He ran his hand up and down her arm, and the words began to pour out faster.

"Joe said that women were always competing in a big beauty contest. He said I was nice and smart and everything, but I didn't rate very high on the head-turning scale. He said he wanted a woman who made other guys think, 'Wow! Joe must really be cool if he's got a gal like *that*.'"

"The idiot must have been blind," Austin muttered.

"Nathan asked him who he had in mind to replace me, and Joe said, 'Frannie's new roommate.' And then he went into a crude description of the size of her chest. He said he planned to dump me after the dance that night."

Frannie glanced over and found Austin's gaze resting on her, his eyes warm and troubled and filled with concern. "Did you ever let the moron know you were sitting right behind him?"

"No. They left soon after that, and then my friend came back to the table." Frannie gazed out at the sky. The moon was higher now, but still incredibly large and orange. A sprinkling of stars twinkled around it.

"Did you tell your friend what you'd heard?"

"I tried, but I couldn't. I just couldn't bring myself to repeat the words. I—I just kind of sat there. I can't tell you how bad I felt. How inadequate. And then it was time to go give my speech."

Austin's hand stilled on her arm. He pulled her closer.

"It was in a big auditorium," Frannie continued, "and it was nearly filled. Most of the people running for office were in fraternities and sororities, and their whole houses had come out to support them. It was kind of a rowdy crowd. I pulled myself together as best I could. The first candidate for treasurer gave a really good speech. He ended it by throwing candy that looked like little coins out into the crowd.

"And then it was my turn. I walked out on stage, stepped up to the microphone and looked out at the crowd, and then, there in the back, I saw them. There was Joe, standing right beside my roommate."

Frannie's throat started to close up at the memory. "I froze. I couldn't talk. I couldn't move. I just stood there like a statue, paralyzed with fear and hurt. And the room fell completely silent."

Frannie fell silent now, just thinking about it. "And then someone laughed." Her voice came out barely more than a whisper. "And then some more people. And then a guy yelled, 'You want to be class treasurer? Show us how you count money!' And he threw a piece of the candy money at me. And then all of a sudden, everyone was throwing it. I just stood there, getting pelted."

"Ah, Frannie," Austin's hand ran from her neck down her back, then up again.

"It was awful. I finally managed to run off the stage. I felt like the biggest loser in the world."

Austin pulled her close, his arm around her. "But you know you're not, right? You know that this Joe creep is the real loser, don't you?"

Frannie swallowed hard. "That's not how I saw it. I felt like the homeliest, stupidest female on the planet. I decided that if life was a beauty contest, well, I just wouldn't enter it. I wouldn't even *try* to look attractive. I figured that if you don't try, you can't fail. So for years, I refused to do anything to call attention to myself. I tried to just blend in with the background."

Austin gazed at her, his heart heavy, his chest tight. This explained so many things about her. The prickly way she'd acted when he'd told her she'd looked beautiful the night of the ball, her fear of public speaking, the way she liked to hide behind her glasses even though she could see better out of her contacts. And it was all because of a conceited, air-headed jerk who obviously had no taste in women.

A surge of rage pulsed through Austin. He wasn't a violent person, but he'd give anything to be able to smash his fist through the creep's stupid face right now.

Frannie was staring up at the moon. "...And then my cousins started giving me a hard time about turning into a hermit," she continued. "They wanted to make me over and fix me up with a blind date for the Whitehorn Ball. And then I met you, and..."

Austin's heart thudded hard. "And what?"

"Oh, nothing." She looked away, and her voice lowered until it was barely audible over the swirling water. "That's just the beer talking."

"One beer can't say very much."

Frannie stared at the bubbling water. The color in her cheeks might be the result of the hot water, but the way she avoided his gaze spoke of embarrassment.

The ache in his chest tightened. He shifted closer toward her, and gently rubbed her arm. "Let me guess. You were about to say that then you met me, and you could tell I didn't see you the way you saw yourself."

She turned toward him, her eyes wide.

"In fact, you could tell that I thought you had the sexiest legs...." Austin ran his right hand from her calf up her thigh, and was gratified to feel her tremble. "And the most beautiful, kissable lips..." His wet finger drifted to her mouth and softly traced its outline, carefully following the curve of her upper lip.

Frannie's lips parted. Austin leaned closer. "And the softest, warmest, most intriguing eyes..." His hand feathered up her cheek and worked its way into her hair. He was whispering now, his mouth close to her ear. "You could probably tell that I haven't been able to get you off my mind since we met, and that I've lain awake nights fantasizing about you."

His face was close now, very close to hers, close enough to see that her pupils were dilated, her eyes filled with desire. A rush of need throbbed through him, hot and hard.

"Austin," she breathed. Her arms reached up and circled his neck.

And then he was kissing her, devouring her sweet, salty mouth, and she was kissing him back, kissing him with a fervor that was hotter and wilder than the swirling water— hotter and wilder than the last lap at Daytona the time he was three abreast and fighting for the lead. She shifted onto his lap, pressing her bottom against his arousal, and he moaned at the sweet torture.

The denim of her shirt rasped against his chest, making him ache to feel her skin against his. She must have felt the same need, because she reached for her top button. Austin covered her hand with his.

"Let me." He slowly unbuttoned her shirt, one button at a time, trailing kisses on her flesh as he exposed it. He eased the shirt down and off her arms, then tossed it on the deck behind them.

She was wearing a tiny black bikini, and her nipples pushed at the wet fabric in hard, erect peaks. He took one of the tips into his mouth, fabric and all.

"Austin," she murmured. "I want…"

He circled her breast with his palm, reveling in the soft weight, and kissed the peak again. "Yes, sweetheart?"

"I want…"

"Tell me what you want." He ached for her, ached to do anything, anything at all that she wanted.

"You," she whispered. "I want you."

The blood roared in his ears. He put one hand under her knees, the other under her arms, and lifted her as he stood. He carried her out of the steaming tub to the chaise longue where he'd placed the stack of towels.

Propping her on his knee, he picked up several towels, then carried her to a pair of French doors on the west wing of the house. Balancing her again, he turned the doorknob and carried her across the threshold, not setting her down until he reached his bed.

Thirteen

Frannie felt the give of a mattress beneath her, then felt Austin's mouth settle softly upon her lips. She shivered, and he pulled back to settle a towel around her. "You're cold. Let me light a fire."

"You've already lit it," she murmured.

He grinned as he leaned over her in the dimly lit room, rubbing her arms with the soft ends of the towel. "Well, let me light another one."

Frannie hugged the terry cloth around her and watched him stride across the room to a large stone fireplace, where logs were already neatly stacked, just waiting to be set afire. He squatted in front of it and touched a match to the kindling. Flames blazed and crackled, illuminating the room. Frannie glanced around. It was large and masculine and handsome, with taupe adobe walls, oversize Southwest-style furnishings and animal-skin printed fabrics. Frannie picked up the other towel Austin had laid on the bed beside her and padded across the thick cream carpet to the faux fur rug in front of the fireplace, where he was crouched to adjust a screen.

He looked so masculine, so manly in the flickering firelight. A fresh rush of desire pulsed through her as she draped the towel over his muscled shoulders.

He turned and looked up at her, his gaze hotter than the flames leaping in the hearth. "Come here," he growled, pulling her to him.

The next thing Frannie knew, they were lying on the thick, soft fur rug, and Austin's mouth was working its magic, coaxing sensations from her that she never knew existed. She arched toward him, straining for every point of contact her body could make with his, intimately pressing against the rock-hard proof of his desire. She was on fire, aflame, ablaze with wanting, and she moaned softly against him.

His mouth moved to her neck, to her throat. He slid the straps of her bikini top off her shoulders and pushed her top down around her waist. His gaze moved over her breasts, as warm as a caress, making the hardened tips swell still more. "Frannie... You're even more beautiful than I imagined."

Beautiful. Austin thought she was beautiful. The thought hazily filled her mind and her heart. The words freed something inside of her, something she had always held back, something she had always been afraid to give. She wanted to give everything, everything in her heart and soul, to Austin.

He bent his head and kissed her breast, pulling the sensitive flesh into his mouth. Sweet, hot arrows of pleasure shot through her, firing connections all over her body, pooling into throbbing need at the center of her being. Her hands played over his back, into his soft hair. "Austin," she murmured.

His mouth traveled down, down to her bikini bottom. His fingers toyed with the strings that held the fabric on her hips. "Just like a present, all tied up with bows," he murmured. He tugged at the string with his teeth, unfastening one side, then slowly trailing kisses across her lower belly to the string on the other side.

"Please," Frannie moaned.

"Not just yet."

His fingers moved lower and his kisses followed. Frannie lost all sense of place and time, all sense of anything but an aching, melting need.

"I want you," she whispered. "I want to touch you. I want…"

He slowly slid up her body, trailing kisses across her belly and breasts. He pulled away for a brief moment and shucked off his swim trunks, then returned to reclaim her lips.

He hovered enticingly above her. She reached out and closed her hand softly around the hard length of him, and was gratified to hear him moan. She arched against him, fitting herself against him. Austin gazed at her for a moment, his eyes dark and tender. "Frannie," he whispered, then buried himself inside her.

And then she was flying, racing through space and time, weightless and free, aware of nothing but the lusty, primal, urgent pleasure of loving Austin. She felt the love well up inside of her, felt it fill her to bursting, and when she finally shattered, she wasn't sure if the words spilled out of her lips or were just shouted in her heart. "I love you, love you, love you."

And it was true. With all her being, she loved him, as completely, as fully as any woman had ever loved any man.

She heard him gasp, felt him shudder, and held him close as he followed her into the star-strewn place they had created for each other.

She loved him. And if he couldn't love her back, well, she would just have to love him enough for both of them.

Austin was dreaming of Frannie, dreaming that he was following her alongside a mountain stream. The stream magically turned into a waterfall. Frannie stepped under the water and started taking off her clothes, beckoning for Austin to follow. He reached out for her, and...

Austin's hand reached out, but instead of touching Frannie, it fell on an empty mattress. Opening one eye, he saw that the pillow next to him was empty. A feeling of loss fell over him like a painter's drop cloth. He'd known the waterfall part had been a dream, but had the rest of it been unreal, as well?

He pushed up from the pillow and opened his other eye. The bathroom door was closed, and the sound of running water was faintly audible through the wall. The shower. Frannie was in his shower. He leaned back against his pillow, an immense sense of relief pouring over him.

It was strange—he normally couldn't get women out of his room fast enough the morning after, but with Frannie, he'd felt panicked at the thought she'd left without saying good-bye.

The shower shut off. A minute later, the door opened, to reveal Frannie in her jeans and one of his SeaBreeze Detergent T-shirts.

She gave him a shy smile. "Good morning."

"Mornin'."

She crossed the room and stood by the bed. "I hope you don't mind my borrowing your shirt. Mine was still wet."

Austin grinned. "Well, I sure as heck do mind."

Her eyes widened. "You do?"

"Yeah. I think you should take it off immediately."

Frannie gave him a playful push. He grabbed her and hauled her back onto the bed.

"You're insatiable." She laughed.

"Me? Who kept me up till all hours in the kitchen?"

"You promised me dinner. I was hungry."

"Yeah, well, so was I. And our steaks were just about

cooked to perfection when you lured me away from cooking duties.''

''You didn't seem to mind at the time.''

''Oh, I didn't mind.'' Not at all. He smiled at the memory of making love to her in the kitchen while she'd been perched on the countertop. ''But our steaks burned to a crisp, and I had to start all over with fresh ones.''

''Well, maybe I'm responsible for the kitchen episode. But who woke who up in the middle of the night?'' She arched an eyebrow. ''Not once, but twice?'' She wagged two fingers at him.

He was incapable of even pretending remorse. His grin widening, he pulled her down and gave her a thorough kiss.

She reluctantly pulled away. ''I need to go.'' She rolled off the bed and ran a hand through her hair. ''I want to get home before Aunt Celeste and Jasmine so I won't have to make any awkward explanations.''

Austin nodded. He understood, but the prospect of her leaving made him feel as empty and deflated as a punctured hot-air balloon.

She picked up her purse and slung it over her shoulder. At some point in the night, all of her belongings had ended up in his bedroom. ''What time do you leave for New York?''

''I have to be at the airport in Bozeman at three.''

''How long will you be gone?''

''Three weeks, if we qualify for all the races. Then I'll have a week off before the final race in Denver. I hope to spend at least part of that here.''

Frannie adjusted the strap of her purse. ''I'll miss you.''

Ah, hell, he didn't want things to get all heavy and serious. That wasn't his style. He swallowed hard. ''Look— I'm, uh, not very good about calling. I mean, I don't like to have any distractions while I'm focused on a race, and, well..." He let his words trail off. Damn, this was awkward. He felt like a heel. He cleared his throat. "I'll call you when I get back to Whitehorn, okay?"

"Okay." Her mouth smiled, but her eyes looked hurt. "I understand."

He was afraid she did. A funny ache settled in his chest as she looked away.

She pulled her car keys out of a side compartment on her purse. "Well, I'd better be going."

"I'll walk you out." Austin flung back the covers.

To his surprise, Frannie blushed at the sight of his naked body. After all they'd shared, she still blushed. He grabbed a towel and wound it around him, feeling oddly touched and more than a little guilty. Why did everything about her this morning have to remind him that she wasn't the type of woman who made love lightly?

He walked her through the main house. She stopped at the front door and gave him a quick kiss. It would have been no more than a peck if he hadn't grabbed her shoulders and deepened the kiss. He immediately regretted it, because he felt an undeniable surge of fresh desire.

She did, too. He could see it in her eyes, see it in the way she backed away and smoothed her hair. When she spoke, her voice was breathless. "Well, thanks for everything."

"The pleasure was all mine."

She opened the door and gave him a Mona Lisa-type smile over her shoulder. "No, it wasn't. Not entirely."

A slight drizzle was falling. He watched her walk to her car, her keys in her hand. She opened the driver's side door, then paused. "Good luck at the races."

"Thanks." He tightened the towel around his waist and watched her duck down to enter her car. "Hey!" he called.

She turned and straightened. "The roads are wet, so they'll be slick. Drive safely."

She looked directly at him, and her gaze hit him like something tangible, something with weight and warmth and depth, something that socked him right in the chest. "You, too."

And then she was in her car, driving away, and he was more alone than he'd been in years.

Drive safely. Hell's bells—he didn't want to drive safely. He wanted to drive as though he had nothing to lose. Furthermore, he didn't want to give a damn about how safely somebody else drove, either. What the hell was the matter with him?

He slammed the door harder than necessary and strode into the living room. Through the floor-to-ceiling windows, he saw a cream-colored towel sitting on the chaise longue, a taunting reminder of how he and Frannie had begun their lovemaking the night before.

Mumbling an oath, he turned away and stalked into the kitchen, only to face the dirty dishes left over from their midnight feast.

He heaved an exasperated sigh. Maybe he should just go back to bed and get some more shut-eye. He started toward the bedroom, then stopped. Hell. If the kitchen made him think of Frannie, the bedroom was bound to be ten times worse. Dad-blast it, even the thought of taking a shower brought Frannie to mind.

He fell heavily on his leather sofa. What the devil was the matter with him? He didn't feel at all like himself. He'd been with women before, lots of women, and none of them had ever left him feeling this way—mooney-eyed and sad and forlorn, missing her like crazy when her scent still hovered in the air.

Well, it was a darn good thing he was leaving town this

afternoon, he thought. Time and distance were just the ticket to cool things down. The sooner he put some miles between himself and Little Miss Hap, the better off he'd be. He'd take a shower in another bathroom, throw his things together, then get the hell out of Dodge. He'd leave the kitchen mess and rumpled bed for his housekeeper to deal with.

There was no room in his life for sentimental soggy-headedness, he told himself, rising to his feet. No room at all.

Across town, Lyle Brooks stood as a tall, silver-haired man strode toward his table in the dining room of the Whitehorn Country Club. At seventy-two, Garrett Kincaid still cut an intimidating figure. Lyle swallowed down his nervousness and pasted on what he hoped was a warm smile. "Grandfather. So glad you could make it."

"It's good to see you." The athletically built older man seated himself at the table. "You could come out to the ranch once in a while, you know."

Lyle lowered himself back into his chair, trying not to let his grandfather's chastisement rattle him. "I'm afraid I've been very busy lately, what with the construction project up in the air."

Garrett's blue eyes cut across the table like the blade of a hunting knife. "What do you mean, up in the air?"

Lyle shrugged. "The Indians are all upset about the two deaths at the construction site. Seems they've gotten it in their heads that the location is cursed." Lyle took a sip of water, trying to play it cool. "There was even an article about it in today's paper." Lyle had planted the story himself by making an anonymous call to the business reporter.

"I haven't seen the paper yet." Garrett spread his napkin

in his lap and took a menu from the white-jacketed waiter who'd silently materialized at their table.

Lyle accepted a menu, as well. He paused until the waiter had filled both of their cups with coffee and moved away. "Well, it has to with the fact that the land is the burial ground of ancient Cheyenne warriors. The Indians think their spirits will return to bring death and destruction to anyone who disturbs their graves."

"You don't say." Garrett took a long slurp of steaming coffee, his face inscrutable. Lyle nervously took a sip of coffee, too. Damn, but the old man gave him a case of the jitters! Sometimes it felt as if the old goat could see right through him and somehow read his mind.

Lyle leaned forward, trying hard to look earnest. "Some of the Indians are really up in arms. They think the land is sacred. It could bring all sorts of problems for us if the tribe decides to stop the project."

"Are they threatening to?"

"Well, not yet. But you know how these things spread like forest fires, especially if any more accidents happen. That's why I want to bring up another option for your consideration."

Garrett squinted at him. "And just what might that be?"

Lyle carefully added a packet of sugar to his coffee. "Well, we're not too far into this project yet. It's not too late to move the site to another location."

Garrett's jaw twitched. "And would that location happen to be on your land?"

Lyle squirmed. Damn, but the old man was shrewd. "Not exactly. Under my proposal, the land would no longer be mine. It would be Gabriel's."

Garrett's gaze fastened on his face like a bear trap. "What are you sayin', boy? You're going to give your land to Gabriel?"

"Well, no, not exactly." Lyle picked up another packet of sugar, wanting an excuse not to look his grandfather in the eye. "It wouldn't be an outright gift. I would simply swap my land for his."

The old man's eyes turned cold. "We've already covered this ground, and I've told you no. I'm not trading your land for Gabriel's."

"But this curse business puts everything in a whole new light! If the resort is moved, then the northern land becomes the more valuable property."

"And you'd want Gabriel to have the more valuable property out of the goodness of your heart?" Garrett snorted. "Pardon my skepticism, son, but I wasn't born yesterday. What's in it for you?"

Damn. Lyle inwardly squirmed. "A guarantee that the project won't be held up indefinitely by some legal injunction."

The hard set to Garrett's mouth softened, but he still looked less than convinced. Lyle decided to try to appeal to the old man's emotional side. "There's another reason, too. A couple of them, actually."

"I figured there was." The old man drummed his fingers on the table. "Well, let's have it."

"Well, I've, uh, gotten real interested in Indian history lately. And the fact is, I hate to disturb the burial grounds myself."

"Is that a fact." Garrett looked as if he'd have an easier time believing the table in front of him would sprout wings and fly. "What's the other reason?"

Lyle swallowed nervously. "This is kind of embarrassing to admit because it's not very business-like, and I pride myself on being business-like, but, well, I spotted a bear and a couple of cubs. I hate to destroy their home."

"That's funny." Garrett's voice was curt. "I don't recall

you bein' much of a nature lover. In fact, I don't recall you havin' much use for the wildlife at all.''

"Well, I don't let most people see my softer side." Lyle reached for yet another sugar packet, trying hard to appear confident and chipper. "So, what do you say? If I can convince the Indians to move the resort to the land up north, will you let me swap that land for Gabriel's?''

"No.''

The old man was impossible. A burst of rage shot through Lyle. He tried to tamp it down. "It would be in the child's best interests. How can you possibly object?''

"Because you're up to something." Garrett stared at him hard over the rim of his coffee cup. "But I'll be damned if I know what it is.''

Lyle sat back and did his best to look wounded. "Granddad, how can you think that? I'm your own flesh and blood. It hurts me that you distrust me.''

"Yeah, well, it hurts me that you'd try to pull the wool over my eyes.''

"I don't know what you're talking about.''

"Don't you?'' Garrett slammed down his coffee cup, making the saucer rattle. Coffee sloshed over the sides as he leaned forward over the table. "That land's no burial ground. If you were half as interested in Cheyenne history as you say you are, you'd know they used to place their dead up on tall stilts, not bury them in the ground.''

Oh, hell. Why hadn't he checked his facts? He should have known the old goat would know all about the customs of the Cheyenne. Lyle's hands knotted into sweaty fists under the table. "Well, maybe a lot of them were put on stilts on that land. Or..." Lyle thought fast. "...Or perhaps they died in battle there. I don't know all the details. All I know is the Indians are saying the land is cursed.''

Garrett stared at him across the table, his eyes as cold as

the eyes of a trout. "I've got good friends among the Cheyenne. My own grandmother was Cheyenne, and I've never heard that tale before now." Garrett plopped his napkin onto the table. "I don't know why you want that land, boy, but I've designated it for Gabriel, and that's not going to change. Cursed or not cursed, that land is his." Garrett scooted back his chair and rose.

"Granddad, wait a minute." Lyle stood and reached out his arm, wanting to restrain the old man. "Where are you going? We haven't even ordered."

Garrett shrugged off Lyle's hand. "I seem to have lost my appetite. I'll talk to you later."

The old man stalked out, leaving Lyle to stare after him. Lyle slowly sank back into his chair, his spirits sinking with him.

Hell. He'd been sure the curse approach would work. Instead of convincing his grandfather to give him the deed to the land he wanted, he'd only managed to make him suspicious.

The waiter stopped at Lyle's table and gave a solicitous smile. "Are you ready to place your order, sir?"

"Yeah. Bring me a bloody Mary. Make it a double. Hell, bring me two doubles."

"Yes, sir."

He watched the waiter scurry away, his dejection hardening into anger. He'd have to come up with another plan. He wanted that land, and by damn, whatever he wanted, he got. He could do anything he set his mind to. Hell, he'd already gotten away with murder.

And it had been surprisingly easy, Lyle thought, drumming his fingers on the table with satisfaction. Peter Cook had met him at the construction site that night, just as Lyle had asked him to. The heavy equipment operator had been excited at the prospect of getting his hands on some money.

When Lyle had asked him to point out exactly where in the pit he'd found the sapphire, he'd been more than eager to comply. The unsuspecting construction worker had crept close to the ledge and bent to point out the location. By the time he realized Lyle was about to shove him in, it was too late. He'd put up a fight, but Lyle had been on solid footing, and Peter had been too close to the edge. After a brief struggle, the sucker had lost his balance and fallen to his death.

Lyle had no intention of giving up his quest for the land now. No, sirree. His grandfather wasn't buying his story about the curse, and Jackson Hawk hadn't believed it, either, but that didn't mean they couldn't be persuaded to change their minds. It might take another accident to do it, but it could be done.

Somehow, some way, Lyle Brooks always made sure he got what he wanted.

Fourteen

"Frannie, come quick!" Celeste's voice called from the hallway. "The sports news is coming on, and they're about to interview Austin."

Just the mention of Austin's name was enough to make Frannie's heart pound. Lately it seemed as if everything elicited an emotional response from her—the ringing of a phone, the delivery of the mail, the opening of a door. He'd been gone for two and a half weeks, but instead of becoming accustomed to his absence, she felt it more deeply with every passing day.

He'd told her he wouldn't contact her until he came back to town, she reminded herself. It made no sense that she should feel so awful about not hearing from him when he was only keeping his word.

He'd said he didn't want to be distracted from concentrating on each race, but she knew it was something more. He was deliberately keeping his distance. He didn't want to be attached to anyone or anything.

"Hurry, Frannie! They're almost back from the commercials!"

Putting down her book, Frannie rose from her bed and padded barefoot into Aunt Celeste's room to watch the end of the ten o'clock evening news.

"Austin Parker was today's top finisher at the qualifying race for the Daytona 500 in the Winston Cup series," the dark-haired newscaster said. "We have a reporter at the track who talked with Austin after the race."

Frannie sank onto Aunt Celeste's bed, her hand over her stomach, as Austin's face filled the screen. The reporter thrust a microphone toward him. "Austin, you've been on a roll here lately—a win last week in Atlanta, and now finishing first here in the qualifier. To what do you attribute your winning streak?"

Frannie's heart jumped in her chest as the camera zoomed in on Austin. "I have the best crew in the business. All the credit belongs to them."

"Well, your driving is certainly a major component," the reporter said.

"I just try to do my best."

"Austin, we were all touched to read about how you and your girlfriend saved a baby and her mother from drowning in a cold Montana pond this summer."

"Did you hear that?" Aunt Celeste said, squeezing Frannie's hand. "He called you his girlfriend!"

Would that it were so, Frannie thought. She watched Austin tuck his helmet under one hand and run a hand through his hair. "We, uh, just happened to be at the right place at the right time."

"Well, I understand our network is airing the story about that rescue on next week's 'Celebrity Spotlight' show." The reporter grinned. "What does your girlfriend have to say about your performance at the tracks lately?"

"I, uh, haven't had a chance to talk to anyone except you and my crew since finishing here today."

"Well, I'm sure she'll be proud. Have you got a strategy for the race on Sunday?"

"Just to make sure that the car's in top shape and to drive my best. There are a lot of excellent drivers here. It's a tough race, but I'm looking forward to it."

"We are, too. Best of luck to you, Austin. Steve, back to you."

Celeste hit the remote control, turning the TV set off, then turned to Frannie, her eyes glowing. "They talked about you nearly as much as they talked about Austin."

Frannie traced a rose in Celeste's floral comforter with the tip of her finger, trying to blink back the tears that threatened her eyes. "I noticed he managed to change the subject every time that interviewer brought it up."

Celeste's hand landed on Frannie's shoulder. Frannie could feel her aunt's eyes on her. "Honey, are you all right?"

Frannie nodded. "Sure. Why wouldn't I be?"

"There's just something about you..." Celeste regarded her silently for a moment. Her voice grew soft and low. "Frannie, are you pregnant?"

Frannie looked up, startled. Her eyes filled with tears. "How did you know?"

"Oh, Frannie." Celeste reached out and hugged her.

"How did you know?" Frannie asked again.

Celeste slowly released her. "Your hand. You put it on your stomach just the way Blanche always did. I remember doing that myself with Cleo and Jasmine." Celeste patted Frannie's hand. "Oh, Frannie, is it Austin's?"

She nodded. The tears she'd held back so long came pouring out, along with a rush of words. "I just found out this morning. I did a home test, and it was positive, so I called my doctor. She worked me in on my lunch hour, and when she checked me, she confirmed it. It's very early— I'm just a few days late. But I'm definitely pregnant."

"Well, honey," Celeste crooned, stroking her hair, "don't cry. This will all work out. A baby—why, that's wonderful."

"I'm not sure Austin will feel that way." Celeste reached

over and pulled a tissue out of a box on her nightstand.
Frannie blew her nose into it. "He hasn't even called."

"When he left, you said you didn't expect him to," Celeste reminded Frannie.

"I know. But on some level, I—I kept hoping." Frannie twisted the tissue until it looked like a paper tornado. "I wanted to believe he feels about me the way I feel about him."

"You love him."

Frannie nodded miserably. "And he doesn't want to love anyone. He told me so."

"What a person wants to feel isn't always what he ends up feeling," Celeste said matter-of-factly. "Besides, love has a way of changing the things people think they want."

Frannie sighed. "If he cared about me half as much as I care about him, I would have heard from him by now."

Celeste patted her hand. "Men have odd ways of dealing with their emotions. For some reason, most men don't want to show them. Not at first, anyway."

That was true. Frannie knew from her cousins's experience how easily that could be the case.

"When will Austin be back in Whitehorn?" Celeste asked.

"The race is Sunday. I guess he'll be back Monday or Tuesday."

"All right. You'll see him then, and you'll talk. This will all work out. I know it may not feel that way now, but it will. Just wait and see."

Frannie took a deep breath. "Waiting seems like the hardest part."

Celeste smiled, her eyes full of empathy. "It always does, honey. It always does."

The phone rang Sunday evening as Frannie was loading the dishwasher after dinner. She picked up the kitchen phone, her other hand holding a dirty plate. "Hello?"

"Frannie?" said a deep, familiar voice.

The plate nearly slipped from her fingers. Frannie grabbed it, her heart pounding hard. "Austin! Are you already back in town?"

"Not yet. But I should be there late tomorrow."

"Congratulations on the race."

"You heard, huh?"

"I watched it on TV."

She could almost hear the smile in his voice. "Don't tell me you're turning into a NASCAR fan."

"Well, I'm a fan of one particular driver." She swallowed around a lump in her throat. "You were great."

"Thanks."

Silence beat between them. Frannie felt a current of electricity racing through the phone line.

"I was calling to see if you'd have dinner with me Tuesday night."

"Gee, I'll have to check my social calendar to see if I'm scheduled to dine with any other race car drivers that evening. If not, well, I suppose I could find time."

"Good."

I've missed you, Frannie thought, willing him to say the words. *I love you.* "How long will you be in Whitehorn?" she finally asked.

"Just a couple of days. And I'm afraid it's going to be crazy while I'm there. Five members of my crew are coming out to rework the suspension on the cars, my main sponsor wants to see the ranch and I'm being trailed by a bunch of sports media."

She shifted the phone to her other ear. "Where's your next race?"

"In Denver. I leave Thursday morning for the qualifying race on Friday."

He'd be here for just two days—and he'd be surrounded by a throng of people the whole time. Somehow, in the midst of all that, she'd have to find a way to talk to him.

"Well, I'll look forward to Tuesday."

"Me, too." In the background, she could hear laughter and loud voices. She heard Austin's muffled voice call, "Keep it down a second, guys!" She could picture him pulling his hand from the mouthpiece and turning back to the phone. "Listen, I've got three separate schmoozing events I have to go to tonight, so I'd better get going. See you Tuesday evening. I'll pick you up around six-thirty, okay?"

"Okay."

"Oh, and Frannie, that show about our rescue airs Wednesday. I thought you'd want to know."

Frannie was fully aware of the air date. Mr. Billings, all her co-workers and half the population of Whitehorn had mentioned it to her, telling her they couldn't wait to see it.

"I'll try to watch."

"Me, too."

Frannie hung up the phone, her emotions jumbled and raw. He'd called before he'd come home—that was something. In the back of her mind, she'd secretly harbored the notion that if he called before he said he would, it meant she'd broken through his wall, that he cared for her more than he wanted to.

On the other hand, the call left her feeling more disconnected from him than ever. This was a man who drove race cars at two hundred miles per hour, who had thousands of devoted fans, who regularly got doused with champagne on national TV. He inhabited a world of fame and excitement and endless parties about as far removed from her own quiet life as she could imagine. Could a man with such a thrilling exciting life ever find happiness with an ordinary, everyday kind of woman such as her? Could two people so dissimilar ever build a life together?

She didn't know about building a life, but they'd already created one. Frannie placed a protective hand on her stomach and prayed that she'd find the right time to tell him in the right way.

Jasmine peered out the front parlor window Tuesday evening as a car pulled into the long drive. "He's here, Frannie! He's here!"

Frannie smoothed her new black dress, wishing she knew how to smooth her nerves, as well.

"You look wonderful," Jasmine told her.

"Thanks." She'd pulled out every trick in the book to look her best, but she still didn't feel equal to the task in front of her. How was she supposed to tell a man who didn't want any emotional involvement that he was about to become a father?

"I can't wait to see how he greets you. I bet he's going to kiss you the moment he sees you."

Frannie shot her cousin a meaningful glance. "Don't you have something to do in another room?"

Jasmine grinned. "No, not really."

Celeste stepped into the hallway and firmly took her daughter's arm. "Come on, Jasmine. Let's give Frannie a little space."

Frannie cast a grateful smile at her aunt as she ushered Jasmine out of the room. She was nervous enough about seeing Austin without having an audience.

The doorbell rang. Frannie silently counted to three before crossing the foyer to open the door, not wanting to look too eager.

The impact of seeing Austin face-to-face nearly took her breath away. He was taller and more handsome than she remembered. Her voice came out low and breathy. "Hi."

"Hi, yourself." Grinning widely, her pulled her into his arms and gave her a hard kiss. He held her at arm's length and let his gaze run over her. "Wow. You look terrific." He kissed her again, and this time it was a slow, lingering kiss that made her blood tingle. "Taste good, too."

A shiver coursed up her spine. In all of her thoughts about seeing him, she'd underestimated the power of the physical attraction she felt for him. "I've missed you," she whispered.

"Me, too." Sexual energy surged between them. They stood there, just looking at each other. "You make me want to skip dinner and head right for dessert."

Frannie's heart pounded.

He grinned ruefully. "I wanted to take you to my house for a nice quiet dinner, but my place is crawling with people."

"This place is, too."

"Well, then, I guess we'll just have to go to a restaurant. Maybe we can form a plan for dessert over dinner."

He walked her to his truck, and the drive to the restaurant passed in a flurry of conversation. From watching the races on television, Frannie was filled with questions. She asked about restrictor plates, fabricators, and drivetrains. She asked about the problems he'd had with a tire in the qualifying race at Atlanta, and about the two-way communication system between him and Tommy at Daytona.

"You've really been following the races, haven't you?" Austin said.

Frannie nodded.

He smiled in a way that made her think it pleased him.

Her spirits soared. Maybe, just maybe, he cared more than a little.

Before she knew it, he'd pulled the truck into the parking lot of the Lakeside Inn. "I didn't know where to take you, but I have great memories of this place."

"So do I."

They walked to the door and were promptly escorted to a lakeside table. "It feels great to have a night off," Austin said. "The last few weeks have really been hectic."

"It's good to have you back." Maybe I should just go ahead and tell him, Frannie thought. Get it out in the open, and get it over with.

Austin leaned his elbows on the table. "You know, as great as racing is, sometimes it just feels like an endless series of decisions. Should we put more air in the tires? Tighten or loosen the steering? It feels really good to be with someone who's not going to expect me to make a major decision in the next few minutes."

Uh-oh. Now was evidently not the time. After dinner—after they'd had a chance to reconnect—she'd find a way to tell him about the baby.

He reached out and covered her hand with his. "I missed you."

Frannie swallowed. "I missed you, too." She looked away. "I kept hoping you'd call."

"I started to. I actually picked up the phone a few times, and then I put it down."

"Why?"

Austin lifted his shoulders. "I didn't know what to say."

"Hello would have been a nice start."

"I wasn't sure what to say after that."

A flash suddenly went off in Frannie's eyes, momentarily blinding her. She blinked, startled, and as her vision cleared, she saw a tall, wiry man with a large, professional-looking camera standing beside the table. A shorter, heavier man stood beside him, holding a small tape recorder and a flash attachment connected to the camera.

"Hey, Austin, can you give us a smile?" the photographer asked.

Austin scowled. "We're out for a private evening here. Do you mind?"

"Ah, come on. I've got to make a living."

Austin raised his hand and signaled the waiter. "Could you get the manager, please?"

"Hey, Frannie, how 'bout a smile?" the photographer wheedled.

"How does he know my name?" Frannie asked Austin.

The photographer answered before Austin got a chance. "Saw your picture in the paper, sweetheart. And after that episode about your rescue airs on TV this week, you'll be even more famous." He clicked another picture. "The readers of the *National Reporter* will want to know all about you." He clicked another photo.

The reporter held the tape recorder close to Austin. "Are things getting serious between you two?"

"Frannie and I are just friends," Austin said flatly.

"Any chance of wedding bells?"

Austin looked around, obviously searching for the manager.

"Any chance at all?"

Austin tried to ignore him, but Frannie saw a muscle flex in his jaw.

"You've been quoted as saying you're not the marrying kind. Is that an accurate statement?"

Austin hissed out an impatient breath. "Look, I have nothing further to say."

"So your statement stands?"

"I have nothing new to say."

The reporter turned to Frannie. "What do you think of that, sweetheart? Must be pretty disappointing to hear Think you can get this confirmed bachelor to change his mind?"

Frannie looked down at the tablecloth, trying to follow Austin's lead, trying to ignore the man.

"I'll bet you want to be more than just his friend, huh?" the reporter persisted.

To her horror, Frannie's eyes filled with tears. The photographer snapped another picture, blinding her. And then another. And another.

"Hey!" Austin's mouth grew tight and his eyes spat fire. He was halfway out of his chair when a man in a dark suit strode up and bent to talk to him.

After a brief exchange, the man turned to the reporter and the photographer. "Excuse me. I'm the manager here, and I'm going to have to ask you to leave."

The photographer fired off one last shot of Frannie, then waved his hand in a little salute. The reporter gave a smug smile. "Well, I think we've gotten all we need. Nice meeting you, Frannie."

The two men left the restaurant, escorted by the manager. Frannie was mortified to realize a tear was still drizzling down her cheek. She quickly rubbed it away with the back of her hand.

Austin regarded her, his eyes worried. "Hey, are you all right?"

"I'm fine."

"I'm really sorry about that. I know how much you hate being in the spotlight."

Frannie nodded, grateful to have an excuse. Anything would be better than explaining she was heartbroken at the quick way he'd described their relationship as "just friends."

She'd claimed the same thing, she thought ruefully—up until they'd made love. It had been her way of mitigating her emotions, of trying to avoid the fact that Austin had stolen her heart. But she'd been deluding herself, denying what her heart had secretly known all along.

Austin, on the other hand, was simply stating the truth. Friendship was casual. It made no demands, it wasn't exclusive, it didn't require commitment. If it ceased to be mutually beneficial, friends could drift away and fall out of touch.

Friendship was all he wanted, she thought forlornly. She was a friend—someone he liked, someone he was even romantically involved with, but nevertheless, just a friend. A friend didn't hold your heart in the palm of his hand. A friend didn't promise to share a lifetime, to be there through good times and bad, to create children and raise them together. A friend was just…friendly. Like a dog.

Frannie blinked back a fresh onslaught of tears. She'd known Austin wasn't interested in a serious relationship. So why did it hurt so much to hear him say it out loud?

Somehow, in the time he'd been gone, she'd started believing in dreams and fairy tales. Somehow she'd fooled herself into imagining that once she told Austin she was pregnant, he'd do a complete one-eighty. In her mind's eye, she'd pictured him being happy and excited, eager to take on marriage and an instant family.

How had she deluded herself so thoroughly? She was usually so logical and practical. It must be the hormones. Pregnant women were notoriously emotional and sentimental. Austin had said he didn't want commitment, and it didn't come in any bigger packages than with a wife and child. What had she been thinking?

The manager returned to the table, his mouth creased in an apologetic smile. "I'm very sorry, Mr. Parker. I've given instructions to the staff not to allow any more photographers in. And I'm sending a bottle of wine to your table with my compliments.''

''Thanks. I appreciate it.''

Frannie struggled to pull herself together. ''Does that happen a lot?'' she asked when the manager left.

Austin grinned ruefully. ''It's starting to, now that I've won a few races. And our little tag-team rescue at the lake really sped things along publicity-wise. My sponsors are thrilled. I'm sorry I had to drag you into it, though.''

Frannie managed a weak smile. She was grateful when the waiter arrived with the wine, and took their orders.

''So what's been going on in Whitehorn while I've been gone?''

Frannie played with her napkin, trying to compose herself. ''Nothing nearly as exciting as the things in your life.''

''Oh, I don't know about that. I read about the controversy concerning the casino site in some of the Atlanta newspapers.''

Frannie nodded, grateful for the neutral topic. ''That's been front-page news around here. I don't think the Cheyenne really want to move the site, though. Jackson Hawk was quoted in yesterday's paper as saying that everything is going to go ahead as planned.''

''What's new with you?''

Frannie's heart thudded hard against her ribs. She stared at the tablecloth. She couldn't tell him. Not now. ''Nothing much,'' she managed.

''Have you mailed off those manuscripts of your children's books?''

Frannie looked up. ''As a matter of fact, I did.''

''Good for you!'' A soft, high-pitched ring sounded. Austin frowned apologetically and pulled a phone out of his jacket pocket. "Excuse me." He opened the cell phone, punched a button and spoke into the receiver. "Yes?"

Frannie watched his mouth tighten as he listened. His eyes grew dark and troubled.

"Is anyone hurt?"

Frannie's stomach clenched. Something had happened—something bad.

"Is there much damage?" Austin asked curtly.

His forehead eased a bit. "All right. Get on the phone and see of you can locate another dyno. Then give Buddy a call and get him out here by tomorrow morning. I'll be there as soon as possible."

Austin gave a heavy sigh as he clicked off the phone and folded it.

"What happened?" Frannie asked.

"An engine blew while Tommy was testing it on the dyno. No one was hurt, thank God. And the cars and engines are all okay. But I really need another engine to take to Denver, so that means we're going to be working around the clock to build one by tomorrow night."

"Dyno? What's a dyno?"

"It's a machine that records engine performance. It tells us where in the powerband the engine is making its power." Austin looked at her ruefully. "I hate to run out on you, but I'm afraid I need to go. The shop is in shambles, and they need me there."

Frannie forced a smile she didn't feel. "Go ahead. I'll call Jasmine to give me a ride home."

"No. I brought you. I'll take you home."

"You'd lose forty-five minutes running me to the Big Sky, then turning around and going back to your ranch."

"But I don't want to abandon you here."

"I'll be fine." She leaned forward and placed her palm on his hand. "Go on and take care of things at your shop."

"Are you sure?"

"I'm sure."

He rose from the chair, circled around and kissed her soundly on the lips. "I'm really sorry about this."

"It's not your fault. Stuff happens."

"Thanks for being so understanding." He gave her another quick kiss, then strode for the door, stopping to talk to the manager on the way.

Understanding. Her eyes filled with tears again as she gazed out at the lake. Oh, she was understanding, all right. She understood that Austin didn't have the time or the inclination for a relationship. She understood that she was just a diversion in his very busy, very full life. She understood that he might like her and even care for her, but he wasn't looking for marriage or parenthood. He was looking for an escape from pressure and problems, not a whole new set of them.

But she also understood that he was a good-hearted man, the kind who would want to do the right thing. If she told him she was carrying his child, he would no doubt ask her to marry him out of a sense of duty.

Did she really want a husband who'd married her as an obligation? Did she really want a loveless marriage—one that left Austin feeling trapped, one that was sure to breed resentment, one that sooner or later would almost certainly end in divorce?

Wouldn't everyone be better off—her, Austin and their child—if she dealt with the situation by herself from the very beginning?

Her heart knew the answer, but it hurt, letting go of her dreams and hopes. It hurt, accepting the truth.

And the truth was that Austin's abandonment issues ran too deep. He didn't want to get close, didn't want to commit. Even if he married her, he'd never let her close enough to truly share his life, to truly know his heart. And Frannie was certain that a loveless marriage would leave her feeling more lonely than she'd ever feel on her own.

No. Marriage was out of the question. She would make a life for herself and the child without him. And it would be easier on everyone involved if she made it somewhere besides Whitehorn.

Austin pushed through the door of the Hip Hop Café early the following afternoon, scanning the room for Frannie. He'd stopped at the bank looking for her, and the receptionist had told him she'd come here to have lunch with Summer.

He spotted Frannie in a corner booth, and a feeling of delight welled up in his chest. She was wearing a sky-blue dress that reminded him of the day they'd spent together at his ranch. Good grief, but he was crazy about her! Just seeing her across the room made his heart seem to swell.

He'd been wanting to tell her as much, but he'd wanted to do it in an appropriate way. That was why every time he'd picked up the phone to call her over the past few weeks, he'd abruptly put it down without dialing her number. He was afraid he'd just blurt out "I love you" the moment she answered the phone, and he didn't want to tell her that way.

He'd never felt this way about anyone. The need to tell her he loved her was burning a hole inside of him, but he wanted to do it in a romantic setting, when the two of them were alone. He guessed he'd have to wait until he returned to Whitehorn.

But he couldn't wait that long to see her again. That was why he'd tracked her here.

He strode up to the booth, and both women turned toward

him. From the grim looks on their faces, they were in the middle of a serious discussion.

He looked from Frannie to Summer, then back again. "Hi. Is everything okay?"

Frannie's face went pale at the sight of him. Her cousin blanched, too, but she quickly recovered, pasting an unnaturally bright smile on her face. "Why, Austin! Good to see you again." She scooted out of the booth. "Here, take my seat. I was just about to leave and go back to work." She patted Frannie's hand, gave her a long look, then quickly headed to the register, the bill in her hand.

Austin slid across from Frannie into the booth and looked at her questioningly. "You two looked like you were having a serious discussion. I hope I didn't interrupt something important."

"Oh. N-no. We were just finishing up. I have to get back to the bank in a minute."

"Well, I didn't want to leave town without seeing you again. I'm awfully sorry about last night. I hated running out and leaving you like that."

"Is everything under control?"

"More or less. A swarm of contractors is buzzing around repairing the shop. When that engine blew, it took out half a wall that held a lot of our spare parts. My engine specialist is nearly finished building a new engine for an intermediate track, and Tommy is beating the bushes getting all the extra parts that we need. But it looks like it'll all come together in time to make it to Denver."

"Good."

Austin reached out and covered Frannie's hand with his. "I'm sorry I couldn't spend more time with you this week. After this race is over, I'll be back for three weeks in a row, and then…"

Frannie's chin tilted up slightly. She pulled back her hand

and swept a strand of hair behind her ear. "I, uh, won't be here."

Austin's heart seemed to stop. "What do you mean?"

"I won't be here. I'm moving to Billings."

"But, Frannie—what for? Where did this come from?"

"The bank has a satellite office there, and they've been after me to transfer for some time. I finally decided to do it."

"But, Frannie..." Austin ran a hand through his hair, completely bewildered. "When did this come up?"

"I made the decision to accept the offer this morning. It will be a big step up. I'll be in line for a vice presidency."

Austin stared at her, dumbfounded. "I thought you were more interested in staying near your family and writing children's books than climbing some corporate ladder."

Frannie shrugged. "Circumstances change. It seemed like too good of an opportunity to pass up."

It struck Austin as mighty odd, but if it was what she wanted, he'd support Frannie's decision. More than anything, he wanted Frannie to be happy. "Well, then, I'll come to Billings and see you there."

Frannie looked down at the green-flecked Formica-topped table. "I don't think that would be a good idea."

"What do you mean?" Austin leaned forward. She was acting distant, not at all like herself. He tightened his clutch on her hand. "Frannie, what's going on?"

Frannie sucked in a deep breath. "I don't think we should see each other anymore."

Austin's stomach knotted hard. "Why the hell not?"

She looked up at him. Her eyes were filled with pain. "I'm not cut out for this. I don't want a part-time, long-distance relationship. I can't make love with my body and keep my heart out of it. I'm an all-the-way, in-over-my-head, till-death-do-us-part kind of woman. I'm not what you need.''

"Frannie—"

She put up her hand. "Your life is too different from mine, and I can't handle it. I never should have gotten involved with you in the first place."

Hurt. It burned through him, hot and fierce, cutting into his chest. This was what happened when you let someone get close. His father had been right. "So you're blowing me off? Is that what's happening here?"

"Don't put this all on me." She looked up at him. "You're the one who left for two and half weeks and didn't call or drop a note or send an e-mail."

She had no idea how many times he'd nearly done just that. "Now, look here, Frannie," he began.

But she was in no mood to listen. She shook her head. "Don't give me excuses or tell me what you think I want to hear. I prefer being straightforward about this. We never should have gotten involved in the first place. It'll never work. And I don't want to pretend that it will." She gathered up her purse and slung it over her shoulder.

"Can't we talk about this?"

"There's nothing to talk about, Austin. We want different things out of life. You want to risk your life on a racetrack every week, and I want a man who'll be around to raise children and grow old with me."

Her words hit him like a sledgehammer, the weight of their meaning pounding his heart. She was right. He wasn't very good marriage material, and a woman such as Frannie was cut out for having a family.

She gazed at him pleadingly. "If you care for me at all, even a little bit, you'll leave me alone. Please don't make this any harder than it already is."

He watched her slip out of the booth and hurry away, taking his heart with her.

He banged his fist on his thigh, hard enough to leave a bruise, but he hardly felt it. The pain in his chest was too all-consuming, too hot, too fierce.

Damn. The last thing he'd ever intended to do was to hurt Frannie, and it looked as if he had. And the way she'd left things, if he tried to make amends, he'd only hurt her more.

Damn, damn and double damn! He'd never felt about a woman the way he felt about Frannie, and she hadn't even given him a chance to tell her.

Not that telling her would make any difference. She wanted a home and marriage. And he wanted…

Hell. Just what the heck *did* he want? He no longer knew. He used to think he just wanted to win races. But now he was winning, and he'd never been more miserable in his life.

He propped his elbows on the table and sank his face in his hands. It wasn't fair. He was at the top of his career. By all rights, he should be on top of the world. If he did well at the race in Denver, he would win the Winston Cup. It was the granddaddy of all wins, the dream of every race car driver out there. He should be thrilled and excited, chomping at the bit for that checkered flag to drop. So why did the prospect of heading to Denver leave him as flat as a can of cola that had sat open overnight?

Because all he wanted was Frannie, and all she wanted was to be left alone.

His father had been right, he thought bitterly. He could almost hear his old man's voice, low and rumbly, barely audible over the rusty engine of his ancient pickup as they'd headed down the highway one hot day in June. Austin had been eight years old, and he'd tried hard to keep the tears from rolling down his cheeks as he waved goodbye to his best friend out the dusty rear window of the truck.

"If you let someone close, you give 'em the power to hurt you," his father had said. "Don't give away your heart, boy, unless you're willin' to live without it."

Austin hadn't meant to let it happen, but he'd given his heart away to Frannie.

The old man had been right, he thought grimly. It hurt like hell.

Fifteen

"You didn't tell him?" Summer stared at Frannie incredulously.

"I never got the chance." Frannie pulled a stack of folded knit shirts from her dresser drawer, then turned and placed them in the open suitcase on her bed. She was packing to move to Billings tomorrow. She didn't yet have a place to live, but that was all right. She'd stay in a motel until she could locate an apartment and at least minimally furnish it. The important thing was to make a clean break, and the easiest way to do it was as quickly as possible.

Aunt Celeste sat beside Summer and Jasmine on Frannie's bed, watching her pack.

"He's the father of your baby," she said, her face lined with concern. "He has a right to know, a right to be a part of his child's life. You can't just run away."

"I know. I intend to tell him." Frannie opened another drawer and pulled out a stack of underwear. "And I will. But right now, I just need some time to get over him."

"Frannie, you're making no sense."

"I'm making perfect sense." She placed the undies in the suitcase. "All my life I've wanted one simple, old-fashioned thing—marriage and a family. I want a loving, faithful, committed relationship with a man who loves me just as much as I love him. And Austin can't give me that."

"You're not even giving him a chance!" Jasmine exclaimed.

"Yes, I am. I'm giving him a chance to live his life the way he wants to live it." Frannie crossed to the closet and pulled a pair of slacks off a hanger. "That's the best I can give."

Aunt Celeste's eyes were warm with concern. "But, Frannie, why do you have to move? You need the support of your family at a time like this!"

"Don't you see? The media is constantly following Austin. He lives under a microscope. And because of the publicity from that rescue, I'm linked with him. If I stay in town and start sprouting a pregnant belly, well, it won't take anyone very long to put two and two together. And a scandal would ruin his career. He's a spokesman for a detergent company, for heaven's sake. He needs to keep his image squeaky-clean in order to keep his sponsors."

Summer eyed her soberly. "You really do love him, don't you?"

Frannie nodded.

"But, Frannie," Aunt Celeste said, "if Austin knew you were pregnant, I'm sure he'd want to marry you."

Frannie plopped onto the bed and sighed. "I don't want him marrying me out of a sense of obligation. It would kill me, living with a man I'd trapped into marriage. No. I won't do that. Not to Austin, and not to myself." Frannie picked up the slacks and started folding them. "For the first time in my life, I feel like I deserve to be loved. Austin helped me see that. He helped me put that whole college episode behind me, once and for all. And I'm not going to throw away all that hard-won self-esteem by entering into a one-sided marriage where I love a man and he doesn't love me."

"Marriages don't always start off even," Summer said gently. "In time, Austin might grow to love you."

"It's more likely he'd just grow to resent me. No, thanks." Frannie shook her head. "It's not an option."

"But you shouldn't be alone at a time like this," Jasmine said, her brow furrowed with concern.

"I know." Frannie looked into Jasmine's warm eyes. "Promise me you'll come see me often. And after some time has gone by and the baby's born, I'll come back and visit here, too. But I can't for a while. Not until this whole media thing has died down."

The telephone rang in the hall. Celeste rose to go get it. She returned, her forehead puckered. "Frannie, it's Tommy. He says he needs to talk to you right away."

"Tommy? Austin's crew chief?"

Celeste nodded.

Frannie felt the blood drain from her face. "Has something happened to Austin?"

"I don't know."

Frannie dashed to the phone, her heart in her throat, and grabbed the phone. "Yes?"

"Frannie, it's Tommy."

"Is Austin all right?"

"Well, not really."

Frannie's heart skipped a beat, then drubbed madly. "What happened? Was there an accident?"

"Nothing major. He crunched the nose of his car, but he's all right. And he managed to qualify for the race, but just barely."

"So, what— Why—"

"Frannie, he's not himself. He's drivin' reckless. Makin' stupid mistakes. I'm worried about him."

"Why…why are you calling me?"

"Well, because it's kinda your fault."

"My fault?"

"That didn't come out right. What I mean is, he's all torn up over you breakin' up with him."

"Tommy, Austin's the one who didn't want a relationship."

"That's not what he told me."

Frannie couldn't believe her ears. "What?"

"He got pretty loaded Wednesday night, drank more than I ever saw him drink. We sat up, talkin'. An' he told me he loves you, but he doesn't know how to handle it. Says he's never loved before, and he acted like a jackass, and now he's gone and lost you. An' he hasn't been himself ever since."

He loved her? Austin loved her? The concept whirled around her brain, then spun into her chest, where it grew and expanded like a hurricane, gaining force and strength, until her heart felt as if it would explode.

"He...loves me?" Frannie's voice was just a whisper.

"Yes, ma'am. That's what he said. I tried to get him to call you, but he tol' me some nonsense 'bout you sayin' that if he tried to call you, it would mean he'd never cared about you at all."

That was what she'd told him, all right. She'd said as much just before she walked out of the café.

"Now, I don't know what this is all about," Tommy continued, "but I know this—if you care the least little bit about him, why, you'll get your tail down here to Denver as fast as you can. 'Cause the frame of mind he's in, he's not drivin' worth a damn. I'm not worried about him not winnin'. I'm worried about him crashin'."

Frannie didn't hesitate. The words were out before she knew she'd even said them. "I'll come."

"Thank heaven!" Relief flooded the older man's voice. "Now, listen—I've already got you booked on a plane. It eaves from Bozeman tomorrow mornin' at six. Can you make it?''

''I'll be there.''

''I'll send someone to meet you at the Denver airport nd bring you straight to the track. Austin will already be acin' by the time you get here, but we'll get you seated where he can see you, and hopefully that'll pull him out of his black state of mind.''

''Okay.'' Frannie hung up the phone and turned to find Celeste, Summer and Jasmine staring at her in fascination.

''Well?'' Jasmine said.

''He loves me. Austin loves me!''

Amid war whoops and squeals of delight, the women hugged Frannie. ''Come on, I've got to pack,'' she said abruptly.

Summer frowned. ''But, Frannie, surely you're not still planning to go to Billings!''

''No.'' Frannie smiled so wide her face hurt. ''I'm going o Denver.''

''One more lap, and it's time to hit the pit.'' Tommy's voice crackled in Austin's ear over the headset. During the ace, the two men were in constant communication. 'How's she runnin'?''

''The car's fine, but I'm about half speed.''

''Roger that. You're down a lap, but you're still in the unnin'. I've got a little somethin' to perk you up when you stop.''

''Oh, hell. Not more of your coffee.''

''Nope. Not coffee.''

''What is it, then?''

''Come on in and see. You're clear to change lanes. Atta way. Bring it on down.''

Tires squealing, Austin expertly pulled into the pit. Half

a dozen men ran out and started working on the car—on
on each tire, one refueling, one checking under the hood
Austin leaned out the window.

"Take a look in the stands," Tommy shouted. "Fron
row."

Austin scowled. "Hell, I'm in no mood to play bab
watch."

"That's not what this is. Take a look, damm it! Righ
behind the pit."

Austin had never heard Tommy so worked up about any
thing other than the car in all the years he'd known him
Unfastening his seat belt, he reluctantly pulled himsel
through the window and sat on the frame, lifting his eye
to the spot the Tommy had indicated.

He blinked, then blinked again. *Frannie.*

It couldn't be. But it was.

She stood and shyly waved. Austin waved back. Sh
broke into a grin, and a weight seemed to lift from Austin'
chest. The feeling was so strong, it almost seemed as if the
law of gravity had just been repealed. His heart was float
ing, flying to the sky, soaring higher than the Goodyear
blimp hovering overhead.

Frannie. Here. Waving at him and smiling. And her eye:
held everything that felt as if it were about to burst wide
open inside him.

She was wearing red and yellow—his race colors—and
she looked as bright as a ray of sunshine. Seeing her
warmed him like sunshine. Her smile was a golden ray
beaming down like a benediction. He stood there and
basked in it, smiling back, and suddenly everything wa:
clear, as clear as a cloudless sky on a sunny day.

His father had been wrong. Love wasn't something to be
avoided. Love was something to be embraced, to be nur-

ured, to be cherished. It was something to be accepted, something to be given.

From Frannie. To Frannie.

How could he have been such an idiot? He didn't need to worry about giving her his heart. It was safe in her keeping, safe and cared for. It belonged to Frannie. It always had. He just hadn't known it.

Not until this second.

"Four more seconds, and you're ready to roll," Tommy said.

His eyes on Frannie, Austin touched his chest and mouthed the word "I." He crossed his hands across his heart, and his lips formed the word "love." Then he pointed right at Frannie. "You."

Even from this distance, he could see tears glitter in her eyes. She rapidly returned the hand signal, adding two fingers at the end. *I love you, too.* She blew him a kiss.

Austin pretended to catch it and clutched it to his heart.

"Okay," Tommy said. "Time to go, Romeo. The sooner you finish the race, the sooner you'll get to kiss her."

Austin climbed back in the seat, switched on the ignition and roared back out onto the raceway. He might be a lap down now, but he wouldn't stay that way for long. No, sirree. No one on the track had a bigger incentive to get across that finish line than he did.

"And the winner is…Austin Parker!"

The black-and-white flag dropped in a blur as Austin zoomed past. His pulse was racing harder than his car's engine and his adrenaline level was somewhere near the ozone. But it wasn't the joy of winning the race that had him lit up on the inside like the sky on the Fourth of July. It wasn't the wildly cheering crowd, or his jubilant crew jumping up and down in the pit. It was the thought of the

woman in the grandstand, the woman he loved with all hi
heart and soul.

He steered his Monte Carlo around the curved end of th
track on his slow-down lap, his eyes searching the stands
He reluctantly drove a victory lap, then headed into th
winner's circle.

And that was where he saw the face he'd been searchin
for. The face he'd been searching for his entire life, bu
hadn't known until now.

He jerked the car to a stop and hauled himself out th
open window. "Frannie."

She hurled herself into his arms, her eyes shining, he
cheeks wet, her face ablaze with love. Around him th
crowd roared, but Austin only heard the roar of the bloo
in his own ears as he kissed the woman he loved.

At long last he pulled back. "Frannie, Frannie, I lov
you."

"I love you, too."

"I can't live without you. Will you marry me?"

Frannie's smile would forever be etched in his memory
would forever be burned on his heart. The moment wa
golden, as gold as the sun on her light-brown hair, as gol
as the ring he longed to put on her finger.

Her eyes twinkled in that impish way he loved.

"Well, that depends."

"On what?"

Her gaze grew serious. "On whether you're willing t
take on a baby as well as a wife."

It took a few seconds for the words to sink in. He woul
have thought he couldn't feel any happier, thought his hear
couldn't contain any more joy, but he was wrong. His hand
tightened over hers. "You mean…you're…"

Frannie nodded.

With a wild whoop of joy, Austin picked her up and

swung her around in a wide circle. He abruptly set her down and leaned over her. "Oh, hey, are you all right? I didn't hurt you or the baby, did I? Oh, Frannie, I don't ever want to hurt you."

"I know. And I'm fine. The baby's fine. We've never been finer. And, Austin, I don't ever want to hurt you, either. I love you so!"

Austin gathered her into his arms, a feeling of love, overwhelming and complete, filling his chest, choking his throat, pulsing through his veins. He'd do anything, anything at all, to keep from ever hurting her.

"This is my last race," he murmured abruptly. "I'll quit NASCAR."

"No, you won't. I love you just the way you are. I want to add to your life, not detract from it. The baby and I will come to the races with you and cheer you on." Looping her arms around his neck, she pulled him down and gave him a kiss that all but made him forget his surroundings.

Tommy's elbow dug into his ribs. "Uh, boss, the cameras are rollin'. Everybody's waitin' to see what you have to say."

Austin reluctantly ended the kiss, but kept an arm firmly clenched around Frannie, pinning her to his side. Six separate microphones were thrust in his face. "Folks, I've won something far more important than a race today." He glanced down at Frannie, his throat swelling with tenderness. "I've won the heart of the most wonderful woman in the world, and she's just agreed to become my wife."

The crowd went crazy. Flashbulbs and strobes went off his face. He looked down at Frannie, worried that she'd be overwhelmed, but she beamed like the sun, bright and steady.

"What are your plans?" called a reporter.

"Well, the first thing we intend to do is get back to Whitehorn and get married as soon as possible."

"Hey, Austin," another reporter called. "Will you keep on racing?"

Austin opened his mouth to answer, but Frannie beat him to it. "Yes," she said emphatically. "I wouldn't dream of asking him to give up his first true love."

The crowd burst into cheers and applause. Someone threw paper money all over the car, and someone else popped the cork on a champagne bottle. "I thought you couldn't speak in public," Austin murmured in her ear.

Frannie smiled up at him. "As long as you're by my side, I feel like I can do anything."

Austin's heart was so full, he thought it would burst from his chest. "That's how you make me feel, too. But you've got one thing wrong."

"I do?"

"Yeah. Racing's not my first true love. You are."

"I am?"

"My first, and my last."

He heard another cork pop.

As a shimmering spray of champagne rained down, he drew her near and lost himself in the intoxicating sweetness of her lips.

*   *   *   *   *

M O N T A N A
Bred

From the bestselling series

MONTANA MAVERICKS

Wed in Whitehorn

Two more tales that capture living and loving
beneath the Big Sky.

JUST PRETENDING by Myrna Mackenzie

FBI Agent David Hannon's plans for a quiet vacation
were overturned by a murder investigation—and by
officer Gretchen Neal!

STORMING WHITEHORN by Christine Scott

Native American Storm Hunter's return to Whitehorn
sent tremors through the town—and shock waves of
desire through Jasmine Kincaid Monroe....

Silhouette®

Where love comes alive™

Silhouette Books presents a dazzling keepsake
collection featuring two full-length novels by
international bestselling author

DIANA PALMER

Brides To Be

(On sale May 2002)

THE AUSTRALIAN
*Will rugged outback rancher Jonathan Sterling
be roped into marriage?*

HEART OF ICE
*Close proximity sparks a breathtaking attraction between a
feisty young woman and a hardheaded bachelor!*

You'll be swept off your feet by Diana Palmer's BRIDES TO BE.

Don't miss out on this special two-in-one volume, available soon.

*Available only from Silhouette Books
at your favorite retail outlet.*

Where love comes alive™

PSBTB

*Silhouette presents an exciting
new continuity series:*

When a royal family rolls out the red carpet for love, power and deception, will their lives change forever?

The saga begins in April 2002 with:

The Princess Is Pregnant!

by Laurie Paige (SE #1459)

**May: THE PRINCESS AND THE DUKE by Allison Leigh
(SE #1465)**

**June: ROYAL PROTOCOL by Christine Flynn
(SE #1471)**

Be sure to catch all nine Crown and Glory stories: the first three appear in
Silhouette Special Edition, the next three continue in Silhouette Romance
and the saga concludes with three books in Silhouette Desire.

And be sure not to miss more royal stories,
from Silhouette Intimate Moments'

Romancing
the Crown,

running January through December.